JOSHUA RAYMOND

IN SEARCH OF THE RETURN

COURTING THE MAGIC OF THE DREAMSCAPE

In Search of the Return
Courting the Magic of the Dreamscape
Joshua Raymond

Published by:
Lumen Fidei Press, LC
308 E. High St.,
Jefferson City, MO 65101

ISBN:
Paperback: 979-8-9884300-2-5
Hardcover: 979-8-9884300-3-2
Digital: 979-8-9884300-1-8

Library of Congress Control Number: 2024939444

Cover Design by Miblart

Printed in the United States of America

Disclaimer:
This is a work of fiction. Names, characters, businesses, places, events, and incidents are either the products of the author's imagination or used in a fictitious manner. Any resemblance to actual persons, living or dead, or actual events is purely coincidental.

Publisher's Note:
Any trademarks, service marks, product names, or named features are assumed to be the property of their respective owners, and are used only for reference. There is no implied endorsement if any of these terms are used.

For Permissions:
For permission requests, write to the publisher at:
308 E. High St., Jefferson City, MO 65101 or email lumenfideipress@gmail.com

PROLOGUE

During the editing and prescreening of this book, many have asked the same question. "Is any of this true; any of it at all?" The short answer is that yes, most of it is, though anyone who reads this account will find it hard to imagine how this can be so. In reference to the individual characters in this work, however, their specific identities are decidedly fictitious, as a measure of protection from those in positions of great geopolitical power. The characters in this book are designed to tell a very real story based on the lives of real people and the occurrences of improbable timing that they experienced toward the creation of something both beautiful and inimitable. It is this author's great privilege to have had access to study the lives inspiring this work and to have been given the chance to create a vessel channeling the Truth found in the connection of these lives to one another.

Public historical occurrences in this work have been verified, and in many cases so too have the individual histories of relationships and other semi-private facts relating to the characters themselves. Regarding the *subjective* experiences described in this work, many have been verified by the accounts of multiple parties as the original purported experiences that were conveyed at the time of their occurrence. However, inward spiritual experiences can never be verified beyond the bounds of the experiential phenomena known as 'minds'.

The genesis of this story's design in book form is the author's own, and as such, there are aspects of it that are purely artistic, or which take their inspiration from the author's life experiences. The artistic variants throughout this work are intended to highlight the experiential core of the human narrative.

This adventure is crafted in a non-linear fashion, making use of multiple tenses and points of view, including specific chapters conveyed through first-person narration. The passive voice is also used frequently throughout this work. There is a marked difference between the passive thought and the active one, and it is an error to force the active where the passive best suits the approach of the mind's intention. Furthermore, first-person narration is reflective of the mind's living experience of the 'self', which it constructs out of its past. The present awareness of an individual as an unfolding storyline is the basis of that person's conception of present reality, and it colors the world of their subjective dreams. This perspective is thus integral to the presentation of this shared narrative, where 'You', 'I', 'He', and 'She' all find a place in common. We seldom experience our own personal stories without the subjective internal "I", and yet we are always aware of our place in a greater saga, where we are seen as third person characters. The mingling of "I" and "You", while rare in our experience, holds a great magic when it is found.

In addition to the present mind's awareness of the past, some minds occasionally reach forward into a future that conventional logic and reason dictate cannot yet exist. It is the epic ability of the mind to understand both *across* and *through* time, as well as *through* and sometimes conversely *without* logical explanation, which this story seeks to relate. The profound capacity of the human mind is at once infinite inside of its perception, and yet forever limited by its own framework of existence; a derivative of the world perceived.

Emerging, flourishing, dissolving back again

This is the eternal process of return

To know this process brings enlightenment

To miss this process brings disaster

Be still

Stillness reveals the secret of eternity

Eternity embraces the all-possible

The all-possible leads to a vision of oneness

A vision of oneness brings about universal love

Universal love supports the great Truth of Nature

The great Truth of Nature is Tao

Whoever knows this Truth lives forever

The body may perish, deeds may be forgotten

But he who has Tao has all eternity

- Lao Tzu

CHAPTER

One

The forest was steeped in rainy fog, obscuring everything beyond the intimately near. The tree in front of me was a grand specimen, perhaps two thousand years old, and those just ahead of and behind were only slightly younger. They were Redwoods to be sure, though I was uncertain of how I knew what to call them, as my mind held few details of the life left behind. All the same, I did know certain things; like the fact that these trees were *Sequoia sempervirens.* This was their Latin name. They were commonly known as Coastal Redwoods in English, which was the language of the land known as America. They had grown there once upon a time, in a place called California.

My mind confronted only those thoughts closely connected to the reality around, though memories from another world seemed to inform my understanding. My eyes saw a tree, and then thoughts of its name emerged in two forms. These forms then led to the recognition of languages once learned, the place the trees had grown, and of a story being told in that time.

I walked along under the giant trees, carefully seeking to avoid stepping on the beautifully delicate ferns that seemed to be everywhere. There was no way for the mind to grasp where on Earth this forest might be, but it was clear that it wasn't in America.

"How do I know this?" I asked myself, crouching down near the base of another large tree, eyeing a small plant. I had seen this type of plant before and sensed a subtle meaning in my past connection to it. It stood out among the ferns, for it was a broadleaf plant, which had once grown wild in the mountains near Oaxaca, Mexico amidst the cloud forests. Still kneeling, I extended my hand to stroke a large leaf. It possessed a healthy sheen that seemed to radiate energy from within.

"Twelve leaves, you are supposed to chew twelve leaves." The thought flowed into the mind as if the trees themselves bore the message.

"Why?" my mind enquired of itself and the trees even as I began to pluck the most appealing of the plant's members. The herbage had a particular flavor that my taste seemed to recall.

Looking up, my eyes captured a light beam that had found its way through the dense forest canopy far above. The light here was different from the light I was used to. It was thicker; it seemed almost to have mass. No, this was not California. This place was older, the land of an archaic time.

Vision left the canopy and traveled down the long straight bodies of the trees until they met with the ground beneath my feet. I was standing on a narrow but well-worn path. The path was the formation of directional understanding amidst the endless potential reality of the forest. The forest itself defined the reality of its own existence, but the experience of that reality by those moving through it was defined by the character, direction, and frequency of the movements made. This, in turn, refined the existence contemplated by the forest, and the forest's understanding of itself grew to include the visions of those beings that existed as travelers through its world.

When looking for direction in the forest, the application of thought as to the direction preferred was repeated by countless individual minds over time. This kinetic repetition of potential understanding formed a channel, and thus created the path, giving direction and meaning to the efforts of those seeking to find their way. With each new decision to walk the path, the clearer it became, and the more harmony flowed.

I began walking along the path that had been gifted to me. It was only just wide enough for a man's body to pass through without trampling any vegetation, and this fact was deeply moving to my spirit. What was needed to avoid trampling the plants was provided, a sacrifice of the plant world to the mobile. The path could be ignored if one wished, but there was no need to blaze my own trail in this moment. There was a time for wandering and for stepping out into the unknown in search of new understanding, but my soul was searching for what the forest had to offer and that would only come through understanding the harmony that had already formed here. You had to walk the path before you could know it, and you needed to know the path before you stood a chance of finding meaning in the wilds beyond, where the magic of the path's genesis lay hidden.

Harmony flows from balance and an understanding of it. The path is the balance manifest.

I stopped under another large tree, this one perhaps even larger than the first one seen, which had long since succumbed to the foggy mist behind. Then again, perhaps this was the same tree.

My hand rose to meet the trunk of the magnificent being. It was so clear that it was alive, so clear that it had a soul; whatever that was. This had once been a source of much argument amongst men. Perhaps it still was.

Man drew his breath in rhythm, in and out, in and out. Man circulated his life force to an internal beat. He ate in cycles, he slept in cycles, he did everything in cycles. And all the while he thought about his world and sought to manipulate it, either for good or 'evil'.

The tree was different. It did not breathe in and out in cycles. There was no rhythm, only a constant flow of air through its essence. So long as conditions would allow, the tree was ever inhaling, ever exhaling, ever drinking in water, ever growing, ever living, and it was not set to a beat; it was constant. All the while it sought to do nothing other than 'be'. Man was different from plants, and even from other animals, chiefly because he had the ability to conceive of what the world 'ought to be', and to create that world by altering the natural state of things in fundamental ways. But to deny the worth of all that you are not, is to miss the point of your own existence. Man's blessing was in being able to search for what *should be* and to do so of his own free will. What a sad fate to use that blessing to curse creation.

I stood with my hand on the seemingly invincible giant, recalling the forests of California. In another time and place, the land of California had been the last refuge of these giants. Many men had arrived there, and rather than marveling at their worth, they had cut them all down, almost to the last tree. Two million acres were logged for human pursuits, leaving less than five percent of the species to live on in areas too difficult to penetrate with machines. If he could have accessed them, man would have killed them all long before any resistance had formed among his ranks.

Man's heart had not even considered the sacrifice that was made, and this could never be justified. Man had a right to take because he was an intelligence, and it was his fate to shape his world to his understandings of what was good. However, man was never supposed to harm others without reflecting carefully on his understandings of goodness, respecting the sacrifices he requested, and appreciating that he should not take simply because he can. Thousands of years of growth multiplied by millions of individuals, brought to an end for the sake of an industry; this should have been cause for reflection.

The tree could not think, but it could sense. The tree accepted me. She liked me. I too could sense the tree and felt a strange compulsion to walk around to her other side. The tree wanted to be explored a bit more. I circled the base, stepping on and killing my first plant this day, an infant fern that had only just emerged from the ground. The ferns were thick here, and the decision to circle the tree was a decision to end several lives as a direct incident.

As the body walked, my hand ran along the dense wet bark, taking in its texture and its essence. The energy leapt from the tree and into my hand as my own life connected to something beyond 'self'.

Approaching the far side of the trunk from the path, I saw that it had been largely hollowed out in one area by fire. Mind marveled at the way these subtle feelings had led to what was needed, precisely *when* it was needed. Both body and mind had become incredibly tired, struggling to stay awake. I had begun fighting the desire to sleep earlier on the path, having been far too exposed in the open forest to entertain the idea of a nap. But now here was a tree-cave, provided just for me, and in perfect time.

My eyes surveyed the surroundings, contemplating what else the forest had to offer for rest. Soft conifer needles were in abundance, and I gathered these and spread them over the bare earth inside the tree, creating a soft, dry place to lie down. When this was finished, I began looking for something to cover the opening to the tree's inner world.

I walked back up the path in search of a fallen pine seen earlier only a short distance away. It had come down recently, ripping its root system right out of the ground as it fell. The top would provide small branches dense with foliage which would serve as a perfect make-shift door.

I had just reached the place where the branches lay when an awareness suddenly emerged. Heat was radiating from above. Traces of light penetrated this world's great canopy. The slight beams that made their way to the forest floor had not changed since I had come to this place, and yet suddenly they had become sources of intense warmth. My mind recognized that the light had not changed, but rather, perception had shifted. It had done so dramatically, yet the change had come in the most subtle of ways. The light broke through the trees in trickles emanating from thousands of cracks in the canopy. Each and every one of them could suddenly be felt on skin individually. My body had been absorbing this light throughout its walk in this ancient land, but this truth had not been felt before perception had shifted. Now, I marveled at the sensation of it soaking into skin while gathering the branches needed for my return.

I had only just woken up to this land of path and plant, but it seemed that the time had come to set down this new awareness. The gateway would be closed so that it might be reopened to another world.

I approached the opening to the living cave, and then lowered my head to enter her inner space. The floor area was wide enough to lie in comfortably, and amidst the soft bed of earth and green, I found rest.

After blocking the entrance with the branches that had been gathered, I shut the eyes. Body and awareness sat in the dim light, as thoughts of another realm began to emerge. It was becoming clearer now, almost as if I was fading back to a land from another time.

As awareness drifted between consciousness and the dreamscape, the life of a young man began to emerge. In another time and place, all of his existence had become subject to law and rule. Men had been steeped in knowledge, and there had been a great war of ideology. Man's ability to conceive of good had driven him to see himself as the enforcer, rather than the student. With the best of intentions, many had sought to force the world's inhabitants to observe their conceptions, but these had all failed. They had not understood that good could never be forced; it had to be yielded to by the individual out of a love for the goodness itself. The failure to understand this had resulted in confusion, and the world of man turned on itself, creating a sea of misperception over what good was. This led many to deny the existence of the 'Good' entirely. Some even began to deny the Spirit of Truth itself. Much had gone wrong, and the young man had grown up in the middle of it all.

Eventually he found himself emerging from the darkness of his world, into the light of understanding. This emergence had begun in early adulthood, near a time when he was all but destroyed by a young woman. She had said that she loved him, but this had not been enough to see past the lies that she wanted to believe in.

Then one day, an unseen force took hold of his experience. The days of old, lost in confusion and despair were gone. In their place was an idea, and a dream. It was a dream of a love unlike any known, and yet it was the story of every human being. Through this love a new reality was struggling to be born, and the dream set its hook in his mind. There was no turning back now, the Truth could not be un-thought. Now all he could hope for was a way to make some sense of it all inside of her, so that he might find a way to bring the ideas forward from the chaos without losing his sanity. This was the time he needed her to understand. Now that she was finally here, this was the time he needed to understand for himself all the more.

His emergence had begun, and it was a beautiful time.

The Light of Understanding
Consciousness refined
Dynamic process beyond define

Two shores were made
Two shores for mind
The Deep crossable only through Design

Life contemplates journey
Journey contemplates The Deep
Still many fear to sail on waters so grand

I will stand for the life lived
For the shore distant
For the gateway Divine

Our world is destined to lose its way
For the way of our world has become
One shore

Alone

CHAPTER
Two

The truck's wheels gave off an almost inaudible hum, which couldn't really be appreciated with the windows tightly closed. But with the windows down, the sound of them spinning across the pavement introduced a hypnotic resonance into Walker's world, though it was nearly hidden behind the noise of the air rushing past the window opening. Walker concentrated on the noise as his hand floated on the air rushing past at seventy miles per hour. Air had such density at speed. At seventy, it felt thick enough to swim in. In fact, this was quite possible in a manner of speaking.

Flight was essentially just swimming in air. He had once done an experiment on a motorcycle, accelerating to 150 miles per hour and then sitting up suddenly from behind the aerodynamic windshield and cowling while closing the throttle. Walker wanted to know how much force would be applied by the wind, and how quickly it would slow him down. The air had hit with the same intensity as water when a person jumps from a slow-moving boat, nearly ripping his body off the bike. In a matter of seconds, he decelerated to ninety without the use of the machine's brakes.

Walker thought of this, and other experiences had over the years with air and its properties. It was a curious thing to study, and he enjoyed that study very much. It was funny that one could claim to study the dynamics of air by almost killing himself on a motorcycle, but it was a study of aerodynamics nonetheless. To study was to seek to understand, and this often resulted in the testing of ideas in peculiar ways.

His life had been nothing but a study. He studied air, water, earth, fire, space, plants, animals, thoughts, concepts, languages, cultures, beliefs, and countless other divisions of reality. But above all else, he studied women. He had no formal methods regarding his most favored of subjects, just a never-ending curiosity for what they were, and a desire to experience and appreciate them. As a young high school student, the simple line of a young woman's calf transitioning to ankle had held enough wonder to occupy his mind for an entire semester of classes designed to teach Latin. The class rubric focused on a language structure that had taken men centuries to develop, and he enjoyed immersing himself in Latin's particular vision of reality. Yet ten thousand times the amount of meaning found in all the languages of the world was contained in the perfection of form that had manifested itself across the room.

This appreciation for the beauty of women had nearly killed him. He had escaped that fate, and now found himself taking on a new reality; one based in an understanding beyond his old conceptions of life. Walker was profoundly excited for his future; driving alone towards Canada, full of hope and a sense of what should be. The past had not gone as it should have, but then again, he had invited that reality. He had not taken the right path and that failure had brought on suffering. Now he understood this. He was determined to live life rightly from this point on, or at least to intend on it.

This trip to Toronto was a step towards living out that future, and it was thrilling to be on his way; pursuing the symbol of the dream he had found. Logic told him only that he *might* find a symbol there, but his heart knew something beyond the dictates of that logic. His heart understood that there was but one intended symbol, and it had been set aside for her alone. It was faith for its own sake that drove him toward Toronto, and it whispered of a blessed path to come. His friend's father would show him how to find it.

Toronto was a long drive from his parents' house in Missouri, and so the trip was broken into two segments to avoid driving a thousand miles in one day. As chance would have it, his uncle lived several hundred miles from his home, and in the right direction.

Walker thought of his uncle and of his grandfather's farm, which he had visited often as a young boy. Coming here felt like stepping back into a forgotten history. His uncle now lived on the original plot of land settled centuries prior by his relatives. For years, his grandparents had lived in a much more modern home, built in 1876 as the window above the front door had proclaimed in gold stained-glass letters. He remembered the house vividly. His mother's family had moved there from the original homestead when she was a small child, and only years later had his uncle moved back to their ancestral home, which was located just five miles away.

Now his grandparents were gone from the Earth, and the farm they had built, so deeply etched into his memory, had become an empty field. The home his mother had known from childhood was destroyed by a young couple, who set fire to it and four other houses one night on a drugged-out arson adventure. Walker mourned the way people sought out darkness, and the way they gave themselves over to dark chemical experiences.

Walker's eyes struggled to make out the old driveway entrance as he passed by, but it could no longer be seen, having been completely swallowed up by the callous cornfields that were once restrained by barns, sheds, and a giant willow tree. The tree too had gone, blown down in a storm just prior to the arson. The barns were torn down after the house burned. It had been time for the old reality to pass away, it seemed. One year the farm was there to touch, the next it was a memory.

His truck crossed the rough railroad tracks near the local farm supply distributor and continued a mile or so until the road led to a stop sign. He turned, and then continued for another mile, exiting yet again onto a still smaller lane. He pulled off onto a gravel driveway and took in the sight of the familiar homestead, parking his truck next to an old equipment barn in the side yard.

"Hey there Mr. World Traveler nephew!" his uncle Brad called as he stepped from the vehicle.

Walker always felt troubled by the recognition of the things he had done, feeling that they somehow came to be recognized out of a sense of separation by those noticing them. Perhaps his uncle looked down on him, or maybe up at him for having lived in England. He wanted neither to be true. All he could do was let the comment go, and perhaps in time and with the help of a little conversation, he could show that he was still cut from common cloth.

"You want something to drink? Soda, water, beer, whiskey?" Brad laughed as he slapped Walker on the back.

"I'll have a beer."

"I don't have any of that tar you love so much, sorry."

His uncle was referring to Guinness. Walker had become very fond of it while studying abroad in England a few years before but had acquired a taste for it even in high school, his friend Ben having been infatuated with the brew and the innovation of the widget that came in every can. The device spewed forth a magic gas that was supposed to transform canned beer into draught beer. It worked remarkably well, though he now knew that the best Guinness could only be found in the circular Gravity Bar atop the Guinness Storehouse in Dublin.

He would have loved to explain the magic of Guinness and Ireland to his uncle, but Brad's question required that he refrain. Brad was fishing for something in Walker he hoped not to find, fueled by his memory of the time his nephew had shown up at a family camping holiday with a fancy black foreign beer. Brad had given him trouble over it then, as did most of Walker's friends. Walker had challenged him to try it. That experience had not gone well.

"Oh my god, it tastes like charcoal flavored piss!" his uncle said as he committed an Irish felony, spitting the holy elixir out onto the ground.

Following his crime, they had engaged in a healthy debate while sitting around the campfire. They spoke of culture and beer and the benefits of being open to new ideas and experiences. His uncle had agreed that new ideas could be good things and that so too could new beers, "just not when it involves drinking tar mixed with piss," he had said.

"No, I'm in the mood for a good old American beer, a St. Louis beer if you have one...or were you a Miller man?" Walker asked accusatorily.

"Miller? Are you on drugs? I ought to throw you out!"

Brad was smiling, happy to have been pushed back; it showed that his nephew wasn't afraid, and that he still understood what his roots were. Budweiser was based out of St. Louis, just across the mighty Mississippi River in his home state of Missouri. In that time, there was a strong sense of pride for Budweiser in their area of the world, and neither of them was above it. Miller was from the North, and Miller drinkers were second class citizens in Budweiser country. The same was true for those who drank Coors, which came from the Rocky Mountains in the West.

The pride of St. Louis in its beer was a force all its own. Yet as much as Budweiser held sway there, it seemed rather unimportant next to the fervor the Irish showed for Guinness. Dublin had given new meaning to Walker's understanding of pride in a beverage.

During his second stay in England several years before, Walker's younger brother Lucas had come to visit him. Walker had lived in England for a year's time during his fourth year at college, attending Lancaster University in the North. He had moved home following his studies, only to discover that he had left his heart in Lancashire. So, he returned for a time. His brother's decision to come and visit him meant a lot, and he arranged to show him a good time while he was visiting. After enjoying the club scene together in Lancaster for a few days, they had crossed the Irish Sea by ferry to stay in Dublin for a few more. On their first night out, his brother asked for a Bud Light at a bar and received only a blank stare.

"He means Budweiser," Walker had said to the barkeep.

"No, I want a Bud Light," Lucas protested as the man retrieved a bottle of Budweiser.

"They don't have it, Luke."

"Who in the hell doesn't have Bud Light?" he asked, rather indiscreetly.

"The Irish don't have Bud Light. You're lucky to get a Budweiser. Really you are wasting a perfect chance to experience Irish culture. You should be drinking a Murphy's or a Guinness."

"Aww, that black shit?"

Walker froze and waited for an uproar to commence, but no one had heard.

"Shut up Luke, you'll get us killed."

He wasn't joking. The Irish loved their beloved drink as much as they loved the Irish flag, probably more. To insult Guinness was to insult Ireland. He took his brother aside to explain.

"You know how you would feel if some European guy was in a bar back home saying that Budweiser was a shit beer made of piss? Do you think that guy would last very long?"

"No, he'd get his ass kicked."

"Exactly. The same thing is true in Ireland, only here, they might kill you."

"Kill you?! I thought you said it was so much safer here!"

"Overall, yes, it is much safer, but you don't understand the level of pride involved with Guinness. The beer is holy."

Lucas looked down at his brother's pint with subtle amazement, and then reluctantly, took the glass into his hand and tipped it up for a drink. He cringed as the sacred liquid went to work on his taste buds, refraining from ill comment. Walker was glad to see that his brother had gotten the message, and that he was beginning to open to the experience in front of him.

Later that night they found themselves in a busy pub near the Temple Bar section of Dublin. Lucas sat at a side table with Walker's good friend Zalman, whom Walker had met during his year of study in Lancaster. Walker went to the bar to purchase two pints of Guinness and a bottle of Budweiser. While awaiting the drinks, he had a revelation. "Why not get an Irishman to explain Guinness to his brother?" An Irishman knew his own religion far better than Walker ever could. What was needed was a holy man, at least in a sense of the word.

Walker happened to be next to an old man that seemed to fit the part. He was clearly wise in the ways of alcohol, weathered and beaten by its effects, yet he had never succumbed to it. He was as close to a drunk as a person could get without becoming one. There was a clear sense of pride and honor that seemed to dwell alongside his love of intoxication, such that it struck one almost as principled and dignified. He loved his mistress, but she did not rule him. He was well over seventy years old, with scruffy grey whiskers and peppered hair. He wore an old green army jacket from a life lived long ago, and he seemed lost in thought.

"Excuse me, sir?"

The man looked up with skepticism at the young American next to him, in his tight blue jeans and collared shirt.

"I'm sorry to bother you, but I need an Irishman to help me out."

"You're American, aren't you?"

"Yes sir, I am, but you see that's the problem right now. See that guy over there? He's my brother, and he came over to visit me in England."

"England?!" the man exclaimed as he sat back in alarm. "You live in England?! I hate to see a nice American lad caught up with the English."

"I just live there at the moment because I was on a course of study there for a time. Now they are the only friends I really have."

"That's too bad. You should make some Irish friends if I'm honest."

"Listen, I love England, but I also love Ireland, and I love Guinness. Naturally, I thought it was important to show my brother what Ireland was all about when he came to visit me, so I brought him here this morning on the ferry from Holyhead in Wales. I've been trying to explain to him the meaning of Guinness and help him to love it as much as I do, but he doesn't like it."

The man stopped him before he could continue. "What the hell do you mean he doesn't like it?!" he said, leaning in toward Walker. "That's

God damned sacrilege!"

The excitement began welling up; Walker had found exactly whom he was looking for.

"I know, but he doesn't understand that! I am trying to teach him, but he's just a boy, and I don't know enough myself to help him. Would you try?"

"Try! By God, it's my duty!"

The man yelled to the barkeep, "I need a Guinness, and fast!"

The barman was incredibly busy, as the bar was packed full, crowded with five times as many people as there were seats. Still, he dropped what he was doing, grabbed a drink he had been preparing for another customer and handed it across the bar.

"Let's go," the man ordered.

The customer waiting didn't mind sacrificing his pint. He seemed to understand that something important was happening, something for Ireland. He would wait for another 119.53 seconds, the time that it took to pour the perfect pint of Guinness.

"Are you the boy who doesn't like Guinness?!" the man pointed with a crooked finger and shouted in a thick Irish accent.

"Aw, crap!" Lucas prepared to be mauled by every able-bodied man in the pub.

"It's alright, he's here to help," Walker insisted, patting the man on the shoulder as he moved past to his own seat against the wall.

Their new friend sat down and pulled his chair up next to their table. What ensued was a forty-five-minute history of Ireland and Guinness, which left the three friends awestruck and silent. The man might as well have been a famous Irish historian; maybe he was. He concluded by telling Lucas that he was not leaving the bar until he drank the pint he had been given.

"You'll drink it and like it or you and I are going to have to step outside."

"Holy crap, are you serious?"

"God damn right I'm serious. You've sat there this whole time pissing about and sipping on that pint I bought you, even after I've explained to you that to disrespect Guinness is to disrespect Ireland. I will not sit here and let you disrespect Ireland. I don't want to fight you, especially at my age, but principle is principle. Now drink."

Lucas looked at Walker, who just shrugged, so he took the glass and drank it up in a single go. The man began to laugh and slapped him on the back. "There you go son, that's the way," he said enthusiastically. "Now you don't even need to eat dinner. Guinness has everything you need, all your vitamins and minerals and such. It's like a meal in a glass. Well, I guess that's me job done. Nice to meet you lads."

And with that, he got up and returned to the bar, wearing an enormous smile that he couldn't subdue.

One beer turned into several, plus three bottles of wine shared with his aunt and uncle, and the three of them stayed up later than planned, talking and getting to know one another better than they had ever had occasion to do in the past. Despite the long night, Walker felt well rested in the morning.

When he had left home the day before, the air had been warm and soft, and he could feel the light beginning to intensify in his corner of the world. The energy had moved away for months, but now it was preparing to come back, with plans on a hot, muggy midwestern summer. But after the late night with his aunt and uncle, when he rose to pack the tent, the wind blew cold and hard, chilling his flesh as he worked to scrape the ice from the windows of his pickup. Winter was not yet through with the midwestern United States, after all. Toronto would be much colder, he suspected.

Walker climbed into his truck and waved goodbye to his uncle, who was already up and working at six A.M. The time for planting corn and soybeans rapidly approached, and Brad could feel the anticipation of another year of growing; another year of working with the connection between the Earth and its plants.

Most people in the modern world did not comprehend the beauty and meaning inherent in growing and nurturing plants, but there were still those few who understood. The farmer was still connected to the land, and so among farmers many still appreciated the truth about plants and life.

When a man plants a seed and then gives his time and effort to ensure that the young emerging seedling grows into its potential, the man's energy quite literally deposits into the body of the plant itself. After the plant has lived its life, the man's energy returns to him when he takes of the plant's body and eats. What is more, the strength of the energy man gives is greatly multiplied through the plant's relationship to light, and the man's pleasure is also the plant's pleasure in this regard. Man harnesses the power of sunlight through his relationship to plants, which understand the light and know how to create life and physical beauty from its energy.

This symbiosis of living beings trading in energy and lifeforce is a holy thing, a deeply spiritual and meaningful thing. We are part of a sacred and beautiful connection, bound up in the majesty of the natural order that ordains the path's design. Our connection with light through the pathway of the plant exists on multiple levels, and in multiple dimensions.

CHAPTER
Three

Walker thought back several years to that visit with his uncle as he sat looking out over Table Bay. He had gone to Toronto in search of something of sacred importance. He had known then that the reason behind his search necessitated following a new life path, but he had no idea just how far that path would diverge from his expectations. Being here now, under these pretenses, seemed something out of a science fiction novel. Only this was palpably real.

Table Mountain loomed behind his rented apartment, the characteristic tablecloth of clouds hanging just over the edge of the cliffs that defined its limits. He was sitting in a wicker chair, on a small veranda outside the bedroom. The house he had been given for the two-month period he was to be in Cape Town was situated partway up the beginnings of Signal Hill, adjacent to the small mountain spire known as Lion's Head. The elevated setting provided a wonderful view of the city and bay below.

In the distance, Robben Island sat empty. The island had been home to the prison which housed many who had opposed South African apartheid, including Nelson Mandela, who after years on the island prison had risen to the presidency of the country. Much had changed in this land, and yet much was still the same.

This fact more than any other made Cape Town a fitting meeting place for the upcoming Council, as it mirrored the truth he hoped to confront about the state of the modern world. Though he had once thought he understood the origins of the Council and their purpose, his mind had lost its bearing by this point. His reality had become much more complex than he could fully understand, and he now found himself lost in the pursuit of whatever it was. He was no longer in control of many of the ideas that made up his reality in this regard. All he knew for sure now, was that this meeting had the potential to change the course of his life.

Walker had begun a career as a defense attorney in New York only a few years prior, and in that capacity, he had become acutely aware of the power of government. The official government was like a lumbering giant that you could fight if you were so inclined, but the odds were always strongly against you. This was true even when you were completely innocent of any wrongdoing.

Then there was the unofficial government. If the official government was a lumbering giant, the unofficial government was an unspeakable demon. It took when it desired to take, destroyed when it decided to destroy, and killed when it desired to kill. If a person posed a big enough threat to the status quo, that person was handled without invoking the legal system. In those situations, your attorney simply never came into the discussion. Death squads and mercenaries were not only real in his world, they were much more active than almost anyone realized. This was particularly true in relation to the international drug control apparatus, which he had chosen to challenge openly in his capacity as a lawyer.

The world's underground power gave Walker pause as he sat staring out over Table Bay. By all rights, the entire construct of the Council might have been gamed to bring him to a place where he could be questioned and dealt with. Yet, this seemed doubtful given the Council's origins. Plus, he was not important enough in the movement to warrant attention. Was he?

He picked up the glass of water sitting on the small wicker table in front of him and took a long, slow drink. Below his apartment, a group of friends were passing by on the typically quiet street, laughing and talking about the upcoming World Cup which was to take place in South Africa. They were clearly foreigners, as South Africa had little to celebrate in-spite-of the event location, having failed to qualify this time around. Behind the noise of their conversation was the constant, quiet hum of cars and people several blocks away, out on the main road.

The sounds danced around Walker as he slowly raised his glass again, concentrating slightly to steady his hand while taking another drink. He believed in his heart that he was here for a real reason and that what he was doing was still under the radar of the powers he feared. Still, the risk Walker was taking in trying to change the state of affairs present in his world caused a deep anxiety that was hard for his physiology to ignore. He looked at the faint disturbance still visible on the surface of the water in his hand.

"Fear is such a powerful thing," he thought to himself.

His mind continued, "But if you can overcome it, you might just change the world."

Then another thought crossed his mind, "Or you might end up dead."

Walker smiled at the gift of life in all its complexity and challenge. He was truly blessed to have been given this chance, and for the success in business that allowed him to step away from his career for a time so that he might pursue deeper things. His law firm still required his attention, but the days of needing to be physically present were over. Success in business had opened the gate to the hunting grounds where success lived on another level.

He had arrived at Cape Town International Airport the day before at around five A.M., officially coming to the city for a course of legal study, which served two purposes. First, it gave him a reason to be in the area while awaiting the announcement of exactly when and where the Council would be held. The Council would meet in South Africa, during a three-week window of time; that was as specific as they had been. Second, the legal program provided a genuine opportunity to exercise his mind and hone the presentation of ideas in difficult forums, away from the distractions of his law firm.

He wasn't sure how to approach this so-called Council. He had been given no information about how one worked. He didn't know how long it lasted, what sort of material to prepare, or even the nature and number of his audience. Walker wasn't fully prepared for what lay ahead of him, and he knew it. It reminded him of his first week of law school, so many years before.

Above all else, law school, like the practice of law, was about being as prepared as possible through knowledge of your subject matter. It was also about being ready to improvise and adapt to the unforeseen. You could plan for an argument, but in the end, arguments were fluid, evolving things that required you to think in the moment and respond to challenges you may not have expected. It was a lot like a physical fight. You couldn't just plan for physical fights or arguments; you had to train for them.

For this reason, he had chosen the course of study at the University of the Western Cape to pass the time until the Council was announced. The classes would last for nearly two months, and the timing happened to work out. Thus, he had become a student again, at least for purposes of appearance. It was almost comical to him how difficult it had been to recreate himself as a student for purposes of admission. He remembered his good friend from the American Bar Association on the day Walker had approached him with the request. His face had become a mess of confusion and suspicion as he tried to conjure a rationale for such a backward intention. The memory of his reaction always made Walker smile.

At the airport, Walker had met up with several other law students and then booked a taxi into town. All of them were staying in De Waterkant Village, which was supposed to be one of the safest areas in Cape Town. The group was made up of students from prominent American law schools, and there was noticeable excitement among them about the opportunity to study and live in such an exotic location. They had spent much of the morning talking about the flight to Africa and how they had been treated on their respective airlines. Everyone had agreed; South African Airways was the best airline any of them had ever flown. There were personal television screens with movies, games, and flight data. There were steaming hot hand towels following a real dinner, sleeping masks, and a free pair of neon-colored socks. What more could a law student ask for?

Their accommodations had not been ready when the taxi driver dropped them off in the village, and consequently they spent much of the morning together, getting acquainted in a small coffee shop. In the span of a single morning, Walker had already managed to make several new friends.

As he sat twirling the last of the water in his glass, he contemplated what to do with the remainder of the evening. Then he heard another group of people approaching on the street below.

"Hey, Walker? You up there?" one of the guys in the group shouted.

Walker leant out over the veranda wall and acknowledged his presence with a wave.

"We're heading out to do some shopping in town, and then we thought we'd catch some food. You in?"

That night, dinner was at Café Manhattan, a popular restaurant less than a block from most of the student residences. Upon arrival, Walker noticed something different about his surroundings, though he couldn't quite place what it was. He sat down and visited for a while with his student colleagues. The waiter brought some menus, and each opened them to see what was available. Walker was immediately struck by the strange image next to the listing of salads. Pictured was a plate of salad held by a man's muscular arm that was protruding from a cutoff shirt. He didn't know what to make of such a thing, so he turned the page to find the seafood selections next to a picture of five men in speedo style bathing suits with their arms around each other.

Walker began to consciously question what manner of culture he had walked into. He turned the page again to find the burger menu, only to come across a rather artistic photograph of a man's body. The camera had been placed on a man's chest and focused on a bulge in his tight white underpants, leaving the rest of the picture out of focus.

He leant forward cautiously.

"Are we in a gay restaurant?" he asked one of his new friends.

"We are in a gay village," was the reply.

Walker sat back in bewilderment. It seemed that this could be a source of tension for some of his fellow students, as the gay rights movement had sparked a large amount of controversy in recent times. Many people simply didn't know what to do with the issue, and as such it had become polarizing to those of various political and religious backgrounds. Walker was sure there were those among his classmates who would be quite uncomfortable when they came to find out that the University had purposefully placed them in an outwardly gay neighborhood. He suspected it was probably the University's intention in the first place.

In Walker's part of the world, the inclusion of sexually themed photos in a restaurant menu simply didn't exist, let alone in connection with such a divisive issue. Yet in Cape Town, everyone took such a presentation in stride, and after a moment of reflection, Walker chuckled at the complexities of juxtaposed cultural identities, and then left the thoughts aside.

They had seated themselves outside, and after their waiter brought them their food, an older man in raggedy clothing came to the edge of the railing that fenced in the elevated patio. He peered up at the table in front of them and tried to sell some socks to the students dining there. Walker watched this situation unfold, witnessing each of them decline the man's offer. He felt genuine empathy for the old man's struggle to make a living and decided to purchase some socks. He could use a few new pairs anyway.

The man moved down to Walker's table, and peering up between the bars of the railing, he asked, "I am so sorry to bother you at dinner, but can you please help me and buy some socks? I have children to feed, and this is how I make money."

Walker's new friends each turned their gaze away from the man, but Walker leant over and said he would take some socks. His compatriots were mildly shocked by this announcement. The man began to thank him and livened up considerably.

"How many pair do you want?" he asked.

"How much for each pair?" Walker asked.

"Three pair are thirty-five rand."

Walker looked in his wallet, he only had perhaps twenty-five rand to spare after accounting for the anticipated cost of dinner.

"How much for two pairs?" he inquired over the table.

"I only sell in three pairs."

"I only have twenty-five rand."

"The price is thirty-five rand. You said you want socks, now give me thirty-five rand for three pairs!"

"But I don't have thirty-five rand to spare."

"The price is thirty-five rand!" the man barked.

"Well then I guess I don't want any socks," Walker said indignantly.

The man had become visibly angry and began to cuss and yell through the fence. "You laugh at me. You think I am stupid? You waste my time!"

He was convinced that Walker had asked him for socks specifically so that he could tell him he didn't want any. He thought Walker was mocking his position in life for the fun of it. Walker tried to interject and explain that he was honestly down to twenty-five rand, but it was no use. The man screamed and yelled and caused quite a scene.

"You horrible, horrible person. You think it is funny? You think it is funny? You god damn, you god damn, you god damn sock tease!"

At this point, he ran to the front of the patio and tried to come in to fight. Walker was scared to death. What would he do when the man reached him? Win or lose, a fight with a homeless person just trying to feed his family would not reflect well on him.

A waiter stopped the man at the gate and shoved him back off the patio into the street. Then he came over to apologize.

"Sorry for him, he knows he is not supposed to bother our guests."

"I don't know what I would have done if he came in here," Walker admitted, standing to shake the waiter's hand.

"You would have sorted him out," said the waiter. "You are much stronger than him, I think."

Walker explained that he was mostly happy that an incident had not occurred that would have involved the authorities. The waiter smirked and patted Walker on the shoulder.

"You are from America, yes?"

Walker said that he was.

"You are in South Africa now," he said with a gleaming smile. "The police don't concern themselves with such trivia here."

Walker sat back down at the table and looked at his fellow diners.

"What did he call you?" one of the men among them asked with a hidden smile.

"I think he called me a sock tease," he laughed.

"That's what I thought I heard," the man said, chuckling quietly. Walker finished his meal with one eye on the front patio gate.

The weeks that followed opened-up a new understanding of Africa far removed from the typical images conceived of by most Americans. South Africa, in fact, was much the same as parts of the United States. It was rather reminiscent of the wine country of California. The climate in winter was wonderful, the landscape rich with vineyards beneath pristine mountains. Architecturally, Cape Town itself might as well have been any number of first-world cities.

The only real differences were subtle ones, but they made an enormous impact on the day-to-day experience of the place. The cook at the internet café, for instance, had simply sat down with the students at their table after serving them. In America, such occurrences were rare. In Africa, they happened frequently.

"You were talking about the Rastafari?" the cook, Zach, had asked curiously.

"Yes, indeed we were. Are you familiar?"

Zach claimed to be a Rastafarian and began to explain a famous case he had heard the students discussing. Walker thought that the man knew an enormous amount about law given his position as a cook in an internet café. When this was pointed out, he beamed a smile and said he had always been far too curious, seeking to learn whenever he had the chance. Zach had never been to school and yet taught himself to read newspapers by the age of four.

He explained that he would like to deepen his understanding further of the court's decision if anyone had time to discuss it with him. Walker happily obliged and they spent the following three hours tearing the case apart, even getting into the way similar cases had played out in America. Zach had a better handle on the Constitutional Law of the United States than most of the American law students.

At the end of the conversation, Zach came clean, admitting that he was not truly a Rastafarian. He explained rather that he was a Christian, albeit one who had incorporated some of the Rastafarian religion into his belief structure. Individuals like Zach were abundant in Cape Town, dismantling stereotypes and overturning paradigms that were commonly understood in the West. The people seemed to rub off on the city, giving it a different sort of soul. Or was it the other way around? It wasn't just the people that made South Africa seem so subtly different though; there was also the transparency of problems created by the country's history. The abundance of crime was so obviously an incident of the unmistakable divide between the affluent inner city and the markedly impoverished townships outside of it. In turn, this divide was historically created through layers of imperialist policies based on racial caste structures.

Walker thought daily about the law and economics and his understanding of human nature. Those with money and power had asked for the current crime problem. Law had been used to subjugate the black man in South Africa, much as it had been all over the world. Now economics was perpetuating the 'evil' that the law had officially let go of. In response to this, more 'evil' arose from the subjugated community. The problems in South Africa were much the same as they were in the States, only more apparent. Apartheid had ended just twelve years prior in 1994.

Though most have never had occasion to consider it, law is in-point-of-fact a tool of colonization. Law is used to create a framework suitable to the colonizer, and then, once firmly established, the architects of the system can leave. The law can even be repealed in time, but economics and human nature will perpetuate the reality that law has forced into being. This doesn't have to come from an invading army; it can come from within the society as well. Mankind has been conditioned to view colonization as a concept applicable to Nation-States alone. But the Nation-State itself is but an incident of a stated cultural identity, which is never anything less than schizophrenic in its conception. Cultures are always made up of multiple separate but pseudo-harmonious subcultures, existing in tandem with various aspects of incongruent countercultures. These cultures are no less at war than those separated by an ocean or a wall. Each plots a future for his enemies defined by principles which will destroy all oppositional defiance, subsuming the 'other'.

Those who believe in a principle do not need a law to pressure their behavior toward compliance with that principle. Law is only necessary to create a framework in which dissenters can be controlled. Once law came to subjugate a people or some aspect of individual freedom, the inertia of history was almost impossible to reverse entirely, but Walker intended to find a way, nonetheless.

Each morning when he woke, he looked out from the balcony and considered the scale of misery that went unnoticed by the privileged. A few weeks after arrival, he had visited a South African prison as part of a class. The students walked freely among the inmates along with a couple of guards and spoke to them about the adequacy of their care and the availability of legal counsel. The prisoners expressed much frustration regarding both.

Walker asked a guard why there were boxes of condoms on the walls in the prison's hallways. The answer was that rape was a sad truth in the prison that could not be controlled. The condoms were provided, along with education about AIDS, in the hope that some dent could be made in the rise of HIV among inmates. At the time, it was estimated that over forty percent of South Africa's prison population was carrying the virus.

Walker learned that when a person was accused of a crime in South Africa, he was either released on bond or was housed in a prison among the general population while awaiting trial. If the person was poor, he was facing a possible death sentence simply by being accused, because his chances of being raped by someone or even multiple people with HIV while awaiting trial were actually quite high. These and other issues became the focus of the comparative law coursework, highlighting distinctions in Criminal Procedure, Alternative Dispute Resolution, and Constitutional Law in each country.

The current paradigm ensured such a reality would persist. The world was helpless to stop the rapes that would occur at the prison that night, and the thought made Walker feel sick.

The physical reality in the prisons could change little without changing multiple layers of society, which would require time and dedication, and not only by South Africa itself. South Africa was part of a complex international structure that was governed by legal and geopolitical realities few understood. For South Africa to change, the whole world would have to change, and not just functionally, but fundamentally. The only hope lay far in the future, and the only true solution required that the entire modern thought construct be restructured. It was a tall order.

As Walker rode the school's charter bus home following the prison visit, he reflected on what he was trying to do in seeking out this experience. He prayed that somehow, through it all, he might find a way to create the beginnings of a new perception that would free others to do what he could not do on his own.

As the days wore on, Walker found his classes an excellent venue for practicing the art of persuasion, and even found occasion to touch on the areas of law that were at the core of what he needed to explain to the Council. In his criminal defense practice, arguments were always limited to what practically applied to the client's situation, and Walker was glad for the opportunity to brush up on his ability to persuade orally with unbounded legal theories. He had nearly forgotten what a joy law school could be at times. He would read through the cases and legal materials for classes each morning, attend seminars for debate most afternoons, and then retire to his veranda, where he would set about trying to grasp the story that was his life. Even more than the legal theory Walker needed to convey, it was his life story that would matter most when he went in front of the Council.

In his mind, it was unlikely that the details of his life would be inquired into directly, but those same details were at the heart of what he needed to explain. For the depth of what he knew, as with all true understanding, was born not of static theory, but dynamic experience. Walker's experience had not come to him in a straight line, nor even in ordered time. The journey he had walked was as complicated and impossible to explain as it was beautiful.

It had begun on a well-worn and comfortable path traveled by many in his corner of the world. But then he had departed that path in favor of a new road, a magnificent wide road full of so many travelers that one never had to walk without company. This new direction led through extravagance and pleasure, but also moved ever closer to a place of darkness and despair. The darkness had been distant enough at first to ignore. Yet as he drew nearer, it became clear that the delights around him were not in keeping with the obvious and steady march toward the pit. Disingenuous beauty is always conceived with sinister purpose, and the lover of beauty is thus betrayed by the same false path that offers it. The effective lure accomplishes its task by hiding the danger amidst sparkle and shine.

Walker had stopped then and considered the inconsistency of his journey with his purpose. The lesson considered was the lesson taught. Resolved, he had first returned to the path of his youth. Then one day, he left it entirely. He set about wandering through the forest of reality in search of a higher plane. As he wandered, he learned to trust his 'self' to feel the direction meant for his life. Soon he walked in confidence, without concern for the routes others had traveled in their search for meaning. He thus came to yearn for an ancient and beautiful path, one which could not be seen unless it was first walked in the blind.

His soul came to understand what the path should look like, and as it did, he began to walk as if he were already on it. In seeking to walk where the path should be, he came to understand. The true path is hidden behind a million lies and a million half-truths, and yet to pursue the hidden Truth is to behold it.

He had the path beneath him; he knew it with a conviction beyond logic or reason. It would lead him home to the sacred place that she had prepared. She that tended the eternal garden. Aiyana.

CHAPTER
Four

A voice called his mind backward in time.

"Open your heart, that I may feel the pain you lived in the time of your first dream's end." The voice floated through his awareness in an airy feminine whisper.

"If you want to know me, you must first know all of you. If you are open with your fear and your loss, I will join you in it so that together we can walk out of that place. I am not afraid to feel the loss of her. Show me that you do not covet your experience of pain. Show me that you want to let her go."

He had fallen in love with the voice over time. It seemed to come to him as do dreams. Suddenly you are in the middle of one, and you cannot recall from where you have come. Your mind awakens to the reality of the dream, and it is all there is, all that ever has been. The reality of the dream is accepted as the definitive 'real' in that moment of first impression, and the 'self' is birthed into its new world fully formed, from some forgotten place outside of time. You know who you are without any context, and your new reality is all that matters.

Her voice was always like that; it was tangible reality without need for precondition. Walker yielded to its power and influence without hesitation, for he knew intuitively that her purpose was to heal a wound he had no hope of treating on his own.

The truth was that Walker had reached a point not long before where suicide became intriguing, if not planned or seriously considered. A young woman named Alizée had found her way into his heart, and then she had chosen to leave, but not before poisoning his understanding of purpose. Losing her had been hard to bear, but it was the mental disease Alizée left behind that began killing him from within. He struggled on for almost a year and a half without her, trying to rid himself of what she had taught him, but to no avail.

Then everything changed in a single evening, the night of his little brother Lucas' high school prom. In that time, Walker's insecurity and failures hijacked the inner world of his mind. In this unstable state, the mind simply lost its ability to maintain control of itself, and it snapped. This was a great blessing to a perception that had been warped into contentment with the careful tending of an internal hell.

On the night of prom, his mother had come home understandably perturbed with Lucas for failing to pick up the house in preparation for dinner with his girlfriend and several other high school couples. She had agreed to host on the condition that the dining room was made presentable for such an occasion. Presentable, it was not.

His mother had begun yelling at Lucas and a fairly strong argument erupted. This all took place at a very fragile moment for Walker. He couldn't seem to stop his mind from racing out of control. He was used to having numerous thoughts running through his head at once, especially since Alizée had left, but lately it had become unbearable. He left his college library that day and came home early. It was only around four o'clock, but he desperately needed to get to sleep so that the thoughts could stop. Sleep was the only way he could escape them, and so each day had become an effort to return to the unconscious state. He simply couldn't stand being aware any longer.

Walker had listened as his mother berated Lucas for his lack of respect and for going back on his agreement. He was struggling to block the negativity out as memories of shattered dreams ran through his head. As the argument escalated, he retreated into his mind to escape it, only to be met with everything he had so desperately been trying to avoid. Alizée was there, or at least the sound of her voice was, calling him back to a time he could not bear to remember.

She had come down from Michigan over Christmas the year before, and Walker had hoped to find a way through to her again. After all, she made the effort to visit, and this had to mean there was a chance. But he had been wrong, and now all he had was the sickening knowledge gained from their time together, coupled with the memories of a love that he could no longer hold.

He heard her voice, the sweet voice he knew in England. "Walker, I want to say something to you, but I don't know if I should."

He heard his own voice responding tentatively. "I want to say something to you too, but I don't know if I should either."

"I wish you would tell me... Walker."

She had gazed at him longingly, desperately. Walker looked down at his hands for a moment, thinking about what he was about to do.

"I love you," he said softly, looking up and into her eyes.

An indescribable look came over her face; it said too many things at once, all of which were good. Something opened inside of her in that moment as she smiled and began to cry.

"I love you so much, Walker."

He could see the time following those words when they had made love, but it was not a pleasant memory. It brought no joy, only sadness, for even as these scenes raced through his mind, others were also playing out.

From another time he heard her say, "Walker, I don't think you should come to stay with me when you get back to the States, it just isn't a good idea anymore."

He could hear her speaking still other things, from that night when they sat in a hot-tub kissing during her visit over Christmas.

"I don't want to be with you anymore Walker, why can't you understand that? It's not that I don't miss you in a lot of ways, I just don't want to be emotionally involved."

He remembered his question. "What do you mean: 'it's not that you don't miss me in a lot of ways'?"

And her words, "I mean like right now, you're so upset, and down, and annoying with all this pressure about 'us', and it is such a turn-off. But at the same time, I look at you and I still feel a lot. I mean, I want to kiss you and to be with you. I miss being with you like that. I miss the way you used to touch me; do you remember?" She smiled coyly. "I want to feel your hands on me again, I think about being with you like that a lot. I just don't want it to mess you up, you know?"

Walker remembered the way he had tried to let go of the love issue so that he might touch her once more, and the way his breathing had nearly stopped when his left hand ran along her thigh while he traced the contours of her face with his right. As his hands first met with her inner world again that night, his mind became overwhelmed with the magic of the things he had tried to forget. Walker could not explain it to himself, but there was an enchantment that occurred when he stroked his hand over her cheek and then back into her hair. Her face felt unlike any other woman's that he had ever caressed, and her inner space was more sacred still. She was unique and beautiful, and every curve was memorized and loved, every line and texture adored.

He heard her words in the car when he had driven to Michigan to see her, and they had gone out to dinner. "Walker, I don't know how to help you understand this, but I just don't want to be tied down. I mean, I really do miss you in a way, but I still want to be young, you know?"

"You mean you want to have sex with other men?"

"Oh my god, I can't believe you just said that."

"You mean that isn't what you meant?"

"No, I mean, actually... it is, but I can't believe you just said it like that."

There had been a long pause and then he asked if she had been with other men already, to which she replied yes, in fact there were three since they had last been together. Those words had stung, but it was what she had said next that rang most loudly in his mind as he lay there on his mother's couch remembering.

"So, who are you with now?" he had asked.

"Mike," she replied, smiling to herself.

"What happened to Paul or whatever his name was?"

She had made an unpleasant face and said, with a disappointed and yet playful tone, "Eh, he was crap."

The meaning of the words had been immediately apparent, and they cut deeply. The other guy simply wasn't any good in bed. Evidently, Mike was. Walker struggled with the concept inherent in the words his beloved had just spoken. He strained to push the thought away, to keep his faith that Alizée loved him for more than sex, that their spirits had been united. She had believed it in England, or at least he had thought this was true. Though even as he fought, the 'truth' was sinking in; his worth was in his ability to bring a woman sexual pleasure, and little more.

He could hardly breathe following those words, sitting silently in her car as she drove along. His mind relived countless unions over their many months together in England. When their schedules would allow, they had often stayed in bed all day, enjoying one another's physical opportunity almost continually. They paused only for an occasional break to eat hunks of chocolate and take drinks of water from the sink next to the bed. The two just focused on being one body as the rain fell against the window, day after English winter day. They didn't need anything else. They were happy just being together.

Walker had thought that they were this way because they felt that much, loved that much, and belonged together that much. He didn't want to believe that he was simply a guy who was up to the task. He attempted to take satisfaction in knowing that he had been a difficult man to replace in this regard, requiring three attempts. But this understanding only spun around on itself, toward realization that it had only taken three attempts to find a comparable specimen. That is all he seemed to be, a good specimen, but certainly replaceable. That understanding had really stuck, and it worked on his soul like a spiritual poison, coloring his world black.

As the memories raced, one thought grew louder and louder. "Eh, he was crap... eh, he was crap... eh, he was crap... eh, he was crap... eh, he was crap..." He couldn't stay here inside his thoughts any longer; he had to leave these things behind.

Walker opened his eyes and let the environment pour in.

"This place looks like a damn pigpen, Lucas. And you just don't give a crap, do you? Because you know that I will do it for you if you just jerk me around long enough huh?"

"No! That's not it! I told you I just forgot!"

The voices around him continued to tighten and elevate in both tone and volume, and he began to feel as if he needed to scream. "Easy, easy, easy," Walker repeated to himself.

He was afraid he couldn't keep his mind under control any longer. He had never felt this unstable before. "Eh, he was crap." The thoughts began to break back in.

"Easy, easy." He tried to fight back the volcano that was finally ready to make itself known.

His mind had already broken at this point, but something beyond it held him together in spite of this. He lay there on the couch staring at the ceiling, and then suddenly, for the first time in years, he had no awareness of anything external. The input simply stopped, and this allowed his mind a moment in which he could feel himself again. His mother's voice went away, as did the many voices from the past, and all he saw was the white of the ceiling. He contemplated The White and remembered what it had once shown him in the way of Truth. In every moment since his first journey into that world, he had known that he would someday face this trial because there was no way to skirt the truth of his love for a woman now gone. His spirit was prepared to face this, he just hadn't understood how badly the loss would fracture his mind. Walker considered his pain from afar and resolved to sit for a time with The White again, as he had once done in those formative days when he first saw beyond the confines of the explicable. After months of torment, he had found a moment of reprieve and peace in spite of all that was around him.

This breakthrough immediately became the source of a torrent of emotion, as the peace was destroyed only moments after it had been found. His mother shouted his name. Then she shouted it again. He shook his head and looked away from the ceiling with indignation for his surroundings. Being called back to reality surprised his mind, and this stirred a great wave of rage.

"How dare you!" This was all he could think. His mother walked up to the couch where he was reclining and began grabbing the half-dozen or so things Walker kept on the end table, making numerous remarks about how he was no better than his brother. She spoke of his rotten depressing mood and 'poor me, poor me' attitude over 'nothing' and stormed out of the room.

Walker's mother had been nothing but supportive of his situation up until this moment, and she had genuinely tried to help him more than anyone else. But in truth, Walker had nearly worn her out, being unable as it were to see anything but his own pain. He had been sleeping on the couch for nearly a year by this point, and he refused to move into a bedroom, saying that he was just passing through. He was a sad and broken version of the son she thought she knew, and it grieved her to see him mired in depression all the time.

Walker did not consider any of this, for he took enormous offense at his mother's assertion that his pain was for 'nothing', and the idea filled his mind like a boiling liquid. He stood, picked up a thirty-pound backpack of economics and ecology books, and walked towards the stairs without any plan, yet aware that a reckoning was at hand. He didn't know what he would destroy, but he understood that something was about to get very broken. His higher 'self' struggled to avoid the loss of control that the rest of him had already committed to, and Walker felt his body begin to choke physically on the emotion as he fought to keep it down. As he neared the stairway, control slipped away, and the volcano erupted. It started with a low roar in the back of his throat and then surfaced as a deep-toned yell of immense volume. Even as the sound waves were beginning to flow, his arm was already in motion. He swung the backpack like a sling and threw all thirty pounds of it twenty feet across the stairway where it smashed a small hole in the plastered drywall.

Having never seen this kind of behavior from her son, his mother came into the room and shouted to stop in a commanding voice. Walker gave her one look and then punched a hole straight through the wall next to her face while screaming at her to shut her mouth. She shut up immediately.

Time slowed and nothing seemed to happen for a while. Then gradually, it began to move again. He had buried his hand inside of the wall, and he focused on it as he wrenched it back out. As Walker stood there panting, blood dripping from his knuckles, he realized that his mother had begun crying, though she was trying to conceal it out of sheer terror.

He looked at what he had done. There was a large crack and a small hole in the wall near the bottom of the stairs from where the backpack had impacted it. Two feet from his face was a cavern the size of a fist. He had gone straight through the plaster and the drywall like a hole-punch, despite having hit the edge of a wooden stud in the wall. His hand had even splintered it, which had, in turn, cut his first two knuckles open.

Walker looked at his mom who, realizing that he was in control of himself, began to cry loudly, saying that he had wanted to hit her. He didn't know what to say. She was wrong. He wished that he had the strength to stop her from pursuing her fears, but he simply didn't have any emotional capacity left. He backed up, eyes glazed in confusion, and let himself out of the house.

Walker sat in the front yard on the wooden porch swing for a good long while, looking at his hand. It was utterly amazing, the power that had just been unleashed. The skin on the index knuckle had been pulverized, and the middle knuckle had been cut open by a wood splinter. It was hard enough to punch through drywall, let alone to sheer it off along a stud. And thick plaster? Plaster added a lot of strength to a wall. But his hand had blown through it like it wasn't even there. Even now, it didn't really hurt. He just sat there staring at his hand, marveling at the power he had exerted, yet genuinely confused by the use he had put that power to.

After an hour or so, his father came home and went into the house. It was at this time that Walker began to feel truly ashamed. His father had done nothing to him. At least with his mom, he could tell himself that she shouldn't have called his loss of Alizée 'nothing'. His father had gotten up at five-thirty in the morning as he did six days every week and gone to work building custom homes. He had worked until six-thirty at night, and then come home to the house that he had crafted years ago using his own two hands, out of love for his young wife and new baby boy. What could Walker possibly say to him? There was nothing to say. He understood that he would probably be told to leave.

As expected, his father came outside and told him that they needed to talk. They walked down to the end of the cul-de-sac and back and he explained to Walker that he was sorry for what he was going through and that he thought it understandable that it was tearing him up like it was. He said he understood that Alizée was important to him, but that it had been over a year, and it didn't look like she was going to honor what he wanted her to.

"I'm not saying you should give up Walker, I'm just saying that you shouldn't let the fact that one person is refusing to love you blind you to the fact that you have a whole family that loves you right here, even if it feels like they don't care. The truth is that your family does care, and the woman you love doesn't seem to. Your mother is frustrated over being unable to help. How many nights has she sat up talking with you over the past year? She gives and gives, and nothing seems to work. She's getting desperate.

"She wants to help but understands deep down that she is powerless to stop the hurt. It isn't the natural order of things for you to find an answer in her. But a mother cannot bear to see her son suffering. She wants to believe that you're bigger than this pain, but she fears you are not."

Walker glanced at his father to verify that he knew how far his son's mind had descended. His dad confirmed this knowledge with his gaze.

"You must remember," he continued, "once upon a time, your mother and I shared a love that became who you are. Think of your love for Alizée, only imagine it had manifest as a new human being. Then imagine your love survived and grew and thrived, but then forgot its origin because it lost the love of another. You would suffer deeply watching the son you love struggle because of those who are unworthy of him. It is right that you should seek to carry your heritage forward, to recreate the love that made you. But letting the search for that Return destroy the love that already came to be, which is literally *you,* Walker, is a blasphemy against all that *you* are and all that *you* come from. If Alizée would believe that she does not need you, then she is not worthy of your intention. You cannot fulfill your heritage with a woman who wants less than who you are. Don't you know that you are born of something much greater than she is willing to see? I know the love from which you are made, and it is beyond what you have found in her.

"Let me tell you what I believe. I believe that we are all searching for our path, and for the One who creates the path in the first place. Each of us must search out the direction we are meant for, and for some of us, that is more difficult than for others. There is a hidden trail that you have yet to find, and I pray that you find it soon. On it you will discover the beauty that your soul longs for. I believe in you, Walker, and in a woman still unseen. You are a man. You are my son. Your heritage is to rise above this, and you will. Honor me in this and stand up now. Don't let the fact that Alizée isn't who she should be pollute your ability to be who you should be. You can only control who *you* will be, but that is enough once you understand it."

His father stopped mid-step and looked at the ground with sudden purpose. His voice tensed as he considered the limits of his ability to save his son. "I will not let you do this to your mother and your brothers and sisters." He looked back up, continuing, "We love you Walker, and we want to be here for you right now, but you're going to have to decide if you can respect that. If you can't promise me that you won't do anything like this again, then you have to leave. Can you promise me this won't happen again?"

Walker promised his father that day that he would change, in fact, that he had already changed, which was true. In the days that followed, he would sit outside on the porch swing and talk with his sister Rochelle and watch their younger siblings play. He'd throw the football around with Lucas and their younger brother Isaac and chase their youngest sister, Hanna. He apologized sincerely to his mother and began to think positive thoughts again, though they remained in the minority. Alizée and the pain and the questions still plagued most of his days, but the voices from the past had grown softer. Now they had competition from the sounds of his brother laughing as he chased their sister around the yard and his father's 360 cubic inch Dodge Ram rounding the corner as he would return home from work each night. Walker began coming home in time for dinner with his family, and he moved off the couch and into his childhood room in the loft of their home. He had reached the bottom, and he had turned around.

A Personal Letter from Walker:

I must take this opportunity to speak into this story, as it is my hope that all who read these words will come to see what I have seen regarding the gift of life, and regarding the lie that opens the door to leaving your own story behind.

Suicide isn't always about believing things can't get better, as many suggest. Lack of faith is rarely the problem. For many, suicide is simply a desperate attempt to stop the torture which has taken root inside the mind. The individual gives in, to a desire for the pain to cease, to a desperate want for a break from reality and thought, even if that break is eternal. The decision is more instinctual than rational, though it manifests through rationality. The moment becomes too much to bear, and the person's will to live on gives way to a desire to find a way out of the pain, like someone in a burning building jumping to their death. To be aware is to be in pain, and to sleep is to escape awareness. Eternal sleep becomes the goal.

I never reached that point, but I understood it clearly and personally. I slept to avoid being conscious of my life as much as I could, and I worked to occupy my mind during waking hours. I often thought of the ease of suicide and felt almost cheated because I was not allowed that way out.

It seemed to me, in the midst of my pain, that I was paying for the mistakes I had made, and that suicide would make those mistakes permanent rather than bring relief. I believed this because I knew the soul was eternal. You cannot end suffering by removing yourself from the reality you know, for this only solidifies the reality you seek to escape. For life is, by its very nature, the process of growth and change. To abandon it is to accept the current reality, and to preclude evolving into something better.

In my childhood, I was always told that people possessed a soul, and that the soul was eternal. I had always believed this, but that belief had been fragile, and as years passed it continually waned in the face of my 'education'. But then I journeyed to the far shore of this experience we call reality, against all advice, and I experienced firsthand the perfection of that white land. The purity that my mind encountered there changed everything in my perception.

Although it took me some time to work through the wrongs that pervaded my mind after my first journey beyond, I immediately understood that the Truth required me to endure this part of my story, no matter how much it hurt. It was for this reason that I never abandoned my life in the midst of the pain and confusion over Alizée. Had I not seen the far shore with my own eyes, suicide might have remained an option. Most could never understand or believe this to be true, for in reality, my problems were rather small. But reality is not the way of the mind; rather, it is perception that is key to the mindscape.

Man is not wrong for being unable to handle everything that life can throw at him; he is wrong for believing that he *can* handle it, rather than admitting of his need for strength from beyond. What is more, man is not wrong for being unable to handle the idea that life has no meaning, rather he is quite right to be unable to handle such a concept. Man is meant to realize that the idea is simply untrue. Man is only wrong for failing to believe in the Truth. The Truth is that life is not only meaningful, life is meaning itself.

The question, therefore, is not "can you handle reality", but rather "what do you choose to believe reality is?" Given the wrong vision of reality, no person can handle it. Given the correct vision of reality, however, a human being cannot be broken. The key to happiness lies in finding the Truth of Life amidst an endless sea of falsehoods.

The truth is that the world is never better off without you. It is, however, true that the world may be better off with a different you. The gift of your life lies in realizing you can *be* and *become*, and it's your birthright to find joy in *both*. I pray that you will never lose your life to your own deception. Always remember that if you feel your life isn't worth living, then it may be time to find yourself another life. The good news is that you have the power to do just that at any point in time. This is the nature of Grace. We can all begin again. It is noble to hold onto your understanding of yourself, but not to the point of letting your own thoughts destroy you and everything that you love.

The enemy of Truth has the advantage of being able to claim that *it* is the Truth, but this advantage is forever limited by the intrinsic nature of what a lie is. There is power in the ability to counterfeit, but it can never equal the power of the genuine article without losing its essence in favor of that which it tries to copy. The counterfeit implies a divergence from the original, not a perfect clone.

The pretender always runs the risk of succeeding in its deception to the full, and in-so-doing yielding itself to the authentic reality by actually becoming what it seeks to corrupt. In point-of-fact, this is the inevitable end to all who pretend and deceive. They cannot survive forever. Truth is different, Truth never ceases to Be.

I reached inside a world unseen
And found in her the stuff of dreams
These dreams unfolded like a page
A secret book I alone could read

Her world was poisoned
Though I did not know
Mind was young
Spirit far too bold

Upon a moment my dream did turn
A detail missed
A snake unseen
My world unmade before my eyes

Darkness and death then took my gaze
Upon another's altar my 'self' degrade

Still the light shines in from behind my wall

CHAPTER

Five

There was once a day, though precisely when it came to pass can no longer be recalled, in which I decided to take a drive. The drive went on for an entire day and into the next until it brought me to the base of a great mountain range. The drive then turned into a walk, and the walk turned into a climb. The climb, in turn, took me to a place from which I again chose to ascend; this time not by effort, but by a focus on the sublime as I sat on the tundra and soaked in the sun. The day had come sometime after the heartache had ended, but before the answer had been found.

I pursued the physical climb for an entire afternoon and evening, so that the known reality might be left behind and something new discovered. Mile after mile, the hike went on until the path was abandoned entirely in favor of direct ascension. My body strived skyward into the night by light of the moon, and then, just before dawn, in a state of euphoria brought on by the altitude and exhaustion; I lay down under the stars and slept. Upon awakening in the morning, there was no sense of concern with these actions. Where it seemed there should have been a self-critical opinion regarding apparent irresponsibility for the flouting of nature without precaution or regard for safety, there was instead an all-encompassing trust and faith that no harm could befall me. I had hiked and camped quite a lot in my life and learned that one should never venture into an unknown wilderness without provisions. The weather could turn quickly, and on many occasions, I had confronted storms and weather that would have killed me but for my preparations. But this journey was different, nothing bad would happen, and somehow this was known completely.

Something was pulling me to it, and I would follow without question. I had felt it almost a thousand miles away, begging me to come and to come *now*. I had taken the week off work and driven to somewhere unknown. "West." That was all the mind could think until my eyes beheld the mountains. My spirit had followed these feelings here and only stopped when my body gave out from exhaustion. As eyes took in the morning light, I suddenly knew that I had reached the place that had pulled me to journey westward, and I saw that my awareness had already begun to meld into the scene beyond. I felt my 'self' as 'I', present and fully aware, which had not happened for several years now in mundane reality. Something was calling me into a deeper realization of myself, and toward a unification of worlds.

I sat up on my bed of tundra and saw the place that time had in mind for me. A river of sun was pouring through the clouds as if a mighty waterfall had emerged from Heaven. It spilled out onto the center of a vast tundra prairie, light flowing outward from the place where the falls plunged into a great rippling lake of liquid energy which moved atop the alpine realm in shallow transparency. My body stood and waded through the waters of the liquid-golden, toward the place where Heaven's Light met Earth's substance. Upon reaching it, I lay down and stared into the sky, bathed in the warmth from above.

Eyes closed only for a moment, but when they reopened, reality had shifted dramatically again, and I beheld another place and time entirely. Much as moments before, upon awakening for the first time this day, my eyes took in the light of their new surroundings timidly. Where the field had been set ablaze by the intensity pouring from the heavens, its glow here was soft, and thin, and diffused, despite an obvious power. The contrast could not have been more pronounced. The mountain and the fields of golden tundra were gone, as was the river which illuminated that world. I was now in a dimly lit cave of sorts, and my body was lying on a bed of conifer needles. Though the light here was thin, it had an almost tangible quality to it, as if it could be gathered and drank. Still, only a sliver of its energy was finding its way into this world of earth and wood. This place seemed familiar, reminiscent of a memory from a time long ago.

I marveled at the small beams breaking through the dense foliage that blocked the cave opening, laying bare the contents of the air for my eyes to perceive. Removing the pine branches, I recognized them as those taken from the tree which had fallen along the path that lived in the outer world, and I remembered my search. As my body emerged from the tree's inner space, it was delivered into a world of ethereal enchantment. The sun had come out, and the fresh scent of a newly fallen rain carried on the slight breeze, entwined with the subtle fragrances of moist wood and dirt. I looked to my left, remembering my surroundings, and focused on the place the branch had been found earlier that morning, or perhaps a thousand years ago. Time made no sense in this place.

Thoughts were now of little other than the splendor of this nearly forgotten land as I began to walk around the giant trunk of the mighty tree inside of which reality had drifted. My body felt amazing, my muscles seemed full of energy and life, and I felt like running for no reason other than the appreciation of the ability to do so. As my body came around to the front of the tree where the path pertained, it took off in a sprint.

A half-mile later, I slowed to a jog, having made record time for the distance covered, but having also overrun my ability to keep up with the effort. Some time was needed to recover; my sides were hurting badly, and my muscles were refusing to maintain the pace. Feeling gratified and accomplished for my effort, the run slowed again, and I returned to the walk.

Sauntering along now with my hands above my head, exhilarated and still panting, my ears began to focus on something in the distance. At first, it was difficult to make anything of the sounds, and my mind struggled to sort through its catalogue of possibilities to find a match. It was a complex sound, and it was being crafted by something, but at this distance, I could not determine anything more. As I continued to close in, the sounds suddenly leapt forward, now originating from directly in front of me. I stopped abruptly. It was the voice of a man, and though I could not understand the reason, it was instantly apparent that he was from a time far before my own. His voice moved again, the chants seeming to weave among the spires of wood as if he were directing them consciously. The sound returned first to the distance, then moved quickly to the left of the path, then to the right, and then began to emanate from each of them in stereo. The language was one unlike any I had ever heard, though it mimicked the patterns of Native American songs once heard during a lifetime faintly recalled.

I began moving forward again, cautiously seeking to avoid disturbing the author of the sounds. Walking to the edge of the path nearest the place where the sounds seemed to have settled, I peered out from behind a large boulder into a clearing. An ancient man was there, dressed in animal skins and covered in ferns and purple flowers. He possessed a flowing beard that spoke the color of snow, and his hair joined with it to form a frame which contrasted with his bronzed face, which was expertly chiseled to convey strength, wisdom, vigor, and age. He sat cross-legged between two great trees that had grown closer and closer together across the millennia until they had arrived at a place where a man could sit between them and rest one hand on each. This was their purpose in this place, it seemed. The man appeared to communicate with them, or perhaps for them.

I stepped out from behind the boulder and walked toward the man until only a few steps away, then stopped and sat down amidst the ferns as he chanted. For a long while, he remained lost in his experience. Finally, the man finished, and his eyes opened as he removed his hands from the trees in time. He looked at me with complete acceptance and stood slowly to greet me. I rose and stepped forward to offer my hand in friendship. The man stared at it strangely, and then, perhaps remembering a life he had once lived, he extended his own.

He smiled as we shook hands and then spoke in a language that we both knew from the other world.

"Please… sit."

I looked at him curiously as he motioned for me to sit in the place that he had just occupied between the two trees.

"Please… sit," he offered again.

I walked over to the spot that the man seemed insistent upon and then sat down on the mat of conifer needles covering the ground. The man went over to a nearby satchel I had not previously seen and removed some sticks and tools from it. He then sat in front of me, leaving enough space between us to pile the sticks in anticipation of a small fire. He reached into a small pouch around his waist and removed a tightly bound bundle of dry grass wrapped in a leaf, which was smoldering faintly. I watched, intrigued as the man breathed gently into it. Smoke began to flow, and then, with a few more breaths, fire burst forth.

"I prepared this when I awoke today, as I knew I would be in need of fire," he said, eyes focused on the tender flame. "I saw it in my dreams. But I did not know the purpose would be so noble or so personal to me. I saw a stranger in my mind, and he was in need of fire."

The man spoke very slowly and deliberately.

"I understood that you would come, but I did not know who you would be. Now I understand who you are. I am very happy to be a part of this creation. In seeking to obey the spirit for the benefit of another, I have found happiness and the rebirth of all that I have ever desired to be true."

"What do you mean? Who am I exactly? I don't understand."

"You are the one who is searching for that which should be found. I too once searched and found what I sought amidst the trees, and the rain, and the fog. You will find what you seek. She is my creation, born of the creation of lovers from another time. You will find completion inside the world she has designed and tended for you, and then one day, you too will desire what I desire. The love that was born of the love seeks to find its way to still more love. I see now that it is to be found again. There is no greater joy than this."

The man reached up and began to untie an amber necklace that he wore, and as he did, he began to speak in the ancient language from his song, which came in a rhythmic sort of cadence. The amber pendant was a perfect sphere, with a small, curved hole tunneled through one side. It hung on a rope of hemp that had been wound and braided in an exquisite fashion. He placed the rope around my neck and tied it in place as he chanted what seemed to be a prayer or blessing.

I looked the man in the eyes and thanked him with a nod. He had long since placed the burning grass under the small pile of sticks, and they were beginning to crackle and pop as their energies released into the air around us.

"You are going to find the way," he continued. "But you must understand that you are not yet there. You must open your heart and your spirit to what I must tell you; to what you have to tell your 'self'. But most importantly, you must remain open to the world of the spirit and the light. Much is yet to be done, and you must finish that process before completion can be found. Do not despair the learning, for it is the heart of what you will find. Look always forward to where you long to be, and be always ready to go there when you come to see the way. But be happy in today as well, for what has already been found and understood. The understandings of today give birth to the understandings of the future that you will share with her. Tell me what you know of your mistakes with the women you tried to love. Let us help each other find the understanding."

I thought for a moment and then spoke tentatively. "I know that I began with a pure heart, but then I compromised what I desired when I could not find what I sought. I was intent on having what I longed for in my own time, and so I looked for someone to love, even if they were not forever. I fell in love with a woman named Nadia, and I treated her as if she were forever, sharing all that I was, yet neglecting to commit. I should not have compromised the dream this way. I should have either sought union or awaited it; I should not have tried to do both at once.

"I became confused and promised her that I would always stay with her, even though I was not ready to promise such a thing. I hated her for the mistakes she had made that hurt me, and for sharing herself with another, and I destroyed what was good with hate for the things that were not. Then I rebelled against my wrongness with wrongness of an opposite kind, offering all that I was to a woman yet again, but this time insisting that love need not be exclusive, even in the moment, and that each person should remain unburdened by commitment. Two promises were made, and each destroyed the other, and nearly my sense of 'self' along with them."

"You think about the women you loved often. You still love them," the man stated.

"Always," Walker confirmed his assertion with steady eyes.

"Good. They should not be forgotten. You have failed by betraying yourself and the path, but this is not beyond repair. You already understand this well. Grace is the greatest gift the Creator has ever given a creature such as man. It is Grace that we should all seek. But I wonder... do you understand the way your soul was set up to lose itself? Do you see the trap that lies in wait for our kind?"

"I believe so."

"Tell me."

"By trying to force love, I ended up driving it away, which caused me great pain. I responded in ways that drove love away still further, causing even deeper pain. Slowly but surely, I was broken down until my will was almost destroyed. I realized that I had made eternal promises and then failed to honor my 'self' by failing to honor those promises. Ultimately, it was I who betrayed both Nadia and Alizée at the outset of those relationships, by trying to partake of their beauty at the highest level without committing to give myself in a way that sufficiently honored what they gave.

"This then sprung the trap. The world told me to see myself as innocent. The world said I need not continue to hurt over my loss. This lie would have destroyed me had I not been so suspicious of it. In truth, the way forward is to understand that you have failed by your own standard as to what you truly want, and that your innocence is granted by the Grace of the spirit in-spite-of your personal culpability in betraying your own ideal. Freedom from our sins is not deserved; it is gifted from that which lies beyond."

The man looked at me intently, eyes unwavering and kind.

"Yes. Even as we speak, understanding is with you, though we must speak nonetheless. Knowing what one feels in his heart is essential to the pursuit of happiness. Lying to one's 'self' about what he believes and feels does absolutely no good to anyone. Perfecting the 'self' is the end to which all life is geared, and it can never be sought through false understanding.

"When a person claims to believe in something eternal, and then later betrays that claim, this person has cast a curse on all future attempts to believe in things of an eternal nature. This curse is the knowledge that your most fundamental ideas of 'who you are' have been manipulated by your 'self' to keep you from the truth: you do not truly believe in what you purport to.

"It has been said that a house divided against itself cannot stand. Know this: where the house is the temple of the human body, its collapse results in defilement of the sacred.

"Human beings allow themselves to believe that they are static phenomena, either x or y. They are, however, dynamic entities that can engage in support of x or y one minute, then change their support to the other in the next, or divide it among the two, without becoming either.

"This comes from a need to categorize, implicit in a life where survival depends on studying and distinguishing the environment and its inhabitants; knowing who to depend on, who to fear, and who to trust. Thus, man's perception is driven by this way of thinking.

"This equating of concepts saves time and effort mentally, but its utility comes with a cost. For unlike the inanimate portions of existence, mankind is truly defined only by the fact that he is indefinable and unpredictable. Free Will is the fundamental core making man what he is.

In equating a human being to a constant idea, we diminish the person's identity as an evolving dynamic.

"The truth can be seen clearly in the failure of the world that championed the idea that human beings were static things to be categorized. There is one particular aspect of reality that exposes the fallacy of equating people with their labels: the fact that people do not always stick to what they say they are or what they have shown themselves to be by the world's definitions.

"People are often adamant that they are something but then decide later that they are the opposite of that something. These occurrences are frequent in our world, because we insist on applying static theories to dynamic entities. Individuals beholden to the lie of static existence must still confront this reality, and they typically do so by conceiving of the 'self' as something that changes from one categorized thing to another over time.

"This allows a person to see the actions he took and the commitments he made in the past as being separate from his current understanding of 'self'. In his mind, he is not bound by his past promises if they did not contemplate the present reality that he now understands. In effect, a man believes that he is freed of pledges he makes under one circumstance if circumstances change in relation to the pledge. But this understanding is faulty and destructive to the premise of both oath and covenant.

"We both must understand this if we are to fulfill the purposes for which we are created, and so I do not wish to simply preach to you but invite you to tell me what you know of these things yourself."

Walker contemplated the invitation for a few moments. Understanding seemed to seep in from the forest world around him.

"Since the purpose of life is to grow, a static conception of 'self' is the antithesis of life. It is quite literally a death force. Many people ground their identity in membership to groups that mirror their choices, whether they be political organizations, social causes, corporate sports teams, or a particular sexual inclination. The main problem isn't making choices of any particular variety or identifying with a certain group or way of living. The problem is failing to own our choices as expressions of an intentional 'self'. We must recognize that we are not bound to a static framework where we must continue identifying with anything in particular. We retain our ability to choose in each moment. We are not our thoughts, and we are not our choices. The moment we forget this, we reduce ourselves to slaves for the force behind the lie designed to destroy us.

"It is accurate in a sense to say that a person is 'who he is' in a given moment, but not in any meaningful sense, because he cannot stay in that moment. He must progress, but to where? Wherever he progresses will necessarily redefine 'who he is' in this sense. If a man starts with a definition of 'self', it is redefined in each successive instant in some form or fashion simply because the man is unable to remain unaffected by his experiences. This is true even in his dreams. His progression through time creates a chain of infinite changes to his 'self' so minute as to become impossible to identify or even comprehend. This is the nature of flux, it is not actually a succession of changes, but rather a state of perpetual change. No matter how refined our digital conception of 'self' becomes, it can never be True, because life and Truth are not digital, they are analog."

The man smiled and leant forward intently. "In truth, the one correct understanding of your present 'self' is that you are quite literally a 'being' that has constant occasion to understand and shape your own conception. When your existence is defined by 'being', you cannot separate it from 'becoming', because when you choose to 'become' you already 'are'. But until a 'being' understands that it should '*seek* to become'; it has not yet become *aware* of itself as a 'being'. There is no such thing as 'who you are', rather there is only the continual evolution of the way your essence flows, guided and shaped by the intention of your mind and the messages hidden in our souls.

"Our continual evolution is the purpose to which our awareness of 'self' is geared. It is this awareness that gives us the power to grow into what we want to be. We can go anywhere, save one place. We cannot decide to go back to a present past, where 'we are' what 'we were' again, excluding the experiences that have transpired. This is true because of what the present is. It is awareness of the very state of flux that defines the existence that we have internalized into our own conceptions, and our experience of the present as living beings is defined by the nature of that flux. The difference between the present time, and every other time, is that we are in between our future choices and our past storyline. We must admit of our history, but we must understand that we do not live in it. Rather, we live at the edge of our own creation, building who we are even as we struggle to understand who we want to become. When we lose our connection to the present by setting down our understanding of 'self' as fluid, we are dead because we are done changing."

I sat for a few moments in quiet contemplation amidst the sensation of warmth radiating out from the man's small fire. The ironic and profoundly sad truth of the world was that once a person saw himself statically, his desire to remain whole became the very tool with which he was fractured. Having fallen for the greatest of lies, man came to believe something untrue. He came to understand himself as a *something*, rather than as a *someone*. He came to believe that he needed to guard his definitions of self, rather than guard his intention as one who transcends definition entirely.

The ancient man continued to sit, tending his fire now and then with a stick procured from the forest floor. It was beginning to die down a bit, and there were no longer any significant flames, but the small bed of red coals remained warm enough to feel from where I was sitting several feet away. After a few minutes sitting in silence, the man stood slowly and retrieved his satchel. He removed some herbs and then returned to the warmth, placing them atop the coals where they began to smolder. They gave off a thick smoke and a pungent scent that I instantly adored.

"There is one more thing which you must understand before I go," he said as he watched the gases billowing into the air. "Listen closely to these words, though you will scarcely understand them, and let their meaning open to you in time's own preference."

He paused, and then began slowly as if he were quoting, "Know that any given life is itself, the presence of a collective internal preference for a given ordered state, in relation to the components of that which makes up a given ordered reality in a particular region of space-time.

"Self-awareness is the recognition of the preference of the given collective, or the identified physical 'self', if you like, experienced by the mind, which is evolved by the 'self' toward the purpose of guarding and perpetuating the preference it holds. The individual is, in point of fact, a collective unification of billions of diverse cells coded to think of themselves as unitary. This preference is exclusive to the individual and is opposed to all that are not a part of its vision.

"Love is then the bending of this collective self-awareness to comprehend that its own preference may favor the preference of another, separate, and normally adverse collective awareness. Do you understand?"

"I'm following as best I can."

"Sexual union is the process of two self-aware collectives submitting themselves to a shared vision of a future collective so that their 'self' might Return to the place of beginning rather than submit to death.

"True Love is this sexual union, but born of Love. Namely, two collectives submitting themselves to a shared vision of a future collective through process of cosmic synergy produced from the mingling of their intentions. When two individual human beings each come to insist on the preference of the other, intention comes to a halt, and the way forward becomes unknown to either of them. A vision must then materialize to resolve the schism. Thus, an 'as yet unmade awareness', a child of their love, becomes the new identity of 'self', and the fulfillment of a legacy twice believed.

"The purpose of a universe in motion through both space and time is mirrored by all life within it. Though dependent on the greater Universe for its existence, all life seeks to assert the Truth inherent in the code it carries, even if only in the microcosm. Life honors the unending nature of the whole beyond it, by laying claim to a shadow of the power which calls creation forward from the unmade and unknown. Life proclaims, 'I AM HERE', and 'I AM GOING TO BECOME'. Becoming necessitates setting down the current 'self', in favor of that which calls to us. Thus, we move about, searching for tomorrow. Some lose their way, and some find it, but only those who *love* can find the path to the dream of rebirth as a new soul.

"You must come to understand this truth, and you must come to see the power present in the dance of 'self' with 'other'; so that you may also come to see the false one's plan for humanity. There is a growing counterfeit which mimics and then debases the divine-human model. You must learn to see it and to understand how it has wormed its way into the world of man's concocted ethics. Only then will you have the power to challenge the lies. For the lie that remains hidden from recognition, enjoys the accolades of truth."

When he finished speaking, he motioned for me to place my hands on the trees as he had done earlier. Then placing his own together as if in prayer, he bowed slightly, which I mimicked in return. With this gesture, he turned and walked away. To my surprise, upon reaching the trail he broke into a fast jog, chanting as he moved out of my reality. As the sound of his voice faded, I reflected on the truth that was now so clear. I was going to love her so much.

The Love born of THE LOVE
Seeks to be born again
I have searched through space and time
And now I understand

I am awake
I am free
LOVE has gifted these to me

Now I know why I long to be
Back inside of mystery
Searching in the hidden place
Where all is right and pure

Love pines to make a nascent flesh
So I shall come into your dream

Come my love
Return

CHAPTER
Six

One Saturday morning, half a year after his fight with the wall, Walker pulled into a small municipal airport on the cusp of sunrise. The temperature had dropped overnight, and a slight frost had formed on the trees and grass. Everything was a muted, white version of its typical self. He parked the car, shut off the engine, and stepped out.

"Holy shifters, where did you get this? Is this yours?" Preston walked up and shook his hand, admiring the car.

Walker replied that it was.

"Sweet. Can you start it back up for a minute?"

Preston was Walker's flight instructor. He had agreed to take him on as a student when Walker took a job at the airport a few months before.

Walker fired the car's engine again.

"What's it got in it?" Preston wanted to know. Walker popped the hood and revealed the chromed-out, 350 cubic-inch, Chevrolet engine.

"Sweet, what's it do in the quarter?"

"Thirteen-point-four seconds at 104 miles per hour."

"Nice. How much quicker is your FZR? What's it, 12 flat?"

"I hit 118 miles per hour in eleven-point-seven seconds with it."

"Good Lord! That's haulin'!'"

"You gonna' walk out with me?" Walker asked.

"No, I think I'll go inside and get a coffee. I like having a drink in my hand when I'm watching a show."

Walker smiled and shut the car off again, giving Preston a casual salute as he turned and began walking toward the plane.

He looked the aircraft over carefully, checking the lights and the control surfaces: the ailerons, the flaps, the elevator, and the rudder. He made note of the fact that the frost was melting rapidly under the increasing energy from the sun and was completely gone from the wings. He checked the pitot tube opening and the static port, as well as each of the plane's structural components. He checked the oil and fuel levels and drained the fuel sump to remove any moisture. Then he climbed inside the cockpit.

Preston shouted some last-minute advice and encouragement from the door to the flying service, and then retired to a plastic chair he had set just outside. Today was a big day. Today was Walker's first solo flight. Preston would not be there to bail him out if he botched things up like he had often done in the beginning.

Walker recorded the number on the Hobbs meter so that he could verify the engine run time after the flight. Then he began his checklist.

"Seatbelts fastened? Check."

"Fuel shut off valve on? Check."

"Radios and electrical equipment off? Check."

"Brakes set? Check."

"Mixture to rich. Carburetor heat set to cold. Electrical master switch back on. Priming one, two, three pumps, throttle open a quarter inch. Well, this is it."

He opened the little window and yelled, "Clear," waited a second and then fired the starter switch. The prop turned and spun to life.

"Okay, okay." The nerves really started to set in now.

"Oil pressure in the green? Check."

He turned on his radio and tuned it to ASOS frequency to listen to the weather and wind information.

"Automated weather observation one two three one zulu, wind zero five zero at zero four, visibility one zero, sky condition broken at eight thousand, temperature zero two Celsius, dew point zero four Celsius, altimeter three zero two eight." He set his altimeter and then switched the radio to tower frequency.

"Tower this is Seven-Two Quebec Whiskey at the flying service, ready to taxi with the numbers."

He waited for a response.

"Roger, Quebec Whiskey, you are clear to taxi."

He released the brake and throttled the engine up to about a thousand RPM. The plane eased into motion. Thirty seconds later, it was at the run-up area for takeoff. Time for another checklist.

After surveying all the important instruments, Walker keyed the microphone. "Tower, Seven-Two Quebec Whiskey is holding short of One-Two for closed traffic."

"Roger, Quebec Whiskey, you are clear for closed traffic."

He throttled the plane up and drove onto the runway – this was about to get real.

Twenty minutes later, his feet were back on the ground. He was soon talking to Preston and a group of veteran pilots; the back of his shirt having been ceremonially cut out as is the custom for solo-flight survivors.

"How'd you hold up, get freaked out at all?" asked Preston.

"No, not really. It was kind of strange though. Those three takeoffs and landings just now were the smoothest and most precise I've ever done. It's like my mind knew it was time to perform at a higher level."

"Awesome."

"Yeah, awesome," he thought to himself. He had just flown a plane, something that he had dreamt of doing since he was a boy.

"You want to grab something to eat?" Preston suggested.

"Sure."

They crossed the airport parking lot and entered a small restaurant overlooking the airfield. They sat down at a table and spent a few minutes talking about the details of the flight and Preston's plans for the weekend, before wading into the deeper conversation that each of them knew they were going to have. They had started making a point of seeking these moments out with one another. It soon became obvious that Preston had a specific question he wanted to ask.

"What is it, Preston?" Walker asked, looking over his glass as he took a slow drink of water.

"What are you talkin' about?" Preston smirked.

"What is it you want to know?"

There was a long, uncertain silence, and then Preston asked his question.

"Well, I don't want to be nosey or pushy or all evangelical or anything, but are you a Christian?"

"Walker's expression was difficult to decipher, and he looked steadily at Preston as he responded, "That's a question I have trouble answering for some pretty complex reasons."

"Fair enough. Do you pray?"

The truth was, Walker had been praying a lot at that time, but he didn't want to expose his inner thoughts to Preston too hastily. Preston was a devout Christian, and though Walker appreciated his goodness in this regard, he also felt a degree of hesitancy around him. He feared that Preston might be unwilling to entertain his liberal understanding of some things that were viewed by most Christians as clearly wrong. Walker valued having a good friend like Preston and didn't want to lose him over a misunderstanding.

After setting down the pursuit of women, he had found himself truly alone. This had been a source of added strain on his mind at first and was certainly a factor in his battle with the wall at his parent's house. Slowly but surely, prayers had emerged.

The act of praying, Walker had begun to understand, was simply responding to the recognition that you are not alone, even when you are by yourself. Religious people seemed to believe that this is because God is with us. Atheists seemed to attribute it to the mind talking to itself. They were both right in Walker's estimation.

He related some of these ideas to Preston, telling him that he had not prayed much in his life until these harder times had come, though he had not realized this until recently.

"What do you mean?" Preston asked.

"I mean, as a kid I would pray, but it was always the same thing. God please keep me safe, keep my family safe, bless this food, help me do good in school and finally hit a home run in little league. Oh, and help the Cardinals win the World Series. You know, it was all boilerplate stuff. I wasn't really seeking God, or his advice or will, I was just asking for stuff."

"I get ya," Preston said.

"Now it's different," Walker told him. "Now I pray to understand what should be, to see what is good and what is not, and to have the will to follow what is good even when I prefer what is not."

"Why would you ever want to do what's 'evil'?"

"I didn't say anything about 'evil', but now I suppose I have to. 'Evil' isn't what people think it is, Preston. You probably see the world in terms of good and 'evil', because that is how we have been taught. Most people seem to think they are opposites, but I don't think it's that simple. See, only good exists in truth. 'Evil' is a non-thing, a nothing. The concept exists, but that is all it is... a concept."

"Where did you get that from?" Preston laughed playfully.

"From inside The White," Walker smiled back, almost embarrassed.

"Huh?"

"Never mind that. Look, 'evil' doesn't exist. Only good exists. This is why 'evil' cannot overcome good. When I was a kid, the question to my mom was always, 'what if the Devil wins in the end? How can we know that God will win?' In my childhood understanding, a day was literally coming when good and 'evil' would fight to decide things. I figured that there was no reason to fight if the conclusion was foreclosed. So, I began to worry that 'evil' might prevail. But my thoughts were only those of the unsophisticated mind, the child's mind. In a physical sense, there may indeed be a battle one day, I cannot say that there will not be. But in the sense of what force will prevail through time, the so-called 'battle' is anything but.

"When you turn on the lights, can it be said that light and dark battle one another, but light wins? You see the flaw in this way of looking at it. Light simply illuminates the room when the lights come on. It is undoubtedly the victor when it shows up, the question is where it shows up, and when, and why. The same is true of what is good and right, also called Truth, or God.

Walker continued, "'Evil' is just a word to describe the conscious choice of those capable of disavowing the good, the preferable, the correct. 'Evil' is denying what is good, denying 'that which is', or the 'I AM' of existence. Thus, though a tree and a man can both do what is good, only the man can do what is 'evil', because he thinks he can understand it.

"Blinded by the idea that 'evil' exists, man ignores the fact that it is only he that can choose to ignore what is good and right. 'Evil' is born in him because he chooses to conjure it, and it grows in his world because he ignores his responsibility in creating it. Man would rather blame God and creation for his own inability to live rightly than admit the truth and blame himself."

Preston interjected. "But once man creates 'evil', then doesn't it exist?"

"I don't believe so. It seems to me that man's problem is that he thinks in ways that do not completely comport with Truth. He can't see this flaw because his way of thinking is based on the idea that the flaw is not there. He cannot see because he is not looking at or perceiving his reality. Rather, he is projecting what he wants to see onto reality, and then claiming that his observations are proof that these projections are right.

"When we fail to see the goodness of Reality, or 'What Is', our ability to perceive The Good itself diminishes, confusing the issue further. Though, the nature of 'What Is' remains pure outside of our subjective conceptions of it. We quickly find ourselves falling further and further into a trap of perception because we do not know how to step beyond it."

Preston gave a friendly smirk. "Okay, so let me rephrase. Why would you want to do what isn't right and good then?"

"I wouldn't in truth, but see that is part of my point. Just because a man desires what is good does not mean that he will not follow the wrong path based on that good desire. This is the human condition: only a few of us identify with and desire to serve 'evil', but every one of us is twisted into serving it at some level because we all love and desire good things. Take sex, for instance. Sex is probably the most perfect thing that there is in life. Yet it has nearly destroyed me. How is this? The answer is that I loved something good so much that my mind let it work wrongness into my life and the lives of others. I pursued sex because of its goodness, even when that pursuit caused me to debase the beauty that underlies it.

"Soon, I began to pursue lesser forms of sex because of the frustration created by failing to find what I desired and the need for beauty to fill the void that its pursuit created. This is how so-called 'evil' works. It works off of people's desire for good, convincing them to settle for less than what should be. Faith in what one truly desires is set down, and in its place, something less is found. Once a person buys into this method of thinking, he soon finds himself settling for less and less, and eventually accepting that he prefers this feeling through self-justification. Such a person will suffer emotionally for reasons he cannot consciously understand due to his own methodology."

"This is kind of like what you were saying about drugs the other day with that guy, isn't it?"

Walker recalled the middle-aged man Preston was referring to. They had encountered him at another airport after flying in for lunch together the week prior. It had been clear from the discussion that he had substance issues, and that he couldn't get control of the spiral that had developed in his life.

"I feel bad for that guy," Walker admitted.

"Me too."

Walker continued. "You know, I hope you didn't think I was trying to patronize him or paternalize him, but I just don't think a guy like that is capable of hearing what he really needs, so I didn't even try to go there. Instead, I tried to open one small window into his mind. He's like so many people in our culture, he views psychoactive substances as a way of escaping reality, rather than as a tool for connecting with it. The modern term is 'recreational drug', right?

"Have you ever thought about why this is? Some Native American tribes view the peyote cactus as a sacrament. Think about the identification of a plant as an embodiment of the sacred, versus the words we use to describe alcohol and drug use in our culture. People say they are going to get 'wasted', 'trashed', 'smashed', 'fucked', 'obliterated', even 'destroyed'. Is this the goal of our friends and neighbors when they set about inducing an altered state of consciousness? No wonder so many people have problems with substance abuse; they've gone looking for them."

Walker paused as a waitress approached and began to refill the glasses of water on the table, not wanting to air his ideas to those without context. He contemplated the way the liquid caught the light as it fell from the carafe on its way to his cup as they sat silently for a moment. When she had left, he began again.

"The problem isn't that the people partake of 'evil' substances that eventually corrupt them. The problem is the artificial classification of nature as the source of wrong, when in fact, all of God's creation is good. Good is all that exists. It is only in warring against this truth, that 'evil' is born. Of course, there is a distinction here with manmade potions, which are themselves a manipulation of the created order. God designed everything to work in harmony, and seeking this harmony out is what we are here to do. Helping others to understand what is good and right *is* good and right. Telling others what is 'evil' and wrong *is* 'evil' and wrong."

"Good grief. It looks like you've thought about this stuff for a while." Preston declared.

Walker smiled at this recognition of what he considered to be his life's work. "Sorry."

"No, it's alright. I'm not sure I agree with everything you just said, but you made some interesting points I hadn't thought of before. I really think you might be onto something with the idea that 'evil' doesn't exist, but I'm not sure you can reconcile that with what the Bible teaches. I mean, the Bible teaches that Satan is very real."

"I wasn't trying to say that spirits and people cannot serve what is wrong, I am only saying that what they serve is nonexistent." Walker added.

"So, Satan can be real as a spirit, and people can seek to destroy what is good, but no one can overcome God by serving a false idea. That is what you are saying right?"

Walker smiled at the fact that Preston's mind was running ahead. He leaned forward excitedly. "It seems to me Preston, that it is quite possible to be a real warrior, fighting for a real leader, who oversees a kingdom based on lies and false understandings. In fact," he said sitting back again, "this is the only way you can challenge the Truth; you must lie. And now that you mention it, only a personified, named concept such as 'Satan' makes any sense as a potential challenge to Truth. Truth has no fundamental enemy, only practical, personal enemies. So, though it sounds antiquated to speak of 'demons' or 'Satan', these ideas are actually much more intellectually persuasive than they often appear.

When you look at 'evil' in the world, you always find a self-aware intellect causing it. No one accuses the wolf of it because the animal mind cannot contemplate the idea. The truly dark things in life can only be found through those with the ability to understand goodness, who then choose to war against it. 'Evil' is an action and a verb, never a noun. It is the failure of an intellectual being to acknowledge the Truth and what it requires of us, not an alternative vision in and of itself. If we all choose to reject it, it ceases to exist.

"You can call those in the service against Truth and the Light 'evil spirits' if you like, but that doesn't make 'evil' itself real. It just means intellect allows for active rebellion even against its own premises."

Preston looked out the window as a small plane touched down on the runway in the distance.

"Just promise me that you won't let these thoughts go too far. I don't want to see you ruined by addiction to some chemical."

"I promise, Preston," Walker smiled broadly. "You don't have to worry about that with me. I have seen too much of the far shore to entertain the idea of kicking in the door to that realm with manmade potions. The only safe way to sail those waters is in humility and service to the botanical paths that God ordained. These I have known, and these I cannot discount. Though lately, I find that I am generally content to search for the other world without them."

CHAPTER

Seven

It had been over a month since Walker arrived in Cape Town, and there was still no word regarding the Council. He had become lost in the memories of years gone by, of how he had come to find his way. He thought often and in detail about his first love, the transition to his second, and the degradation of his 'self' that had followed the loss of both. But there was no longer any sorrow in the memories. Aiyana's theory of mind was right, and the therapy was working. He could sense her soft presence in his awareness daily, as she worked to move the darkness out of his memory.

The reality of his past had been hard to face, but it was now becoming a source of pride. Walker could see exactly where he had faltered. He had been trying to walk where he did not belong. But he never quit, and he didn't accept the defeat he had handed himself. This, in turn, opened the door to Grace.

Walker understood now, he wouldn't follow another path just because it existed. Now he would insist on walking where the path should be, rather than where it seemed to appear. This is how the true path was found. Aiyana's love for him was proof of this. She was a blessing beyond any he could have imagined before he came to understand the way the sacred path was made. He knew that they belonged together, but that he needed to stay by himself here in Africa, at least for a time. She would find a way to join him soon.

Classes at the university had become increasingly focused on the issue of human rights, which helped to ground him in the present.

Understanding them would be central to his presentation to the Council.

During the previous couple of days, the class had been discussing the similarities and differences in the South African and United States Constitutions concerning the protection of fundamental individual rights. They had spent a good deal of time in class talking about gay rights in particular. South Africa had made specific provisions for the protection of these rights, but the United States had not. This was a distinction between the two countries' systems of law. However, the United States had recently interpreted its Constitution as protecting an individual's right to engage in private consensual homosexual conduct through the concept of Equal Protection. This concept originates in the Fourteenth Amendment to the United States Constitution and applies to individual states directly. It is defined largely by case law and applied to the federal government through reverse incorporation of the Fourteenth Amendment Equal Protection concept into the Fifth Amendment by way of the Due Process Clause, which makes sense only to a lawyer.

The class had discussed the legitimacy of the concept that some rights were beyond the will of the people to ignore. Those with the power to say what the law meant had decided that gay rights were beyond the will of the people to ignore, and thanks to the case of *Lawrence v Texas*, now they were. This had not been a movement of the People, nor a triumph of democracy, rather it had been a change made by those in power due to an understanding of liberty, over the objection of the democratic will. The people of Texas wanted homosexuality to be a crime, but in the minds of the Supreme Court justices, the concept of what it meant to be free had evolved to include a right to be free from Government persecution based on one's sexuality. Walker could quote Justice Kennedy's sweeping declaration on cue:

"Had those who drew and ratified the Due Process Clauses of the Fifth Amendment or the Fourteenth Amendment known the components of liberty in its manifold possibilities, they might have been more specific. They did not presume to have this insight. They knew times can blind us to certain truths and later generations can see that laws once thought necessary and proper in fact serve only to oppress. As the Constitution endures, persons in every generation can invoke its principles in their own search for greater freedom."

South Africa, on the other hand, had made gay rights explicit by banning discrimination based on sexual orientation in the Constitution itself. Yet, some court cases were still required to firmly establish these rights.

The class had discussed the developments within both countries systems and then made its way into discussions concerning abortion, the right to die, and the right to freedom of religion.

The morning they were to reach the concept of freedom of religion, Walker was excited. In preparation for this discussion, a number of case readings had been assigned. Two were particularly important, the first of which Walker was already extremely familiar with. This was the United States Supreme Court case known as *Employment Division v. Smith*, decided in 1990. The second was the South African Constitutional Court case known as *Prince v. President of the Cape Law Society and Others*, decided in 2002.

In the *Smith* case, two men had been fired after it was determined that they had ingested peyote. The men were then denied unemployment benefits because they had been fired for what was termed 'misconduct'. The men challenged the law, claiming that their religion required them to ingest peyote from time to time and that the enforcement of the laws against them was a violation of their right to freedom of religion. The court rejected these men's argument, stating that:

"[t]he Government's ability to enforce generally applicable prohibitions of socially harmful conduct, like its ability to carry out other aspects of public policy, 'cannot depend on measuring the effects of a Governmental action on a religious objector's spiritual development.'"

Walker had long found this rationale rather inconsistent with the sweeping generalizations put forward by the court in support of their findings regarding abortion and homosexuality. In both *Planned Parenthood v Casey* and *Lawrence v Texas*, which addressed each of the issues, the court had asserted that:

"These matters, involving the most intimate and personal choices a person may make in a lifetime, choices central to personal dignity and autonomy, are central to the liberty protected by the Fourteenth Amendment. At the heart of liberty is the right to define one's own concept of existence, of meaning, of the universe, and of the mystery of human life. Beliefs about these matters could not define the attributes of personhood were they formed under compulsion of the State."

Walker wanted to know how it was that a court that protected a person's right to engage in abortion and homosexuality based on these notions of liberty, did not focus on the applicability of these same rationales to protect the rights of Native Americans relating to their ingestion of peyote. Instead of directing their focus at ensuring that Native religious ceremony was not stifled by law, the Court focused on explaining that, when it came to religion, it was only direct, explicit infringement done for the purposes of infringement that rose to the level of unconstitutionality. The state was free to ban something for the general welfare, so long as it banned everyone equally from the practice without ill motive. The court said that the government didn't need a compelling justification unless a suspect class was involved, just a rational basis for its law.

Conveniently, however, this meant that the Native minority religion could be suppressed simply by banning a substance necessary to its practice. The religious traditions implicated in the *Smith* decision were thousands of years old among some native peoples, and the plants themselves existed before humanity had even been conceived.

Yet, the majority culture considered the minority culture's beliefs to be a threat to their way of life. This was exactly the point the Texans had made regarding homosexuality. Texas didn't want a future where individuals decided for themselves whether or not homosexual conduct was right or wrong. The people of Texas thought it was wrong and that it was harmful to society, and they wanted a law requiring dissenters among them to abstain from ruining the Texan ideal.

Why, in the Court's opinion, were homosexual practitioners worthy of more protection than religious peyote users? Who chose what behaviors rose to the level of identity, and what choices were merely incidental? Why did the Court suddenly see the need to protect society from 'socially harmful conduct' regardless of the impact on individual freedom when the issue shifted from private consensual homosexual conduct to private consensual drug use for religious purposes? The answer to Walker lay in the fact that the Court itself believed that 'drugs' were socially harmful.

South Africa had followed a somewhat different path, though it too disturbed him. In the *Prince* case, a young man had gone to law school and subsequently passed the bar exam. When the man had his interview to determine whether-or-not he had the requisite character to practice law, he was found to be a Rastafarian. He admitted to smoking marijuana in the past and said he would continue to do so in the future, as it was part of his religious observance. As a consequence of this admission, the man was not allowed to register to complete the community service required to be admitted to practice as an attorney.

He sued and, eventually, the case made its way into the Constitutional Court. The Court made several sweeping declarations that seemed worthy of attention in the classroom discussion that was to come. One particular set of quotations had struck Walker. They stated that:

"There can be no doubt that the right to freedom of religion, belief and opinion in the open and democratic society contemplated by the Constitution is important. The right to believe or not to believe, and to act or not to act according to his or her beliefs or non-beliefs, is one of the key ingredients of any person's dignity. Yet freedom of religion goes beyond protecting the inviolability of the individual conscience. For many believers, their relationship with God or creation is central to all their activities. It concerns their capacity to relate in an intensely meaningful fashion to their sense of themselves, their community and their universe.

For millions in all walks of life, religion provides support and nurture and a framework for individual and social stability and growth. Religious belief has the capacity to awake concepts of self-worth and human dignity which form the cornerstone of human rights."

Based on this language, the Court asserted that: "[t]he right to freedom of religion is probably one of the most important of all human rights." Working outward from this position, the Court reasoned that:

"[t]he effect of the prohibition is to state that in the eyes of the legal system all Rastafari are criminals... There can be no doubt that the existence of the law which effectively punishes the practice of the Rastafari religion degrades and devalues the followers of the Rastafari religion in our society. It is a palpable invasion of their dignity. It strikes at the very core of their human dignity. It says that their religion is not worthy of protection. The impact of the limitation is profound indeed."

The Government went on to add, however, that:

"... there can be little doubt about the importance of the limitation in the war on drugs. That war serves an important pressing social purpose: the prevention of harm caused by the abuse of dependence-producing drugs and the suppression of trafficking in those drugs. The abuse of drugs is harmful to those who abuse them and therefore to society."

Walker admired the straightforward talk of South Africa's high court regarding the truth about the interplay of human rights, religion, and drug usage among the Rastafarians. But he was struck by the fact that a drug-free society was seen as healthy, while a drug-using society was seen as socially harmful. This seemed particularly odd considering the prevalence and acceptance of the pharmaceutical industry in the modern world, not to mention the cultural phenomena surrounding both alcohol and caffeine.

The Court then said:

"Any exemption to accommodate the religious use of cannabis will of course, have to be strictly controlled and regulated by the government. Such control and regulation may include restrictions on the individuals who may be authorised (sic) to possess cannabis; the source from which it may be obtained; the amount that can be kept in possession; and the purpose for which it may be used."

In regard to the South African Constitutional Court's decision in *Prince*, it was this concept with which Walker took the most issue, and it was this concept that he planned to attack in the class discussion. How could a court that had so much insight into law and policy, and which was so dedicated to freedom, end up with a conclusion like that? They were going to regulate the sincerity of a person's beliefs? The difference between prison and freedom would be the Government's understanding of *your* sincerity regarding the need to use 'drugs' based on *their* understanding of the requirements of *your* 'religion'? Who would define religion, the Government? He was appalled that the Court had suggested such insanity.

The class began, and the discussion proceeded smoothly, though little real thinking seemed to be going on from Walker's point of view. He paid this little mind, as it was not uncommon in law school to spend the first half of a class playing with surface-level issues before delving deeper. What did bother Walker, was that everyone in the room seemed to accept the premise that 'drugs' were inherently destructive and that their use had nothing to do with human rights directly. Everyone also seemed to accept that when drug use indirectly implicated human rights such as religious freedom, these rights were trumped by the great need to protect society from drug use. The discussion was dominated by the fact that it required a good deal of thought just to understand what the actual law was in these areas, given the complexity of the decisions and the way they interacted with other legal developments, such as the fight over the reach of the Religious Freedom Restoration Act (RFRA).

At several points, Walker attempted to press the issue of the inconsistency in the logic behind rationales for protecting various human rights. He made little headway and soon became enormously frustrated. Many of his points were foundational, and the foundation could not be properly laid without invoking the entire thesis of his work, which necessitated challenging the system's classifications. Unfortunately for Walker, in order to engage in a discussion of 'human rights' as a legal construct, you have to first accept the parameters of what human rights are under law. It is impossible to have a 'human rights' discussion without honoring the definition of what everyone believes they are discussing.

Yet it is only the reason, or 'objective' behind the creation of the human rights construct that gives any need to have the construct in the first instance. Thus, it is the objective that drives the definition, and where the definition does not fulfill the reason for its own existence, it is necessarily incorrect in some fundamental way. In other words, human rights are not conjured, they just 'are'. They weren't invented, they were discovered. Our understanding of them, however, is fundamentally flawed, which ensures that a full understanding of the truth of Human Dignity is precluded by the very frameworks that we have designed to explain and protect this dignity. An evolved understanding is necessary to fulfill the objective.

A simple class discussion did not allow Walker the latitude to challenge the logical fallacy inherent in the identification of specific 'fundamental' rights. Walker's chances of succeeding in his arguments that day were slim.

As he continued his attempt to change the nature of the discussion, Walker became rather upset by the fact that he could not seem to hold his own. He was trying to get a foothold in the discussion, but numerous students were actively opposing what they saw as nonsensical points of argument. These defenders of the modern paradigm would not let someone equate fundamental rights like the right to abortion and gay rights with the destructive scourge of drug use. They were totally different considerations, they mandated. Walker was frustrated and confused. He couldn't help but wonder, "If this is the best I can do at explaining this, how am I supposed to confront the Council?"

He attempted to center his emotions and levied more of his argument, drawing South Africa's Constitutional Court into the fray.

Eventually, a South African student took on a father-like tone and said, "Listen, you cannot say that the right to be free to choose what to do with your own body, be it in regard to sex or procreation, is the same as the right to destroy yourself with drugs."

"Why can't I say that?"

"Well, you can, but it doesn't matter if you say it, it doesn't make sense."

"On the contrary, I think *your* point doesn't make sense. You just said explicitly that the unifying theme between the right to abortion and gay rights is the power to do with one's own body as one sees fit. If that is the rationale behind the idea that government has no place in matters of personal choice, then why is a person's right to put a plant into his stomach or his lungs any different?"

"Because drugs harm society and destroy your health!" The man shouted in frustration.

"Who says?"

"Everyone knows drugs harm society!"

"Yes, and twenty years ago, everyone in power knew that apartheid was necessary because mixing the races harmed society. Wasn't that wrong? So how then can you say that 'drugs' harm society just because that is what 'everyone knows'? This is what you believe because it is your culture to believe this, your upbringing. What about the freedom to disagree with your vision of society? What about those who see a healthy society as one that has marijuana in stores? What about the Rastafari? Miscegenation was a very real harm in the minds of the leaders of this country as well as in the United States until very recent times. Did their subjective belief in the importance of racial purity have anything to do with their right to force that belief as an objective norm under penalty of pain?"

Walker had hit a major nerve. Everyone was looking at him with wide eyes, and he was glad. They would have to chew on his point for a while now, for none of them was willing to stand up for apartheid or miscegenation laws, and one of the South African student's own classmates was a Rastafarian, though he was unfortunately not a part of this particular class.

Just as Walker began to think he had broken through, the man retorted.

"The reason it is different," he told the class, teaching again, "is that the harm drugs cause is evident. Miscegenation and other racially bigoted laws are based on the illogical idea that a certain class of people are less deserving of human membership. Furthermore, homosexuality and abortion only deal with the immediate person involved, and so the only harm possibly caused is moral; they are not societal issues in any direct sense. Drugs, on the other hand, make people do all sorts of things to others, and this harms society directly. The harms are not moral, they are actual and identifiable."

Walker made mental note of the man's argument and decided to look for a chance to point out that abortion quite possibly dealt with more than the immediate person involved, depending on the definition of 'person', and that a dead fetus was an obvious identifiable harm regardless of the moral weight attributed to it. In his estimation, private drug use was a stronger example of a right that only dealt with the immediate person involved, and it was demonstrably an issue of personal morality alone. But Walker decided to clarify the man's vague mention of 'all sorts of things' first.

"What are these 'sorts of things'?" he asked inquisitively.

"They make people violent for one thing," the man retorted.

"The use of some substances which you refer to under the generic label of 'drugs' can be associated with violence, this is true, but we are talking about peyote and marijuana."

"Marijuana makes people very violent."

This assertion was ludicrous. Walker didn't have proof that the man's statement was untrue, but he had been around long enough to know that the only violence someone smoking marijuana was capable of was towards a tub of ice cream or maybe a pizza.

"Where are you getting your information from?" Walker asked as politely as he could.

"I don't need a source, it's common knowledge," was the reply.

Walker was appalled. If this was common knowledge, then the constructed reality propagated by the engineers of the 'War on Drugs' was more absurd than he had previously understood.

"That just isn't true. I'm sorry, but marijuana does not make people violent... ever."

"Where are *you* getting *your* information from?" the man seemed to accuse.

"It's common knowledge," Walker quipped, precipitating a quite chuckle that spread across the room.

The man gave him a disgusted look. Walker was slightly upset with himself for getting fresh with the man; he was only trying to stand up for what he believed, even if his beliefs were based on propaganda and bullshit. He was being true to himself, and for this reason, it was hard to be truly angry with him. Walker was actually angrier with his other classmates. As he began to pick them out in his mind, the man remembered a case that supported his theory.

"You wanted to know where my information is from, and now I have asked you the same thing. I didn't give you an answer, but only because I wasn't able to remember the name of the case. We read a case in our first year here, where a bunch of men went out and raped several little girls and then murdered them all and did horrible things to their bodies after they had killed them, and it all came out in the end that they were smoking marijuana. Do any of you remember that case?" he asked his fellow South Africans.

"I remember that case, but I think it might have been crack-cocaine that they smoked," another South African student replied.

"Wait, yes it was crack-cocaine in that case," the man admitted. This would be the end of the discussion, and the only support Walker received that day.

"The effects of crack are much more in line with that type of behavior," Walker added. "And even in the case of crack, we should not conflate association with causation, nor the choice to use it with some false idea of victimization at the hands of an inanimate substance."

The professor announced that the class needed to move on, he had other points he had hoped to get to.

Normally, Walker could engage in heated discussions without being angry at those disagreeing with him. After all, it was just healthy debate. But this discussion was different. He was disgusted with what he perceived as the cowardice of his classmates. Not one of them had helped to defend their drug. He thought of it as 'their drug' because he had yet to touch marijuana in South Africa, though it was sold by the security guards in De Waterkant village. In fact, he hadn't smoked in several years by this point in time. The same was not true for many of his classmates.

There were thirty American students in class that day, from over half a dozen American law schools, and twelve South Africans. Walker knew several students among his fellow Americans who smoked back in the States, but who had not, to his knowledge, been smoking since arriving in South Africa. He knew of another dozen that were most definitely smoking just the night before. He had sat with them as they passed around a joint and talked about the price the security guards had charged them. All-in-all there were sixteen of thirty Americans that he knew were either currently smoking or had in the past six months, and five of twelve South Africans that had told him they smoked marijuana frequently.

It was appalling. Walker understood the framework clearly. His classmates wouldn't stand up for the principle because they didn't need to. They weren't caught up in the supply side of economics; they were going to be lawyers after all, but it was they who drove the demand for their drug, which necessitated a supplier. If they were caught, it would be for simple possession, and they would have the resources to defend themselves. They might get fined, or scolded, or both. None of them, however, would go to prison. That would be reserved for the 'drug dealers' that emerged to supply them with access to the plant they enjoyed smoking. They were his friends in many regards, but he was very disappointed in them that day. Hypocrisy! The legacy of apartheid was alive and well, as was the legacy of slavery in America. Law had driven the wedge that opened the chasm between the races, and now everyone turned their heads while economics and facially neutral laws ensured that it endured.

"Damn it!" he thought as he waited for the class to end. He rode the bus home in silence.

That night, Walker began to feel bad about his anger for his classmates and so decided to join them at the Kurdish hookah bar for a communal tobacco smoke. They were not standing up for what they believed in, but who could blame them? The last thing they wanted was to openly admit that they broke the law on a monthly or even weekly basis. According to the U.S. Department of Health, ninety-seven million Americans had smoked marijuana at one time or another in their lives. And according to the World Health Organization, the figure was even higher, with over forty-two percent of the U.S. population having imbibed the plant at one point or another. One out of every three citizens, possibly more, lived a double life, touting the law and the 'war on drugs', while secretly sharing a joint with friends, or at least remembering the times when they had.

As the students passed the pipe around, Walker apologized for the anger he had made so abundantly clear on the bus ride home that afternoon and asked why no one would speak up against the misinformation being asserted in class. He didn't bother to hear the answers they gave; he didn't really care. He did want them to at least consider the way they had left him alone on the front lines, but mostly he just wanted to smoke some tobacco with friends in an amazing place and forgive them.

Underneath, he suspected that his criticism of them was ultimately based on his own fear. He still felt doubt about confronting this 'Council' or whatever it was really. It had begun to take on an almost make-believe quality. Whatever he might have once thought he understood had given way to a sort of mental fog when he tried to make sense of it. Day-in and day-out, he continued to try to hone his arguments and work through his memories. "All this in an effort to be ready for what?" Walker asked himself.

He had been told that someone would contact him here, but he hadn't been approached by anyone, and no one seemed to be aware of him as anything other than a law student. The thought that he might be walking into a trap came suddenly back to the front of his mind. Walker immediately pushed it aside and took another puff from the hookah, reflecting again on his quest for the true path. It had created him as he now existed. It was the search that had made him whole.

For far too long, he had not understood his own worth, and had spent many years lost and scared. Then one day, he realized that he was not alone, and everything began to change. As his mind opened, he saw past the rational, into an understanding beyond comprehension. He grew in faith towards accepting the Will of Reality and began actively searching for what It desired to write into his story. Then Reality itself reached out to him, coming in the form of a message scribbled on a bank deposit slip. The year he learned to fly.

There can be no room for GOD
Where man insists he be,

Man's worship of the law,
Destroys what is FREE.

Law has been waged,
And as a consequence,

Freedom must be cured;
EARTH made a place

CHAPTER
Eight

"Walker... Walker... Walker..." Her sweet voice had called to him from somewhere unseen. It was the same voice he would one day come to know and trust, but at the time her identity remained a mystery. It was, in fact, his first encounter with the melodic tone that emanated from her mouth; yet he was still years away from his first encounter with her in the physical world.

In front of him, the darkness had given way to a translucent flower. There was no foreground, and no background, only the flower. Through its folds, a form could be seen, though the details were muted. It opened slowly, the petals relaxing and gently curving back and away. As they parted, his awareness began to center on the form at the flower's core. It was becoming clearer. It was a woman. She was obviously beautiful, though her features remained partially hidden from his view. The soft glow of something like a miniature moon that she held in her hands seemed to take all of her focus, and she was mesmerized by its aura. He tried to make sense of this magic without context.

"Walker." Her voice changed suddenly. It had been distant before, echoing. Now the voice was right here beside him, sounding in a whisper.

His eyes opened, and the white plastered ceiling above flooded into his conscious mind. It was just over half a year since he had promised his father that he would change, and Walker had been making good on that promise in a big way. Each day he made more progress than the last. He was smiling again, eating well, flying weekly, and praying more than ever before.

Walker remembered that it was Saturday morning and he needed to get to work. Ten or so years before, Walker's father had built a school in the neighboring town, which aimed to help children with special needs. Since that time, he had gone back to build on a large addition and had also worked on a playground for free because he wanted to give something of himself to the mission of the school. They appreciated his generosity greatly, and over the years, he had begun taking care of the lawn maintenance as his relationship with the school continued to grow.

This summer, the job had passed to his son. His father was busy, and the school insisted on paying for the continued maintenance work. This worked for Walker, as he had more time than money.

He loaded up his father's lawn equipment and hitched the trailer to his truck before pulling out onto the street. As he drove towards town, his mind began to drift.

"Walker... Walker... Walker..." The woman's voice had provoked a deep feeling that he couldn't make sense of. She seemed to search for him.

"Who was she?" he wondered. She was beautiful, regardless. He had not seen her face, and he hadn't needed to. The soul was beautiful. "Perhaps it is my mind focusing on what it is that I want in a woman," he thought. "Or perhaps it is someone connecting to me somehow. Someone living, or maybe someone who is not?"

He didn't have answers, but he was happy just to have heard her and to carry the peace that followed being in the presence of such a creature, even if she might have been wholly imaginary.

Walker arrived at the school feeling quite removed from reality, almost as if half awake. He unloaded the riding mower and began the three-hour process of cutting the main areas of the lawn. He had cut this grass all summer, and the approach had become second nature. His body drove the machine around and around as his conscious awareness focused on his life and the changes that had occurred in it.

His life had always been built on the assumption that he should seek out love with a woman; now he didn't know if that was true. He had fallen into a world where his love of women nearly destroyed him, where he had ceased to stand for anything beyond himself due to his need for feminine attention. He loved the female body more than anything on Earth, save true feminine personality. True femininity was the pinnacle of existence from his perspective. But his love of this ideal had caused him to seek it out at all costs, even at the cost of settling for something less.

He had never known women as they should be, for he had not been open to knowing any of them in their true depth, nor they to him. Yet he had seen deeply enough into each of them to catch glimpses of the ideal.

With every glimpse, his mind became more addicted to the pursuit and enjoyment of women, and slowly but surely, Walker had lost his ability to see himself as having any worth. For a time, he only felt legitimate when women believed in his legitimacy. Sex then became proof of his worth, and soon this held a power over him so strong that he had betrayed his understanding of both love and loyalty for this reassurance. The loss of Alizée had precipitated much of this, as his mind sought to unmake the values of his heart that had come to hurt so much. He had been fortunate to see what was happening to him; many traveled the entire road before realizing where they were going. But Walker had stopped, and by now he had been free of his addiction to women for nearly a year.

Good things were happening to him since he had quit women, and he was determined to avoid any regression. Yet underneath, Walker still felt that he had been seeking a beautiful dream, one that he hated to give up on because of his own weakness. Was true happiness found in seeking out love? If it was, then how could he seek it out correctly? Or was he to understand that his walk would not include love? How did sex play into all this? He could not see a way to ever know a woman intimately again unless he found true love, and he could not see how this was ever going to happen. To find a woman, one presumably had to pursue women, and to pursue them would be to lose himself again in the pursuit.

Walker felt he could be past women and sex, yet he still dreamt of love. He missed the way he had been as a young man, when the beauty of sex and the power of love were still one and the same to him. How could he ever bring them together again?

He circled one area of the grounds for a while, then another. Along the way, he listened for the sound of the machine's engine to change the way it did when the bagger was full. The grass would begin to clog the chute when it had nowhere else to go, and this put an added load on the motor, changing its sound ever so slightly. When the bagger was full, he would drive to the rear of the school, then down a gravel path to a gully where he dumped the bags. Then he would return to fill them all over again.

As the machine continued to cut, Walker began to speak to God. He spoke not with his mouth, but with mind alone. The message was pure and simple.

"Please God, please help me. I cannot see the way. I believe in Alizée still, somewhere in my heart, but what am I to do with that, Lord? How am I to move on? Am I to move on? I wasn't faking when I gave her my heart, and I don't know how to take that back entirely. Does this mean I am now to find happiness alone? Please Father, please help me. I do not want my will, but Yours, for I am blind as to where happiness lies."

The prayer was continuous and unrelenting in its sincerity. Walker thought of nothing else for nearly three hours. Then something happened that forever altered his perspective on life and prayer.

Walker had just finished the last patch of yard that was accessible to the riding mower and was on the way to the gully to make the last dump of the day before beginning the task of finish-trimming. He drove onto the gravel path, still in the middle of sincere reflection and prayer. As he did, a thought crossed his mind suddenly, cutting off those he had been previously immersed in.

"Turn on the blade."

He pushed the thought away, as he was driving on rocks.

"Turn on the blade; these weeds need to be cut down." The thought was almost audible.

He stopped the mower and raised the mowing deck a few inches with the large lever on the side of the contraption. If he was going to mow these rocks, the blade needed to be as high as possible to avoid dulling it. He engaged the blade and put the machine in gear again. As the rock path was mowed without incident, Walker thought it silly how long it had taken to make the decision. He hadn't attended to the path all year, and by this point, two-foot-tall weeds were growing in the rocks everywhere.

After fifteen seconds of rock-mowing, Walker shut off the blade and finished the drive to the place where he had been dumping the grass. He switched off the engine, went around to the rear, and flipped open the hood to the three bags of cuttings. He grabbed the first bag and wound up for the throw. Spinning to the left, he felt the muscles in his back stretch taut.

"Look in the bag."

His conscious mind pushed the thought away as the muscles began to contract. The bag was in motion now and gaining speed. Time to let the grass fly. His pseudo-conscious thought wouldn't allow it. Rather than stopping abruptly and sending the grass into the air, his muscles continued the throw, up and around, putting his body into a full spin to keep from tossing the grass out of the bag. Now, his conscious mind was committed to looking inside it.

As Walker spun back around for the second time and gained control, he set it down. Not a single blade of grass had been lost. He felt very strange for having been so intent on following this thought, that he had danced around in circles, twirling a bag of grass for the entire world to see.

"Not that anyone is looking down here," he counseled himself.

Walker looked down at the grass in its container. Atop the blades was a square piece of paper. He reached down with a peculiar sense of inquisitiveness and picked it up. It was a bank deposit slip for a woman named Verna, folded in half, with some words handwritten on the back of it.

His eyes took in the writing on the discarded piece of paper while his mind contemplated the oddity that it was. To have gone through the mower and remained uncut... that didn't seem normal. Possible yes, given that paper is likely to be sucked up in such a way as to have its thin edge parallel to the blades of the mower, but certainly it was not the normal course of things in his experience. Most often, when he ran over paper it was shredded, or at least cut up a bit. But this looked as if it had just come out of a checkbook.

There were three phrases in quotation marks. The first phrase read, "Hiding from love". The second read, "How people grow". The third read, "God will make a way (10 real-life principles)". Walker did not feel he was reading the words of another person written on paper, but rather these words seemed to have come to him from some place unseen. His mind was racing over the fact that the paper was uncut, that he had decided to turn on the blade at a place where he had never mowed, and how this had resulted in the note being placed atop of all the grass in the bag, the only practical way he ever would have found it. He recalled his mind's bizarre refusal to allow his body to throw the bag. It had been as if his mind was arguing with itself the entire time, or with something else.

And here were these words, which cut straight to the heart of what he knew to be true. He was hiding from love. The concept of how people grew also seemed to make some sense to his emotional plight. But it was the third set of words that brought tears to his eyes. "God will make a way". Walker stood there, holding his note, just staring at it for a time, and then he looked up to see who was there. He saw no one. No one was watching, no one was aware of the moment but him. He was by himself, and yet he knew that he was anything but alone. A presence suddenly enveloped him, one that he had previously felt only once, several years before in the other world. But where the experiences of that world were difficult to remember in his conscious mind, this experience was clear and accessible, born of the language of his conscious reality.

For the first time in his waking life, he was consciously aware that

God was speaking to him *as* He was speaking to him. This was different than realizing that God had sent a message, or that an experience in the past had been one where God was involved. This was realizing that God was delivering a message here and now in the physical world of earth and sky. God was here. Every cell in Walker's body began to resonate with deep corporeal pleasure, unlike any he had ever felt. His physical form stood silently, just feeling perfect for a time, and barely able to breathe in-the-midst of such total perfection of physical feeling.

He would never know for sure how long he stood there, but around a full hour of his day seemed to have evaporated when he later noticed the time. In his experience, however, only seconds passed. Then just like that, everything was normal again.

The sound of cars passing down the road some distance away traced through the air, as did the sounds of the insects and birds in the marshy gully and adjacent woods. He smiled openly, trying to grasp the memory of his surroundings, which had somehow been forgotten in what seemed mere moments. He felt strangely happy, yet completely befuddled. Had this just happened?

Walker's mind began to entertain the rational, the reasons that he may have come to this note. He took notice of the fact that he was looking for comfort and answers. He was aware that what his mind needed most of all was a sense that everything would be alright. Walker did not believe he could create this random occurrence, but was it possible that his unconscious awareness of his desire was simply looking for a moment such as this to cling to? He was always suspicious of those who attributed happenings to forces outside of themselves, without considering their own desire to see these happenings in some particularly meaningful way.

The more he thought about the practical explanations for the event, however, the more amazed he became. This woman, Verna; she had written these words for some unknown reason, perhaps a similar life situation to his own. These words were not written with him in mind. Then the paper fell out of her car, or something of that nature, and found its way to this area of the world, where it lodged in vegetation seeking to reclaim the gravel path. If it had been anywhere else, it would have been buried in the bagger, and he would never have seen it. But the note was at the only spot where his mower could pick it up and deposit it on top of all the clippings, that is given his choice of timing and cutting pattern. And then there were the schizophrenic thoughts that had guided it all.

So, the words of this woman had come to him, saying something unrelated to that which she intended to write. She had written to herself most likely, but in doing so, she had also written to him. Writing to her 'self' was her decision; writing to Walker had been God's.

It was unlikely that a person should find anything in such a manner, but to find a message that spoke to the very thing that someone was praying about only moments before was highly improbable. He unfolded the paper and noticed one additional notation in the upper right-hand corner. It read: "Proverbs 5".

"Alright," he told himself. "I will go home and read Proverbs 5 and see what it says."

As he made his way home after finishing the job, Walker wondered if Proverbs 5 would be germane to his situation. He told himself it was important to remain as objective in the meaning of this Biblical reference as possible. His mind would be looking to draw meaning out of this verse in order to validate the feelings he had experienced upon finding the note. But Walker didn't want to talk himself into believing things just because they were found to be comforting or expedient to his own sense of wellbeing. He would not draw meaning from what was not there if he could help it.

"This experience is valid and meaningful as it stands now," he told himself. "I do not need to read more 'meaning' into it."

He arrived home and went to the large Bible that his mother kept on a stand near the front door. His fingers paged to Proverbs 5, and as he began to read, wonder and intrigue flooded into his mind.

"My son, attend unto my wisdom,
and bow thine ear to my understanding:

That thou mayest regard discretion,
and *that* thy lips may keep knowledge.

For the lips of a strange woman drop *as* a honeycomb,
and her mouth *is* smoother than oil:

But her end is bitter as wormwood,
sharp as a two-edged sword.

Her feet go down to death;
her steps take hold on hell.

Lest thou shouldest ponder the path of life,
her ways are movable, *that* thou canst not know them.

Here me now therefore, O ye children,
and depart not from the words of my mouth.

Remove thy way far from her,
and come not nigh the door of her house:

lest thou give thine honor unto others,
and thy years unto the cruel:

lest strangers be filled with thy wealth;
and thy labors *be* in the house of a stranger,

and thou morn at the last,
when thy flesh and thy body are consumed,

and say, How have I hated instruction,
and my heart despised reproof;

and have not obeyed the voice of my teachers,
nor inclined mine ear to them that instructed me!

I was almost in all evil
In the midst of the congregation and assembly.

Drink waters out of thine own cistern,
and running waters out of thine own well.

Let thy fountains be dispersed abroad,
and rivers of waters in the streets.

Let them be only thine own,
and not strangers' with thee.

Let thy fountain be blessed:
and rejoice with the wife of thy youth.

Let her be as the loving hind and pleasant roe;
let her breasts satisfy thee at all times;
and be thou ravished always with her love.

And why wilt thou, my son, be ravished with a strange woman,
and embrace the bosom of a stranger?

For the ways of man *are* before the eyes of the LORD,

and he pondereth all his goings.

His own iniquities shall take the wicked himself,
and he shall be holden with the cords of his sins.

He shall die without instruction;
and in the greatness of his folly he shall go astray."

In whom do you believe?
Is it 'self' alone?

From where do you come?
Do you answer 'self' again?

Why does he thirst for her and she for him?
If each is already whole?

What is love's purpose?
Is it not to guide us home?

Her love opens as a flower
Why is this so?

Why does she take his flesh inside?
Why not simply embrace?

Can't you see that also she
Is in search of the Return?

As with FLESH
As with SPIRIT
So too all things DIVINE

CHAPTER
Nine

As I sat silently, taking in the soft quiet of the forest, the sweet smell of the plant that the ancient man had placed on the embers rose to enrich my interaction with the world around me. At first, the smoke billowed in thick rivers from the smoldering herbs, then divided into smaller streams which looped and fanned out, up to where I was seated. The smaller streams seemed to maneuver almost consciously around my body in a mesmerizing display of color and form.

I looked at the two trees, which were easily twice as large as the giant which I had once slept under. *Sequoiadendron giganteum*; the Giant Sequoia. I had never seen them among Coastal Redwoods before. They were easily distinguishable, even apart from their size. Unlike the Coastal Redwoods, the bark of the Giant Sequoia was a deep orange-red, and it seemed spongy to the touch. These two particular trees were almost identical in size, though one was slightly taller and larger. Just beneath and behind them were four or five other trees ranging between ten to thirty years of age. I did not know if the sexual processes of trees worked in this land as they did in the place where I had studied them, but this was immaterial to my understanding. This was a family.

I placed my hands on each of the two trees, closed my eyes as the ancient man had done, and searched both my mind and spirit for what might be there. Slowly something began to make itself known. It was a sweet, soft, green presence, and it took the form of a beautiful young woman. She caressed my left arm gently as my hand lay upon her skin. Her essence and form were fully human, and yet she was also fully tree.

At her touch, my mind opened to the scene of a new beginning, and a whisper traced my ear. "Eden's call," what did that mean? The phrase hung in my awareness as she continued to caress and court.

I do not know if I chanted like the ancient man, or if I simply remained still and silent, for my awareness departed that reality and traveled with the woman to a violet light at the end of a river painted with indigo hues. The river flowed quickly but calmly, and we rode amidst its waters on a giant floating lily. The great waters carried our delicate awareness in smooth arcs until we came to a place where they spilled seemingly off the edge of existence. Beyond the water's end was a brilliant sphere of violet light, many times larger than the yellow sun I remembered from my time on Earth. Here, a stone's throw from the edge, the woman commanded the lily to stop and then offered her hand. I took it in my own, and together we ventured across the expanse of the lily pad to the base of its brilliant flower, which though violet in one sense, the mind saw more clearly as simultaneously pink and blue.

The spiked flesh of this flower had towered above our heads through-out the journey, and disappearing into its folds was an idea I longed to consummate. Still holding my hand, the woman turned to the side and slipped in among the dew-covered petals, pulling me in behind her. The lily pressed tightly against our bodies as we moved further inside, searching for her center. Soon we were deep inside and covered in the flower's dew. It took some time to find our way through, but eventually we emerged into a great clearing and the woman gently released my hand.

We now stood at the edge of the flower's center and could see a vast circular field. The inner ring seemed many miles across, and the sheer expanse of the petal barrier needed to form its boundary made little sense. In light of the proportions we had seen only moments before from outside the folds, the center of the flower seemed a great many orders of magnitude larger than was possible given a constant perspective. I contemplated this truth, along with the greater truth that was becoming clear; my perspective was shifting, and had been since leaving the forest clearing. As it shifted, so too did my conception of "self".

I began to understand what I was here to do and the power behind my reason for being in this world. I had been called back to Purpose by The Reason. Hidden inside of every human journey was a call, born of a purpose older than time, and there was a magic that came when you opened yourself to it. It pervaded one's awareness until that awareness returned to its origins... here in the land where the soul contemplated the design of its incarnation. I began to understand that to continue being, I would have to become. I would have to set my awareness of "self" down in order to find it anew.

All along the edge of this circular field, small waterfalls and streams emerged here and there, flowing into larger streams, onward into the great lake which dominated the center of this world. The woman walked tentatively to where two of the flower's folds met. Here, they created a channel around head height, and from there flowed a small cascade of clear liquid, which fell into a shallow pool below. The pool was almost perfectly round, and though it was liquid, it was also light. It shimmered as fragments of luminosity entered its form and then came to life on its undulating surface. The liquid and the luster seemed to communicate, driving one another's essence to meld into a living fabric beyond either of them.

The woman moved to the edge of the pool, stopping briefly before stepping into the shimmering liquid. It was scarcely waist high at its deepest point just below the flow, and only three or four body lengths across. I watched the light of the pool lapping first at the skin of the woman's calves, then at her thighs as she walked in deeper. She knelt in a shallow area just to the side of the stream, fed by millions of droplets converging across the great expanses of flesh high above. She faced away from the small falls and sat back onto her heels, offering me a glimpse of the limitless beauty that was possible when form began to play with motion.

She did not thirst for this living water, rather she longed for me to yearn for it, and for the vision she desired to gift me. I contemplated my thirst for her and for this liquid light, and the way these desires married with her passion for sharing with me. She wanted me to know her secrets, but there was one beyond them all that she held special and reserved. It could belong to only one, and I resolved to convince her to tell me.

"Come. Drink," the woman invited.

I walked into the pool, out to where she was kneeling, and placed my hands into the flowing luminescence. The scent inside the lily was captivating, and every breath brought pleasure. I knelt beside the green woman and drank deeply of the emergent dew. The taste was not only a taste but a feeling of innocence. Purity and passion and all that is alive radiated through my being as I indulged in the flavor, in the fragrance, and in the experience. Each drink seemed a rebirth of all that I longed for.

When I had taken my fill, I leant back in the water, in search of breath, now deeply in love with both the pool and the world which had caused it to form. I looked over at my guide and asked her to help me understand. There, amidst the deepening color of the now violet-blue petals, and bathed in the glistening wetness of the inner world, she explained. I sat in a drunken state of contentment and peace, listening intently as she counseled.

"In the beginning, there was only what we now call darkness. Then the light came to be. Darkness in that time was not viewed as equal and opposite to light, a consequence of the fact that all intelligence was still pure. It is only the pseudo-intelligent that can make the error of equating darkness with light. But pseudo-intellect did come to be, and this evolved through time until it began to manifest the human form. Within a short frame of time, humans began to categorize existence. Because their intelligence was not pure, it had to be manufactured.

"It was the revolution of the *label* that allowed man to create categories of thought with which he worked to alter his environment in favor of himself. He was not the first nor only creature to use this power, rather he was the master of the technique. As time progressed, mankind's mastery of categorization grew, and with it the complexity of that which he could understand.

"But it was not the truth that man found in his quest with labels and classification that made him a slave; it was his *perception* of the ideas themselves that gave birth to the problem. He simply wasn't ready to handle his own ability. He perceived two where there was only one. When man conceived of darkness and then gave it a label of its own, a peculiar thing happened that had never been before in all his history. Darkness became the equal of the light in the minds of intelligent beings by the billions.

"It seemed darkness too could be understood and thus manipulated. But mankind was venturing outside of his element, for he was not the product of shadow, but of illumination. He was not a child of that which 'was not', but of that which 'was', and chasing after the darkness poisoned his existence as one born of light.

"Man chose to focus on what made him different as a species, as a race, and as an individual. This focus led man to prefer himself above all else, his race to all races, and his species to all species. He began to plot a new design for existence with his understanding of himself at the center. As his plan progressed, his world became plagued with 'evils' he could not escape from.

"Rather than stepping back from his worship of knowledge by seeking to understand its limitations, at every opportunity, he intensified it. If mankind would have opened his eyes and seen that his manufactured reality was flawed, if he would have only seen the light and understood that it alone exists, he could have cured himself of his disease long ago. But he did not understand, and because of this, he tried to apply his knowledge to eliminate diseases from the world that his flawed understandings had brought into it. Morality and law had come into being.

"In the blink of an eye, these concepts took on a life of their own and evolved into a symbiotic relationship, each ensuring the perpetuation of the other. Religion took hold of the world, and because men thought they understood Truth, they killed each other in the name of the force that animated them all.

"Reasoning from his knowledge of history and the state of his present world, man then concluded that religion and belief in unverifiable principles were the enemies. He began to attempt the removal of religion from his reality, along with anything that drew the mind toward the far shore of his existence."

My mind absorbed her every word, and I resolved to reflect deeply on her teachings in the future, though I could not presently make any sense of them with such perfected form bathing before my gaze. Her lines and curves seemed to reach out across the water, infusing my awareness with a deep and satisfying truth beyond the bounds of the rational.

She continued, "The surest way to lead the mind away from Truth is to hijack Truth's name and apply it to something false, and man is easily manipulated into facilitating such endeavors. It was the reduction of the ethereal to the categorical and intellectual that tainted the spiritual basis underlying the religions. It is this same misguided reductionism that now calls for a post-religious, post-spiritual existence.

"There are forces moving in your world that would see science as the sole arbiter of legitimacy and truth. They will stop at nothing to cure mankind of his addiction to fancy and superstition. Know this, however. Genius comes in posing the correct hypothesis, not in testing it. Science does not hold the answers; rather, science helps people to understand the answers when they are already believed in. Even then, it can only provide a level of detail proportional to the questions you have posed.

"The utility of math and science cannot be denied, nor can it be denied that they offer something uniquely informative about the nature of reality. But math and science do not make reality; they are born of it. The mind, if it is to remain free, must be capable of contemplating the irrational, the illogical, and the unscientific. The existence of the free and intuitive mind forms the foundation of scientific engagement, for without it, there can be no hypotheses.

"There is a Truth beyond mankind's ability to understand, and to survive, he must stay connected to it. In your world, a few ancient pathways remain that sidestep the walls built by mankind's logic. Because of these pathways, even the most thoroughly ruined minds can sometimes be freed. These paths cannot be closed by man's continually evolving mental strategies because they operate on the premise of experience without the limitations of reason. Authentic understanding without reason sidesteps reason, and in the process, it sidesteps all reason-based defenses built up in the mind.

"The fact that these ancient pathways cannot be closed is most troubling to the *false* collective consciousness, which man insists on forcing into being at all costs. The false collective consciousness is defined by its subversion of the individual minds within the collective itself. It demands that individual liberty yield to a static framework of law and order concocted by men. This framework supplants the primacy of living human entities with alternative entities that man himself has pretended into existence, such as governments and corporations.

"*True* collective consciousness does not seek to usurp the individual experience. Rather, it operates because of the free experience of individuality. Beware, the false collective seeks above all to see order and control brought to the confusion and excitement of the lives of individual human beings, and final success in this is rapidly approaching. Only the emergence of a true collective consciousness can displace the emergent false consciousness that mankind has opened himself to.

"For individuals lost in the lie of a static sanctity, the path to Truth can nonetheless be found by connecting to those still linked with what lies beyond. Those living things who remain closest to the Earth and the Light, the plants and their kindred, sometimes come to embody aspects of the Truth."

My mind suddenly recalled that I had once learned of this connection through plants in grand fashion, somewhere far from the world around me. I thought of that time for a moment, and then found that my gaze had again taken over, focusing now on the way the woman's hand and arm flirted with the water as she played with its surface gently.

"Because they stand in the way of the total enslavement of humanity by offering a way back to the transcendental, powerful men now seek to wipe their understanding from what they see as *their* world. They must silence those among us who still wish to conceive of mankind as an integral part of a system that was created by a higher power, with whom we were designed to commune as a community of beings. These powers desire to see the Spirit taken from the world, and this can never be accomplished so long as the gateway to Truth remains open.

"In your world, sacred plants were made to appear 'evil', and their use was punished and vilified. This led to societies where their purpose was no longer seen as a gateway to connect to something higher, but rather as a way to indulge in an imaginary and 'dark' reality. The prophecy fulfilled itself, and though the gateways remained, the world saw only the falsity they had been indistinguishably linked with. The gateways were forgotten by all but a few, and the masses blasphemed the sacred by equating them with the false, the meaningless, and the destructive. Thus equated, they became increasingly sought by those bent toward pursuit of 'dark' places, reinforcing the narrative of those who could not understand.

"Know this: if minds can be confined to a created logic, then the thoughts of men can be allowed to run anywhere they please within this, and the results will never stray outside of the bounds that this logic dictates. Thus, the false collective consciousness of mankind seeks to weave a logic for all and to subordinate the created order to itself.

"There is no singular conspiracy, at least not amongst men. The coup is unintentional in most regards, not driven by a group of scholars or a man behind a curtain, but rather by the false collective consciousness of mankind itself, which is becoming 'self'-aware. This emergent consciousness can only become aware to the extent that its individual components, which are still free men, are made into slaves for the thought process. Logic and reason themselves are quite literally seeking to own man by enlisting many of the brightest and bravest into submissive servitude to knowledge. The human experience of freedom is being replaced with a mandate of obedience to law and logical constructs. This is not in keeping with mankind's origins, for the Force behind creation chose to make man not as a predictable component of a higher-ordered intellect, but as a stand-alone creature in community with others of equal worth.

"God does not need to rationalize; He Is because He Is. Logic and reason, however, preclude such thinking where they are based on the fallacy that nothing lays beyond their reach. Because of this, once law and fact come to fully control man, the spirit will no longer dwell with him. When the spirit leaves, so his story will end. The disease will have destroyed its host. Man cannot be what he is not... He cannot become God.

"Mankind cannot see this reality coming to pass because he only sees that he is still individual. If he opened his eyes, he would understand that he is becoming less and less so every day, as laws replace his ability to confront what should and shouldn't be in his life, and facts replace his ability to wonder and to worship the unknown. The world has become a system run by humans, rather than a miracle enjoyed by them.

"The path home remains passable to those who are willing to fight, but the struggle is great for much of mankind. He must deal not only with those who would seek to confine him in his pursuits, but also with a far greater foe: himself. For even as the law plots to control the actions of man by removing his ability to be free, modern thought is also working on his mind to convince him that he already is, or that he doesn't want to be.

"You are incapable of knowing everything, Walker, and you must always admit as much. Do not rely on yourself to know what is right; rely instead on yourself to try to find it and feel it. Always be ready to admit your failure in this search, and yet do not let those who speak lies unmake what you believe you have found to be true. You are a failure by nature because you are not the Whole and can never be. Grace is necessary if you are to find The Path home. The Power animating our Universe understands this; it is why Grace was established as the only Way."

I sat forward and reconnected with the woman's hypnotic eyes as I came to understand who she was, and what that must mean about myself and the other tree I was touching. "I know why I must touch both of you in the forest world. It is so that I can be here too; that is why, isn't it?"

She looked at me softly, smiling but saying nothing. Suddenly, I felt the gaze of a man upon me from the side. I turned my head to meet a face that I had never seen before, though his features were my own. He had some things he needed to tell me, and I was open to his counsel and advice. Yet I would not suffer seeing him for very long, as I had not come to marvel at my own way, but rather to lose my 'self' in the majesty and splendor of her intricate and consecrated design.

I awoke to the darkness
Yet the light was my preference
The light is my origin
I am a child of the light

I awoke in the dry
Yet the wet was my preference
Born of a love for the lily's dew
To the wet I long to Return

I awoke to find myself subdued
A prisoner inside my own mind
Cast off thy chains young man
See your future

It is not here
It is not among such as these
Immerse yourself in her light
In the dew of Heaven, you shall swim

CHAPTER
Ten

Walker's eyes surveyed the jewelry case in front of him. There were around thirty rings in total, each of which was gorgeous. However, one caught his eye. It looked like an antique and was made from a miniature superstructure of white-gold, like a tiny bridge built to hold up the brilliant-cut round stone which crowned the design. The stone was of reasonable size, at .81 carats, and it possessed flawless color.

"That ring you are looking at has a center stone that is D in color," Abraham told him.

Abraham was Zalman's father, and Zal had promised that he could supply Walker with twice the ring that could be bought anywhere else, as Abraham was an Israeli diamond importer. All Walker had to do was drive a thousand miles to his office in Toronto.

"What does it mean that it's D in color?"

"It means it is the absolute finest color grade that there is."

The silver radiance of the stone was captivating; he had never seen a jewel as beautiful. Running down each side of the ring were baguette diamonds that began nearly the width of the center stone and tapered slowly down, followed by small round diamonds further down, and finally detailed gold etching.

He was mesmerized by the object, but he didn't want to be too hasty, so he perused the other rings in Abraham's collection. Soon he discovered another, which reminded him of a royal crown in its shape, with two spherical sapphires on each side of the center diamond. The diamond from the first ring could be transferred to the sapphire ring, Abraham offered. Walker began to struggle between the two possibilities. Sapphires had found their way into his heart at a young age, and he had never quite let them go.

At age five, he had been intent on building a laser-blaster and read that precious stones such as rubies were utilized in the building of lasers. He decided to read about the different precious stones one could buy and found that among them there were three that held a special status: emeralds, rubies, and sapphires. Walker struggled to rank the beauty of these stones into a hierarchy, finding the choice between emeralds and sapphires to be incredibly difficult. In the end though, he felt that a blue laser beam would be most useful for his purposes, and the sapphire became the object of his affection.

"Mom, can we go buy a sapphire?" His mother said no. "What about an emerald?" Again, the answer had been no. A few weeks after the sapphire request, he eventually decided that a ruby would do, but she still wouldn't give him the money he needed. She wouldn't even take him to the jewelry store at the mall so he could browse. It seemed quite unfair at the time.

As he struggled with the decision, Abraham asked, "Can I help you choose?"

"No, I want to choose."

"I didn't ask if you wanted me to choose, I asked if I could help you."

Walker thought about his proposal for a few seconds.

"Sure," he said, making a trust exception on account of Abraham's generosity.

"Why do you like this ring?" Abraham took the sapphire ring from his hand. Walker explained his infatuation with lasers. "And why do you like this ring?" Abraham held up the antique-looking ring that Walker had been so absorbed with at the beginning of his perusal.

"I don't know," he admitted. "I think it is because the stone in the center is so clear and silver, and because Aiyana is set on either an emerald-cut diamond, or a circular-cut diamond, and this ring kind of provides both geometries all at once, which I feel like Aiyana would like. And this bridge-like superstructure is unlike anything I have ever seen. It seems rather antique too, which I know Aiyana would appreciate."

"So, you like this ring because you want a sapphire for yourself, and you like this ring because you think your future wife will love it?"

Walker smiled sheepishly. "You're right. I just really want a sapphire," he laughed.

Abraham threw his hands in the air, then walked to the corner of the room and rummaged around in a small box on the floor. He produced a rather large, but very poor-quality sapphire, offering to include it in the deal for free, but admitting that it was not of sufficient quality for use in laser-based weaponry.

"There is no wrong decision," Abraham counseled. "Put that out of your mind. You make a choice, and then you invest in it until you find that you can scarcely remember what the others looked like. It is this way with everything, including your bride. You begin with a good choice, and then you perfect it by giving yourself to that goodness."

Walker agreed, laughing at himself as he took the sapphire and placed it next to the ring he would offer to his beloved.

Walker and Aiyana had met almost eight months before, and in their short time with one another, they had already come to understand that something beyond them was at work in their meeting. Love was certainly at the heart of their relationship, but it was also more than that. They shared a common path and a common destiny, and signs of that truth seemed to show up everywhere. Walker held no doubt in his mind as to the decision to ask his newfound love for her hand in marriage.

They met in the most uncanny of circumstances; the product of a series of chance occurrences that left each of them considering the improbability that they had come to meet at all, let alone learn of their shared focus in life. From their first meeting they had both felt strongly that their stars were entwined, though neither could make sense of why, for it would be years before they knew of the magical story behind their initial meeting. Yet from the beginning, just being together created a palpable feeling of completion that neither could deny. They seemed to connect on almost everything, and in peculiar ways. Without a doubt, they were different in many respects, and yet their differences seemed to double back to form more connections. These then tied into still other aspects of personality, creating a complex interconnectedness far more intriguing than simple compatibility of like personalities.

Nearly every week they discovered more inexplicable connections of time and space linking their histories and choices. These frequently discovered linkages seemed to them to be a matter of fate or spiritual resonance. It was as if each had once been part of the same whole, but had fractured into two separate visions, each carrying with them a small piece of the other so that one day, they might find their love again. Daily they pondered the oddity of the way their energies seemed to synergize, and they puzzled at the depth of their connection.

Both were open-minded thinkers, but at this point in their lives, such incredible spiritual possibilities seemed the stuff of make-believe and possibly mental illness, making each cautious. Yet, Walker and Aiyana were both intense personalities, and they thrived on the complexity and the bizarreness of their otherworldly connection, as frightening and socially dicey as it often was. Life was too short to play it safe, and the whole purpose of existence seemed to each of them to necessitate wanting to reach as far as possible into the higher realms of meaning and love.

They soon discovered that they were both independently working on rectifying the same fundamental flaw in the modern human rights paradigm, and in this they found more than simple common ground. Each was working to understand the spiritual implications linked to this effort. As a lawyer, Walker had become deeply connected to a legal movement seeking to expose the fundamental shortcomings of the human rights framework itself, while Aiyana had become equally immersed as a psychiatrist in a movement working to identify the mind's role in the cosmic fabric. Aiyana believed that the nature of cognition was much richer than anything that had yet to be conceived of or tested by science. Cutting edge theories in physics were rapidly unraveling many of the mysteries of the Universe, but these theories had not yet been incorporated into what Aiyana saw as one of the most fundamental aspects of reality: the role of the mind. She said that coming to even a shallow understanding of the true role of cognition in the makeup of reality would start something akin to the Copernican revolution. This would in time, utterly transform mankind's comprehension of the fundamental inviolability of personal freedom. Her ideas fit almost magically with the concepts Walker sought to bring into the world of law.

As their time together grew, they began to discover or experience something inexplicable almost daily, ranging from the curiously simple to the truly bizarre. There were books that neither intended to pick up, but that each came to read by quirks of fate, independently and within days of one another. There were chance meetings with one another's parents and family members years before in separate circumstances and geography, the details of which should never have been uncovered based on chance alone. There were frequent phone calls placed at the moment of the other's need, and a sudden compulsion that had driven Walker to pay Aiyana a surprise visit, only to arrive at the exact moment necessary to save her life.

Walker wasn't even supposed to be in the same town that night, and yet she felt her love coming for her as he ran into the parking garage three floors below. She smiled at the man with the knife as he ordered her into her own car, as she offered up a quick diversion. It was only a gaze, but it confused the man greatly, and he found himself staring blankly across the roof of the car, the knife dropping to his side. He looked at her longingly, almost hypnotized by the very beauty he sought to capture and to ravage. For a moment, he no longer wanted to harm her at all, but he never got the chance to retract his threat, for Walker had dispensed with any time for questions upon reaching him. The man was lucky that the knife disappeared under a car in the struggle, or he might have suffered more than a few broken bones.

Then there were the duplicate dreams of unearthly places that each had held in their hearts for years, and the lessons they had both learned from them. Aiyana had once painted, and Walker had once drawn, each seeking to capture the majesty of the lands that they had dreamt of. The first time Walker had seen Aiyana's painting above the fireplace in her mother's home, his heart had nearly stopped. He walked up and studied the forest scene, which portrayed the same world he had sketched and given to his own mother as a gift many Christmases before. His mother had hung the drawing above her fireplace in the same manner as Aiyana's. The parallel was so striking to him that he could only stare. His gaze swam in the pigment and the memory as they mingled in front of him on the wall. The portrayal of the world was accurate down to the last detail. The only real difference between her art and his own was that Aiyana had brought color to her memories. What touched his soul most, was that the color scheme was just as bizarre and other-worldly as he remembered from his own travels in that realm.

When she found him standing there in front of her painting in a daze, Aiyana intuited that something profound was at work. But after being taken to view his penciled drawing later that day, her mind began to swim as well. The signs around them had already stirred a great curiosity concerning the reason behind their relationship, but upon realizing that they had walked in the same dream for years, this curiosity morphed into full-fledged wonder. The cosmic fabric, woven from so many threads of meaning and connection, became a source of staunch faith in their collective purpose and identity.

It became clear to each of them that their dream was not mere whimsy, but a directive from somewhere beyond, counseling them to venture further into the world of their shared visions. Slowly, they began to learn the art of walking together in the world of dream, and eventually, they found a way to play in a shared reality which neither could explain, and that both refused to deny.

I hear through the night
It is your voice
You who live in eternal light

Take me away
Beyond this world of time and place
To ancient lands bathed in elysian luster

Light sings a constant beam of Pure
The Pure is the ONE
The ONE has gifted her to me

She with voice that pierces night
She that has chosen to be mine
GRACE

The Miracle

CHAPTER

Eleven

"There is a hidden trail that you have yet to find." My father's words echoed in my dreams, then faded out of perception as focus gave way to the power of the distant shore. I opened my eyes and found myself back inside of mystery.

As I recalled my surroundings, I noticed that awareness had shifted backward slightly in time from my recollection. I was no longer inside the folds of the flower, but was again standing at the edge of the great floating lily pad near the water's edge. The flower itself was towering above as before. Hadn't we gone in yet?

I looked toward the spiked petals only a short distance away and contemplated the desire to return to the warmth and pressure. Then I remembered what had pulled my awareness back from the pool inside the world of pink and blue. I remembered his presence and turned to meet his eyes.

He was a handsome man, green like the woman, but otherwise the definition of a Greek sculpture.

"My husband," the woman said, motioning to him.

"Trees as spouses?" I said quietly as my mind struggled to reopen to another way.

"Is it so strange a concept?" the man asked.

"To a man? Yes. It is a wonder I am willing to see it at all."

"With this, I agree," he smiled. "Human beings are such strange creatures with their need to understand in order to accept. What has driven this quest to be like God? If you yourself were *everything*, you could not experience the miracle of being a traveler inside of wonder. Your limited nature is a gift. You embody the opportunity for the unlimited to dwell inside a finite and personal vessel. Thus, you are the fulfillment of the only thing that God lacks without you, which is the joy of discovering what is beyond understanding. It is your great joy to experience such divine duality so personally."

"I cannot speak for mankind, but I will endeavor to revel in the discovery of the highest perfection I can perceive."

He stepped forward and put his hand on my shoulder. "This is as it should be. Your spirit is so focused on beauty, we knew you would listen to it," he continued.

Understanding found me. "That is why I only saw her." I turned to look upon the woman's emerald glow, speaking aloud now. "True beauty lies with the female."

"Yes," the man answered. "That which is whole is half male, half female, and each half is completely distinct and completely one at the same time. The female is the beauty, and the male is the lover of her design, which the female loves. The purpose of life is thus born of the reason for living, and the reason is born of the purpose. We are bound to recognize the majesty of creation when it blooms and to honor the power of those who give themselves over to the path's design. This is the dance of female and male."

"Like Yin Yang I suppose?" I muttered to myself.

"Yes, very much like Yin Yang," said the man. "Perhaps more so than you have yet realized. Your energy fits together perfectly with that of the woman you are discovering, in case you haven't noticed. I know this, because I am your own energy reimagined through the medium of the tree, and I understand the exquisite nature of my own complement very well." He offered a flirting glance to his wife, who grinned bashfully.

"Your energies have begun to mingle in the world of dream, and already it is possible for you to explore the insides of the connection you have formed there. This is why it does not offend me for you to look upon my wife, for she is but a mirror of the woman I am destined to find through you. My wife and I are both derivatives of the love the two of you are building together in your shared world of path and plant. Finding one another here is the beginning of something profound that will manifest there. Yet it is only you that has come this day to perceive your connection with your conscious mind. Though she is right here with us now, she will not remember what happens in this time and place, though she will certainly feel the gift you leave behind. My own energy goes with you in this world, and so you only need suffer looking at me for a short time."

I thought for a moment, and then rather than attempting to speak, I began to draw the symbol we spoke of onto the lily pad with my finger. I could lay color with my hands in this land, and this ability came without effort or thought. I was mesmerized by the exercise of the ability as I played with the color in front of me, painting the white half of the symbol perfectly. Then I attempted to trace the other half of the circle, but nothing appeared. I tried again, but nothing emerged. The two regarded my half symbol for a few moments and then looked at each other and laughed softly.

"This is a light world," the man counseled. "These are not pigmented items capturing some colors and reflecting the rest," he said, pointing to our surroundings. "These are composed of light itself. This lily is made of it, and in this place, you paint with its energy. Light cannot be covered up with its absence. Darkness can never cover violet or white. Here, in this world, the radiance of Creation paints existence with the ultimate dimension."

I considered the ideas of 'black' and 'white' and how they differed in the realm of light and the realm of matter. Suddenly, the violet world around me made a great deal of sense. 'Green', as I had known it in the physical reality, was the capture of all light other than itself by the object encountering it. So, a tree might well be seen in truth as being any color other than green from an orientation focused on the type of light that is claimed by an object. Green was the only color of light plants couldn't care less about. Why would identity be bound up in the one thing you did not identify with? This seemed counter-intuitive. If trees were any color, they were actually a sort of reddish violet, the complement of the yellow-green light that plants rejected.

I walked to the edge of the lily pad and stared into the river. "Do you understand the way pigments work?" I asked.

"We are trees," the man replied with surprise at the lack of perception.

"Of course, your existence depends on it. Then I needn't explain to you the reason the symbol can only be made in the other world; I needn't explain what is different about that place. You already understand. The other world is the fallen reality. I understood that darkness cannot cover light; I just failed to understand that this place was not of that realm. I have only ever seen through the veil of the fallen. I do not understand how I have come here, but I am happy that I have. In the other world, the symbol was always made of 'black' and 'white', whatever those are.

"Is an object to be defined by the light it absorbs or the light it reflects? In a world of light, you do not have this problem, but in a physical world, it gets very confusing if you attempt to ponder an answer."

"Why do you conflate pigments and light?" the man asked. "The object can be whatever it wants, and you can call it whatever you like. Objects in the fallen world are only animated by light. Don't you understand? An object is simply whatever it is. The rays of the Sun inform the objects of the Earth, not the other way around. Pigments reflect some truth, and hold fast to the rest, and yet they are immaterial to the fundamental, which soaks our world in cosmogonic enchantment.

"What is important in the other world is what the objects and their pigments draw your mind to understand about the world of light, and of the way its power floods even the fallen realms."

The man returned to the spot where my half symbol remained painted on the lily pad. "Let us try to make this symbol as it should be," he said, reaching down and painting it in green and violet.

"Why these colors?" I asked.

"Because I like them," said the man. "The color is just my preference, born of my love for a soul that is violet and a body that radiates green," he said, looking to his wife as he spoke. "Draw it for your 'self' any way you like, but for the sake of the light, draw something. What good is a focus on nothing?"

"No good at all, I suppose. Tell me, if the soul of a tree is violet, then why do you appear to me in green in this place?"

"Did you think I was the soul of the tree? I am only the intelligence. This is why you speak to me, and not water or the sky. The soul is everything that you see," he said, motioning to the reality around.

I looked at the violet world, then back at the man. "The intelligence is not the soul?" I questioned.

"The intelligence is not the entire soul, but only an intentional, 'self' reflective component of soul. It is distinguished from the soul as a whole, in that it baths in its own essence by force of choice alone, which is to say that it is the portion of the soul that is conscious of itself. This is why I am green. I am aware of my physical existence. I choose to remain in this energy, just as you choose to remain in yours, even as you visit here in our world.

"Soul and mind exist in a mirror, created by the flux of a world where spirit opens to experience through the miracle of the exquisite language of genetics, which mirrors its own existential dichotomy in the created vessel as the body/mind dichotomy. Human experience is thus one of journey through the spirit's own cosmos in submission to 'time' and a specific physical blueprint. When the mirror is set down at the end of this reflection, only soul remains, and intelligence returns to its origin. In that moment, death is found in the physical world. The derivative mind thus ceases to be because the intelligence responsible for the body's primary process has gone out from him. Sometimes this is driven by forces on the far shore, and other times by those on the near, but the outcome is always the same. Thus, dust to dust for the body, and something entirely different for the soul, the energy the mind reflects. You cannot destroy energy by breaking the mirror you see it reflecting in.

"It is necessary, if my evolution through life is to continue, that I should see myself as green, even here in the world of the soul. For if I saw myself as violet, I would cease to remain with my body. I would die in the physical sense because I would have let go of the idea of what I am physically in the world of reflection and change."

"But what of the soul, how do you keep from losing it if you do not see yourself as violet?" I inquired.

"The soul is a very different thing from the body in that way. You do not lose your soul by seeing yourself as a body, so long as you do not disown the soul by denying that it exists. You only lose it by actively asserting that the body is all there is. Even then, because the soul is the power behind the manifestation of the code responsible for the body, it is never truly lost until the capacity to change is extinguished through the body's death. The body is derivative, but the soul is primary, an intelligence leaking in from beyond the veil. It is this incomprehensible intellect from beyond which manifests in the genome itself.

There is an iterative phenomenon of intelligence flowing in and out of the potential and the kinetic realities. It is easy to say that the mind is a phenomenon of the brain, until we see the mind used to operate on the underlying physical structure, which we call brain surgery. Then the power of the mind takes center stage over the bodily structure and form. The world of the soul is much the same in this regard. Thus, the balance is found in seeing the 'self' as a body, to be used and enjoyed for what it is, while honoring it as the temple of the soul. The temple is used until it falls, and then, the soul goes somewhere else, perhaps to another temple, perhaps to a world where bodies do not exist."

"You do not know what happens to the soul when the body dies?"

"Of course not, I am still green. If I were not, you would not see me in this place. Just because you can see the plan, doesn't mean you know the story."

I walked to the edge of the lily's flower and ran my hand over the flesh of the plant, pink and blue, as I thought about my own color. "Are the rules the same with man? Do I have a color?"

"Plants must feed on the light to survive, and thus light informs all that we do. Man is different. Man is free to pursue any truth, even non-truth. He may focus on darkness if he chooses, though darkness is nothing. A tree cannot do this; a tree must worship the light. But a man can ignore it if he chooses because he can feed off the tree, and the bush, and the grass, or others that do. This does not make man 'evil'; it only means that his conception of life can grow more complex. He is still bound to the light, just not in the inflexible way a plant is. Man should not pursue the fallacy of darkness, but the rules of how he should find the light are not as cut and dry.

"This is why human beings are so fond of creating art with pigments. Man is drawn to create his own eternal focus through his representational understandings."

I stood silently for a moment, contemplating all that the man had spoken.

"How would you draw this image if you were to create it as you would have it be?" the woman asked curiously.

"I will draw my future love's half in porcelain one day because that is the color of both her body and her soul," I said, looking out across the violet world.

"Do you know who she is?" asked the woman.

"I cannot remember. I feel her, but I'm not sure why. It is almost as if I recall that she and I found one another once, rather than believing we someday will. The fact that we are here together must mean that we have already found one another in the world beyond. Yet I cannot remember anything, and I certainly do not recognize you. How can that make sense?"

"It makes all the sense in the world," she said, smiling. "Your intelligence is here in this world, and it draws what it knows from the world where your understanding now sits among the trees. You must join with your lover's energy first here inside of the connection that you created together in your shared world. Here in this place, you can learn to see the energy of her garden, and thus find a way to mingle your perspective into it so that it may become more than it could ever be without you. This will cause her to open to you in a new way, and you will know how to find her in the world of your dreams. Then you will find yourselves ready to produce the fruit intended in the world of decision and action. She is your moonflower."

"I don't know what you are saying."

"That's okay, you don't need to. Your internal guide knows what to do, and both halves of the whole are here to help you see the way."

I considered this point, and the way I had become entangled with these entities, which was still somewhat unclear, but then left the thought behind, as I was beginning to lose track of all the concepts that had been coming at me in such density. I suddenly felt the need for a mental break and noticed that I had become incredibly thirsty.

"Tell me, can a man drink of this water? I am ever so thirsty."

I knelt, running my hands into the caerulean waters of the river as I spoke.

"Of course," said the woman as she walked to the water's edge.

She caught a leaf that was floating by and formed it into the shape of a bowl, filling it with violet-blue water. She accomplished all this in one quick dipping motion of her arm.

"Drink," she said, holding her creation out to me.

I marveled at her artwork for a moment and then took the leaf and drank deeply. It had a familiar taste that I couldn't place. It was really more of a smell, a fragrant, pungent smell experienced before.

"This is interesting water."

"Yes, said the woman. "And it will take you where you need to go."

"Am I to return to the land where my awareness sits in the forest?"

"In time. But first, you must return to the other world."

"The other world? Do you mean to England?"

"That is the correct world, but I am speaking of another time."

"I don't understand, how do I know that I came here from England? I thought I had been sitting in the mountains when I opened up to all of this."

"At one point, you were sitting in the mountains, that is true."

"That is when I came here, I am sure of it. I remember rising through the cascade of light."

"That is only one time through which you entered. This is not a story bound to a singular timeline. You are outside of that limitation. Embrace this truth. Remember the symbol that you found for her, the one you chose to give when you asked her to join you in forever. You were searching for that moment with her. Remember?"

"How is all this happening? It doesn't make any sense."

"*How* can be understood later, and everything makes sense, you simply don't know enough to make sense of it yet. For now, try to focus on the why. Why are you going there? What is this moment you need to find? What is it you want to show her? You were driving, and she was sleeping. So how is it that *you* returned to the forest that *you* have always known, when *she* is the one who is dreaming? Do you think that this is all *your* doing?"

"I feel suddenly very tired. Is that the water?"

"Yes," said the green man. "And it is high time you two got moving if you are going to conceive your future before you leave this place. The lily is in bloom, and the purity of morning has come to rest upon its splendid design. You mustn't miss the walk that was made for you."

I shook my head to clear it, as I was struggling to understand where I ended and the thoughts began. They sounded in madness, and yet my mind identified with them deeply. I wanted to understand them, but my capacity had begun to wane substantially under the weight of the intellectual effort. And so, my mind came to let go of control, and as it did, I opened to the beauty of conception.

Inside her dream I conceive my plan
Immersed in her garden, hand in hand

Love to channel through the pure
Soaked in dew of Yin

Sacred code and sacred way
Love flows unto itself again

Garden for Seed
TRUTH for Journey

Behold Eternal Beauty

The man smiled more broadly now. "You belong here together with the beautiful one that tends the garden. The ancients who gifted this to you are proud, and so too should the both of you be. There are many paths through the forest of existence, and still more that are to be made someday. But when it comes to the Return, there is one path alone, and it is this way by sacred intention. We may disregard it, and we may find enjoyment in pursuing shadows of it, but only those in search of the Return can ever fulfill their own reason for existence. Those who search will only ever find it on the one sacred path that leads back to where your soul first became aware.

"Now go and experience the true Yin in which you are destined to swim. You have found your way to her flower, and into it, you must now go. Let your own Yin guide you through the flower's folds. Her Yin thirsts for Yang to exploit the understandings reserved to it alone. This dream is often lost because it is so hard for Yang to conceive of its own Yin, and to let it lead without destroying its own essence. Find your Yin, and listen to its counsel inside the lily, but remain steadfastly Yang throughout. Create, but only create from a place of resonance with the song you hear her singing. She will show you what she has in mind, and if you will trust in her and in the garden she has prepared, the creative power that lives in you will find occasion to conceive an idea that might one day change the world."

The man finished speaking, then quietly and suddenly stepped backward off the edge of the lily pad and into the water. He disappeared momentarily, then resurfaced and began to swim slowly away, against the current, eyes facing the sky.

"Don't worry," said the woman, "This is what is meant to be for our journey. It is the path we must follow. It is a good path. Come."

She pulled my arm gently and led me away from the lily's edge, back toward the great flower at its center. My gaze took in the radiance of its flesh as we approached. The soft skin held a sheen that was at once velvet and yet somehow liquid to my eye. But the petals were neither, rather they were a material all their own, set aside from the others as first among all.

The lily pulled our awareness into her folds, leading us back through the dew-soaked pink and blue. The petals had thickened since our last immersion, and now their flesh seemed to come alive as we slipped through the great pressure of the flower's inner world. They contracted around us, gripping our bodies firmly, sometimes halting our progress entirely and holding us in place for a time. In these moments, we held our intention, waiting for the flower to offer invitation to deeper journey. In time and in rhythm, the petals would relax, though only just, allowing us to slide forward once more. Then the pressure would mount, and once again we would be still, concentrating on the pulsating energy flowing from the flesh pressing against our bodies on all sides.

The petals transmitted sensations in vibrating waves. These sensations went beyond the mere power of the contraction, stopping not simply as pressure on the skin, but penetrating deep into our flesh in a stimulating current of pleasure and awareness. Each of us moved forward almost instinctively in response to the feelings generated and imparted from our motion. Breaths were short and quick, and little else was needed apart from the immense pleasure that radiated through both our bodies.

Soon we passed through the last of the folds and crossed into the familiar circular field. Here, all was as I remembered, save for the conspicuous blue hues that had attached themselves translucently to everything from the petals to the field and the flowing water. We held hands and walked along a stream that fed into the great lake occupying the center of our beloved flower.

When we came to the place where the water fed into the deep pool, we waded in together and then swam to the center of all that we could perceive.

The design of this land was from beyond, but it was she that had built it, she that had nourished it and protected it in anticipation of my arrival. Here in her own world, beauty was already in bloom, and I had come to partake of it with her. She loved me for this, for the chance to share her glory, and for the opportunity to dream a new experience into existence as one. As we floated there together with eyes facing the sky, I found the thought I had been courting. She had always believed in my ability to find the part of her that she could not, and as I whispered what it was to her, a peace unlike any she had known before washed over her spirit. She cried openly and thanked me for my love of her, and for the infatuation that had allowed me to see through the veil. Then she softly whispered her secret to me, and we each closed our eyes and began a new dream as we drifted there in the pink and blue center of all that was loved, bathed in the fragrance of our Return.

Green amidst violet
Bodies showered with soul
The Cosmos is among us
It fills the forest full

Pink surrounds blue
Half and half is whole
Inside her I am blooming
Our future here shall grow

Nothing and then White
No leaf to cover skin
Two sacred worlds thus merging
Return and Return again

CHAPTER
Twelve

Walker had returned home from purchasing the ring just in time to meet up with Aiyana for a vacation they had planned together. Her heart told her that something meaningful was at work, but she didn't really trust the feeling entirely. She knew all too well that human desires can cloud our ability to see what is true and what is fantasy. Her heart was too invested to toy with the idea that Walker might want to commit his life to her. She wanted to enjoy this love for what it was, and not to hope too much too soon, lest this cause it to go awry.

They left Missouri and headed south by car toward Texas. They had decided to spend some time camping together on North Padre Island after first exploring San Antonio for a few days. Walker planned to propose somewhere along the city's famous River Walk.

However, just outside Ardmore, Oklahoma, their car had broken down, and they were resigned to spend two nights in a hotel, awaiting the repairs. The night before the work was to be finished, Walker suddenly felt that the River Walk was not the right place for his proposal. An idea had hit him just as he began to drift off to sleep. He needed to be on the beach at the national seashore in North Padre, the day after tomorrow, at sunrise.

He didn't understand the reason, and he took no issue with this fact. Such was the drive behind the idea, that he just chose to follow it and accept the change of route. Aiyana sensed this drive and offered only support for the way Walker's spirit sought to lead her. She had begun to trust him intuitively. This drove her deeper into their connection, which fed back into Walker, creating a resonance they could both feel.

The next morning at the dealership, they found that the car wasn't ready as had been promised. The repair of the intake manifold had gone smoothly, but the water pump assembly didn't work for some reason, and the mechanics were trying to get another one. The manager said they had called around town, but none were available. They would have to order the part again and have it shipped. But Walker wasn't even slightly worried by this alleged reality; he had to leave Ardmore with Aiyana in three hours as a matter of fate. His mind understood it with such conviction that he knew the part was on its way, even if the mechanics said it wasn't.

He told Aiyana they should sit and wait in the lobby for it to arrive in spite of the man's assertion. The part would be here soon, he mandated. Aiyana asked what on Earth would possess him to believe the opposite of what the mechanic had said. "Logically?" he asked with a smile. "Absolutely nothing."

Aiyana smiled back as she grasped his hand and led him to the corner of the waiting room where two metal chairs sat by a window. "Okay, we'll wait then. Something is going to happen; I can feel it too."

Five minutes later, the mechanic came hurriedly through the door to the shop. "Oh good, you're still here. One of the shops across town just called back, they have your part after all. We should have it in twenty minutes, rest of the job won't be more than a couple of hours."

Aiyana leant over as the man disappeared back into the workshop. "I see you've been playing with a few things," she whispered.

They both beamed as they pondered the absurdity of their faith in the ridiculous and the fact that, through this faith, they were coming to see beyond the rational limitations of their reality.

A few hours later, just after noon, the car was ready. They began to steam south once again. When darkness fell, and they had yet to reach Corpus Christi, Aiyana decided to call ahead to obtain information concerning the campground and how to find it.

"What did they say?" Walker asked as she closed her flip-style cellular phone.

"They have plenty of room, and the office is open 'til eleven."

"We should make that easily, don't you think?"

"I don't know, I'll check the map."

A few minutes of calculating and Aiyana settled on an arrival time of ten o'clock.

"We can't afford to stop and eat though," Walker said. "We'll have to grab some fast food."

"Yeah, I think that's probably a good idea. I didn't imagine a candlelit dinner was in the works anyway," Aiyana joked.

Walker gave her a playful grin and touched her shoulder gently. "We could grab some candles when we stop. I'll put them all over the dash right there," he said motioning in front of Aiyana's seat.

"I don't trust you that much yet," she teased.

Eventually, they drove into the campground, having fallen behind on time due to severe weather a few hours earlier on the highway. The air was fresh and clean, and you could feel the ocean, even though it couldn't be heard distinctly. The sea had a sort of presence to it, like the mighty Rockies or the Alps, or any other great mountain range. If it was behind you, or you were in the dark, you still knew it was there. You could feel where it was, even without the sound. Walker wanted to go straight to it and return to the office after, but there was little time left. They went inside to purchase a site for the next two nights.

Aiyana rang the little silver bell on the counter. "Ding, ding."

"Such a pleasant sound," she thought to herself as a short and curious-looking fellow emerged from an adjacent room.

"You just made it, folks. I close in twenty minutes."

"How much for a basic tent site?" Aiyana asked.

"Twelve dollars."

That was a good price these days; they had expected sixteen or maybe even twenty or more. As Walker began to retrieve his money, a seal on the wall caught the eye. "Is this a state park campground?" he asked.

"Yes, it is."

"Where is the national seashore?"

"It's down the road a way, further down the island."

"They have camping there too, right?"

Aiyana had not called the campground Walker had in mind. They were at the top of the island, nearer the city. This was not what he wanted. When you were camping, the further removed from people the better. He wasn't keen on city lights interfering with their sunrise, or bratty kids fighting in the distance as he proposed. If the romance of the moment was based on culturally built environments like the River Walk or the Eiffel Tower, then, of course, the presence of people added to it. But if the romance was based on serenity, then anything that disturbed that serenity was to be avoided, including other people.

"We'll just be needing the one night," he told the man. "I want to head further down the island tomorrow." In Walker's mind, he had decided that where he slept wasn't the point, it was the morning that mattered. He just needed to be in range of the national seashore.

"Oh, you don't want to do that," the man said after ascertaining where Walker planned to go in the morning.

"Do what?"

"Go down there," the man said as he looked in the direction of the southern part of the island. His eyes stared as if he could see straight through the walls of the building toward some monstrous basilisk in the distance. Aiyana was slightly taken aback by the man's behavior.

"I thought it was a national seashore down there," she said, studying the man's emotion.

"Oh, it is, but that doesn't mean it's safe. There's no law down there you see, the law is afraid to go down there. There are people down there who never leave. They just live there, and they do whatever they want to. Down there, they are in control, you see."

"No law? On federally controlled land?" Walker thought to himself, beginning to suspect that the man was out of his mind.

"Tell me, have you ever been down there yourself?" Walker asked, looking him in the eye to get a sense of his soul.

"Good God, no, never. I wouldn't go down there if you paid me. Yep. I stay up here, where it is safe." He seemed genuine in a way, but Walker couldn't be sure, he had been wrong before.

"You do what you like, but if you go down there, be very careful, and keep your eyes open. Remember, there is no law to help you if something goes wrong. And *they, they* always pretend that they know nothing about anything that goes on down there. So, don't expect *them* to come looking for you."

"Do lots of things go wrong?"

"Even more than *they* like to admit. But even *they* can't ignore it entirely. Lots of *robberies*, but not just robberies. Now and then, someone is *raped* or *murdered*, or just *disappears*." The man inflected his words theatrically.

"Well, I'll have to think about it tomorrow when I'm rested, thanks for the tip. Just one night, please," Walker said, ending the man's foray into his plan. The man gave them a look that neither knew quite how to interpret. He seemed angry, and yet somehow gleeful in a way that disturbed Walker's soul. He handed the man twelve dollars, and the young couple went out to find their site.

The campground was set up in alternating fifteen-foot-wide strips of asphalt and grass. There were half a dozen or so rows of each. It was the single ugliest, most industrial campground either had ever seen, and they each got a good look at it in spite of it being eleven at night, as the grounds were lit up like a stadium, with orange sodium ballast lighting everywhere. The rain added to the gloom provided by their artificial glow and the asphalt covering what should have been green. It was falling hard now, and neither of them wanted to set up the tent for one night if it was going to be in a parking lot anyway. They would sleep in the car and spare themselves the fuss with the tent.

They resigned to eating bread for dinner, and Aiyana rummaged in the back seat looking for it. "Get a couple of waters too," Walker said.

Aiyana fished around in the cooler. "There's still a package of beef in here!" Her voice seemed to announce a miracle.

"No!"

"Yes!"

They were saved. Both were starving by this point.

"I thought we ate all the cold cuts. I checked," Walker insisted.

"I did too, twice."

"Where was it?"

"Right on top."

They ate their sandwiches with some corn-curls they had bought when they left Ardmore and settled in for bed, much happier after this small miracle of sustenance. But all was not right. Walker was troubled by both the man and the location.

"Get out of here," his mind told him repeatedly. He couldn't shut the thought out. Again, it repeated, "This place is all wrong. LEAVE!"

He sat up in his now reclined seat as Aiyana tried to drift to sleep. "Aiyana?"

"Yeah?"

"I don't want to stay here."

"Where do you want to go?"

"To the national seashore."

"What, after what that guy said? I get that something was wrong with him, but he is local, so he should know a thing or two about the area. Aren't you at least a little worried about what is down there?"

"I'm actually more worried about him than about the lawless bandits he was talking about. I got the distinct feeling that he was playing with ideas that he wants to be true. The problem here might be him."

"Yeah, that makes a lot of sense. He talked like a schizophrenic. Did you notice the amorphous *they* that he kept referring to?"

As a psychiatrist, Aiyana knew a thing or two about mental instability.

Her agreement only increased Walker's resolve. They were leaving. Yet it was love, even more than fear, that was driving his actions.

"I shouldn't have let my mind accept this reality, this place made of asphalt and orange sodium lights," he thought to himself. "I almost chose to stop short when I was this close. Why, because I was sleepy? I would have woken up in a sea of manmade filth and possibly missed the exquisite offerings of nature, all while knowing that my prize was only a few miles away. Regret would have been inevitable."

They pulled out of the grounds and headed south. Walker felt his heart race as he cast off feelings that sought to hold him in that inferior reality.

"You already paid. You should get something for your money." The thought tried to infect his mind, but he laughed at it. That was a trap designed to keep him from where he was supposed to go. He drove the thought away, and once it was gone, there was a heightened sense of the spiritual at work in his heart. Two forces were at war. One was trying to keep them from something, and the other called them to find Its Will for their lives and love. There was a place and time that was designed for them together, and if they were willing to search, they were going to find their way to it. There was no understanding the spiritual forces in the world, but he knew that they were present, and he could feel them intensely in that moment as they sped through the darkness toward an unknown morning.

Nervous anticipation seemed to exist all around, and as they drove further south, they felt the energy grow. They were like two explorers setting out for a world beyond their own. Aiyana loved this feeling. It felt quite simply like being alive. She adored this excitement and the sensitivity of perception that resulted from it. Her heart told her that something good existed in the unknown which lay before them. There was no information on which to base this belief, and she had direct information to refute it.

This unknown land supposedly held danger, and she had no concrete reason to ignore the man who had warned against this course of action, crazy or not. However, Aiyana had learned to trust her spirit's inner understanding, in spite of logical process, if need be. The man was sick and lost in delusion, and she could see right through to his soul, which was defeated and alone. He was not a mere schizophrenic, but something darker. He desired to inject fear where he could, and he took pleasure in watching others struggle with pain and loss. She had been asleep to this truth initially, not wanting to judge, but Walker had woken her up. He didn't like to judge either, but he made no qualms about doing so when it came to protecting her. She looked over at him and smiled to herself as she considered the way they complemented one another.

Aiyana had learned to see through to the inner person, to the motivation behind the speaker's ideas. It was important to understand when to listen and when to ignore. Often, as on this night, she discerned that the unknown was preferable to the reality the speaker offered for her life. Besides, Walker was with her now, and she knew why he believed as he did. She trusted him completely.

Walker had heard the man's message before. "You mustn't venture into the unknown, it is dangerous." He knew now that these messages were born of defeat, true or not. Danger often did exist in the unknown, it was true, but this truth was used to keep the spirit from finding what it was meant to find. Danger existed, but that was no reason to refrain from pursuing what one felt in his heart. The key to life was to search out the good, and this could not be done if one was afraid to explore the unknown. It was, therefore, vital that a person develop the ability to sense the path for himself and to trust that in walking it, he would be delivered from anything beyond his capacity to safely navigate.

He was an explorer and always had been. Walker had found wonder in foreign lands, beauty in the pursuit of love, and meaning in the exploration of his own mind and the world beyond. He had found all of this despite advice from almost everyone that he should be afraid. Those who did not believe in one thing or the other wanted everyone else to agree with them, and so they used fear of harm to convince others to fear the pursuit of life. Often, they did so without even understanding what they were doing, or even who they were talking to. They believed that they spoke to others, but in fact, they were speaking to themselves.

He hadn't always been so aware of this truth, or of just how special moments like these were. But as the headlamps of their car cut through the darkness that night, he was fully aware of the blessing they were living.

Walker was eternally grateful for his spiritual enlightenment and for the pathway that had opened between his world and the radiance of the far shore. He had nearly succumbed to the lies around him as a young man, but then the light had pierced a hole in the canvas of his reality, and he found himself venturing through the opening.

CHAPTER

Thirteen

"**D**o you still want more of me? Are you willing to give more of you? I am eager to follow, but I need to understand the far shore from your perspective and experience alone. This is how we will refine what you can see. It is also the only way I will be able to trust in this. Then I will be capable of going there with you, so that together we may write our song."

Her sweet voice was with him again, inviting him to remember more. She wanted to step into the stories he had shared in the traditional therapies concerning parts of the world beyond that she did not know. His descriptions intrigued her, and she desired to feel the power that had changed the course of her lover's life so profoundly. She wanted to experience The White for herself, and to know the Force behind it more fully. Even more than that, she desired to tend to the hurt inside the man she now loved. Walker concentrated on his intention to take her there, inside of his recollection. He was afraid, but always open in these moments when she asked to journey into his memories.

The only hope he had for a future with her was to find true meaning inside of their union. True meaning only comes from understanding the real. Their connection could never survive if all she loved was a false image he chose to portray in place of his true identity. Thus, he would open himself to her like a book, so that they might find something everlasting.

Walker would take her with him, back into the annals of his mind, where there existed an awareness of things not born of their fallen world. He would let her sit with him inside the memories, reliving every detail, so that she might come to see the exquisite truths that he had found inside the tilt of the psychotropic. He would gift her the beauty, without the wounds, so that she could hold the purity and innocence of the forest inside of herself. This was the only way she would ever come to understand how to heal him.

Years earlier, after completing his first semester in Lancaster, Walker had traveled to Amsterdam with his friend Zalman just after the New Year. At the time, his love for Alizée was in full swing, and though this would soon cause him great pain, he was still oblivious to the wrong in his life due to the magical power of England and the excitement that new love counsels for.

It was on this trip with Zalman that he finally ventured into the part of reality he had been warned about more than any other. Teachers, and politicians, and even religious leaders had warned him again and again of the dangers of what they referred to as 'drugs'. It was his first encounter with the world beyond the constructs we call knowledge and reason. It was also there in that time, in the city of canals, that he first contemplated the true nature of the thought construct 'drugs'. He had been brought up in a culture that force-fed the message that 'drugs' were 'evil'. They brought death and suffering, he was told, and turned good people into murderers and rapists.

His government had made every attempt to train his mind to fear and despise 'drugs', and the people who used them. From the age of eight, he was wearing the Government's propaganda around, advising others to 'Just Say No' to a world he had no experience with. Later, in the 'DARE' program, his 'education' continued with counseling on the penalties that existed for those who were foolish enough to throw their lives away by taking 'drugs'.

The 'DARE' program did seek to present both sides of the coin, but only from the perspective of those who thought the other side should be eliminated.

Even as a twelve-year-old, Walker had been suspicious. The officer in the 'DARE' program thought he was being objective and open, but that simply wasn't true. He had his conclusion, and he wanted to make sure you had his conclusion too. He was the prototypical example of how good people with good intentions could be used by those in power to harm freedom and to war against the human condition. If he were truly objective and open, he wouldn't have been able to enforce a policy that took away the rights of people to choose differently than he believed they should. But he could not see this, because he was honorable. The system had turned that fact against him. He didn't want to see kids dying from heroin overdose, and the system used this fact to subjugate him and his community to a predefined conception of how life should be lived.

The officer only wanted to see a better world, a safer world. All the same, the law was his master and he bowed to it, subordinating his ability to feel to the understanding it had constructed for him. You were free to come to your own conclusions, sure, just so long as you concluded as the system said you should.

The truth was that some substances were indeed nothing but poison. Their production and use was a plague which fed on the naïve and the broken. Other substances, however, were quite the opposite, with the potential to pull awareness towards meaning and contentment. The impact of various 'drugs' on the lives of individuals were as varied as the personalities of the individuals themselves. What was not variable was the uniquely caustic nature of policies which sought to replace personal choice with subservience to a blanket prohibition against psychedelic exploration of any kind. More harm resulted from the war against 'drugs' than from the 'drugs' themselves, even as the war catalyzed an increase in the numbers of those falling victim to the horrors of drug addiction itself.

As a young high school freshman, Walker saw firsthand the true face of law enforcement's stance on 'drugs'. One afternoon, he had asked to go to his first party, but his mother, who was of the mind that he was too young, refused. After three hours of talking, she finally gave in.

"Fine," she said, "but if there are drugs or alcohol you will call?"

True to his word, he forwent having a drink and didn't concern himself with the presence of pot, as he never smoked, being concerned that the 'drug' might be too much to handle responsibly. He wasn't going to call home early however, as he needed to maintain some sense of independence from his mother's will.

His friend Corey explained that they couldn't go into the basement due to his twenty-year-old brother, who was using it for his own party. As a result, the night consisted mainly of sitting around upstairs, drunk and high, at least for most of the group. One of the boys eventually raided the home's medicine cabinet and powdered up some Nuprin and Tylenol and a few other pills and then snorted them up his nose. He went into a seizure and was placed in a back room by his closest friends to recover. Walker was most concerned for the boy's state, but his friends insisted that he would be alright. Eventually he did indeed recover and then left the house on foot. Walker was amazed at how disrespectful some people were to their own bodies.

By midnight, almost everyone Walker's age had left, and his mom was on her way to pick him up.

There was a knock at the door.

"I'll get it," Walker shouted to Corey. He walked around the corner of the hall towards the front door. "Wham!" The front door came bursting in, and a piece of the door frame splintered off and hit him in the leg. A policeman entered with his gun drawn. He pointed it at Walker.

"On the ground, now!"

Walker turned to run, taking one step towards the basement. Before taking another, he realized that they were downstairs too. He could hear them yelling and people screaming. He turned to his right. Dead end. Corey's mom kept so much junk piled against the rear door that it couldn't be opened.

"I said on the ground! Do it now, or you're dead!"

Realizing that he was trapped, Walker got on the ground as instructed. Corey had come out of his room and ended up on the floor as well, less than two feet away. They stared at one another, a cop standing over them, as other officers ransacked the house.

Outside another policeman could be heard screaming. "Don't you throw it! Don't you drop it! I will blow your fucking head off; do you understand me?! Do you want to die tonight, son?!"

The cops lined everyone up and searched them one at a time. Corey and Walker were the only ninth-graders left, the other twenty or so detainees were all several years older.

A policewoman came over to search a female named Tabitha. Walker seemed to remember that she had attended his elementary school three grades ahead of him. The policewoman stood behind Tabitha, running her hands up and down the girl's extremities. Then the cop put her fingers down the front of Tabitha's bra. She came out with a small plastic bag with sheets of something in it. Walker figured it must be what acid sheets looked like.

"I've got something here," the cop said and turned towards the other officers. Tabitha was a heavy young woman, a good fifty pounds bigger than the athletic policewoman, and she decided to make a break for it. She made it about six inches before the cop reacted, catching her around the throat from behind and then dragging her to the floor. Once there, however, it was anyone's fight. Tabitha seemed to be getting the better of the cop for a second, but then the cavalry arrived.

He was around six feet tall and a solid 350 pounds. Despite his size, he covered the length of the hall in scarcely more than a second, diving as he reached his fellow officer at the end.

The officer gave Tabitha one solid cuff with the back of his hand across the face and then dragged her to her feet and slammed her face against the wall. Walker watched the blood run out of her broken nose and down across the painted white surface as she struggled to breathe through her mouth. She began to sob. He handcuffed her and then spun her around and forced her down onto her butt.

"Sit down!" he shouted.

Twenty minutes later, Walker sat in a side room with Corey. One of the undercover narcotics officers pulled a chair up in front of them and sat down, looking directly at Walker. "What are you doing here, son?" he asked in a friendly but stern voice. They had already determined that Corey lived there.

"I haven't done anything, I promise. I don't even use 'drugs,'" Walker said.

"I can tell that," the officer replied. "Why are you here?"

Then Walker's mom appeared in the doorway.

"Oh God, I hope she can fix this," he thought to himself.

His mom talked with the policemen. She explained the argument earlier that night and the respective positions that both she and her son had advanced. The policemen took her side. After being lectured thoroughly and presented with the possible legal avenues for the police to pursue, including one related to associative guilt, Walker was allowed to go home with his mother without charge.

The drive was quiet. His mother said only a few words related to how he was growing up and how he would need to quickly learn what it meant to be responsible for his own future. His conception of personal responsibility almost immediately evolved into a realization that he could get into a lot of trouble doing what so many other guys his age were doing. He needed to be more careful. Parties were out.

As time went on, Walker often thought about the officers he met that night. When the law was 'just', cops were indispensable heroes. When the law was 'unjust' however, the police became the enemies of free men. Many free societies have descended into tyranny because of this one bare fact.

It was inherently disrespectful to tell your fellow man what he had to do with his own body and mind, regardless of the reason. Disregard for this reality contributed significantly to the widespread public disdain for the police in twenty-first-century America. To the many millions who did not agree with the government's control of their minds and bodies in relation to plants or other substances, the police were perceived as self-righteous bullies. This perception led to a counterculture of violence towards them, which was also entangled with racial tensions inextricably intertwined with the reality of drug use and demand. The predicable and perverse result was the mass incarceration of young black men. Songs such as 'Cop Killer' made no sense to older generations, but to the youth of America, they were disturbingly adored.

The truth of the matter, however, was that the police were just as duped as everyone else. The law used the honor and the good in people to attract them to public service. Then it twisted this noble ethic from one where the weak were protected from predators, to one where all men were protected from everything, including themselves.

Truth is often more nuanced than people like to admit. It is more comforting to believe in what is simple. Thus, God is viewed as a man in the sky, and other more complex notions are ignored. In an equally simplistic vein, 'drugs' are viewed as 'evil' because this allows for a response to the 'evil' that we can see. Man sets up phantom targets that he claims are the sources of the problems in his world, and this ensures that he fights a foe that cannot be defeated. The foe is imaginary; a distraction that ensures that the real problem goes unaddressed.

The worst part about overly simplistic understandings is not the bare fact that they are counterproductive. Rather, the true damage lies in the way that simplistic solutions to complex problems tend to breed contempt for more foundational aspects of reality. The idea of God as a man in the sky becomes entrenched until it is the dominant vision being offered of what He is. This leads intellectuals to disavow Him completely, seeing God as an elementary idea born of ignorance. This is a tragedy of the highest order. In like manner, viewing 'drugs' as 'evil' ensures that they will become exactly that, and that many who seek them out will decide that they like what is 'evil'. Once categorized this way, other 'wrongs' are naturally married to drug use. This creates a dangerous culture of drug abuse, where the goal is to seek out what is 'wrong', predisposing users to self-destruction. This is what comes of giving credence to that which 'is not'.

Mankind seems determined to run from himself, casting the blame of 'evil' onto God's creation. He attempts to stomp out 'drugs' so that he won't have to confront his own weakness and inability to handle them responsibly. This is the epitome of 'evil'.

Right living cannot be reduced to laws because they cannot perceive the dynamic nature of reality; the law cannot learn. The law can evolve, but it is static at any given moment, whereas the human is a dynamic. Therefore, a pursuit of 'what is right' through the law will always be inferior to the pursuit of 'what is right' through lived experience. In fact, because the law is designed to substitute for the autonomous moral compass of man, it is not only inferior, but it wars against the pursuit of what it is supposedly intent on advancing.

Man is not meant to cast blame onto God and His creation. To see 'evil' in God's creation, and to believe it is out to harm man, is to see the 'self' with pride, and God as the source of wrong. This is a reversal of the Truth and a blasphemy. Man was meant to live intimately with gardens and rivers and all things green, but he abandoned that pursuit long ago. He had always seen plants as inconsequential, felling even the mightiest of trees without giving them a second thought. Yet quite suddenly in his history, mankind came to see them as the source of wrong in the world, and against all logic, he declared war on the least aggressive form of life on Earth.

Man believes that he is pure and that 'evil' pollutes him. So, man wages a war against vegetation to protect him from himself, and in the process, he destroys anything which challenges his motives or methods, including his brothers, his sisters, and even his own soul. Man's pride does not allow him to view his own responsibility in ignoring Truth and goodness. He must blame something else for his weakness, and this gives life to his ultimate foe. His foe cannot be beaten without the Grace of the Divine, because his foe is himself.

CHAPTER

Fourteen

His first experience with smoking marijuana had gone well in most respects, and so had three others that first semester at Lancaster University. On each occasion, his new friends sat around in a circle, conversing in a communal atmosphere of friendship and mutual respect. There was only one problem, Walker never seemed to get 'high', whatever that was supposed to be. In the north of England, it was common to smoke hashish, which is a solid resin of hardened plant matter. To smoke it, it is commonly broken into little rocks and sprinkled into tobacco, which is then rolled into a cigarette.

The problem with this is that to smoke the hashish, you must smoke the tobacco, and tobacco is a harsh plant to inhale. He enjoyed occasional cigars and pipe tobacco, but these were not inhaled, merely puffed upon. Cigarette smoke made him feel ill if he breathed in too much, and on at least one occasion, he ended up 'in the toilet' as they say in England, on account of smoking too much tobacco in a vain attempt to inhale enough marijuana to get 'high'. His friends got 'high' while he got sick.

Zalman was both a Canadian and an Israeli citizen. He had trained in the Israeli Army and had a way of making things happen when solutions were needed. Walker saw him as honorable and trustworthy. They had become best friends by the end of the Michaelmas term, and after speaking to Walker about his frustration with tobacco and hashish, Zalman had insisted that they travel to Amsterdam for what he called "real weed", as opposed to "this English shit". He seemed to feel responsible for helping Walker succeed in his quest.

By the time they finally made the trip to Amsterdam, Walker's anticipation had become well developed. He would, at last, get 'high', his friend promised. They found a café with a neon sign in the shape of a coffee mug, and the words 'Coffee Shop' written beneath it. Inside they asked for a menu and received a small, laminated paper that listed dozens of varieties of marijuana, and one type of coffee, which was obtained from a small automatic dispensing machine in the corner. The situation was hilarious. Walker had indeed gotten high that day, and the experience introduced him to the lands beyond logic. But the experience itself was rather mild. It was only later that he would dive headlong into the world beyond.

The waiter had recommended ordering one of two varieties of marijuana, one called Bubble Gum, and the other called Orange. He chose one and then rolled his first pure marijuana cigarette. He smoked it while Zal smoked his own. When they had finished, Walker asked Zal if he was high.

"You have got to be kidding me?" he said. "You don't feel anything?"

"Nope."

"I saw you inhale, you did it right, and this is nice stuff. You are high, you just don't know it."

"I'm not high. I promise you that."

"No, you are, you just don't recognize it because you've never experienced it before."

"If it's so subtle that I can't recognize it without already knowing what it is, then how can it be a big enough deal to warrant doing in the first place? That doesn't make much sense."

"Sure it does, if you understand *why* it does. Look, you need to focus on the right things. Forget what you are looking for and focus on what you feel."

Walker tried this for a few minutes, but nothing happened. "It isn't working," he said finally. "Maybe I should smoke some more?"

"No, you don't need any more, the chemical isn't the problem, it's your mind's unwillingness to step out of the boundaries it has been taught to observe."

Zal thought for a moment. "When I first got high, I didn't realize I was at first, and a friend of mine told me to look at the lights. I looked at the lights, and he asked me to see if anything looked different or strange about them. That was the key for me. I looked at the lights, and I got it. Try looking at those lights. Do they seem different?"

Walker looked at the Christmas lights, as they were called in the States. They were known as fairy lights in England. He wasn't sure what the Dutch called them. They were strung all around the ceiling. He hesitated for a moment, seeing them as they had appeared all night, and then something shifted, something very subtle. The difference was analogous to standing in one spot looking at the same scene for days on end, and then moving to the side to view the same scenery from a different position. Such a shift in position lays bare the three-dimensional reality of the scene in a way that cannot be observed from one perspective. Our ability to move around and inside of the scenes that our eyes perceive, fails to trigger our sense of wonder, only because we do it every day. When a person is limited to a singular physical perspective for any length of time however, and is then given back his ability to move about in his world, the surreal wonder experienced is often overwhelming.

"Holy shit," he said under his breath.

"Yeah?!" His buddy sat up excitedly.

"Yeah, something is definitely different!" Walker exclaimed with a huge triumphant smile.

"Welcome."

"Glad to finally be here," he answered, looking at his new world.

Then, only five seconds after first realizing what it was to be 'high,' he began to feel contempt for the lies he had been fed. "This is all this is?" he asked his friend.

"This is all it is. Well, maybe there is more, but this is the basic idea."

"That's a bunch of bullshit!" Walker stated, noticeably perturbed.

"This is what I had to argue with Nadia about and what my friends were labeled as 'druggies' over? This is a damned conspiracy!"

"Isn't it though?" Zal smiled.

The rest of the trip was a deep and thorough exploration of the depths of marijuana. The two friends bought the strongest, most potent cannabis strains on the planet, and for a week, they smoked joints and made water bongs and spent their time taking in the sights and museums of the beautiful city. The most potent weed they found on that trip was known as AK-47. Later, Walker would sample marijuana from the Tora Bora Mountains of Afghanistan, as well as other fine varieties such as Diesel, White Widow, Silver Haze, Swazi Gold, Canna Sutra, and Skywalker among many others.

His government's propaganda often spoke of 'new marijuana'. The premise the government offered was that the marijuana of the sixties was entirely different from the super-potent and dangerous marijuana of the modern world. This was a clear ploy to remove some of the supporters of the growing legalization and decriminalization movements who had experience with the drug decades in the past.

The assertion was ironic, considering that it was the illegality of the drug that caused people to engineer the plant into stronger and stronger strains in order to make it easier to hide and ship. Walker couldn't stand his government's phony rationales and scare tactics. On the one hand, they tried to delegitimize marijuana by referring to the so-called 'new marijuana', with its higher concentrations of THC. On the other hand, a patented synthetic pharmaceutical drug which was 100 % pure synthetic THC was a legal prescription medication. Some state governments even took it further and banned the use of the plant's non-intoxicating components such as CBD, even when used as the safest and most effective treatment for children with epilepsy. The government was supposed to ensure individual freedom for its citizens, not profits for pharmaceutical companies at the cost of human suffering. Such was the hypocrisy of those days, that the human endocannabinoid system had only just been discovered, research having been stifled by prohibition for decades.

The AK-47 strain of cannabis was claimed to be the strongest thing on the market at the time, and this mustn't have been far from the truth. On the last night of their trip, they smoked it for the first time in the small attic space of a little-known shop called the Bushdoctor. Walker looked up from the glass of water he had been contemplating as he rotated it in his hand, and suddenly noticed pink elephants playing various sports on the wall.

One elephant was playing tennis, another baseball, another soccer. Walker looked at his friend. "Man, this stuff is really strong. This is way beyond the stuff we had the other day."

"Yeah, how so?"

"There are frickin' pink elephants on the wall, man. And not just regular pink elephants either. These guys are dressed in sports costumes, and they're playing baseball and tennis and all sorts of shit. This is bizarre."

Zalman began to laugh at him.

"What's so funny?" Walker asked.

"The reason you are seeing pink elephants playing sports on the wall is because there *are* pink elephants playing sports on the wall," his friend said with a huge smile. "They're paintings."

Walker looked at the wall more closely and ran his hand over the sporting pachyderms. "Oh. Oops."

They both laughed heartily at their reality.

"I thought I was seeing things," he said, nearly crying with laughter.

"That isn't the way weed works," his friend told him. "You could smoke this stuff all day long and you wouldn't see pink elephants. Weed doesn't make you see things that aren't real; it lets you see things that are real that you might not otherwise notice. It's like these elephants. They've been here this whole time, but you simply didn't notice them until you smoked. Then you saw them and thought, 'what the hell is that all about?' Weed didn't make the weird pictures on the wall; weed caused you to notice how weird they are. Who paints pink elephants playing sports on their wall? Crazy Dutch people."

"It's probably meant to entertain people while they smoke. I think they did it on purpose."

"You're probably right."

Walker looked at him as he smiled, and noticed something familiar about his face, something related to another person. Suddenly, his face changed in the most subtle of ways.

"Your face just changed," he said with a look of shock.

"That isn't good," Zal laughed.

"No, I don't mean it in a weird way; I mean, it didn't really change. You stayed exactly the same, but I saw my cousin for a second."

"That doesn't make any sense. How can I look the same if I look like your cousin?"

"Ahhh, because you look almost exactly alike," Walker said in a voice modeled on a teacher of philosophy he had once known. "Your facial structures, hair, eyes, and eyebrows, all are strikingly similar. I never noticed it before."

"I don't think that's profound. All you're really saying then is that you noticed I look like your cousin?" Zal laughed as he took a drink of water.

"No, I mean, oh God, it did it again."

Walker put his hand over his mouth. He was amazed at what he was seeing. He looked at Zal intensely and opened his mind to the idea, shifting his perception of him, first one way, and then the other. He viewed him as his cousin, then as himself. Back and forth, Walker shifted his perception.

"Wow, this is amazing. I can see you as my cousin, and then as you and then back, and yet, you never really change in appearance."

"I want some of what you're smoking," Zal laughed.

Walker sat back and marveled at what he could do.

"Tell me something. How does what you're saying make sense? I think you've fried your brain," his friend joked.

Walker snickered at his sarcasm. "This is your brain on drugs, right?"

"Seriously though, what are you talking about?" Zal was sincerely curious now.

"I can look at you and see my cousin, simply by changing what I am looking for, because you look just like him in your physical features, or at least very nearly. You have darker skin and darker hair, but the lines are the same."

"I really should tell you something, Walker. I am your cousin."

"Shut up."

"I'm serious, things aren't what they seem. Your friend is under my control. I just came here and took him over."

"Then what's your name?" Walker asked his supposed cousin.

"Damn it! I didn't think you would be able to reason clearly right now."

"Reason is simple enough; I think anyone could manage to think of that."

"You'd be surprised."

"You've done this kind of stuff before, haven't you? Ornery."

"I just like messing around with people's heads sometimes. You're new to pot, so I thought maybe I would freak you out a bit."

"Nice try."

"Thanks. So seriously though, how can you tell us apart if nothing changes?"

Walker raised his hand to his face and stroked his chin as he searched for an authentic explanation of what he was on the cusp of understanding. "Something does change, something profound, yet very subtle."

"What?"

Walker had been looking intently at the table, but now his eyes traveled up to meet his friend's in time with a palpable pause in their dialogue. It seemed as if he were about to disclose a great secret.

"I don't know." He spoke the words sincerely and with a dead-pan seriousness.

"Ahhh! You are worthless."

"Hold on! I'm trying to get there." Walker had begun to laugh at himself now.

"What's different about me, Walker? What?!"

"You know, I'm still not sure, but it's something about your eyes, something in your eyes, but not your eye itself. It's something in the center of your eye." Walker was lost deep in thought again, discovering for himself what he understood moment by moment.

"What is in the center of my eye, Walker?" Zal mocked him openly now, staring right at him with his eyes opened wide. He was trying to expose the idiocy of his friend's thoughts, but instead he unlocked the Truth for him. Understanding washed over Walker's prior perception.

"Oh my God. It's your soul."

Zalman threw his hands up, grasping his head as he leant backward in the chair. "Holy shit! I have seriously got to get some of what you're smoking!"

"You're smoking the same stuff as me."

"Evidently not, my friend!"

Walker sat forward, placing his hands on the table, excited now by what he had found. "You're just closed off to the Truth, that's all. You know how you tried to tell me how to see that the lights were different the other day? That is what I am still doing. You just stopped way back in the process, failed to make the jumps I have made. The student is becoming the teacher."

"Bullshit!" Zal said playfully. "You have one crazy thought and now you think you have eclipsed me? I am light-years beyond you in the world of weed."

"I think not, my brother."

"Ahhh, whatever."

Years later, it became clear to Walker that his friend was indeed more of a shaman than he had given him credit for at the time. Yet Walker could do things with the plant that others could not. Most people who had experienced marijuana did not believe his assertions regarding his abilities with it. He had once taken a clock off the wall with his mind and then rotated the room around the clock, viewing each part of it in its totality, passing behind the stationary timepiece, without a detail missed and without turning his head. Such a feat was technically impossible, and though he knew this on one level, he was also pointedly aware of the reality he had lived. The power of direct experience was hard to devitalize with mere theoretical limitations, however universally understood. He inverted the corners of rooms into cubes and looked into people's souls. A man once approached him on the street when he was under the plant's influence and pushed an object into Walker's side through his coat, demanding money.

"I have a pistol in my pocket," he told him. "Give me your money and you won't get hurt."

Walker had looked deep into the man's eyes and said, "Sure you do friend," and then turned and walked away. He didn't have a gun; it was some sort of prop. Walker was sure of it. He had read it in his eyes with such certainty that he bet his life on it for twenty euros.

But the heights of marijuana were never anything but an amazing experience of the 'self'. One was always in control, capable of making sense of the world in some fashion. The drug never caused paralysis of the mind, where the will was overborne. With this truth came an interesting and mistaken belief. "'Drugs' are not dangerous after all," Walker concluded.

By linking marijuana with cocaine and heroin and methamphetamine, the total abstinence message of 'DARE' and 'Just Say No' had done more damage to their objective of keeping people from destroying their lives than they would ever know. They had transformed marijuana into a gateway for dangerous substances. Luckily, Walker would learn in his first experience with other substances that it was a mistake to think in terms of 'drugs.'

'Drugs' do not exist, there are only individual substances. Marijuana has nothing to do with psychedelic mushrooms, which have nothing to do with cocaine, which has nothing to do with heroin, which has nothing to do with aspirin. Each is entirely different from the others, no matter what similarities one can draw between them. Some are dangerous in ways the others are not, and it is only wise to approach each with the respect that it deserves for being what it is. After all, treating a car as if it were a bicycle simply because both are used as transport can only result in regretful misuse of a potentially deadly machine.

It was in this state of misunderstanding, believing 'drugs' to be a legitimate concept, that he ventured into the world of mushrooms. He had returned to England with Zal for the second of three terms, and soon their mutual friends were calling for another trip to Amsterdam, eager to experience for themselves what Walker had told of in his stories. Eventually, they had arranged for a long weekend trip back to their Dutch playground.

Walker left Amsterdam four days later, a changed man. On the last night of his stay, Zal had convinced him to give mushrooms a try. Walker figured that the experience would be another simple insight into the 'lies' of his 'educators'. Instead, it transformed his understanding of life and helped him to see the Truth of the Whole. He was eternally grateful for what his mind was shown that night. Who knows what type of harm might have befallen him if the misinformation of his 'educators' had led him beyond the evolved natural substances of plant and mushroom, and into the world of manmade poisons such as heroin or methamphetamine. For as true as it is to say that psychedelic nature often opens the eyes to goodness and light, it is equally true to say that manmade counterfeits tend to close them, sometimes permanently.

It is the rare psychoactive plant that cannot be used for good if it is respected, as the pathways inherent in them are evolved by natural processes, just like those of man's brain. A potion, however, may well be specifically designed to deceive and to ruin. It is no secret that some men delight in creating pain and destruction for others, and thus it is wise to stay far away from most manmade chemical visions.

By the time Walker had begun to contemplate the Truth in the center of Zalman's eye, his logical mind was in a profound struggle to keep his faith in God.

Growing up Christian, his mother had always emphasized the importance of faith. But his brain had grown far too confident in its ability to understand, and in the teachings of science and philosophy. He was in his fourth year of college and knew much about the world and how it worked. He wasn't an expert in anything, but his perspective was broad and well-developed academically. He took classes in geology, biology, chemistry, political science, ethics, religion, foreign language, literature, music, athletics, computers, history, photography, and several other areas, in-spite-of working toward completion of a triple major in economics, international relations, and environmental studies, none of which necessitated such a broad selection of courses outside of their direct purview.

If Walker was anything, he was a student of everything. His broad-based perspective caused him to see a host of inconsistencies in what he had been taught about God. His mind began to have trouble swallowing the story told to him so many years before in Sunday school. This was becoming true to a degree, even in his last years of high school. But since his early college years, his faith had been in serious question. He did not want to admit that there was no God and that he was an atheist, but his inner understanding knew that this day was likely coming. Walker simply couldn't ignore the truth about his developing disbelief for much longer.

Then came the mushroom voyage, the single scariest and most powerfully moving experience of his life. He was profoundly grateful for the encounter, profoundly humbled by it, and profoundly in love with his life and with God. Still, for years he couldn't think of eating another mushroom, not even on a pizza. The lives lived that night were almost more than his singular mind could bear. At first, he couldn't make sense of what had happened. It would take years to remember and understand all that had occurred inside the Light.

CHAPTER
Fifteen

The decision had been made, and they were on their way to the store. "What kind of mushrooms are you going to get?" their friend Sylvia wanted to know.

Sylvia wasn't partaking. Nor were Jerry and Kannan, the other two friends on the trip. But the two veterans saw this last night in Amsterdam as an opportunity to branch out and try something new.

"We will probably just ask the shopkeeper; we don't know what we're buying really."

"Oh, that's encouraging," she laughed. She and the two others were willing to chaperone Walker and Zal, though they were not convinced that such a foray was a smart plan.

Zal found a store, and they talked with the shopkeeper about the different varieties available. In the end, they settled on a package each of a dried mushroom called 'Mexican', which was later surmised to have been *Psilocybin Mexicana*.

They took the package around with them that day, and near dusk, they returned to the Hans Brinker Hotel where they were staying in a five-person room together. The two veterans ate the mushrooms and then sat around waiting for something to happen while their friends enjoyed some of the best marijuana in the world. An hour later, nothing had happened.

"You know what's funny?" their friend Jerry said mockingly. "You guys spent what, twenty euros on a disgusting fungus, and we are all stoned out of our minds for about a dollar each?"

He began to laugh to himself and then bobbed his head a bit as his hands directed an imaginary orchestra. "Doooo, doooo, doo, doo, da, doo, doo, da, da, dooo, dooo, dooo, dooo." He smiled as he directed, somehow conveying an incredibly irksome message using utter nonsense as the medium.

"Come on," said Zal. "We aren't going to sit here and waste the night. We decided to do this, so let's do it. We should have bought the fresh ones. These dried Mexican things are shit. Let's go find another shop and talk to someone who knows about these things. I think that other guy was full of crap. We shouldn't have bought the weak stuff; we should have bought the *Psilocybe Cubensis*."

They jumped up and left the hotel hurriedly. It was a long way to walk to reach a shop Zal had remembered from earlier in the day. Upon leaving the front door of the hotel, however, they beheld a shop immediately across the street that they had never seen before. The outside of the store had a purple neon sign reading 'Mushroom Shop'. They looked at each other in amazement.

"Where on Earth did this come from?" Zal asked.

"Beats me, but it's better than walking across town."

They entered the shop and shut the door behind them. Inside, the room was exceptionally long, perhaps fifty feet in all, and the first forty feet of its length had nothing in it. In the back of the shop, there stood a pale woman. She was elegant and beautiful and young. She had short-cropped hair of the darkest tint and wore a thin, flowing dress that glowed slightly from the violet and blue lighting, which mimicked the light of the moon.

"Good evening," she said in an airy and wispy voice. If she hadn't been so beautiful, they might have critiqued the strange manner in which she formed her sounds. "What are you gentlemen looking for? Anything in particular?" she breathed the words across the space softly and effortlessly.

They approached, and Zal explained their predicament to the woman, asking if she had *Psilocybe Cubensis* in stock. She informed them that she only had fresh mushrooms of that variety, which would be better than dried anyway. They bought two packages of fresh 'Thai' mushrooms.

"You must act quickly, if you wait too long, your minds will develop immunity to the experience, and nothing will happen at all this night. If I were you, I would eat them right here, right now."

They looked at each other, opened the packages, and ate the mushrooms. The woman smiled at them pleasantly, and each flirted a bit as they ate. Then they thanked her and headed out the door. "Have a pleasant trip," she said as they left the shop.

"Bizarre, don't you think?" Walker said once they were back outside.

"Yeah, she was strange huh?"

They returned to the hotel and sat for another hour; still, nothing happened.

Zal eventually became agitated by the lack of effect. "This stuff was supposed to kick in after fifty minutes, and now it's been over two hours, and we've done two doses of these crap mushrooms. Come on, we're going back to talk to that girl."

They left the hotel again amidst chiding from their friends who were still enjoying each other's company. Outside, the shop was gone, or at least closed. Neither of them could make out which storefront it had been in. Regardless of this peculiarity, it was nowhere to be found.

"Come on. We *will* get high off these things," said Zal. They made their way to another shop a dozen or so blocks away, and Zal talked in Hebrew with the shop owner while Walker perused other merchandise.

Ten minutes later, Zal found his friend in the back of the store, staring at a display of alien figures under a black light. "Walker, I talked with the guy, and he sold me the good stuff."

He was holding a package of fresh mushrooms, the variety of which neither ever discovered.

"He said one dose was all we needed for both of us."

"To tell you the truth," Walker admitted, "I am starting to feel quite strange."

"Me too," Zal said with a smirk. "But I already bought the things. I was in mid-sentence with the guy when it sort of hit me, but I felt like I was already on a course to obtain these. It was super weird. It was like I felt destined to buy them even though I didn't want to anymore. We may as well eat them, don't you think?"

Walker shrugged his shoulders and opened the container, and they each wolfed down the mushrooms in equal proportions there under the purple glow.

"Have you ever noticed that alien stuff is always under black lights?" Walker asked.

"Now that you mention it, yeah. We had better get back, Walker. I'm feeling weirder and weirder all the time."

Walker agreed, and they set out for the hotel. By the time they got there, each was concentrating deeply on the objective of making it back to the safety of the room. They walked into the hotel and made their way down the hall. The floor suddenly undulated as if the carpet were a wave on the sea, throwing Zal sideways. He had to turn to catch himself as his body careened into the wall. Walker was thrown to the side too, but he had caught the wave before it crested nearer to Zal, and consequently was able to avoid actually hitting the wall like his friend ahead of him. He stumbled around and regained his footing.

"Holy shit, did you just see what happened?!" Walker exclaimed, looking at Zal, who was wide-eyed and nodding, still up against the wall.

"The fucking floor just made a wave," he confirmed. They knocked on the door and were let in by their friends.

Inside, each lay down in his respective bed, and the two talked to one another about what they were experiencing.

"Walker, look at the curtains!"

He looked. The pattern on them was alive, moving like a kaleidoscope. It was mesmerizing. Then the pattern suddenly sucked up into the top six inches of the curtain, compressing into a dense version of its former self, leaving the rest of the curtain a solid hue, devoid of any pattern.

Walker was not doing this on purpose, and he marveled as Zal reacted and described the same scene in detail as it developed. With marijuana, he was always in control, at least partially. But this was happening *to* him; his mind was tossed about like a ship on a great ocean. Still, the experience was interesting, and though it was quickly overwhelming his mental capacity, he didn't fear what was happening... at least not yet.

Some time passed, and Walker's mind began to think deeper and faster than it had ever before. He began to unravel life, and not just his own, but the meaning of life itself. Suddenly the totality of life and meaning was understood in all its complexity. God made sense, or was starting to, and the thought emerged that perhaps he had stumbled upon all that mankind needed to know about who he was and where he was from. He had to write it down.

"Guys, get me a paper and a pencil," he said with difficulty.

"What do you want a paper and pencil for?" they teased.

"I understand the meaning of life. I have to write it down," he said, staring at them intently.

"Woooow!" said Sylvia. "I guess they are really working now, huh?!" she continued in a playful voice. She was a very nice girl, always looking out for others and having a good time, but he didn't have time to address her; he had to write down the meaning of life. His concentration could not be allowed to break, lest the most elusive thing man had ever pursued be lost.

He wrote and wrote and wrote, until eventually, what looked like a dissertation began to take shape. He thumbed back through the pages and cleaned up his work, erasing portions and adding to other ideas to clarify. It seemed that he had worked for days, and then Sylvia came back to him.

"Let's see what you've got there," she said, taking the pencil and paper from his hands.

Walker looked at her. "What does it say?" he asked, genuinely wanting to know what he had written.

She was laughing under her breath.

"What is it?" the other two chaperones wanted to know. Sylvia began to read.

"Jerry is on the top bunk. He likes Sylvia, the girl laying on the bottom bunk. He tried to..." She began to laugh.

"He tried to what?" they asked.

"That's all it says. Then it just trails off in a squiggle like he fell asleep writing it."

She was laughing so hard now that she was crying.

They all laughed heartily at the meaning of life Walker had composed, while he sat motionless, trying to make sense of what was happening.

"I swore I had written. Hadn't I written? I must have. I remembered. Didn't I? I-I-I-wasn't I? I thought I was."

He couldn't keep his thoughts together anymore. They came in strange broken pieces that didn't add up to anything, and he began to stare at the light on the ceiling as his mind began to let go. It was so captivating, a perfectly round white light. It seemed to drive away everything around it. There was something behind it, or in it. Not the light fixture, but rather the energy itself. It seemed it was a portal to somewhere beyond. He focused on the white orb and began to feel his spirit gravitate toward the portal.

It was at this point that their other companion, Kannan, nearly scared the life out of Walker. He was not only inexperienced with mushrooms; he wasn't even partaking of marijuana due to his beliefs regarding 'drugs'. Walker was perfectly okay with his stance on this issue, and they had a fine time on their trip together, as Kannan was accepting of his friends' experiments, much as Walker had once been accepting of his friends in high school and early in college. But Kannan's lack of experience with 'drugs' caused him to react in a most unhelpful way upon seeing his friend lose his ability to function in physical reality.

"Guys, something is wrong with Walker," he heard Kannan saying in a strained voice. Suddenly, Kannan's face was in front of him, and he looked scared, which made Walker scared. Walker couldn't respond, his mind was frozen with fear.

"Look at me buddy! Look at me!" Kannan screamed again and again.

Walker struggled to look at him for a moment, but his face held no power next to the light. It called his eyes back to it. "Walker!" he screamed again. Walker shook his head and looked back at him, mouth opening, eyes struggling to connect. "Stay with me, buddy! Stay with me!"

Walker's head rolled back on the pillow, and his eyes returned to the light once more. He felt his spirit leave his body, no longer seeing anything but the white radiance, which he rose to find. He could still hear his friend screaming. "Guys, we're losing him, we're losing him, we're losing him."

Sylvia had seen this before, and she put a stop to the panic, which was scaring the life out of Walker. "Will you stop it!" she yelled at Kannan.

"Something is seriously wrong, look at him," he yelled back.

"He's fucked on mushrooms, he'll be fine in about eight hours, now just leave him alone. Don't you understand how scared he is right now?"

She asked this as she approached Walker's body, where she began gently stroking his head. "You're going to be just fine Walker, okay? You're still here with us, and we will be here when you get back from wherever you are going?"

Walker paused in his ascent to listen to her words, which were coming from behind him now. He was aware of her stroking his head, though he did not experience it personally; he only perceived that it was occurring. "Don't be scared, I'll take care of you. Remember, you will come back."

She continued to speak from a distance beneath him as he floated slowly toward the ceiling. As he neared the light fixture, he rotated his awareness to look upon his body and the body of the woman tending to his own. Then he rotated his awareness again, into the center of the light. He began to accelerate, slowly at first, then faster and faster. As he began to dive into the irresistible world above him, he forgot about his body and the room. With each passing moment, his acceleration doubled, and in a few seconds, his mind went from moving towards the fixture across the space in the room, to catching up with the cosmic rays themselves.

Soon another world was found, and in this world, he did not have a body, only a presence. There was no scenery, only white space, as he was traveling along with the energy and existing within it. This White wasn't like a blank page, rather it was more akin to a page covered. White was not the absence of information, but the presence of it. People had been conditioned to see it as a blank page because they marked on white spaces with black inks and other stains. But mankind only behaved like this because of the way he thought, and he only thought the way he did because of the nature of the fallen realm in which he lived.

Mankind's entire way of thinking was based on a process of deconstruction. He started with the whole and then began picking it apart into its components. It was a destructive process, rather than a constructive one. Despite the complexity of man's understanding, however, it never satisfied him, because he was understanding in the wrong direction. The complexity of his deconstructed reality could never equal the beauty of the one simplistic Truth.

Yet man's mind seemed unable to refrain from seeking to understand. It was almost an unavoidable truth that mankind was made to divide and to label and to compartmentalize. Naturally, when man sought expression of his labels in evolved form, they came about through another destructive process, which was born of still another. It was easier to stain white surfaces with ink than to overlay black surfaces with white paints, so man utilized black inks to blot out sections of white pages. This was yet another exercise focused on the blocking of the whole. This, in turn, was made possible by the medium for his enterprise, which came about by 'creating' paper. Paper was, in fact, not a 'creation' at all, but rather a destruction of an authentically existent creation in the form of the living forest.

As Walker continued to ponder The White Reality surrounding him, this truth filled the entirety of his mind, and yet he was aware that these thoughts were only part of the picture. For words themselves were not ideas, but rather they were representations of ideas. The ideas were formed by an intelligence, who then passed them to other intelligences through the medium of the written word. It seemed in keeping with the nature of man's deconstruction of his reality that words should be composed by blocking out the whole through the use of black ink on white paper. It was certainly the unquestioned method of conveying information among human beings. Never in all Walker's time on Earth had he seen a book where white letters were brought to the emptiness of a black page.

There was a technical reason for this, which seemed to fit almost magically with mankind's methodology of thought. Black surfaces could not be stained white, only painted or bleached, and staining was much easier than painting or bleaching. It is easier to destroy than to create. It is easier to pull apart than to put together. It is easier to distinguish than to see the whole. Thus, this is the way the written word was used to convey ideas born of man's mental deconstruction of his reality, through the blocking of the light.

Yet to Walker's mind, amidst the simplicity and completeness of the white light with which he now traveled, it seemed clear that the ideas of an enlightened intelligence should be transmitted to others through the opening of light pathways. The written word should begin with a page that absorbed all light, and then it should be overlaid with white paint which allows for the flow of light and truth through an object that was once devoid of both.

He stayed with these thoughts for what would later seem to have been a great many months, thinking about the light and the written word, and thought itself. Man was not wrong for being who he was at any point in time; rather, he was wrong for deciding to travel in the wrong direction. Life was a journey, and the purpose was to find the direction of the whole, but man was constantly looking to deepen his understanding, which required further and further divisions of thought. There was no shortage of division in the world Walker had left behind.

Eventually, an understanding of the Truth came. Despite appearances, the minds of men were capable of more than thought born of division and deconstruction. Spirituality was not a child of man's destructive framework, rather it was born of Reality, and man could connect to it when he chose to engage a higher intellectual plane that did not base understanding on logical constructs. When he stopped trying to understand and sought instead to experience and to wonder, understanding found *him*. Mankind's fully evolved identity is not best conceived of as a thinker, but rather as a seeker. Thought serves the search. The search is primary, and thought is only a tool.

The real was beyond Walker's ability to cognize; it could never be captured and tamed by thought. All he could do was seek it and hope to understand its shadow. Later in his life, he would find that this had also been understood by others, and even written down. It is put perhaps most subtly by Lao Tzu in the Tao Te Ching.

> A way that can be walked is not The Way.
> A name that can be named is not The Name.
> Tao is both Named and Nameless.
> As Nameless, it is the origin of all things.
> As named, it is the mother of all things.
> A mind free of thought, merged within itself,
> beholds the essence of Tao.
> A mind filled with thought, identified with its own
> perceptions, beholds the mere forms of this world.

- Verse 1

He soon found himself reflecting on other thoughts, divining the Truth from the white perfection surrounding him. It seemed to seep in as he questioned.

He posed a thought, and the answer was upon him. The answers came smoothly and without mental effort as if he were listening, but without having to try to understand. It was as natural as noticing that the wind is blowing when one feels the air passing over his body. The interpretation was automatic and took no conscious effort.

He began to think of Alizée, whom he was then losing. He had come home to Lancaster after the vacation between the second and third terms of school to the reality that she was no longer there to hold. She was back in Michigan and they would be apart for at least three months, if not a year. They had agreed that they did not want to restrain each other and that their love for one another did not necessitate jealousy or the preclusion of other romantic interests. In time, he realized that he could not follow through with those feelings, and that he loved her too much to let her be with anyone else, but it had been too late. She had already decided to move on, a consequence of his near decision to sleep with another woman and then admit to this encounter when asked about it.

"I didn't think you would actually take another girl home with you. I mean, I know we said it was okay, but I didn't think you would really do it," she had said over the phone in a broken tone.

"But I didn't follow through with it. Don't you see? I thought about it, but I didn't do it. I was alone with her in that room, yes, and she was offering herself to me, but in that moment, I understood what I wanted, and I just told her that I couldn't be with her because I was in love with you. I turned down all that she offered me, and I told her it was because I love you."

This had not reached her heart. All she felt was the crushing realization that Walker was not the person she had hoped for, for he had genuinely considered sharing himself with another woman. Alizée couldn't see that he was growing into the man he should become. She defined him for what she saw him as being, and then she cast her love away. He begged her not to let this destroy their love. He wasn't perfect, but the error of their shared, laissez-faire approach to sexual freedom had not matured into the reality she feared.

The thoughts of Alizée ran through his mind, and he understood that he truly loved her, and that she was already lost. She had needed him to possess her love, but Walker had failed her in this way because he thought he was respecting her liberation. He had been wrong. Men and women were not meant to join and then part, they were meant to join and become one flesh. He felt the loss in its totality. His heart ached for her, knowing that she was gone, and that another now existed with her... inside of her. He didn't know how he knew, but the knowledge of it filled his mind.

"Ahhhhhhhhh!"

He screamed at the top of his lungs into the space around him. But no sound came forth in that place. He hadn't any lungs to scream with. It was the directing of all his energy to the expression of the pain and heartache felt in his soul. The Truth around him absorbed the pain completely, neither detesting it nor pitying it. It was what it was, and that was all.

If Walker was in hell, he had created it. He began to wonder if he was in hell, or perhaps heaven. It wasn't the heaven or hell he would recognize, that was for sure, but his body was no longer present, and his friends were nowhere to be found. The understanding came that he had died, and his life had ended. He collapsed inward and began to cry spiritually. He directed himself to pity and sorrow. Life had gone so wrong. He had tried to do what was right but had gotten lost. And then he had eaten a fungus that had caused him to die. It had all come so innocently, almost as if he had been set up to fall from the beginning. His mother, father, two brothers, and two sisters would never see him again; they were separated from him forever. And Alizée, oh God Alizée.

"Alizée!"

Screaming without effect again and again; his soul felt sorrow the depths of which cannot be described, and he sat in torment for a thousand years, only there was no time in that place. Walker only saw the thousand years for what it was much later when his mind reflected back. The centuries passed, and he suffered and suffered, unaware that time had been passing. He might have wondered where it had gone, had he been capable of pondering such a concept, but at this point, his mind was at the mercy of time's own conception. All he could contemplate was the life he had left behind, the life he had lived, the loves he had destroyed.

"Nadia!"

Walker began to weep in his soul for the girl he had fallen for as a young man. He struggled to sing to her once again. But words could not be made. Her name had not even sounded in the white around him. His spirit beat itself against The White, but it simply remained as whole and perfect as it had since his arrival. It held him as he thrashed his emotions about, refusing to let go until the rage gave way.

"What have I done?" he eventually asked. Immediately, the answer came. He had not believed. He had turned his back on God, on His instruction, on His Love.

"I never denied you," he protested.

A wave of understanding washed over him. He had not denied, but he had not believed either. Denial precluded belief, but a lack of denial did not mean anything by itself, except that belief might still be found.

"Why haven't you believed?" The message came without sound or words. The White had posed its own question to him for the first time. He felt a shame that cannot be expressed. The White knew the answer, and Walker understood instantly that this was so.

Comfort then found his soul. He was a failure. He knew it, he admitted it, and that was all that was required. The Power beyond him understood that he was not an equal to the Totality of all things. Walker was but a part of an inferior created reality. But being Totality, He or She or It looked upon him with favor and concern, because that Power wanted him to develop.

"The point is that I am supposed to understand my place, isn't it?"

"Yes."

"The point is that I am to admit of your existence, and of my need for your love and forgiveness, which you give freely. You only hate arrogance."

"I cannot nurture those who demand that they need no nurturing, at least not without violating them. I cannot forgive those who believe they are the definition of the way things should be, because they preclude me gifting them anything."

"Of course," he thought. "We should always seek, and we should always understand that we fall short of the glory of perfection. The greatest lie is that there is no ultimate Truth. There is ultimate Truth, but we must not purport to know what it is."

The Presence suddenly surrounded him in a thick emotion of safety, forgiveness, and peace. He knew nothing but this peace and healing for another great span of time, many times longer than an Earthly life. His spirit was filled with the knowledge that he would indeed Return, though the memory of what his life had been about was now gone. The point of his life had come to be understood in a completely general manner. The details of who he had been had left him. But in their place was an understanding of what *all* life was about, and of what it should become.

He and his friends were all eternal beings, and they were in a physical form to learn and to grow. But their eternal nature did not mean they were the ultimate form of life. On the contrary, The Whole was the ultimate Life Force. As beings, however, he and his friends had existed before their walk on Earth, and they would continue to exist after that walk ended. Walker had left his body, though only temporarily, and he still existed. Soon he would return to his body, among the spirits of his friends, who existed to help him learn, and he for them.

After his return, he would have to start over, and he would go through enormous troubles, which had to be endured, as they were outgrowths of the sins of the past. These trials would pressure him into more sin, and this would seek to consume his life in a perpetual spiral. The test would be severe, and he would fall to depths never before known in his mortal journey, but it was the only way back to God's vision for his life. Penitence. The lion's share of his wrongs and sins were behind him, but more were yet to come. He would have to endure his weakness until he could understand it and stop it. God would be there, but Walker would not feel Him again until his belief had been proven in the physical world.

Suddenly, he felt his body. His eyes blinked for the first time in six hours. "Please help me," he said to Sylvia. Immediately she was by his side, helping him down from the top bunk on which his body was lying. He walked to the bathroom.

"Do you need help?"

"No, just leave me be."

She shut the door, and Walker sank in front of the toilet, where he began to vomit. His body was lurching and convulsing as it purged itself of the alien infestation, but he experienced no discomfort. In fact, the sensation was rather pleasant after centuries, or perhaps millennia without a body to sense. He made mental note that his most despised experience of vomiting could in fact be enjoyed the next time he was forced to experience it by whatever illness. He understood the pleasure in it now, at least when it was a cleansing. He finally finished, and then his eyes set about gazing into the waters of the toilet. The mushroom bodies still seemed intact here and there, and they swirled and communicated as the curtains had done earlier.

Walker watched in fascination as they moved about independently, twisting and flowing this way and then that way, around each other and through each other as they met in the water's idea of time. A half an hour or so passed for the people in the other room, and they became concerned for their friend. Perhaps he had drowned in his own vomit?

"Walker, are you okay?"

He stood and opened the door. His guardian angel, Sylvia, was still watching over him like she said she would be. She led him by the hand to her bed, where he sat next to her and one of the other guys as they talked and smoked.

"Am I being okay now?"

"Hey! Welcome back!" Kannan greeted him.

"Did I go away?"

"Yeah, you went away!" Kannan said emphatically, as he placed his hand on Walker's shoulder.

"You haven't spoken or moved in seven hours," his angel told him.

"I did when I got up to puke, I know this is true."

"Well, you moved, yeah, but you haven't spoken 'til now. You just looked like you needed help down off the bed."

"But I said I needed your help down from bed."

"No, you didn't say a word until just now."

"You scared the life out of me, Walker. I thought you were dying," Kannan lightly scolded.

"Will I be made normal again?" Walker asked genuinely. His mind felt completely broken. He could remember very little of the world and knew that he could no longer navigate it alone. Even leaving the room was beyond his capacity to consider.

"Yes, in about another hour."

"What does 'hour' mean?"

"An hour?" asked his angel.

"Yes, what is that meaning to me?"

"Look, you're having trouble making sense of things, you had a really bad trip on mushrooms, but you're getting better, and you'll be fine soon."

"I don't understand 'soon,'" he said. Time was a completely foreign concept. He had existed without it for so long that he could no longer make sense of it.

Sylvia held her watch up for him to examine. "See this? When this hand makes a full circle, you will be better."

Walker studied the face of the mysterious manmade device. It made no sense. He didn't like the object; it seemed all wrong and completely incomprehensible. He began to shake his head and then pushed the watch away. "Get that thing away from me. I don't like it. It isn't right."

"It's okay, you don't have to like the watch." She thought for a minute. "If I take him to get a Coke and something to eat, can you guys watch Zalman?"

"Sure."

"Okay, come on Walker, we're going to McDonald's."

His angel and friend led him by the hand through the streets of

Amsterdam to a McDonald's in the early hours of the morning. Inside, she gave him a Coca-Cola and a fish sandwich with fries. He ate ravenously and was soon given another fish and another order of fries. He finished his food and then sat quietly sipping on his soda and looking at Sylvia and the other people in the restaurant. The material surroundings, such as the building, the furniture, and the street outside with its posts and cars and bikes, were all clear and sharply in focus. The people, however, were not entirely.

Their bodies were mostly in focus, but their faces seemed to blur and shift about as a hologram fading in and out suddenly. Walker looked at his friend's face and noticed that it was quite clear and steady compared to many of the other people, though it too would fade in and out suddenly as if the signal was momentarily lost, then regained. This phenomenon was strange, but it could be comprehended and then left behind when he felt like having a drink of soda. It was sobriety compared to where he had just been.

The fizzy drink seemed to be helping a lot, and Walker was beginning to feel much better. "Thank you so much for helping me tonight. I was really scared earlier by all that 'we're losing him' talk."

"He meant well; he just didn't have a clue about what you were going through."

"Have you ever tripped on mushrooms?" he asked.

"No, I've seen several friends go through things like what you went through, and I have absolutely *no* desire to go through something like that. I tried to tell ya!" she said cheerfully.

Walker began to laugh and feel genuinely perfect in his sobriety. "I thought I was dead," he chuckled, happy to be alive. "How is my fellow mushroom eater doing?"

"He's still pretty bad. You threw up, and that brought you out of it. He may be an hour or so behind you, but it shouldn't be much longer than that. It's been nearly nine hours already. He should be stirring when we get back, but leave him alone until he feels up to talking, okay?"

"Don't worry, I understand. I'm not going to push him. He'll be okay though?"

"He'll be fine, but you guys both really had a bad trip. I've seen a few, but never anything like this. You were both completely catatonic for almost seven hours. You looked like you had died, but from what I know it's impossible to die from overdosing on mushrooms, and you were breathing fine, so I told the others to just give you some time. What did you guys end up taking?"

Walker explained the double dosage of 'Mexican' and 'Thai' variety mushrooms followed by the splitting of the "real deal", as Zalman had called them.

"God Walker, what did you think you were dealing with? I told you it wasn't pot."

"Yeah, but all my life pot was supposedly so scary too, and that was complete lies."

"But that was from people who don't know anything, they just run their mouths. Just because some people don't know anything about drugs doesn't mean you shouldn't listen to the ones that do. I'm a *Southern California surfer girl*, you should have listened to *me*." Sylvia's expression backed up her point in sublime fashion.

"I'm sorry. I will never disrespect the other world again."

"It's okay. I just don't like seeing my friends suffering like that. You went through something pretty intense, huh?"

Walker squinted and tilted his head as he tried to answer meaningfully. "I don't even know how to explain. I feel like I just lived a hundred lifetimes. I thought I was dead, and all I could think about was the fact that I could never again try to make it right with Alizée. I was so scared that my life was over and that I had ended it without love, and without faith. My mind has been fractured into perhaps a million pieces this day. It will take a long time to put my 'self' back together. Maybe this time I can build someone I like. The good news is that I believe in God now."

"I thought you already did?"

"I always said I did, but I didn't really know if I did or not, but now I do. I believe without question. I wish you could understand how deeply I've changed. I can't explain it, but God isn't at all what I was trying to make him into, or what the world tried to reduce him to. I feel as if I've been gone for thousands of years. It is hard even to remember what we are doing here in this place."

"You mean Amsterdam?"

"Amsterdam. Yeah. That is what we call it here, isn't it?"

"Wow, Walker. You remember we go back to England tomorrow, right."

"England? Yeah, I suppose that makes sense. God, I feel so shaky," he said, rubbing his arms to combat the feeling. "I don't feel like I'm even completely whole. I feel fragmented. Yet, I'm so happy that I'm no longer blind. I was almost lost, but now I see. Do you understand that I was ready to turn my back on the Power responsible for my own existence? I will never contemplate such wrongness again. Why would the world try to keep me from this understanding?"

"I don't know. Maybe they don't understand it. Or maybe they do, and they recognize the level of the psychic wound that can result from doing what you just did. Just because you've been liberated by this experience, doesn't mean that others aren't ruined by similar decisions."

Though Walker's mind remained clouded, his words came to the room clear and sharp in response. He felt almost as if he were listening to an audio recording of himself. It was like his mind was answering from somewhere off to the side of his body.

"You're right, I can't say what should be for others. Perhaps for many, forcing the mind beyond its own balance leads to harm. But I understand one thing clearly. No one else in this world is capable of saying what is right for others, either. This is my journey, and only I am positioned to choose what to open to, and how to open to it. I had become imprisoned inside my own intellectual walls. I built them using bricks of thought I did not fully understand, which others had given to me from my youth onward. This left me unable to understand my own fortifications. I recognized that I did not possess the skill to deconstruct them, and so, deep inside my subconscious awareness, I must have decided to blow them up. My mind didn't know what it was being led into tonight, but I suspect that my spirit planned for the whole thing. I have definitely suffered a great psychic wound, as you said, but this wound is preferable to spiritual deadness. My mind and soul will heal well enough. I'm glad my walls are gone."

"Well, it's good to hear that the experience wasn't all bad. Your life isn't over, you're still here, and you still have time to find God and all the rest of it. Come on, let's go see how your mushroom partner is coming along."

Walker took the cup of Coke in his hand and stood to face the future. He knew it was going to get rough, but he would never again allow something as flimsy as logic or reason to interfere with the Eternal Truth of God or the timeless importance of Love. He would honor his love for Alizée. So long as there was a chance to find her soul again, he would try, he would wait, and he would endure. He loved her, and he would honor that truth no matter how painful it might become. He would only move on from her if the Truth counseled that it should be, and he would never love another again unless Grace ordained it so.

They returned to their room. Zalman was up, sitting in the corner. He looked at Walker as if they had once been in a war together.

"You alright, buddy?" Walker asked.

"I'm much better than I was. That sucked. I'm never doing mushrooms again."

"No shit," he replied, climbing back into his bed. "Can I go to sleep for a while?" Walker asked his friends.

"Sure, why don't both of you just rest for an hour or two, and then we'll see how you feel."

At that, he lay back against the white emanating from the sheets and closed his eyes.

Behind the veil of good intention
Lies proliferate
Deceived by disease of reason
THE REASON set aside
Brother seeking brother's end

How long shall we remain
Ignorant to Design
For Virtue is real
Though Truth alone can define
Forcing either dawns our demise

Man arbitrates his own delusion
Arrogance weds the fool
He'll save his brother from himself
Logic dictates that logic must prevail
Blue Waters of the mind no more to sail

CHAPTER
Sixteen

A few months following the experience in Amsterdam, Walker found himself sitting on a Sicilian beach. He was smoking a joint with a half dozen Pennsylvanians who were studying in Rome. It was there that he happened upon a vision of the love he would one day come to know. Looking back on that time, he would come to see it as proof that his connection to Aiyana was beyond the reach of their collective intentions with one another's experiences. The connection occurred outside of their relationship and predated their meeting one another, yet it tied everything together across time and through people other than themselves.

He had grappled daily with what the Truth required of him after leaving The White. The mushroom experience had shaken him deeply, and he struggled to put his life right in the months after his return from the place their energy had taken him. This struggle was accentuated by the sheer loss that he felt after the end of his relationship with Alizée. She was all but lost by then, and though he did not know what to do to heal their love, or if it was even possible, he knew that he had to honor the fact that he loved her. He had to try to set things right even if it was impossible, because that was the kind of dedication that he wanted to see in his world. The path a man and woman should walk had become clear to him, and all his desire lay in finding a way through to a place where the two might walk it together. If he was to be worthy of such a love, he had to first demonstrate it himself. He was starting to see, but the pain skewed everything.

Walker was sitting in the sand and thinking of his lost Alizée when he looked up and saw them; Adam and Eve. He was around ten meters from the sea's edge, studying them as they walked along in the wet sand where the ocean was neither present nor absent. He fancied the idea that this young couple was walking in between two worlds. She was an agreeable young creature, with firm, tanned skin, and a tight athletic physique. Her hair was matted, dirty, and beautiful. He thought of her hair as the tail of a fox, and she reminded him of one. He instantly adored her for the way she embraced the natural world, seeming to meld with it in a way that announced the glory of nature.

Holding her hand was a man, a young man, about Walker's age. This man was handsome and athletic, with slightly lighter skin and a thin but muscular build. He had hair similar to hers, though his did not call to Walker's desire to touch and explore. Walker felt pulled to caress the woman, and to hold her slight frame against his own. His mind settled on a conjured image, in which he stood behind the woman, holding her softly and leaning slightly over her shoulder, so that he might lose himself in the beautiful hair that carried the stories of weeks gone by in a thousand captured scents.

His reason for being in Sicily was the result of a hundred random decisions made in days gone by, and his reason for being in this particular town, on this particular beach, was the result of still a hundred more. He had not planned his trip over the break between the lent and summer terms of school at Lancaster and had instead chosen to book a flight into Stockholm, and a flight home from Brussels a month later. There was no itinerary in-between, no reservations. He wandered the continent, traveling from Stockholm to Heidelberg, then on to Venice, Bologna, Florence, and Rome. From Rome, the journey had turned south, as Pompeii and Naples suddenly took his fancy. But upon arriving at the train station in Naples, he was followed by a group of men. They had marked him for something, though for what he could not be sure. There were at least five of them, and they had positioned themselves around him subtly near the various exits. Walker turned in his tracks and went back to the ticket counter, inquiring as to where the next departing train was headed. It was scheduled to leave seven minutes later and bound for Palermo, Sicily. He booked a ticket and boarded the train so that the men could not follow, turning to give a casual salute to one of them as he entered the gated boarding area, just to make his awareness known.

The ride had been interesting, to say the least, as two ticketless stowaways begged their way into his private cabin to avoid being detected by the authorities. Then they lit up a joint of Spanish marijuana, which they offered to him, though he declined for no particular reason. Later he had sat staring silently at the ceiling in the dark as the woman panted and arched only a few feet away, both she and her man completely lost in one another. It seemed something that would offend normal civilized sensibilities, though Walker was anything but offended. He experienced sex that night in a way he had not before. He lay there, happy for her, and for him, though mostly for her. He adored beautiful women, and he loved listening as she struggled to remain quiet for fear of waking him, simply for the fact that such a creature was being pushed to the edge of her ability to contain her love of herself. He pondered what it was that Reality was trying to tell him about his own 'self', and he considered that perhaps he was being prepared to understand something fundamental to his path.

When the train reached the Strait of Messina, it was placed aboard a ferry and floated to the island of Sicily. Walker departed in Palermo and then took a bus to investigate the area around Mondello, traveling eventually by a smaller bus to a campground advertised on a flyer he had found lying on the ground. The campground was in the nearby fishing village of Sferracavallo, and he stayed there for a week in a small cabin. Eventually, he encountered a group of Pennsylvanian students and joined them on an outing back to Mondello, which had a decent beach where a person could enjoy the simple pleasure of absorbing the light of the sun.

The beach there was somewhat dirty, but this was the only noticeable detraction. A large mountain sat just behind the town, on the other side of which was Sferracavallo. Another mountain sat off in the distance in the other direction, and this one resembled a flop-eared dog lying down on its belly. The beach itself was a vibrant place, with young girls lying in the sun and young boys playing football, or soccer as he had once called it. He spent several days there, chatting with local teenagers and joining them in their sport, which was a lesson on how the game was to be played.

Several of the young men practiced music most of the day on large African drums made of wood and furry animal skins. The mood was irrevocably enhanced by the constant beats these young musicians turned out. Walker had spoken with the young men concerning their smoking of marijuana in public. Were they not concerned about the police? He was well-aware of Italy's strict drug enforcement policies.

"That is just the North," one of the young Sicilians said. "This is Sicily. Sicily is not like the rest of Italy, here, we are still free."

So, Walker and the Pennsylvanians had indulged themselves with a smoke that day courtesy of their new Italian friends, and then again the next, which saw Walker reclined in the sand, looking at life as it ought to be lived. Adam and Eve.

He sat contemplating the two creatures as they neared his position on the beach. A dog followed them. He was a wet, matted, mess and must have weighed about forty pounds. Walker knew he was a mutt, but his mind couldn't make out the breeds that had gone into him. He was a mix of perhaps every breed on Earth. He was a magnificent animal, trotting along with his human companions. They carried only a single possession with them other than their tattered clothing. Wrapped around the woman's neck, beneath her foxtail, was a thin, grey blanket that had once been white.

Adam teased the gift God had made for him, pulling at the blanket and nudging her body away as it gravitated towards him with each tug of the cloth. They passed by, oblivious to anyone's presence. They were in love, and this fact filled Walker with deep joy. After progressing another thirty or forty meters down the beach, the woman jumped on the man, and they twirled around laughing and kissing, until they fell in the wet sand, kissing passionately while their sole possession became a bed for their dog.

He regarded the dog and the two humans as a unit. Singularly, each might have seemed sad, with their dirty hair and century-old blanket. But together, they were a marvelous sight to behold. He loved her, and she loved him, and they loved their dog, who also loved. Suddenly, Walker loved her as well. He sat watching them caressing each other in the sand, unconcerned for their appearance or the grit working its way into their hair. He felt so pulled to her, so in need of her, but at the same time he was happy for the man, and he wished him well with his fox. He hoped to know such a creature himself someday.

"Man, can you imagine living like that?" said one of his new American friends.

Walker looked away from the delights in the sand and set his gaze on the silly mind that had uttered such heresy. His new friend had not asked the question to show his approval, but to call attention to the superiority of his own way of life. His voice was thick with bias.

"The problem my friend is that you and I do indeed have trouble imagining living like that," Walker counseled. "You should nurture the ability to imagine such a life. Perhaps in time, you will be able to imagine it fully, and then perhaps with a little more time, you will be able to enjoy what they enjoy. That is what life should be like. That is all there is in life. The rest of the stuff we deal in, the work and possessions, the status and so-called achievements; these are all illusions. None of these things can be held sustainably. We all have to set them down someday. Why not set them down now? These illusions are designed to keep us from one thing, and that thing is what those people have found. May God bless them, and may God bless their union that they never lose what they have found. Or at least, that they never dishonor it by selling it for the shell of a life we live back home."

"You think they are blessed?! Did you see the blanket they were carrying? Did you see their dog? Did you see their hair or their clothes? I have news for you Walker, those people are homeless, and they probably have as many fleas as their poor, mangy dog."

"I don't think the dog has mange," Walker protested.

"Okay, so he isn't mangy, but I'll guarantee he has fleas, and that they do too. You think they like living with fleas?"

"I know they do, look at them," Walker said, turning his eyes back to the rapture rolling around in the sand. What he wouldn't have given at that moment to be her man, her companion, fleas and all. She was as wild and free as any creature he had ever seen. She played and laughed without thought, oblivious to things as fleeting as dirt and sand. This made her all the more attractive. She wasn't caught up in appearances and cleanliness; she was too intent on living. She was alive, truly alive, and he envied her for her life. He wanted to share in it with her. The dirt could do nothing next to her radiance. It merely changed the hue of her skin, which remained just as perfectly stretched over her exquisite feminine form.

He wondered if someday he too could find this level of abandon in his own life. Walker was much freer than the average American back home, with their dreams of career and status and acquirement of possessions. He was even freer than the average Englishman, who was clearly freer than his American brethren by his estimation. But true freedom remained elusive. In spite of all his mental exploration, and all his travel and exposure to life, he remained trapped by something.

Deep in his mind lived a compulsion to justify himself to others. He had always been this way, from his days as a young boy. He wanted those that he loved to see him as a success, and for this reason, he was constantly torn. Walker had gone to college thinking that he would finish with the respect of those around him, but now it was becoming clear that completing college was not an achievement for him, but an expectation. When it was done, he would be viewed as having completed the minimum of his potential, and his friends and family would begin to wonder what graduate school he should attend.

Already, some had suggested law school, or perhaps a graduate school for economics. He didn't want anything to do with these paths; he wanted to possess the soul of the foxtail, and to feel his soul possessed by her. Yet he knew that this could not be, at least not yet. He had to learn to appreciate the reality of the here and now before he could evolve in a healthy manner. And right now, he was a student, most likely on his way to still more schooling, and eventually, an 'important' career. Running from the things that haunted his heart would do him no good; he had to work through them in order to arrive in one piece at the end. Still, there was a fear that in living the life set before him, he would lose track of what was so clear to his heart while watching the two young lovers in the sand.

He continued to watch them, focusing now on the woman's lover. He was the happiest man Walker had ever seen. It was no wonder, considering the wild creature he had locked souls with. Theirs was not a fleeting passion, but a deep one, born of a genuine understanding of something wonderful that remained hidden from most of the world. All they needed was each other, and each one knew that they both believed this to the ends of their being. He could see their fate as he watched them playing near the ocean's limit, laughing and rolling. They would never part because they understood love. They would live together, enjoy together, suffer together, and love together. Then, while they were still quite young, they would die together. Yet, there would be a child. No wait, there would be several. Walker hoped that each would honor the memory of the love their parents had shared by searching for it themselves.

His American friend spoke again, "They're only caught up in the fact that they just started having sex and they think they are in love. In a few months, still homeless, they'll find themselves alone and wishing they had spent their time working to make something of themselves."

The guy was starting to annoy Walker. The voice of 'evil' worked in him, trying to convince the world around him that he himself knew the right path.

The whole world was infested with this way of thinking, perpetuated by the human need to justify one's 'self' to others. It isn't enough for one man to be hooked on an addictive chemical; he has to offer it to everyone around him so that he can feel better about his condition as an addict.

Walker thought back to the soulless eyes of the men in the center of Amsterdam.

"Charlie, Coca, X. Charlie, Coca, X. Charlie, X, Coke. I've got some Coke." The men hissed the words into your ears as you passed by, coming closer and closer with every syllable. During one of Walker's later trips to the city, one man had crowded right up against him, his lips nearly touching his right ear as he spoke. Walker had looked into his eyes, and there had been no soul in them. He seized Walker by the shoulder aggressively when he recognized the fact that Walker could see into the void. An indescribable, inhuman cold had shot through Walker's body. He had immediately closed his eyes, focusing instinctually on his own warmth, forcing the cold away as the man's grip tightened on his frame to the point of pain. Then he snapped his eyes open and batted the man's arm from his shoulder with one hand while simultaneously hitting him in the chest with the open palm of the other. The creature was sent stumbling backward from the blow, struggling to regain his balance as he hunched over in search of breath. Then with an icy glare, and a hand over his heart, he let out an inhuman hiss as he backed into a dark alleyway in retreat.

Walker's American friend had an agenda not so different from that of the soulless man, though his friend still possessed his own future. He wanted others to follow the path that he was treading.

"... they just started having sex and they think they are in love." He wanted Walker to turn his back on the possibility of love because that is what he had done, and he didn't want others to believe because that compromised his decision. This man had chosen to 'understand' that life was about the individual alone. He was, in effect, bound to his conclusion because he could not bear to be alive. To be alive, he would have to wonder and believe and evolve. But he could not bear to do these things because he needed to conclude; to be finished.

To many, the search for what lay beyond was simply too much to hope for. God and love and anything based in a conception that required hope or faith seemed like a waste of time because the minds involved were risk averse. These people wanted to be in control and to know what was coming. In pursuit of this, they focused on concepts they could subjugate to reason and ignored those they could not, even where the uncontrollable concepts were preferable to them in every other way. If something required hope or belief, they analyzed it until they had convinced themselves that it was a pointless dream for the minds of the emotionally weak and intellectually inferior.

As much as Walker despised his new friend's influence on the beauty of the moment, he pitied him as well. What had happened to him that had broken the dreams of his spirit? Was he conditioned from birth by a broken mother and father? Was it a woman that he had risked his heart on, who had abandoned him for a romp with another? The latter was his guess.

Walker pondered his friend's assertions for a time, wondering if he was capable of seeing the truth. Then the man spoke again.

"You know what drives me crazy, is that I can sit here and almost see what you are thinking. You haven't heard a thing I said because you are so incredibly lost in whatever it is you are lost in. I'm not trying to insult you, man. I'm just trying to open your eyes. Move on. 'God bless their union?' What the hell are you talking about? Love is a fantasy, brother. So is God, for that matter."

Walker smiled to himself, realizing that he was reading things perfectly.

"Listen," Walker counseled. "I think you need to hear this."

"Oh, I do?"

"Yes, you do. You think that we are debating the truth of what these people 'are' or 'will be', but in fact, that's silly. Neither of us can say for sure what these people are, at least not in the sense that we can prove it.

Even if we could prove what they are, what would that prove? Nothing, because right now there are nearly identical scenes playing out all over Sicily. What's more, there are additional scenes playing out in other parts of Italy, in France, in Argentina, and all over the world, not to mention across time. In the end, some of those couples will only appear to be truly in love, and will in fact, be fools just as you have pronounced. But in other cases, the couples will be exactly as I believe them to be, in spite of what you think.

"I am guaranteed to be right some of the time, and so are you. But where you are right, you are diminished, and life is diminished because you have predicted defeat and loneliness. Where I am right, life and love are held up and glorified. And yet, you don't have to choose to be diminished.

"Don't you see? You are looking at the wrongness, and in so doing, you guarantee that it is wrongness you will find. But it's only part of the picture. Why not look at what is good, it also exists, you know? In fact, it is all that exists. When something that appears to be true turns out to be false, this only means that you have yet to find the genuine article. It does not create a challenge to the truth, it only shows that it is not yet within your grasp. You want the very thing that I'm saying those two have," Walker said, looking over at the lovers. "You simply don't want to risk believing it can be real in case it fails. But understand, it is only those who neglect to chase the good that are wrong. How will you ever find your own version of the foxtail if you aren't looking for it?"

"Foxtail?" he asked, suspecting that Walker's mind was not all there.

"The girl. She has the tail of a fox on her head."

His new friend turned to look at her, seeking to verify the facts rather than explore the truth of what Walker was saying. Walker hoped that his words were getting through, as he found himself staring again at the beauty in the sand, who now lay still, entwined with her lover. But the Pennsylvanian's heart would not allow it; he had to win, even though he counseled for his own defeat. He would do anything to remain confident in his conclusions to life.

He shook his head. "But you are focusing on the negative too. You condemn a focus on possessions," he said, turning back to teach. "You are just as negative as I am. You just choose to focus your negativity on something else. You're a hypocrite. You are saying that it would be better to live their life, and I am saying it would be better to live a life in a house. We are only disagreeing about what is disagreeable."

"I'm sorry, that is not at all correct. First of all, I am undoubtedly a hypocrite. What does that have to do with the truth that I contemplate? Besides, I'm not saying possessions are inherently wrong, I am saying they are not a predicate to finding meaning and happiness. You are asserting that something clearly agreeable in the minds of the two individuals experiencing it, is in fact, disagreeable or at least falsely loved. You, in other words, are announcing negativity where none seems empirically to exist. I have said nothing in the way of disapproval. I have only stated that goodness, or agreeability if you like, is being experienced by the two individuals in front of me as a matter of observation and that the number of their possessions is irrelevant to their obvious happiness. Mine is an empirical observation of truth seen through the eyes of those experiencing it. Yours is an attack on the majesty in front of you in defense of your own pre-formed world view that cannot admit of what has manifest before your very eyes, because it doesn't acknowledge any need for the possessions you have been taught are so important to happiness."

One of the other Pennsylvanians, who had been listening from a few feet away, spoke suddenly. His name was Oliver, and Walker had already had enough conversation with him in days past to identify him as a man of integrity.

"Look, Walker, if you want to go on believing that is real," he said, indicating with his eyes, "then go ahead, no one can stop you. Only you have the power to end your fantasy. That's not a decision to take lightly. Once you buy into the idea of 'waking up' from your dreams, it's pretty hard to go back, although it can be done. I know, because I made it back myself after I let someone convince me to stop dreaming. I chose to believe again though, at almost the last second." His gaze conveyed wisdom born of years fighting against the same enemy, and of deliverance from ruin.

Walker looked out at the mountain in the distance and to the ocean beyond. "You're absolutely right, Olli. Only I can end my dream."

Oliver smiled and stood to leave. "There is a saying that I am fond of which has its roots in the Buddhist Dhammapada, but in fact was not from Gautama the Buddha. It owes its form to translators who adhered to the Advaita Vedanta school of Hindu philosophy. Weigh this idea against what you know and distill what is hidden inside it. Trust in your ability to see through to the inner truth behind the evolution of this idea.

"I shall make it my intention," Walker promised.

"'We are shaped by our thoughts; we become what we think. When the mind is pure, joy follows like a shadow that never leaves.'"

Walker nodded to his new friend and resolved to sit with the words for a time, neither agreeing nor rejecting so that he might approach them honestly. As Oliver walked away, Walker closed his eyes and focused his energy on what he could feel, and on the peace that he had found in the balance between the known and the unknown.

He resolved in his mind to give himself time. It was okay not to know, because in his heart, he held something truly special. It was an understanding of what the light was, and he could see it everywhere he went, piercing the unmade and unknown with its power and presence. It shined like a beacon, drawing him somewhere beyond. His spirit had come alive inside the light, and he would never again let the creeping desolation of false ideology darken his mind. Walker knew where he was going, though still lost and far away. He could sense his dawn approaching. He could feel tomorrow's rise.

A Personal Letter from Walker:

What is this consciousness we possess? Are our understandings born of this world or another? Does the essence of a person transcend his thoughts? These questions have driven me to wonder from a young age and to search for answers from the wise.

The pure beauty of life, however, eventually led me to understand. An experiential existence must be lived experientially if it is to remain in line with its purpose. Answers are found by waiting on understanding in a timeframe personal to the one seeking. Deep Truth cannot be taught with a rubric, nor on a schedule. Understanding emerges only when and if the preceptive intelligence decides that it should. Thus, the key to wisdom is not found in books or teachings, though much wisdom may reside there. Rather, the key is found in learning to see that more is unknown than is known, and to find comfort with that fact. This is true for the 'self' and also for the collective wisdom of mankind. It is our privilege to scout the frontier.

To those still lost in perceptive ignorance, the physical Universe appears to be generally void; populated only with separate observable manifestations of form. Yet, to he who sees fully, the universe is actually 'full' of 'empty' space, which forms a great potential substrate, defining the character and structure of the bounded 'reality'. This substrate is populated with many tiny miracles of substance and meaning which owe their existence to the hidden Power extracting the 'created' from the 'potential', and the 'potential' from the 'created'. This can be seen in the vastness of space, which births the majesty of a cosmic symphony of light dancing in the dark. It is also seen in the vastness of human understanding, which conducts its own sort of masterpiece, bringing together so many ideas and understandings that they can scarcely be imagined by one human being. Perhaps this is how it was meant to be. Maybe what matters most isn't what we choose to do with what is known. Perhaps all along, it has been a question of what we choose to do with what we are not yet able to understand.

CHAPTER
Seventeen

My hands were touching something. The objects were cool and rough and moist. A lingering fragrance hung in the awareness, and the sensation of floating in water coupled with it inside the mind. I opened my eyes and took in the surroundings. I was sitting between two giant trees that I recognized instantly from a time long ago. It seemed years since I had been here. As my eyes opened, hands departing the trees in time, I recalled the ancient man in the animal skins and ferns and flowers. The image of him sitting between these two giants was reflected by my own body in the present reality. Then the story of the violet river and the emerald woman flooded in, and all that had transpired within the lily's radiant embrace became vividly clear. I looked up at the towering giants above, wondering how this could all be. It was far beyond any dream.

I sat silently for a time on the forest floor, just thinking about my life, or rather my lives, as it seemed. The fog and the mist had returned, and breath was clearly visible, though the air was not exactly cold. Water ran down my face in a steady rush of drops, my hair seeming to attract the mist at an unnatural rate. I remained motionless in the fog, marveling at the sensation of the water as it traversed skin and wondering what the point of all this was. What was I supposed to do in this land? It had never been a question before; the 'self' having been content just to experience the beautiful creation. Now it seemed that I had somewhere to be, that there must be some point to being here. Was there something that needed to be discovered? I had searched in the other world. Why wasn't I searching here?

I thought suddenly of the man and his strange words as he had placed the piece of amber around my neck. Reaching up, I touched the stone that sat precisely where I had anticipated. My fingers untied the rope of hemp from behind the neck, and eyes gazed into the depths of the resin. It was a perfect sphere, yet clearly not born of a machine. The color was a deep orange, and it held a certain ethereal quality to it. It seemed to glow from within. As I held it in my hand, the light inside began to intensify, until a clear but tiny blue center began to form deep in the core. I questioned whether it was simply a blue piece of something buried in the orange material. As awareness swam inside the stone, considering this possibility, the blue continued to intensify and began to grow until it filled a full third of its volume. I marveled at this magic and felt drawn into the sphere as if it sought to offer me something. Then a vision came.

It was a vision of a woman, and she was walking in the forest alone, tracing her hand over the ferns as she moved along the path. Energy seemed to leap from the plant world at the bequest of her caress, and traces of blue light could be seen each time her hands left one frond in search of the next. Her features could not be made out, but she was young and beautiful and had the fairest of skin.

I looked back to the stone, having drifted away from it while focusing on the woman. After staring silently for a few more moments, I stood and returned to the path, tying the amber back around my neck, and pausing for a moment at the trail's edge, unsure of which way to go. As I stood contemplating, the mind became aware of a large branch lying across the path in the direction leading back to the tree under which I had once slept. I resolved that the fallen branch was a sign from something beyond me, and quickly set off in the other direction.

As I walked, my mind struggled to remember and to understand. Thoughts recalled the violet land of the green woman distinctly, and also this forest world where the man had gifted me this orange and blue miracle. The rest of history, however, seemed to come in broken pieces.

When I had left the land of the violet river, I asked if I would return to this land of giant trees. She had said yes, but only after returning first to the other world. England. I asked if she meant England. I had lived there once and fallen in love, but something had gone wrong. Alizée. Yes, that had been her name. She was intoxicatingly alive. She smiled all the time and seemed to bounce through her day as if on springs. She was smart, beautiful, and caring, at least at first. We made love almost constantly for months and months on end. But this had not stopped her from deciding to go her own way.

She had stood there holding the door, looking down on me as I begged her from my knees not to walk away from love.

"Walker, don't make such a big deal out of it. It isn't the end of the world," Alizée said as she shut the door. She left me there on the floor with no reason to get up. I had resolved in my heart not to leave her, not to give up on her, to always love her. This I had done, and it had almost been too much to bear. My life had fallen to pieces, and then I had slowly begun to put it together anew.

It was beginning to come back to me now. I had fallen asleep inside the great tree on a bed of fresh conifer needles, and my spirit had drifted back into the experience of the fallen world. I had a family there. Yes, that was right. I had hurt them, but they stood by me, and I loved them very much. I learned to fly an airplane, a Cessna, two of them, and two Piper Cherokees. I had met a girl; I thought I had met a girl. Was it Nadia? Had I gone back to Nadia? It didn't feel right. I didn't belong with her. I couldn't understand how I knew she was not for me, but I was sure it felt wrong. Alizée? No, it couldn't be. I knew the soul I sought. Alizée was too focused on her separateness to be my complement. But what if she had changed, what if she wanted to create forever?

The memories only carried so far. Bits and pieces of the other world were a part of my awareness, but these all seemed distant in time. More had transpired than the hurt in that world. Things had evolved, and peace had been found. But the mind could not follow these memories forward to their result. It was as if a veil had descended amidst time, separating what *was* from what *might be*. Yet, I had already lived the potential reality behind the veil. If only I could remember it, I was sure it would come to pass.

It was so frustrating. Something significant had happened, and I had gone to England in search of someone. A girl. But who was she, and where did my spirit belong? Was my life here or there? Was it both? Perhaps the girl had been Shaz, my Welsh infatuation.

As I made my way up a steep hill, there was suddenly something hot against my chest. I reached up and grasped the piece of amber. It was incredibly warm, almost too warm to be comfortable against the skin. I untied the rope again and dangled the stone in front of my eyes. It was still glowing inside, and I studied it carefully. It hung straight for a moment and then began to pull to one side. Not knowing what to make of this, I continued to walk, still dangling it in front of me. As I did, it began to change its orientation, until eventually, a quarter mile down the trail, it was pointing back to where I had come from. I decided to follow its suggestion, however strange it seemed, and began walking in the direction the stone leant. It led halfway back to the spot where it had warmed initially, and then directed me off the path and into the wet virgin forest.

The stone was pulling straight to one side, and the pull had grown so strong that I feared it might take flight if I were to let go. The glow too was increasing to the point where light began to shine out from within, slightly cutting the fog and mist that had grown thick as I moved deeper into the untouched world beyond the path.

It became clear that the rope was also of magical origins, as I had to lean backward to balance against the stone's pull, and yet the thin braid of hemp hardly even strained to handle the load.

The enchanted sphere eventually found its way to a small rocky hill, and then pulled my weight up the steep embankment despite my near-complete lack of footing. At the top, it continued to lead for a few steps. Then suddenly, it stopped. The light subsided, and the rope went limp.

I looked at my amber globe as if to find a switch to turn it back on. I shook it a little, wondering if I had done or thought something that had triggered it, or that had caused it to turn off. Perhaps it was the way I had held it, or perhaps it functioned based on my willingness to follow. Perhaps it had been pursuing something and I had not moved fast enough? I didn't know what to make of it, but there was a chance that I would find out if I continued to walk in the direction it had led me.

And so, it came to pass that I began to wander in the forest. At first, I knew the direction the stone had been seeking, but soon I became altogether turned around in the world of endless wood and leaf. I walked for many hours, and when exhaustion finally came, I lay down in the middle of it all and slept.

Upon awakening, I continued my walk, only to set it down again after many more hours of roaming and marveling at the world around. Day after day, the wandering continued, until too many days had come and gone to remember walking any other way. Sleep would come, and then the walk would again hold sway. The mind became a student of its own ability to perceive; riveted in each moment with the body's connection to subtle changes in the consistency of the earthen mat and the density of light penetrating this world's canopy. Eventually, as the days blurred into months and years that I could no longer understand, a feeling began to grow in my conscious awareness concerning the body's wandering and the way this formed the path's beginning inside the mind. The feeling counseled for a direction, and I began to follow it without effort as I came to understand the forest and what it was.

The day soon came when I began to walk with purpose, no longer wandering aimlessly but sensing the path destined. It was getting closer, and I could feel it as I approached, both day and night. Then one morning, again cloaked in fog and mist, my eyes looked down and beheld the path I had come to believe in. It had almost been reclaimed by the plants living at its edge. It was still used, though rarely and by few. Upon seeing it, I instantly preferred it to all others I had known.

As I stood there, giving thanks to the Creator both for my time in the wilderness and for the path that would lead me back to my own story, the long-dead stone burst back to life as if on cue. It began to pull again, guiding along the trail now revealed. Something was stirring inside my world, and it was time to discover what that something was. I followed it for a few miles, reveling in the manifestation of harmony and balance that had come to be. There was no longer any hurry. The stone and the rope would not fail, they would pull to the place where the Creator knew I belonged. The pull was followed with confidence and intrigue and without doubt. Ahead of me, the path led up a small rise. It was the largest I'd seen since being pulled up the rocky hilltop so long ago; the day I had stepped off into the unknown. The pace quickened at this sight, awareness converging on the meaning that was inherent in both the similarity and difference of this setting.

Atop the hill, the stone again went cold, and the rope limp. I paid no mind. Their task had been accomplished; they had deposited me here. The hill on which I now stood was remarkably like the one from so long ago, but this one sat above more than empty forest, in contrast to the other. It was clear now, the stone and the rope had not failed before, their purpose was only ever to deliver my awareness into such a place. The last hill had simply been barren. This one was not. This time, by Grace of Time, my purpose would be fulfilled.

The path dropped away gradually before me, granting me a view of the forest below. It was not a large drop, maybe forty feet, but it was significant in a forest that seemed flat as a rule. The fog was thickest near the ground, and from the top of this rise, I could see further than usual, out over much of the misty vapor, though the trees still towered above me in all directions. I walked a few steps over to another of the forest's giants, near the edge of the rise, and rested my head against its thick charred bark, contemplating the scene that I already knew contained a hidden treasure.

This forest had seen fire, and this tree had felt its sting, but in the end, the fire had passed, and the tree remained. It was like this for most of the trees in this land, though here and there lay the fallen forest kings of the past. Though the land had been burned, little lasting damage seemed to have occurred.

I looked out over the fog and saw something curious. Something seemed to move in the near distance, adjacent to a large fallen tree. Slowly, the reality became clear. It was another person, a female. I pushed my body away from the tree and began to walk quietly across the forest's perfect organic carpeting, approaching virtually without sound. As I neared, I stopped, afraid of startling the young woman.

My gaze fell upon her wet body, soaked in fog and mist. She wore a white gown of fine linen, though the garment was quite old and sodden. The cloth stuck to her body like a second skin, covering only the most intimate details of her perfect femininity. Droplets of water traversed her taut, pale youth in a celebration of the fantasyland that all water dreamt of, trickling through the sweet world of feminine hair, and then racing across the smooth expanses of alabastrine skin. She wore no shoes, and apart from the thin gown, her allure was completely accessible. The porcelain of her skin diminished everything else in the forest; its perfection forced itself upon me.

She was facing away from me and had not heard my approach. I studied her back through the thin, wet linen. Each line in her tight athletic form could be seen, and the muscles in her back shown as if she were nude, tightening near her shoulder blades as she moved. Her lines changed subtly with each motion, her delicate neck and shoulders flowing almost imperceptibly toward the smallness of her waist, then down to the poignantly formed muscles which were designed to overwhelm the mind's capacity to describe.

The woman leant forward, reaching up the side of the fallen tree which she was focused on. She was struggling to grasp a large mushroom that was nearly too high for her slight frame to reach without climbing. She extended her arm, rising up on her toes as she caught her prize with the tips of her outstretched fingers. I watched her lower leg muscles contract and rise beneath the skin as she reached and found in them the most perfect form yet seen in my life. Her legs escaped the gown just above the knee, and where they emerged, a flood of beauty was unleashed. I stood frozen, overwhelmed by the color, the form, the texture, the purity, and the innocence. She felt my gaze upon her suddenly, though she did not react in fear or with alarm. She only paused, already understanding what was to take place between us, though she had yet to even meet my eyes.

The woman seemed to sense a long-held trust of me, and the curiousness of this feeling pulled at my recognition of something I could not decipher. She turned with slow grace, looking back over her shoulder first, her wet hair hanging in front of her features. She gazed at me with brown eyes through the spaces between cords of hair that dripped as she stood motionless, her slow breaths appearing in rhythm as bursts of visible vapor and life. We were still apart in space and time, but already we were making love. She could feel the scene that was to come, and I could see her anticipation building. Her breaths began to come faster, the rise and fall of her breasts increasingly pronounced. I wanted to know this woman, to have her for my own, but I needed more than her body. I needed to know that she was in search of what I longed for and that she believed she had found it, as did I. I tried to think of what to say, but no words could fulfill the purpose for which they were needed.

I looked down, then up again, frustrated by the inability to locate even a single word. My eyes met hers, and all that she felt was instantly clear. She had always loved me; we simply had yet to meet before this day. Words were not needed, words only represented reality. We were intent on experiencing the real, not a representation of what 'real' was. I took a step and watched as her eyes flared. Her frame shuddered while her stare remained wide, her face taking on the look of a creature that has arrived at the moment it has always sought, afraid and yet willing.

I paused with this first step, dropping my head ever so slightly to better catch the glory of her gaze. Our connection intensified, and I told her not to be afraid, even while I stood silently amidst the ferns. Her mouth opened slightly, the water now dripping off her lips. She wasn't trying to speak; she was reacting to a feeling that grew inside her with each passing moment. She took a small step forward, her eyes deepening as she began to openly invite her own arrival.

I watched as her body came to show her own intention for union, and as she came, it suddenly began to hail. Neither of us took notice as the first few stones began to land around us on the forest floor. She stepped forward again, as the ice began to fall more heavily, bouncing off our bodies and quickly covering the forest carpet's soft needles with a layer of white. She continued to walk slowly, both of us now aware and yet unconcerned with the state of the world around us. With each step, one leg crossed the other, accentuating the movements of her thighs, calves, and feet, while sending shots of ecstasy through her body. The sensations leapt across the ever-lessening space between us. I could feel each burst of pleasure as it came to her, and willed her to make each step more exaggerated, increasing the intensity of the pleasure we felt as she moved the way she was made to feel.

I stood still as she made her way across the purity of the ice in absolute silence, her sounds covered by the great noise that washed away everything but our intentions. Her petite frame grew more and more obviously perfect as she drew closer and closer. An arm's length away she stopped, staring into my eyes as God's favor continued to fall upon our bodies.

She was brave, and she wanted me to love this fact, but ultimately, she wanted to be the one to succumb. I reached up and stroked the side of her face, beginning with her cheek and ending where the water still dripped from her chin. I guided her mouth up with my finger, now resting under her delicate lips, and leant forward to kiss her. As our lips touched, I felt an energy that seemed to be the reunion of all that was once whole but had been separated for a lifetime.

I had known love in the other world, I was sure of it now as this woman's energy poured through my body. I had been blessed in meeting her and blessed in my walk with her. I remembered her delightfulness, her blue eyes, her porcelain skin, her wavy dark brown hair. We had gotten engaged, and God had sent us a blessing in that moment to tell us that it was right and good. It had been so beautiful, and it had all come to pass because I had looked past those who would have given me less. The man in the asphalt campground. I remembered him and his vision for my future. But I had driven away from his ideas, and into the unknown 'darkness' of a place that he had said was full of 'evil'.

It was clear to me now. The land of the far shore beckoned.

Conceive in me, thine own perception
A new awareness to perceive

Bathed in journey's consequence
Eternal souls reprieved

Conscious of his arrival
Arrival at my Gate

My Garden is a Forest
My Forest Contemplates

Witness now this Radiance
Bodies washed in hail

Witness we the Storm of Union
Perfection through the veil

CHAPTER

Eighteen

The gate to the national seashore seemed the portal to the abyss. The land around was so dark, or rather, so devoid of light, that nothing could be seen beyond the reach of the car's headlamps. The small outpost shack at the gate was empty; it looked as though it had been abandoned long ago. It stood in the center of the road, a board covering the opening where a window should have been.

"Maybe the guy wasn't full of it after all," Aiyana said as the car rolled slowly past the shack. Something shot out of the brush suddenly, veering past the front of the car and across the road before either of them could make sense of what was happening. Walker froze in place without touching the brake.

"A deer." His mind relayed the image only after the object had disappeared.

"Oh, God! That scared the crap out of me," Aiyana panted.

Walker pushed on the gas pedal and accelerated, now even more determined to see his feelings through. "The deer wasn't meant to scare, but to encourage us. Deer are not vicious, why should one provoke fear?" The thoughts battled as they sped through the night, pulses still racing. After a few miles, there came a sign signaling the campground was just ahead, to the left at a fork in the road. The car wound its way down a small dirt lane that opened into a parking lot filled with motorhomes.

As he pulled into the lot, Walker stopped the car and counted, "four, eight, twelve," there were at least twelve rigs worth a cool hundred thousand dollars apiece. Another twenty or so were easily worth half that. Walker and Aiyana were the poorest people in the area.

"What in the world was that guy talking about?" he said, registering the obvious wealth and age of the occupants. His eyes could not see them behind their walls, but he knew who they were. These were retired software writers and engineers and lawyers and doctors, maybe a few honest laborers who had been smart and saved.

"Bandits, my ass!" Walker said as he drove to the end of the row to pull in.

Aiyana was relieved too, but still a bit flustered and nervous. "It certainly doesn't look dangerous, does it?" she said tentatively.

"You wait here," he said, jumping out of the car.

"Walker, where are you going?!"

"I'll be right back, just sit tight." He approached one of the enormous mobile houses and knocked at the door beneath the glowing porch light. An old woman of about eighty years answered.

"Can I help you, son?"

He explained their desire to camp, and she informed him of the honor-system box at the end of the row.

"Just put your cash in an envelope and stuff it in the box," she said. He thanked her and she shut the door, returning to a game of bridge.

"They were playing bridge," Walker said as he climbed back into the car. "She said we could park at the end of the lot here facing the ocean. I was thinking we just stick to sleeping in the car for the night if it's all the same to you."

"You read my mind," said Aiyana. She sat staring out the window past dozens of luxury motor homes as he pulled the car into their space for the night. She was trying to make sense of the man who had warned against this place. "You know, I really do think that guy might have been a schizophrenic, but there was something else beyond that going on too."

"I think he may have been a serial killer. Or just a dickhead," Walker added.

"Whatever he was, I'm glad we're away from him," Aiyana replied.

"You want to know what is even better?"

"What?"

"That box over there," he said, motioning out of his window. "Yeah, it's full of cash. Honor-system."

"Pfff, makes an easy target for bandits, don't you think?"

They both laughed at the absurdity of the man's ploy to scare them into sleeping in his parking lot. They had done it; they were where they were supposed to be. Walker felt it deep in his soul. And though she did not understand the reason for the feeling, Aiyana felt it too. Her heart told her she was home, though this made little sense to her as she looked out at the small dunes blocking their view of the ocean.

They took a short walk to the bathhouse to investigate the facilities, and then returned to pay their fee at the drop box. After situating their belongings so that they could recline their seats, the young couple lay down in preparation for sleep.

Walker looked at the clock. It was midnight.

"I want you to remember the number seven for me, okay?"

"What?"

"The number seven, I want you to remember it."

"Okay, why are you telling me to remember random numbers lately?"

Walker had begun asking Aiyana to remember numbers ever since deciding on the exact timing of his proposal the previous night in Ardmore. He had asked her to remember the number thirty initially, then later the number twelve as they had driven toward Corpus Christi. He wanted to seed moments into their journey to point out to her in the future so that she might be able to see that he had been counting down the hours to the magic he felt sure was just beyond the horizon.

"They aren't random; they are tied to something I want you to understand."

"What?"

"I can't describe it yet, because I don't know what it will be. Did you notice what time it is?"

Walker played fast and loose with his linking of these numbers to questions directing his love to note the time of day. He would normally have eschewed such a direct presentation of the link, but he had become aware of just how well he was masking his intentions. Aiyana didn't suspect a thing. By the time the proposal happened, whatever miracle it would entail would have direct evidence of having been an anomaly in time, and thus Divine in nature.

Aiyana just stared at him and smirked as she came to understand something for the first time.

"You're hiding your intention from your own awareness so that I can't perceive it? How cool is that?" She was shaking her head and beaming with pride.

"I love you. I didn't even think about this possibility. How are you doing it?"

"I don't know," he admitted.

"Of course not," she beamed again.

"Let's get to sleep, my love," Walker said, leaning over to kiss her on the side of the head.

Aiyana reached up to softly touch his face, before turning to situate herself in search of slumber.

Walker smiled as he lay back in his seat and closed his eyes.

His mind swam in the beauty of a morning believed, yet unplanned. He was being led to something, and though his mind protested and sought control, his spiritual intuition was finding its way past the limits that such control aims to impose. Aiyana was about to step into a morning of untold resplendence, for Walker was courting nature's intention. Rather than rely on himself to make something, he would instead focus on the majesty of creation, and call it forward into its own timing, toward its own vision of connection, power, and meaning. He couldn't wait to see what would happen.

Aiyana lay with thoughts of nature, space, and time. The love she had found had become lost in an innocence that she could scarcely comprehend. At first, she had thought she understood this man and this love. But as time flowed toward their union, a veil of mystery and fog had descended upon her mind, obscuring his intentions. Yet she doubted nothing; believed implicitly. She was perplexed by her inability to intuit the plans he seemed to have hidden in the morning beyond. How was he doing this? Was this veil of fog his intention or her own? It mattered not, because it was beautiful to her, and she owed its existence to their connection. She would let her mind swim in whatever reality God's creation brought to her in the morning light. Walker was courting something for her out there. She loved him for this, and so she closed her eyes that she might see.

CHAPTER

Nineteen

The sound of rain on a metal roof began to take Aiyana's focus as she dreamt. Walker had been dreaming along with her. He had been looking at Aiyana's hand in his own, and she had been studying the ring on her finger as Walker guided it from side to side to catch the sun's essence. She was memorizing the bridge-like structure of the metal, and marveling at the diamond so silver and cool. Suddenly, it would meet a specific angle with the lens of her eye and fire would dance inside them both. Walker's thoughts tracked Aiyana's feelings, so accessible to him in this shared mental space, until the rain had taken her focus. He had looked up to the sky in response to her acuity. The sound seemed to come as if the rain were landing somewhere just above him. The rain was falling, but the wetness of the drops could not be felt. He questioned this subtle incongruency, noting that the sound was metallic, like that of rain on a car roof.

Walker opened his eyes. Yes, rain on a car roof indeed. The rain had been hitting the roof of the car all night, its sound reaching both their ears, but stopping there, with only a trace of its true nature reaching their awareness, at least until now.

Without moving, he looked out from the car toward the horizon, it was beginning to brighten ever so slightly, and sunrise would be in less than half an hour. Walker sat up and checked the alarm. It was set to buzz in exactly one minute, and he shut it off in order to grant his love a better sound with which to wake. Taking special care to remain silent, he opened Aiyana's case of compact discs and searched for the music that was meant for this one moment in time, the music that would become a part of their story. There in the dim twilight of pre-morning, he came across a University Singers CD, which starred Aiyana among several others performing in a professional level university choir. He longed to hear Aiyana's voice, her pure angelic voice. But the feeling would not be right, the music needed to speak to both of them in this moment concerning that which was beyond, and that required something other than their own independent creations. He just felt he knew this somehow.

Still, he was tempted by the thought of her ethereal sound. He thought back to the first time he had heard it. She had stood in front of an assembly of people in a church for her friend's wedding, the healthy fairness of her firm skin shaming the fine peach cloth of her new dress, and he had anticipated something pleasant. What he had heard was something far beyond; he had heard something transcendent. She sang with a sweetness and purity he had only heard from a select few, and they were famous the world over. 'Ave Maria' was transformed in that moment from a song, into the vision of love that he had always sought. The charm of the Latin paled in comparison to the meaning of the sound emanating from inside his new-found treasure. She was an angel, and in that moment, he came to see that truth clearly.

As Walker continued to ponder, he came across an album with a song listed on its cover that he had long adored. His heart settled his mind on the soundtrack for their engagement, and he reached over to insert the key into the ignition, turning the auxiliary power on.

As the sounds began to flow, Walker leant across the artificial vinyl world to the soft flesh that had begun to stir. His lips met the soft velvet of her skin, just beneath her beautiful eyes, which remained hidden behind their velvet curtains.

His hands entered her hair in perfect time with the words as they began to swirl around them. Every touch had purpose, and every moment was set to the lyrics that flowed through the air. Aiyana's eyes were still closed, but her body rose softly in time with the music and with his touch. He kissed along the line of her delicate jaw, her perfect ears. He began to sing softly into them, replacing the musician as the being behind the words.

"Will you stay with me?" Walker joined the song in message.

"Can we promise to forever be?" he played with the lyrics now.

A smile raced across Aiyana's expression, and her hand rose to take his. Then they began to dance, even as they lay there motionless, confined to the car by the dark unknown beyond, and the rain that they knew lived there. As the artist inside the car's speakers began again, Aiyana felt the words change from what she knew them to be, though ever so slightly, and they both found meaning in the words that the author had not even put there. He spoke of his own conceptions, but Aiyana opened to the idea of a 'lover's soul'.

She painted a moving picture in her mind: the Earth with a blanket of wind and clouds circling round and round the globe. The vision coupled with the idea of the 'lover's soul', which echoed audibly in her ears. The wind came from beyond the horizon and traveled to the other side of the world and back again, just so it could repeat the journey it loved so much. It was the same for the soul when it came to know love. Walker would love her like that. The knowledge of it touched her deeply.

They gave the words back over to the voice in the air, and Walker concentrated on the way his hand traversed the small of Aiyana's back, guiding her into a slow rise as the sounds washed through their awareness.

"Let yourself feel the way her body rises." The sounds flowed in time with Walker's touch, though the words continued to change from those the artist had recorded. It was incredible what they could do with reality when they let themselves play together this way.

"I love you," Walker whispered into a brief silence.

"I love you so much," Aiyana said, opening her eyes for the first time. She smiled, considering that they would gift each other this simple phrase a million times over, and then like the winds of the Earth, each would circle back to begin giving all over again.

In the dark, the CD player had inadvertently been set to play songs at random, a setting which neither of them had ever used. And so, it came to be, that God chose the next song. At first, neither of them recognized this as they were still lost in love's spell. Walker was mesmerized by the shape of her face, and Aiyana was absorbed in the way he kissed and touched, and the way he called forward her sensitivity. But then they each felt a cosmic energy shoot through their bodies, as words they had never heard came to them through the atmosphere, only this time they had not played with the lyrics in the least.

The voice around them asked his love to join in marriage and to dream of children and of forever. The voice promised he would give all that he was if she would only say yes to the dream that they had shared the night before. The words came from a recording made in another time and place, but in that moment, they belonged to Walker.

The bolt of energy shot through him first as the ideas began to flow, but then leapt to Aiyana. She felt it pour from Walker's soul as the kiss deepened, the passion escalated, and love began to bloom in their mind's eye, which was beginning to think of itself not as two, but as one.

"Will you promise me something?" Walker said as their lips slowly parted.

"Anything."

"Love the rain."

"Okay."

"You must love the rain. All my life I have been told that rain is depressing, that rain is gloom, that the sun is better. Some even use it as metaphor for the unholy. But I believe the rain was made to dance with the light, not to oppose it. We are born of both water and light, and each is beautiful. We must take the rain back from those who would oppose the light and make it sacred again. They are designed to meld together into a celestial elixir that transcends them both. Rain is what we have in this moment, so the love of it is what we should focus on. If we can do that, I'm sure we'll find the sun. Feel this way with me, please, my love."

Aiyana spoke. "The sun is beautiful when it shines, but our showering grants us immersion into the sublime. Because I understand this, there is something you want to show me on this day of rain. Now, please show me what you've come to see."

"In a little while, it isn't time just yet. Just sit with me for a few minutes until I can see the way."

She said nothing, just agreed without words, and they sat staring at one another, their hands bridging the space between. Walker looked at the clock, sunrise had been ten minutes before, but the clouds had hidden the sun completely. He looked to the horizon as he contemplated the proposal he had envisioned, red sun rising out of the deep blue.

"That wasn't what we were meant to find here." The thought was so clear. Still, without the sunrise, he no longer had a moment to aim for. He had been sure that this would be his moment, and yet he could not help but question how such a dull grey morning could be right. When should they begin their walk into the future, and how could it be cosmic if it was so ordinary? Light grew in unconscious vision, and slowly they began to feel it, out over the ocean. Walker looked up and saw the signal. A single small hole had opened in the bank of clouds, just enough for the sun to peak through in a single ray of light, scattering in a display that hinted of a spectacle that would make the sunrise he'd envisioned look plain.

"Get your shoes on," he commanded suddenly.

"Now?"

"Yes, right now. Please trust me, I need you to come with me now, and quickly."

Within thirty seconds, they were walking toward the beach, hearts racing, the light dancing even more strongly now in almost a dozen rays as the soft drizzle continued to descend. The wooden boardwalk that traversed the vegetation preceding the beach was glowing intensely under the mixture of sun rays and sky drops. It was as if the long-dead planks had reached into the past and found all the life they had once known, and then reconnected with it so that they might radiate it for these rain-soaked lovers to absorb. Their bodies, still so animated, so alive, crossed the long-suspended forms of the mighty trees that had once been. Aiyana felt music in her soul, a sweeping peaceful symphony of light, water, meaning, and emotion.

Walker's hand caressed the smooth, wet wood of the rail, and energy flowed into his hand, through his heart, and out from his other and into hers.

His future wife could feel the energy flow through him, and her free hand rose to meet the rail he could not reach. Her caress was lighter, softer, subtler, and the energy leapt more easily for her. She felt it as surely as one feels the life-giving power of water when she drinks deeply after a hard day in the sun. Walker looked at Aiyana in awe of her power; she was closer to God than anyone he had ever known.

The boardwalk spilled onto a beach bathed in fractured light from a sky that had begun to dazzle in still more rays, breaking through now in a line across the horizon. Walker glanced to the right as his anticipation for direction grew. There was one lone man, with his dog, playing in the sand a half-mile away. That direction was for him and his animal. Walker turned and led his love in the opposite direction, where no one had yet gone this day. As they made their way, the sky intensified its brilliance, and the peace of the morning grew in strength. The light was burning through the clouds everywhere now, and at each break, light beams poured through.

They couldn't have asked for anything more perfect, and yet even more was at work than they could see in the heavens. After walking a few hundred yards in the sand, Aiyana spotted a log on the beach. "Look at the driftwood," she pointed.

This was the spot. Walker led Aiyana to the log and took out his camera. He set it down and initiated a video recording. He wanted to be able to watch their decision to grow old together one day when they were old. He walked back to Aiyana and began to speak, though the words came very slowly, as he was speaking from his heart. Walker had purposefully neglected thinking about what he would say before this moment had arrived, as he wanted the moment to be a spontaneous event in thought and action.

"Aiyana, I want you to understand something about me. I am not who I should be. I know that I tell you all the time that I am more than I have been in the past, and I have struggled to let you know all that I have been, and this is true. I am more now than I have ever been, but I am not what I *should* be. I can't seem to find in my soul what I know should be there. I feel it sometimes, but sometimes I find that I am lost, that I forget. Around most people, this doesn't bother me, but around you, I feel so ashamed. I should be more for you; I should be able to find more of my 'self'.

"You deserve everything that you are, and I can't seem to be that pure. But I want you to know something; I am never going to stop trying. I am never going to stop searching. I will not stop with what makes sense, or with what I am told is sufficient, or with what those around me think is the furthest a person can go. I won't stop when I am beaten, and I won't stop when I have failed. I will persist, and I will seek you always, love you always, be with you always. My heart isn't everything it should be, but I will give you everything that I currently am, and I promise you, that whatever is lacking or wrong with my soul, I will find it, and I will fix it. I believe that you are God's answer to my prayer and that you and I will always be together."

Though she could sense the power of the moment, Aiyana had not yet decided what it was about; she enjoyed feeling the moment too much to think about it and deduce that Walker was trying to propose.

"I know I can never deserve a love like yours, Aiyana, I know that all my efforts can never make me worthy of such beauty, of such peace, such purity. But I will try to deserve you. You are the definition of everything I hope for in life, and you are the woman I want to be with for the rest of time." Walker reached into his pocket and produced the gold-trimmed white box containing the symbol of his commitment, the ring that he had memorized in his dreams only the night before. Aiyana let out a short burst of air, bound in tears and joy, and began to shake and cry openly. "Aiyana, will you stay with me forever? Will you be my wife?"

"Yes!"

Aiyana shined through her tears. Her beauty was radiating from her eyes, which were now caught in the orange light of the sun that had completely broken through. Walker took her hands in his own and placed his forehead against hers as they began to pray.

"Father, thank you for this love. Thank you for this beautiful day you have led us to. Thank you for everything you have done for us. Please help us always to honor you and each other. Please bless the rest of this day, our engagement day."

Aiyana pulled back and looked into Walker's eyes and told him that she loved him. He replied with his gaze, and then pulled her close, holding her tightly as he looked out over an ocean bathed in honeyed light.

Just then, in that most perfect of moments, God sent the first message He had ever addressed to the two as one. The water opened suddenly in time, but to Walker's mind, it was slower. The blue pulled his eye down from the orange ball in the sky, and he focused on a spot not more than twenty feet off the shore. It seemed to him that the sea should have only been waist deep so close to land, but as he stared, his head tilting as he *felt* the water begin to part, the face of a dolphin slowly emerged. Walker watched as the beginnings of the creature rose upward until the eye was revealed, tiny, black, and deep. Then time began to take hold of him again; the face came faster now, and then the whole of the body, which ascended from the water and into the air in a smooth arc. He watched as the dolphin completed the arc and returned to his home among the deep.

"Aiyana! Look!"

She turned her head just in time to see him emerge again, leaping into the sun, water trailing his body in ribbons of silver. But though its substance followed initially, it soon ceased to trail him, unable to travel any further as he took flight, free of the liquid world. The creature was of the water domain, and he loved this truth, though he still sought to dream. Understanding that his home was only one part of the whole, the dolphin contemplated the possibility of connection to what lay beyond the confines of the ocean's intention. And so, he had looked up, and swum towards whatever lay beyond the fundamental reality around him.

The dolphin had thus broken through and into the air, and into love's gaze. For a moment, he was a creature of the heavens above, and for a moment, so too were the lovers on the shore. But he belonged to the sea, at least for now, and the laws of nature slowly turned him back to the deep. His body turned back to face the world that was quickly returning, and he entered it again headfirst, lifted by the experience of that which lay beyond his realm; the land, the sky, and the beings that glowed on the sand.

They had stared back at him; he knew. How was it that they had been there when he chose to rise, looking back at him the way they did? Their energy had been radiant, for something profound had just been joined between them. Had his urge to spring up from his world been given to him by the beings on the shore, or had they all been led there by the same force, a force beyond them all? He would take one more look.

As the dolphin emerged for the third and final time, Aiyana spoke. "This seems so unreal," she said for loss to say more. Something sparked then in her mind, and she caught the first glimpse of a theory she would one day come to believe in. There was a wonder related to animals that every child knew, but most adults had forgotten. For a moment, she remembered what she had learned as a little girl from them, especially the dolphins, who were her friends.

"Yes, it does, doesn't it?" Walker answered. "Perhaps this is what real feels like, and we've just been living in a dream."

Walker couldn't understand how he knew, but something about Aiyana had brought this energy to them, or perhaps she had just been worthy of it being sent. He could not say. All he knew was that he had found the morning he had prayed for in his dreams. No man could deserve this level of gift. He felt humbled and yet overjoyed that the Universe had brought him to this place and moment in time.

Suddenly, they felt a gentle presence approaching behind them. Turning back from the ocean, they watched as an elderly couple walked from the direction of the campground. As they came closer, they could see that the woman was smiling deeply, and her husband seemed full of pride and power from a time gone by.

"Did you see the dolphin?" Aiyana asked them.

"Yes, that must have been amazing for you. You were nearly close enough to touch it! You're very lucky; we've been here for three weeks now and have only seen one before today, way offshore. Would you like us to take your picture?" the woman asked with a peculiar grin.

"Yes, please."

The woman took Walker's camera and snapped a photo.

"Congratulations," she said softly as they departed toward a path of their own making.

"It's a beautiful ring," Aiyana said turning to Walker and looking at her hand.

"I hoped you'd like it."

"It's exactly what I dreamt it would be," she said. "I can't believe what's happened to us these last couple of days. We're really doing it, aren't we? We're finding our way through to one another," Aiyana said, a flood of tears nearly overtaking her as she finished her thought.

"Let us never stop this deepening," Walker beamed. He held her face in his hands, gently stroking the side of her head with his fingers, as he looked longingly into his future, which was lost in the center of his fiancée's magical eyes.

My wife

Beautiful

My wife

Hair – dark

My wife

Skin soft and pale white

My wife

Pure spirit

My wife

Gentle and kind

My wife

My perfect

Please God forever

CHAPTER
Twenty

A few months later, Aiyana and Walker were wed. They traveled to Italy's Cinque Terre shortly afterward for their honeymoon. On the day of their arrival, they strolled along the ancient pathways of Corniglia, walked down the Via dell'Amore, and swam in the blue lagoon in the town of Vernazza, kissing as the sounds of a professional choir floated over the waters from the nearby twelfth-century Church of Santa Margherita d'Antiochia. They ended the day with a beautiful dinner overlooking the Ligurian Sea and then took in the twilight with a bottle of Champagne on the beach in Monterosso. The next day, they boarded a ferry bound for the isle of Elba.

Elba was not the typical destination for a honeymoon, as the climate was semi-arid rather than tropical. But when they walked off the ferry, they forgot about the other places they might have chosen and focused solely on the creation of a beautiful memory bound up in Tuscan charm. The beaches were sandy, the locals were friendly and accommodating, and the cuisine was rustic Italian. They couldn't have asked for more. They sat together each day for seven days, watching the sunset and eating all manner of exquisite dishes, most of which were enjoyed with a bottle of local wine.

By day they walked through the Mediterranean forest that covered much of the small island or traversed the mountain roads on a small, rented motor-scooter. The time was all that it should have been and more.

On the last night of the honeymoon, a cool breeze was blowing in off the ocean, sweeping over their mutual perception. They lay together on their backs, taking in the details of the antique metal fan rotating effortlessly overhead. The honeymoon had been amazing, yet there was something that needed to happen that had not. Walker struggled to understand what it was. It was not a specific romantic act or assertion, all of those had been repeated many, many times already. It was something spiritual, something internal, and something beyond this world, yet connected to it. He had been thinking about it for several days, and though he was not certain, he was getting close to an understanding of how to proceed. He rolled over and looked into his wife's eyes.

"Aiyana?"

"Yes?" she replied, smiling.

"I want to do something with you right now."

"Again?" Aiyana said, raising her eyebrows.

"Surprisingly, no," he responded sheepishly. "That is not what I mean this time."

She looked at him curiously. "Then what do you mean?"

"You know how I have always said that I want you to understand the effects of marijuana?"

"Yes," Aiyana said in a concerned voice.

"Well, you know I always tell you that I don't want to pressure you to smoke anything as a way to justify my own choices, but that I only want to share something I cannot explain. Well, this is still true. I do not want to legitimate my own decisions to smoke in the past by convincing you to try it. I only want to *experience* the reality I understand from that other world with you, that is all. I want us to feel that magic together because I believe it could help us go further than we have gone in our love so far. My love for you is more than I have given, and I understand this is true of your love for me as well. I believe that we are both guarding something from one another at a level beyond our comprehension, and I think that we would find a way to open ourselves up beyond this, if we could just be in that place together. That is why I seek to walk in that world with you. The reason for focusing on marijuana specifically, is that I do not fear for your safety with it as much as I would with some other plants. Yet, I am moved by your purity and innocence, and do not wish to damage that.

"We've already understood the possibility that we can reach the same plane of thought just by following what I know, but how to do this has remained unclear. Plants opened my intellect to the reality of the path, but now I know their secret, so it is accessible through memory and will. Now and then, I have felt as if I was under the influence of marijuana or another plant, though I was not. Several times in my life, I have gotten what people call 'high' off my conversations with others. They were triggers that shifted my mind into present awareness of the transcendent realm. It happens when the discussion touches on the Truth, like that night in Germany, when we spoke to that kind old man about his wife. Do you remember?"

"I remember. I nearly cried when he told us she was dying. His whole world was crumbling as her life faded, and he confided that in us. I know it is strange to say it, but I think that confronting the pain with him changed the course of her disease. I think God heard us that day. I think she is still alive."

"So do I. I felt his reality change as we encountered it together with him. It is hard to explain, but this is the way of the other world. So much in this reality is driven by truths we cannot understand, but we can sometimes affect this reality when we stop trying to understand it and focus instead on what lies beyond."

"You know, you think you're telling me something I don't already know, but in fact, this is what I have long been trying to say to you. I've encountered the same types of experiences as you say you have had with plants. Yet, I have never partaken of any of them. You have assumed that you can see things I do not, but I've been well aware of the powers you have confronted. I felt reality change that night in Germany just as you did.

"I also felt it happen again when you debated that atheist psychiatrist at my conference last year. I watched you fight and fight that man and his logic. I watched both of you position and reposition and honestly didn't know who would win out for what must have been several hours. Then, suddenly, his arguments came full circle, and he dismantled your theory of God, and as he did, the room actually chilled. Thirty degrees left the air almost instantly. I watched everyone in that room realize that you had lost, and I watched you lose your faith. Then, seventeen seconds later, I saw it come flooding back. The walls around us shifted off-center at that moment, and I sat there feeling with you, knowing that you understood, and knowing that you would never be overwhelmed again by such a man."

"You felt it shift?"

"Yes, I did. And several others did too."

"The truth is a funny thing, isn't it? That psychiatrist is one of the greatest minds in the field, and he is beyond brilliant, and yet Truth eludes him. When he proved that my theory was flawed, for a moment, I was lost. But then I realized that Truth and God had not been disproven, only my prior conception of them. This then was the rebirth of a new conception, which is still evolving to this day. It too is necessarily flawed, and I now know that this is as it must be. Meaning can only be found in pursuit of the frontier, and yet the frontier is always defined in reference to places we already perceive. We are creatures of perceptive evolution, and we must thus seek to evolve our conceptions toward a higher iteration, lest we find ourselves at odds with our own blueprint."

"I still can't believe what you said to him."

"What was that?"

"You told him that he had only disproven you, not what you argued on behalf of, and that the only difference between himself and you, was the fact that you were actually aware that you were full of shit. That really pissed him off."

"I tried to say it nicely."

"You did. He wasn't offended by your tone or intention. What offended him was the assault on his own sense of mastery. You pointed out that he could be wrong as well, and that he was limited by his own mistaken belief that he held unlimited capacity and ability to understand.

You made it clear that his own arrogance blinded him to the reality of his insignificance in the war of ideas that he holds so dear. He couldn't conquer you with force of intellect, and that was beyond his ability to understand. His only escape was to mandate your intellectual inferiority and abandon the conversation as a waste of time."

Aiyana reached out to touch the side of his face. "I really love you for taking this on like you do. I want you to know that I will follow you wherever you go, and I do trust you, and I believe in what you want to show me. I hope you can see that, and I hope you will trust me to guide you as you lead."

She paused, giving him a bashful grin.

"What?" he asked.

"I have been feeling your thoughts intensely today," she smiled. "My theory is correct. It's not maybe anymore, this is happening. In fact, I may be a tiny bit responsible for you starting this conversation up like you did."

Walker looked at her in amazement. She was right. His thoughts had evolved without him consciously deciding to evolve them. He simply hadn't paid attention to the subtle shift in cognition. All the same, he wasn't upset, they had both agreed to this experiment.

"Do you still want to go deeper, I mean, inside of what is inside?" she asked. "I'm willing, if you will continue to allow it. That is why I want to be sure to own my influence, so that you can trust it."

Walker became increasingly excited by the deepening shift in conversation. Aiyana was intuiting his intentions by accessing his perception and then inviting him to recognize his ability to do the same with her own. Above all else, Walker desired that they pick up pursuit of one another again in the subconscious realm. They had made enormous progress in their journey into one another's mental conceptions, but even Aiyana's brilliant psychiatric mind had not been able to bypass all of their inborn defenses to 'foreign' thoughts. No technique in therapy, hypnosis or otherwise, had taken them to where they aimed to be. Aiyana's own innovation in cognitive bypassing had taken them furthest, but their dream of an unguarded experience of one another still eluded them. Thus, they had paused and drifted for a while in the pursuit. In the end, however, they were only resting.

Walker offered Aiyana an answer. "I will venture into you as deeply as you will allow," he said playfully.

Aiyana pushed him gently, understanding the accusation as well as the obvious parallel meanings.

"Do you have any idea how we do this?" he asked, genuinely now. "I mean, we have sort of exhausted all the clinical methods. You said it yourself, the techniques we are using have limits based in our psychology."

He sat, contemplating for a moment before continuing. "I know why you drew my thoughts into the marijuana experimentation issue again just a minute ago. It's because we are coming to an awareness of how to bridge the gap. I started in on this idea before you even raised the issue, do you see that? That part wasn't you. You fished this out, but the idea is my own as well. I opened the discussion by focusing on aspects of our converging desire to see our commonality in all this. I have had experiences that you need to live. You must come to these experiences through me if this is to be genuine. Having them yourself through plants wouldn't prove anything. You aren't resisting the experience I want to share with you; you're welcoming it *through* me, while guiding me to share with you in a way that keeps your purity intact. You're amazing. You have literally been letting my mind guide your thoughts because you knew that I would refuse to violate how you choose to be. I don't think I could have put this all together quite so elegantly. How did you pull this off?"

Aiyana pondered a moment. "I'm not sure. But I know I didn't do it alone. It is only *WE* that can think this way. I'm powerless without your understanding of me. *I* understand that *you* understand, even though the reason that you do is *me*. Neither of us can grasp all that this is."

"This is so insane, and beyond cool," Walker said, amused. "I love doing this with you more than you know."

Aiyana smiled bashfully.

"Right. You do know," he smiled back.

"Try not to think in terms of sanity," she counseled. "Sanity is contextual, and our context allows for this way of thinking now." She paused, then reached out to take his hand as she continued. "When you were young, did you ever dream that someday you would be able to communicate like this with anyone?"

Walker shook his head to convey that he had not, and then began to ponder further.

"So, if we aren't going to involve psychoactive substances, then how are we going to sidestep the respective adverse definitions of reality that each of our ego's insists upon?"

"Don't ask me to explain in detail how I came to this," Aiyana replied. "Cause I'm really not sure. But I definitely derived this from your mind's experiences, rather than from my own. I sort of understand it, but then again, it's hazy for me. You know, because your ego is scrambling some of it? But I am confident you will understand it because you authored it. I am also confident of something else."

"What?" he wanted to know.

"That this is it. This is the answer to our prayer. You knew all along, and I knew that you did. I knew my answer was there in the depths of your mind. It's so beautiful."

Aiyana had begun crying openly. She straightened herself and shook her head to clear her mind.

"So, here it goes. I want to go for a walk with you this night, down to the ocean, to lay on the beach and stare with you into the light of the moon," she seemed to quote the words. "I want you to own what you believe and let yourself see somewhere beyond your own conception, to a place where our conceptions mingle. I want you to travel with me tonight inside the luster of my yin. It is my nature to absorb your luminescence, and then shine it back toward you through the filter of the feminine, softer, and more refined. I trust to follow you where you would have me go, because you hold the potential of my essence within the yang that you are. Who you are, contains what I am, and I what you shall be."

"I would have you go where you would have me take you," he said in reply.

"Then we are already together. Come, my darling."

They rose and took a few moments to get ready for an evening stroll. Then they left their small resort, descending onto the street below. The couple made their way along the cobbled path and down a set of ancient stairs to a section of beach that was tucked beneath the small cliff on which the road had been built. As they walked, Aiyana began to address Walker's understanding of the world beyond and of a path that traversed worlds. She seemed to quote again.

"Focus on this, my love." Her voice had become airy and soft. "The Truth is behind the light. To understand this power, you must only let your mind travel behind the source. Look at the flames of that fire on the beach. Look at the lights from those houses over there, and from that ship far out at sea. Each one is like the stars scattered across the night sky above us. Each is like a hole in the canvas of the reality that you and I share every day. If you look at the lights, you will notice that they are different than everything else around them. We already know this, but have we ever really let the thought take us together? Ask yourself how the light is different, and study it closely with me. It radiates from its source and then spreads everywhere. Nothing It reaches fails to be illuminated. This is particularly true of the way it inspires the mind, which looks out on the world of light through the eye. This is truer still of the soul, which the light pours into as it enters the mind's awareness through the portal of the soul, the center of the eye.

"To transcend this fallen world, we need only understand the purpose of illumination, and to lose our respective 'selves' in its pursuit. The purpose of light is to give us color for the canvas of our inner world, which we paint as we experience this walk through physical reality.

"How will we choose to shape what we see as it passes through our core on its way to our awareness? How will *WE* choose to dream? This is the fundamental question we should be focused on. This is the way to meaning and love for an eternity. Let us take in the Light of reflection together."

They had walked to the end of the beach, where the cliffs met the sea and precluded any further path. This was the spot. Aiyana found a large rock, half onshore and half in the ocean, and led Walker out onto it. There the lovers lay on their backs under the spell of the full moon and stared silently up at the great heavenly body. Aiyana's hand lay in his, until seemingly by magic, they forgot time and the limitations of the physical and the rational. They traveled with one another on a moonbeam to the land of another realm. There, dancing in the liquid-light of a moonstorm, they found one another at last.

CHAPTER
Twenty-One

There is a spectrum of light at the edge of violet. It flirts with the world of the ultraviolet and seems to reach into it, though it remains visible to the human eye. This light often accompanies the white beams of the moon, and it infuses everything with a palpable quality of enchantment. It was into this type of light that Aiyana and Walker fell as they rose from their place along the shore. The great water lapped at their bodies as they lay just beyond its reach, atop the noble stone which lay in the shallows. The bodies were safe, and their spirits understood this. So, they took flight together, falling into the light of the moon.

Together they crossed space and time, arriving in a land of white and violet sand. Their new existence seemed to be born on a song, as something like music surrounded their awareness, though it could not be heard, only felt. First one feeling came, then another, then others still; then the first would come again. The feelings repeated in an unmistakable pattern that began to grow in its intricacy, building a song with pure emotion. Each feeling was in keeping with a certain sense of wellbeing and happiness. The experience was altogether pleasant and riveting at the same time. The song was life, and life was the name of the song. It celebrated beauty and purity, and the dance of male and female halves.

Aiyana took to the melody with ease, as did Walker. They smiled at one another now and then in between long periods of wondering at their surroundings, hands locked together as the moon enraptured them.

Eventually, they stopped and stood barefoot amidst the ocean of sand to contemplate the violet hues. The nearly invisible light seemed to soak into the sand grains, and even into the very flesh of their bodies, which glowed softly under it. A vast ocean existed in the distance, and it too was made of the same nearly invisible color. But where the sand was painted, the water was color itself, existing as a large well of liquid, denser, darker, and deeper than it appeared when spread across the ground.

Walker turned to Aiyana and stared into her eyes. They shone with a radiance he had not seen before. She had always loved him, but on this night, she would give her 'self' over to him. They had pledged their lives to one another in front of God and hundreds of witnesses, and they had even ventured, however implausibly, into each other's thoughts and dreams. Yet their souls struggled to find a land in common; a place that both could call home. He had traveled inside her awareness, and she in his, but to continue to remain together, especially when their time on Earth came to an end, they needed to move beyond walking in one another's worlds. True unity would only come from exploring together inside a mutually conjured vision of forever. This would be the night they envisioned their first unified world, born of their collective creativity.

On this night, they had stopped waiting for safety and established their mutual vision. They had to leap from the edge of their prior self-conceptions, and into the light of understanding that shone in the heavens beyond them. They had come to understand that it was their fear of vulnerability that was most dangerous to their connection.

Yet vulnerability contemplated risks beyond their control as well, and both now understood that this was the true reason they had held something back before coming here to this shared space. There was a constant, unspoken understanding present in every human mind that infected it with the idea that it needed to be ready to lose what it loved, because the individual always broke away from all that was not itself, sooner or later.

The dance of souls is, after all, not only one of compatibility, but also of circumstance, and circumstances can change. Both were aware of this fact, having witnessed the end of relationships among some of their friends, and even among some in their families, despite eternal loyalty once pledged. How could the spirit overcome the winds of fate when they swept one off to war and left the other behind in another world? How could the spirit overcome the latent desires of the subconscious when they stirred the heart of a man to love a new woman, or a woman to love a new man, or even another woman for that matter? What of death itself, could it be overcome? These questions had been keeping them from dancing the way they were meant to. But they were past that now.

Tonight, each had come to find the reality they were seeking. The 'self' was *WE*, rather than *I*. The Light had gifted them the full depth of this understanding, seemingly by magic, as bodies lay on a rock at the edge of the sea.

So long as the '*I*' was the point of each life, the '*I*' would remain the point. If rather than the '*I*', it was the '*WE*' that was necessary for happiness and 'self' fulfillment, then the '*WE*' would become the point.

Aiyana was empty without Walker, and she had always known this to be true in the center of her being. She was not content with herself as a singular unit, though she enjoyed her 'self' immensely. She loved being who she was, but only because she was half of a beautiful whole. Her essence drove Walker to confirm The Whole and assert his preference for her, even above his love of 'self', and this touched her deeply.

Walker too loved his own nature. Yet without Aiyana, he could not connect to his reason for being. Separated from his purpose, from his love of his other half, his power could only waste away.

Each saw the same picture from another point of view. Their respective halves were defined by different experiences, physicality, and emotions, but each was made to synergize with the other toward the making of an eternal whole. This was the highest form of union, and it was a privilege to partake in its secrets.

"Aiyana, can you see it?"

"Yes. I can see it."

Walker smiled at her and raised her hand to his mouth, where he kissed her soft, glowing skin.

"We can stay together forever," Aiyana assured. "But not of our own will, we are too weak to ensure such a reality. Only through Grace can we find our way as one. Yet, Grace is freely given. This is why a life as *WE* is superior to a life as *I*. A life as *WE* is dependent upon Grace for survival. It is an enormous risk, and it is one that we have chosen to take because we are truly together now. Our individual appetites and circumstances will remain separate in the physical world, and so we will remain vulnerable to losing our way as a unit, but we have found the key. It is the will of God.

God is the source of Grace, and the key to our future together is in following what God ordains. Yet, I know I am safe with you, because I see now that our meeting is written in the stars. The will of the beyond has ordained that we should be together as one. Every part of you touches every part of me, and in just the way each of us needs. This is not a choice to love, but a recognition of it in purest form. I loved your pattern before I ever saw it in the flesh. You are a miracle to my vision, and I can see clearly that I am the same for you. We are two halves of a puzzle, and the pieces were made to fit. Our connection is thus ordained from beyond our Earthly experience, and this means we exist together outside of its limitations, if only we choose to recognize who we are together."

Aiyana let go of Walker's hand for a moment so that she might place her hands together in prayer. "Lord, please bless this union, and be among us always, and us among one another in love. Draw our minds always back to this new world in common and guide us as we navigate into the land of our shared dream. Amen."

Walker held his hand out for her. She reached out her own and placed it in his once more, and they walked along together in the sand toward the ocean, speaking of their love and of their wedding day. They reminisced over their first trip to Europe as a couple and over their honeymoon, and over the way they had come to this land the night before they were to leave Elba for a whole new life together in England. Both were amazed that such sublimity could be found simply by staring into space. They marveled at the way they had come to travel together to this land where souls unite, to this celestial body where music was born of emotion. It seemed like a fairytale.

As they neared the edge of the water, white light began to dance on its surface, though it remained subdued as the light of the moon is so fond of doing. The violets and the whites maneuvered themselves into curious flows of intermixed color, and as they did, they rose into the sky. They extended up from the water into a great cloud, which began to swirl in a dance set to the rhythm and tune of the song which pervaded the heavens.

"What is it?" Walker asked, taking a few steps forward on his own. He was in awe of the scene.

"It is a moonstorm," Aiyana replied from behind him. "And I believe we are meant to dance in it. I think it is the way we carry this new connection back with us when we Return."

The Light seemed to sense that she had understood. The cloud began to move back from over the water toward the beach, and soon it was above them. As it came overhead, liquid color and emotion fell onto their bodies, and a great and all-encompassing pleasure flowed through their spirits. They stood for a few moments, looking up at the amethyst cascade, then at each other, and then up again. The power of the moment directed his intention, and his gaze was compelled to offer Aiyana a dance.

They swayed softly and quietly in the sand, amidst a torrent of pleasure and emotion bound up in the form of wind and painted water. The two were at one amidst the storm, and the storm was at one with two.

CHAPTER
Twenty-Two

Following their honeymoon, Walker and Aiyana went to live in London for a time; on a work assignment that allowed them to experience another world from the one they called home. A few weeks after their arrival, they took a weekend trip back to Lancaster to see one of Walker's university friends named Joziah.

As they neared the city of Lancaster aboard a train, the soul of the land began to change, growing ever more closely toward the feeling that Walker loved.

Land has a kind of soul, and you can feel it if you open your 'self' to its spell. But the soul of land is unlike the soul of a human being, for though it also manifests many personalities, these all belong to a singular entity. There is no clear line separating places the way there is between people. Even when this is the least true and lands are isolated by ocean, they remain connected to one another beneath the apparent divide. The resonance of the particular location evolves with each step, the feeling of the place changing slightly with every relocation of the human body with which it interacts. The mystique Walker loved was generalized to an area that started somewhere a few miles south of the city of Lancaster and extended all the way into Wordsworth's famed Lake District.

The couple exited the station and called Joziah, who was surprised to hear from them a week early.

"What do you mean a week early? We're here."

"In Lancaster?!"

"Yes, in Lancaster, where else would we be?"

"Ahhh..." Joziah did not sound well. "Walker, I'm in the Lake District doing a massive project for a really important client of mine. I have to work all weekend."

He felt horrible for Joziah. They had both planned on meeting up for weeks, and a simple miscommunication had unmade the entire thing. Thankfully, Joziah quickly arranged for them to stay with his parents at their house near Lancaster University, and they reconciled themselves to seeing Joziah at a reunion planned for a few months in the future.

They took the bus past the Bowerham Hotel and Pub, and into the hills known only from many similar rides during Walker's time in school there. Five buses ran the route from town to university, the 2, the 2A, the 3, the 4, and the X2. He never knew which was which, and consequently often ended up on the winding route through the hillside communities. All he knew was that the X2 was direct, and that you could never find one.

They departed the bus beneath the underpass at the university and made a beeline for Pizzetta Republic. Walker ordered a 'Hot and Spicy' pizza, as he always did, and paid the four pounds and sixty pence plus the cost of Aiyana's meal.

"You know this is the only kind of pizza I have ever gotten here?" he told her as they sat watching the people walking past outside. "I meant to try all of the varieties, but this one was so good that I just kept ordering it... for a whole year. And now, when I come back, picking anything else feels like going home and visiting a stranger instead of your own mother."

"You are such a weirdo," she chuckled.

They finished eating the slices of pepper and meat laden ambrosia and walked to the end of campus, which was composed of nine colleges arranged along a central spine. Pendle College and its bar were located at one end of campus, where he had lived during his time there, and County College and its bar were at the other. Just past County College, there was a path that led into the woods and past the school's infirmary, continuing through fields and woods for a while, before dumping out onto the streets of the small neighborhood where Joziah's parents lived.

Walker had never seen their home before, nor walked the full length of the path that led there. They navigated their way in twilight to start, then in the dark, until they found the neighborhood and a gate with the sign, "Welcome Walker and Aiyana."

After exchanging pleasantries with Joziah's parents, they were offered a seat in the small living room.

"Tea?" the lady of the house inquired.

"Yes, please!" The response was automatic. PG tips was a favorite among the English, and Aiyana was hopelessly addicted to it. Walker was glad tea was a legal substance because his wife would have risked the indulgence of the plant anyway. It really was that good.

They had both expected the night to be rather awkward. Walker had only met Joziah's parents once before when leaving his suitcase at their former house to avoid carting it across Europe for a month. They had been friendly then, but Joziah had been there, and the interaction was brief. This time was different. This time it was just two couples, connected only by a mutual link to Joziah, and separated by culture and a generation of time. But the reality was entirely the opposite of awkward. Within minutes, they spoke like old friends, and within an hour, they were in a deep discussion about life, love, commitment, and meaning.

Trevor had worked as an engineer for years after completing various degrees in his youth and had then gone back to school for a change of career, desiring to try something new. He had completed a master's in business administration, and then, just when he seemed set up to make even more money than he had as an engineer, he left his professional career aspirations behind and transitioned to laying tile for a living. He did this so that he might have time to think and work toward realizing a theoretical shift in mankind's understanding of 'change' and what it was.

He explained this as the four of them indulged in yet another kettle of PG Tips tea. The topic came in response to a question Walker had posed about Joziah's own choice to abandon his career in environmental science to take up the same profession as his father.

"I'm glad to see you guys supported Joziah in his choice. So many people have trouble understanding that life isn't about becoming one thing or another. Joziah didn't follow his degree. So what? He followed his intuition, and now he works on the most prestigious projects in the county. I practice law, but that doesn't make me a lawyer. It means I practice law; nothing less, nothing more. I am a dynamic happening. I am not a thing, and neither is Joziah. Neither are you, Trevor, nor you, Sue."

Trevor's eyes lit up, and Walker felt the world shrink in around them. Suddenly, Walker realized that he was 'high'.

His friend's father also seemed to clue into the shift. He became excited and explained that he understood exactly what Walker was saying. He said that he had set down his career because he was trying to unlock the nature of Truth, and that nothing was worth sacrificing Its pursuit. They had regarded each other warmly upon meeting, but now the two men began to see that their lives were aligned in a profound way. They were kindred spirits in a sense.

Trevor fired off ideas rapidly, weaving them together into a logic all their own. His ideas were not confined to, nor predicated on, logic born of induction and deduction, though these methods of thought certainly played a part in his thinking. Walker struggled to keep up with the man's mind, which was clearly gifted and had obviously spent much time on the topics that he attempted to relate.

The fundamental dynamics of reality were not set, he said, they were changing. Change was a concept that everyone took for granted. People thought they knew what it was. But it was much deeper than anyone had yet proposed. Trevor had been working on a paradigm that would expose the dynamic nature of change itself, and he was sure this idea would ultimately be accepted, whether through his work or someone else's. The truth of the matter would emerge, he said, just as it always had in the world. Trevor believed he was coming to understand exactly what that truth was. Change was changing.

"But if change were to change, it would have to be something other than itself. If the fundamental feature of something is altered, it eliminates its own essence. And if it doesn't, then you are really just playing a semantic game and altering definitions. Right?" Walker asked.

"No, you're looking at it wrong. There are other ways to think this through."

The man's thoughts required incredible flexibility of mind just to keep up with. Many of his points were, by their very nature, nonsensical from the standpoint of traditional notions of what made sense. His argument sought to advance a new understanding of what thinking could be. He argued that man's conception was such that it granted status only to thought premised on that which was reactive. Science was viewed as legitimate because it studied what the rules of the world were and then applied them to predict the future. Logic and reason were also viewed as legitimate because they were based on what was known from the study of current understandings. In Trevor's mind, this wholesale legitimization came at the expense of other types of thought, namely prescriptive thought. Trevor believed that there was a fundamental blueprint which existence was built upon. This blueprint allowed for a conception of Truth that included insights that were rooted in anticipated truth, rather than based exclusively on reactive understandings of It.

Walker enjoyed the complex theories being proposed, as they seemed to touch on some of the work he and Aiyana had been doing in relation to the quantum phenomena in physics whereby perception could be used to affect experimental outcomes. He and Aiyana had even developed a powerful psychotherapeutic technique based largely on the infamous Double Slit Experiments from the 1900's. Despite the depth of their knowledge in the field however, Trevor's explanations eventually lost everyone, and Walker had to stop him. "You lost me," he said suddenly.

Trevor smiled. "That's alright, it isn't easy to follow. Most people don't get any of it."

Walker thought for a moment, considering the obvious opacity of such ideas to the common mindset held by most people. "That is because you are advocating for a new way of thinking. The old way of thinking will not allow for your understandings because they do not make sense from within the construct that defines sense itself. I, for one, think that our conceptions of reality are pathetically inadequate, which almost demands we consider alternative models in my opinion. Although now that I say this, something I once read in the Tao Te Ching comes to mind, so perhaps these thoughts are not new. Perhaps they have just become lost in our culture.

"Verse 41 says that: 'Tao is always becoming what we have need for it to become. If it could not do this it would not be Tao.' Tao is akin to what we call God, if you aren't familiar, though beyond the personified form."

Sue interjected. "We are familiar with the Tao."

"Oh, good. Then you can see where I am going with this. Tao is the force animating everything, and since this is a dynamic process of change through what we call 'time', the Tao Te Ching seems to be saying something along the same lines as what you are saying, Trevor. Do you think?"

"Perhaps," he replied.

Trevor seemed to ponder a new thought for a moment.

"Let me tell you something about yourself, and you tell me if it is correct or not."

"Shoot."

"You are a scout."

"A scout?" Walker questioned.

"Yes, that is your nature, the type of person you are. You seek to understand by venturing where no one has been. You are someone who is always exploring, whether it is coming here to England, or exploring ideas, or your own mind, or simply your own backyard. You don't care so much about being exceptional at anything in particular, as in knowing something about everything. You always want to know what is around the corner, what is beyond what is known. I realize that this is the way all people are in a sense, but I mean that you are more this way than almost everyone you probably know. Am I right?"

"You couldn't have explained me any more accurately."

"I knew it," Trevor said, leaning back in his chair and smiling at his wife. "The difficult thing for a scout," he continued, leaning forward again, "is living in a world where scouts aren't seen as important. For many years the scout was indispensable because there was a frontier, an endless frontier, and not just physically. But now, within the world as we know it, that frontier is vanishing, at least the accessible part. A scout finds himself with little to explore these days, and this makes things difficult for him. Scouts are generalists by nature, and the world is moving towards a focus on specialization. For a spirit that loves to specialize, this is great, but for a generalist, this is very unwelcome. However, the system has overbred specialists. Generalists are badly needed to bridge the gaps between the specialties, which is the new frontier.

"See, all the specialists are working on their little piece of understanding. There are overarching categories like religion and science and social studies and math, and there are subdivisions of each of these into other categories such as biology and chemistry and anthropology and medicine and on and on. These are then divided again into smaller categories, often akin to professions, which individuals spend their lives trying to understand and legitimize. Each is loyal to their own work more than to the work of others, and to the work of others in their own category more than to the work of people in other categories, and so on. The psychiatrists don't want anything to do with psychologists who want even less to do with botanists who want even less to do with philosophers or lawyers. All of mankind is working on figuring out his world, and ultimately, we need people who can unify that effort. We need people who can bridge the gaps between our modes of thinking, perhaps even find the flaw that is dividing everyone from working towards a better future as one mind. There aren't a lot of true scouts anymore."

Aiyana and Walker exchanged a glance and a smile. They were both courting the same thought. Trevor's ideas had awakened something in the fledgling consciousness that they now shared. After their experience in Elba, they began to entertain ideas about uniting their collective intelligence inside a construct that would synergize with each of their respective dreams and visions. She had known the instant that Walker conceived the plan, or was it the other way around? Things had started to get a little murky in that regard.

Five hours later, they sat finishing their time together with lighter conversation, which had emerged after three solid hours of heavy philosophy.

"It's very late, and you two should get some sleep if you're going to go hiking in the morning in Ambleside," said Sue. "Before you turn in, I want to tell you one last thing. Remember to stick together always and believe that life has its own way of seeing you to where you should be, so long as you believe," she counseled.

Life was always surprising Walker, and he wondered at the purpose in all these occurrences. So much happened that seemed so convenient to his search for answers. He *was* a scout. He had been trying to understand how to carry his idea forward without giving sufficient consideration to his own nature. He wasn't supposed to provide the answer. He was supposed to explore answers still unknown. He belonged with uncertainty and flow. From *his* exploration of the unknown, others would find a way to move the ideas forward. He didn't need a conclusion, in fact, it was contrary to his nature to find one.

Walker didn't understand all that Trevor had sought to explain, but he understood much of it, as it was deeply connected to what he had already come to know.

A half-hour later, as he lay with Aiyana amidst cotton sheets, flirting with the dreamscape, his eyes suddenly caught the glimmer of his wife's ring in the moonlight. The room was only dimly lit by the indigo beams, and it was surprising to see the ring casting color with so little light to work with. Still, it did, and the colors in it were blue and beautiful. The ring had proven to be as Abraham had said. Walker scarcely remembered the other ring; this one had burned its image into his soul. No other could ever be its equal in his eyes, no matter the splendor or value to other men.

He reached out and touched his wife's hand. "Aiyana?"

"Yes, lover?"

"Isn't it so clear that there is more to the physical world than itself? It's becoming obvious to me that the spiritual world resides inside the center of the made reality around us."

"It is amazing, isn't it?" Aiyana said. "Are you saying that because of what happened tonight?"

"Partially, but I was also thinking about our ring, and our dolphin, and our seagull."

Aiyana smiled. "I still don't know how we found our ring. It really was a miracle."

"Yes, it was. We seem to find our share of miracles."

He smiled as visions of their dance on the moon flooded into his mind. "You are so beautiful baby. My little moonflower."

Aiyana blushed at his new name for her, remembering the liquid emotion and indigo rain. Their union was unlike anything she had ever imagined, and she adored the way he perceived her. He saw her for who she was, sometimes even before she understood it herself. The girl she had once been, was reborn each day inside of the woman she was becoming. Walker loved her as a woman, with her powerful sexuality and independent spirit, but he also saw the young girl that she still held inside, the innocent one that longed to be pure and loved without sexual pretense. He saw her as a lover, but he also saw her as a work of art.

He wished he could have known her first, back when she was just discovering her identity as a woman, and he no-less himself as a man. Those years had been given to others, and there was no regret in that, for it had led them both here, and with the maturity to see this love for what it was. Yet in his heart, he wished he could have known her in her youthful innocence. He had seen pictures of her from around the time he had dated Nadia in high school, and he wondered what it might have been like to know her back then, at the beginning of discovery. Her face held an innocence and a beauty that was beyond explanation, and though it had transformed and matured over the years, it was eternally perfect in his eyes. He wondered what it would mean for them in their old age.

He closed his eyes and began to dream of her face in that time, memorized from so many pictures she had shared. Then his dreams shifted, and he began to swim in the memory of the second time God had acknowledged their union with one of his creatures. Aiyana had lost her ring only a month before their wedding day, somewhere between the forests of Michigan's upper peninsula and London, Ontario. The two had searched in vain across two days, stopping in every town they had visited in-between to meet with the police and take out ads in the local papers. Eventually, after they had done all they could think to do, they had finally given up, and bowed their heads in prayer, thanking God that they were more than a ring to be lost. They asked God for his Will, and five minutes later, the ring was back on Aiyana's hand, courtesy of a gas station attendant who seemed fated to find them a second time.

It was in that moment of uncanny timing and bizarre coincidence that Aiyana first began to contemplate the connection between animals and the hidden spiritual center of the physical world. As she sat finishing a prayer of thanks with Walker, a seagull had landed on the trunk of her car. She hadn't quite known what to make of the dolphin experience when it occurred, but now that memory coupled with the experience in front of her, calling her mind toward the importance of animals in relation to the call of the Spirit.

Aiyana had long wished for something to remember her dolphin by, but alas, their video had timed out before his emergence. She wouldn't let that happen again with her bird. Within seconds, she produced a camera to snap a photo through her rear window.

The photo was clear, except for the bird's face, which was transparent and blurred. Aiyana understood that this was probably due to the animal turning its head, coupled perhaps with insufficient lighting to allow for a quick shutter speed. Though, this didn't stop her heart from wondering if there might be another, more satisfying explanation. She would keep an eye out for her winged messenger in her dreams.

When Walker awoke in the small guest bedroom provided for them by Trevor and Sue, his heart was filled with joy and love for his wife as he anticipated a moment he had looked forward to for several years. Today he would take his love to one of the most sublime places on Earth, and there he would show her a secret he had once discovered in the shadow of the great peak of Helvellyn. The place held a certain magical power over him, and he delighted in the chance to open her eyes to the reason why.

The day began with a fabulous English breakfast courtesy of Joziah's parents and then melded into an exploration of the wonderland that is the Lake District. While the morning air was still crisp, Trevor and Sue had driven them to a hostel near the headwaters of the lake known as Windermere, and for three days life consisted of hiking in a land of soft green mountains and deep blue waters.

They spent their evenings in the small town of Ambleside, venturing by day into the mountains beyond the town and packing picnic lunches to enjoy among the grass and the trees. They ate amidst the rock walls and green pastures where sheep grazed freely and gazed out over the lake as Aiyana repeatedly burst into song, filling the ancient hills with the beauty of her youthful energy. At night, they drank Lindisfarne Mead and ate to their fill in the area pubs and restaurants. When their time in that land finally closed, they floated out of Ambleside aboard a ferry bound for the lake's distant shore.

Back in London a week later, Aiyana and Walker began work on the next stage of their walk together. Now that they had found one another fully, they no longer had anything to prove. They were simply happy to live life together, sharing in the same mental space at their pleasure.

This, in turn, freed them from having to focus on their own union, and opened the door to the question: "How are we meant to bring forward the gift that this love and ability enables us to see? How can we bring what we have been shown into the world for others to embrace?"

Because the young couple had found so much, they felt that it was time to give something back. They couldn't solve the world's problems, but they both understood how they were meant to help. They knew that because of their particular histories and professions, they were positioned to do something about the fundamental legal assumptions driving one of the most destructive social paradigms in the history of the world.

They also knew that to do anything about the untold suffering generated in the chaos produced by law, they would have to go behind the paradigm itself, to the heart of the logic underlying it. This would open the door for other reformations of thought, which once begun, would continue until the entire illegitimate construction of their reality based on equating light and dark, along with true and false, would topple and fall. Many would contribute to this undoing, and the two of them would have the privilege of holding open the doorway to that future. Neither of them could do this alone. They were refining one another's intentions and ideas into something beyond either of their individual capacities.

It was like Trevor had said, someone had to find the flaw that was dividing the human race from working towards a better future as one mind. Yet it was vital that such a unified intention emerge organically, and in keeping with the laws of nature insisting on individual liberty. Walker and Aiyana could sense that each believed in the other and in their purpose for believing, which enabled them to cast aside fear in favor of what they knew the other felt to be right.

The whole system of thought and feedback of thought was incredibly circular and confusing as to its beginnings, and yet the depth of its certainty was beyond anything experienced in the divided mind of individual understanding. The place they had come to drove its own conclusions in many regards.

Ultimately, they had to find a way to create a vehicle for what they knew so that it might reach the minds of others. Both played with a number of interesting ideas, but in-the-end they settled on keeping things fluid and dynamic, but within a defined framework based on a common storyline. Walker and Aiyana would not seek to force change but would instead seek to support an organic emergence of ideas. By keeping the context primarily focused on the experience of duality in a finite timeframe, their effort could be framed in such a way as to circle back on itself, and in so doing, they could ensure that it would not evolve into something they didn't want it to become. They insisted that *their* journey remain *their* story.

Aiyana was concerned that they remain careful of any experiences beyond their dual conception, and that they not allow connections to others outside of themselves to inform their direction, unless part of an inherently limited scheme. She suspected that expansion of consciousness by way of multiple unknown psychic partners was perfectly possible and highly inadvisable without some method of limiting the outside influences, especially given the fledgling nature of their ability.

Still, it was important that they find a way to make this plan something more than a foray into self-examination and personal growth. They needed to pull in intellects beyond themselves so that they could expand the solutions that would spread and revolutionize mankind's world. They wanted to invite intelligence greater than their own into their story, but they both believed it was vital that they do so in a way that didn't let those other intelligences direct their stories or perceptions of reality. If they lost control of their own narratives to those who were more gifted and cleverer, they might even lose themselves.

Thus, the Council was conceived. An undefined conglomeration of intellects, perhaps even galactic intellect, would be given the right to commission the development of the very frameworks and ideas that Aiyana and Walker already pursued, but in a substantive and documented form that could be shared with the world. These unknown intellects would also be given the right to game the process, and to affect and guide the emergence of a new paradigm using their own particular abilities. But this is where their influence had to end. The terms on which Walker and Aiyana would grant such beings access to their shared mental space, did not allow for any manipulation outside the bounds of the commissioned work itself. This seemed sufficient assurance toward keeping their influence on the couple's inner world under control. The idea of the Council provided a self-contained methodology for encounter with a concept that would undoubtedly morph beyond either of their capacities if allowed, and which would insist on defining itself by virtue of its own constituency if not for the framework.

The parameters of how and when the encounter with the idea would occur were purposefully left open for their minds to fill in. Each of them wanted to surprise one another with hidden meaning and hidden excitement on their journey toward a shared vision for the future. They were setting out on a serious task, but all the same, they were in love, and they could not help but focus on ways to engage one another in play. After all, it was the sheer joy of their connection itself which gave the experience such validity.

They would continue to explore multiple layers of reality along the way, conscious, subconscious, and beyond. Aiyana was ecstatic, and Walker was no less so. Their psychological union was going to bear fruit. They were about to create a channel that others could pour their own efforts into. The primacy of mankind's spiritual condition was the foundational truth on which the legitimacy of all human enterprise depended. The time had come for a proclamation, and it would be made not only to those holding power in the Earthly Realm, but also to those outside of it who had crafted the doctrine keeping that Realm in chains. The message was very simple, "Let My People Go."

What can I seek in this world to compare?
To this fragile existence
So self-aware

A world beyond boxes
A script without time

The making of meaning
The Birth of the Mind

CHAPTER
Twenty-Three

Walker's focus had moved increasingly toward reconciliation with his classmates, as courses on comparative constitutional law gave way to a study of comparative dispute resolution. This subject had a different focus which was much less divisive than black letter law, seeking not to claim a moral truth, but rather a practical and peaceable solution to problems resulting from the law's failure to control reality. Walker certainly had his criticisms of the study, yet engaging it provided a welcome shift in mood. Hookah bars became a common occurrence in the evenings for Walker and the other law students, and meals out at fine restaurants together were the norm.

Seven of them were reclining on the floor of a balcony that was designed for five small adults at most, and which was only three feet high from floor to ceiling. Walker and his friends had to crawl from the top of the ladder at one end of the platform to the other, where a large water pipe sat in the center of a miniature table standing less than one foot high. The water pipe was made of deep blue glass trimmed in gold, with a mesh bowl which stuck up into the air, forming a platform for a cake of tobacco to sit atop its flute-shaped body.

One of the other law students passed the pipe over to Walker. The cake, which had been glowing orange, deepened into a red, and then faded until the light had left its body, with only a brown opaqueness remaining. He put the nozzle to his lips, pulling in deeply, and the cake burst back to light, showing again in vivid orange. Walker struggled not to cough and held the smoke in, counting the seconds in his head. He had learned that tobacco could give a person a high, and he felt like indulging himself in the moment. At one hundred, he breathed out intensely and then drew in a mass of cool air. His head seemed to float a bit, and his muscles relaxed as the feeling washed over.

Nicotine was as much a 'drug' as anything else, and it was not to be trifled with. It did not provide the reward of euphoria at the level of opiates or other drugs known for their addictive potential, but nicotine had made slaves of many men and women over the years, nonetheless. The tobacco plant was chemically addictive, and it needed to be handled with respect. There were certain compounds that created such euphoria that the individual almost always chose to consume them again, but tobacco did not contain such things. The danger of tobacco lay with a more subtle deception. He felt sorry for those around him who smoked cigarettes on a constant basis. They were an ever-present crutch for many of them, something they could no longer do without. His peers had not respected tobacco, and that lack of respect had cost them their freedom. Yet, the hookah bar was allowable for Walker because it was an event in time.

"Walker?" The pipe had made its way back to him again. He waved it past to his wife, who had only arrived in Cape Town a few days before, having concluded a career obligation in the States. Aiyana inhaled some smoke and then began to cough. She looked so miserable, but he was still proud. Upon catching her love's fondness in a glimpse, she smiled, her eyes tearing now from the smoke. One of the other students instructed her on how to better inhale, and she reluctantly tried again. This time there was just a small cough. Walker rubbed his hand on her back.

"I really don't see the appeal," she whispered to him. "Except for the social aspect of it, and a bit of a spacey feeling. It certainly doesn't seem worth becoming a slave to a habit."

"I completely agree," he whispered back. "But tobacco has its place too. Such as here, tonight."

Below in the main bar, music was playing, and the sound carried nicely near the roof where they sat. The air was thick, and not just with smoke, but something else. He tried to place it, but it was difficult. It was as if you could taste the air. It tasted like dirt.

"Do you guys feel that in the air?" he asked.

"Feel what?"

"The air seems so thick, and it's not the smoke. You can taste it."

"Kind of like dirt," said one of their companions.

"Exactly, just like dirt, and grease maybe. Like fried dirt."

Everyone contemplated this as Walker studied the hose emanating from the hookah. He liked Africa, even if his experience of it was limited to this one small piece. The place wasn't safe enough to feel comfortable in, especially now that he needed to protect his wife too, but aside from this one aspect, it was an amazing place to explore and learn. The taste in the air was the taste of life. It wasn't clean and sanitized the way things were in America. One could get a feel for such a flavor in parts of Europe, but Africa was on a level all its own. This place was real, and he cherished that he could taste the earth in the air. Walker looked out at the small, antique wall clock, just visible across the room below. He realized it was time for them to go, and he leant over to Aiyana and whispered in her ear.

They parted company with the other students and made their way back to De Waterkant and past the now infamous Café Manhattan. They were meeting Zach, the man who worked as a cook in the restaurant attached to the internet café where they had discussed the *Prince* case. Zach had approached him earlier that morning, asking for a favor. The two men had become friends over the last several months, and by now they had engaged in numerous discussions about the South African Constitution, drug policy, the nature of right and wrong, Rastafarianism, Christianity, and Yogic philosophy.

"Walker, can you help me with something? You're a person I feel I may ask," he had said that morning as Walker ordered food from his shop.

"Anything for my African friend," Walker shined. Zach was from

Zimbabwe, and he had a way of saying things that made you understand that he was genuine, regardless of the words he spoke. Walker made a point of reflecting this warmth back to him with his affect and intonation.

Zach had motioned toward a back room, behind a curtain that separated it from the café. They traversed a floor cluttered with crates and boxes of this and that, until they reached the back of the store, away from anyone who might seek to pry.

"So, you know of my Yogic and Rastafarian predispositions, and my Christian roots and belief. But I must confess that I have not shared these details about my faith with you for simple conversation's sake. There is something in the way of how these traditions intersect which brought you here to Africa in the first place, so that you might attempt an explanation, am I right?"

"Yes. How do you know this? I haven't let you in on these things."

"I am much like you," he said, avoiding Walker's examination. "More so than you know. I too walked the path that you are on. I know the dangers, and the way you feel right now, but you must not be afraid, and you must trust."

Zach was toying around with Walker, and he struggled to place what it was he was trying to get at. "Trust what? he asked. Do you mean God?"

"Yes, and also me."

Walker looked into his eyes and understood for the first time that Zach was much more important to his time in Africa than he had given him credit for.

"The Council," Walker stated.

"Yes, *The* Council," Zach spoke in a way that conveyed the singular importance of whatever *it* was.

"You must do exactly as I say," he continued. "Meet me back here tonight at closing, and I will explain more. For now, you only need to know that if you had been alone, we could have spoken sooner, but you are not alone, are you?"

"You mean in Africa?"

"No, I mean here in this life."

"My wife?"

"Yes, you would not leave her behind, we knew this."

"Who is 'we'?"

"Again, in time. Bring her with you tonight, and then you will begin to see."

"Whatever this Council is, I know I must confront it. But look me in the eye and tell me that it is safe for my love. I have a responsibility to her." He looked at Zach piercingly.

"My friend." Zach placed his hands as if in prayer and stared directly into Walker's eyes. "I too know love, and I would not have left her either. So, I too was asked to trust the unknown with the treasure that God had given to me. Your love is and will be safe throughout this time. The Council is more than you know, not less. No harm ever comes by their plans. They do not violate free will. They are not the enemy. They are part of the answer you seek. If you disagree with what you find, you can walk back to wherever you want to go with your bride. But you will not disagree, because you will only find what you already seek. I know because Truth is all there is. You cannot ignore It if you are seeking It, as you are. 'Seek and ye shall find.' You already know what it is that you want to know, and for this reason, you are destined to see."

Both their hearts were pounding as they made their way across town toward the internet café. They walked with nervous energy as they reached their neighborhood from the downtown area. Initially, after they had conceived of the idea of the Council, each had felt their design could contain the evolution of what it would become. Almost overnight however, signs began to emerge that suggested they were losing control of where their conception was taking them. They had meant to leave the parameters bounded but sufficiently loose to experience their interactions authentically, but successive developments had pushed each of them to consider that they may have made a mistake in opening to such things at all. What if they couldn't keep themselves grounded in reality? What if they lost their minds to the control of others?

When they arrived, the lights were already off, but the door opened as they approached, and Zach warmly greeted them, then ushered the couple inside. He led them through the curtain to the back room where he had spoken with Walker earlier and opened the door to a walk-in freezer.

"In here," he said stepping into the cold.

Inside, Zach pulled the door shut and flipped a switch on the wall, lighting the inside of the small space. He went to the back of the room and slid an empty pallet to the side, revealing a hidden door which he lifted open by a large metal ring connected to it. Below, a ladder descended to a small earthen chamber which, to Walker's surprise, contained another secret door connecting to a passageway through the raw earth. Aiyana froze at the sight of the tunnel, which disappeared quickly into an unknown darkness.

"Is this your idea?" she asked nervously.

"I don't know anymore," Walker admitted.

"I promise that you are both safe," Zach said, turning to look Aiyana in the eye. She stared deeply back at him and then chose to trust his gaze and set down her fear. With one glance over at her lover, she conveyed, without a word, that she had resolved something in her understanding of their intention, and this reaffirmed Walker's own trust in what he felt was part of the path they were meant to walk. They continued on into the tunnel, their guide's small flashlight cutting through the black's illusion using its magic.

The tunnel descended at a slight grade for what must have been a few hundred yards and then terminated in a large circular room perhaps thirty feet in diameter. There were several doors around its perimeter, and the floor was dry, but earthen.

Zach motioned for his friends to sit, and the three explorers dropped down in the dirt.

"It is very beautiful that you trust him as you do," he said, looking at Aiyana fondly. "You are right to trust. He will find you back, however long it takes. You can have faith in that."

Aiyana's eyes filled with tears. She knew what he spoke of. There was a day coming when she would have to walk apart from Walker for a time, and her heart had known this from early in their relationship. She had hoped the thoughts would change, that she would find a way to see past the idea so that it might not come true. But it was true, and she began to cry a little as the pain she would come to know mixed with the joy of knowing that it would not be forever.

"You are a good person Walker; you are seeking a good thing. A man should desire to share in all that he knows with those that do not, so long as they are ready. This is never truer than with the woman you love.

"Do not be afraid. What I give to you now will help you to find your way together, rather than apart. You understand." Zach told more than asked. "See past that which makes us blind in this world. Stick to what is natural and made by God, and explore your mind and your world respectfully, and no harm can befall you. This plant is good and pure. Use it to see, but never abuse or force an experience. Use it together in the right timing, and to come together. You understand."

Zach went to the edge of the room to one of the doors, and after producing a key, proceeded to unlock and open it. It led to another earthen-walled room, this one little more than a pantry. He retrieved some small sticks and a few split logs, along with an intricately woven satchel covered in a pattern and color scheme that suggested a Mesoamerican influence, possibly Mazatec.

Returning to the middle of the room, Zach set about constructing a fire. The fire lit nicely, and the smoke traveled up to the ceiling, where it then found its way into a small crack at the highest point and disappeared. They sat in silence, watching the smoke travel. "This is a very special plant." Zach counseled. It has been used for millennia to unite what is meant to unite. You understand."

He opened the satchel and sprinkled the contents into the fire's midst. "This is a small fire, and it will fade soon. By the time it does, your minds will be ready. But you may wait longer if you like, there is no rushing these things. And don't worry, you don't have to smoke anything," Zach looked at Aiyana as he teased.

She smiled sheepishly. "How does it work if it isn't imbibed?"

"No one knows, but just being here as the plant releases its understanding is enough. It is incredibly powerful, suffice to say that it operates beyond the limitations of some biochemical reaction in your brain."

He turned to face Aiyana directly. "Cast fear and doubt aside now, for this opportunity will not force itself on you, but it may not come again if you turn away. Embrace now the Light and the Earth it illuminates, and wherever it is that you are going together. May Yahweh bless your eternal union."

Zach then stood and walked to the door through which they had entered, and placing his hands together, bowed slightly. "I trust you can find your own way out," he said before closing the door, leaving them to ponder where they were meant to go.

"Do you think we are going back to the violet beach?" Aiyana asked in a confused tone.

"I honestly have no idea," her love replied.

"You know, it's funny," she said, sitting back on her elbows, staring at the coals. "You have no idea what this plant is, do you?"

"Not by name, no. But I have seen it before. I saw it growing wild once among the cloud forests of Oaxaca, Mexico."

"Is that the reason I keep seeing it in my dreams?"

"Probably. I came upon one of its kind along a trail in the forest, and saw it bent over under a fallen limb. I removed the limb and straightened the plant so it could catch the light again. I regarded its pleasing aesthetics as I stroked the leaves, and felt a strong connection emerge. I did not partake of it further that day, I merely caressed it, and yet my awareness departed my body and I saw past the confines of the physical, to the very edge of existence. There is a veil there, existing between the worlds of the 'made' and the 'potential'. I was so close that I could almost see through to the other side.

Ever since then, I have seen the plant growing many times in my own dreams and visions. In these visions, I always know the plant is good, and I eat of it freely. The last time I saw it, it was growing at the base of a great tree. I chewed twelve leaves and awoke from my dream to find this life."

"How does our dream connection fit into this? And what is the significance of the translucent flower where you first found me?"

"I'm still not sure. Do you want to find out?"

"Most completely," Aiyana smiled.

They lay down next to one another and continued to speak for a time about Zach, pondering who he could be, each more than suspicious of what the other was up to in that regard. They spoke of the strange passageways and the hidden room, and of what they hoped to find beyond.

Walker reached over and took his wife by the hand. Then they just lay together for a long while, as they once had so long ago on the beach below their honeymoon resort in Elba. This time though, there was no guiding light overhead, only the substance of the Earth itself, which barely reflected the glow of the flames. They watched as the fire danced across the earth above them and spoke of its beauty, and of love, and of the majesty of God's creation, until they found themselves beginning to drift.

CHAPTER
Twenty-Four

Reality was pulsing now. It came in waves. The radiance of existence massaged the flesh from all directions with a force that was ever-present, but which differed in intensity from one moment to the next. The force arrived at awareness as does the undulation of the ocean, only it did so from every direction at once. Body began to experience pleasure everywhere as the energy continued to surge against skin. Mind began to accept the sensation of the waves, and with this acceptance came the rising of self-awareness out of the back of the head, like a flower in bloom.

Walker rose up from within himself like a man emerging from a cramped tent where he had spent a long, cold night huddled for warmth. He looked around, and the world was suddenly very old. He was in an opening amidst the trees of a dense jungle unlike any he had ever seen. These trees were different from others he had experienced in his past, though how they differed could not be placed. They seemed tropical and projected a feeling that they were somehow all part of one great organism. Even as he pondered the fact that they were different, however, he could not venture into them, nor was there any inclination to do so. They were the boundary between the place he had come, and all that lay beyond.

He stood in a clearing which was circular in shape. The ground was all dirt, with scarcely a blade of green breaking the surface. There were a few huts, though they were not important enough to focus on. A woman sat in the center of the clearing. She was a young Native American woman in form, though she was ancient all the same. She was chanting something in a language not heard before. It was much like the language of the ancient man remembered from another forest world, but it was different in subtleties of sound and rhythm.

He was focused almost entirely on the woman, but not her physical features, though they were stunningly beautiful. It was the feeling of her spirit that captivated. She chanted of something with an all-encompassing dedication, as if it were her sole purpose in this place. This being was focused and powerful. She was alone, aside from him. His presence went either unnoticed or noticed with the sort of neutral indifference of a person who becomes aware of an ant on the forest floor.

Suddenly, something beyond Walker pulled back toward the woods in a natural fall. He began to feel as if his awareness were reaching the apex of an upward, arching trajectory. His vision had entered this place by breaking through the thick of the trees and into the sacred space of the woman at the center of the circle. He had initially moved across and inward, or upward as it seemed, but then continued past and away from the woman in a consistent arc, having failed to reach her. Walker began to feel as his dolphin must have felt as he left the upper world for his own, gravity refusing to let him stay above the water. He turned to keep his gaze on both the clearing and the woman as his spirit began to leave, not only to the woods, but to his body. As it began to depart, Walker mustered all his power and energy to arrest the descent, yet the clearing began to close around his vision. He struggled to hold the gateway open, to keep his vision in this world beyond. For a moment, this succeeded. Then, like the closing of the water behind the dolphin, the world below swallowed his awareness.

Walker was back with his body, but he was not concerned with the physical 'self'. He felt his thoughts, sharp and powerful. He contemplated the way he had come back to his world, facing backward. He had not been looking forward upon returning as the dolphin had. Pondering his friend from the sea, he lay staring again at the earthen ceiling while holding his wife's hand. It was then that he realized what he was meant to do.

He began thinking of his conceptualization, and of his belief that the Truth of the other world was beyond any Earthly power. Why hadn't he taken the cause there? He decided to go back to the woman in the wooded clearing and plead his case to her. Then a new thought came. "Why put faith in this woman, however powerful, or even in a Council? It would be better to go beyond man's broken world, to the very edge of the far shore of his reality."

He resolved to travel to the limit of his ability to conceive, and from there, to speak into The White and hope that his prayers reached beyond the veil. The White already knew his heart, but his ideas themselves needed to be sanctified through offering. For whatever reason, God desired for human beings to confront their world, and to take a stand for what they came to believe, by speaking the Word.

Walker closed the eyes and concentrated on desire, on flight, on ascension. A sensation that can only be described as that of a jet engine spinning to life began to grow in the mind. He had experienced this phenomenon first-hand many times, both while sitting inside of planes and standing alongside them during his days as a lineman at the airport. But in the past, he had always experienced the phenomenon through sound; he had *heard* the engines start. This was different, it was not a sound; it was a feeling, an understanding, and an experience of a potential kinetic reality.

Though there was no sound, he was aware that the feeling had a sort of pitch. The pitch was low but had already begun to heighten as the feeling gained power. Like the countless jet engines in his memory, it continued to rise in strength and volume, elevating in a continual climb toward the inaudible, or its analog. Soon, he felt full of an energy beyond the bounds of space and time and understood that he was controlling it, channeling it. He resolved to take it back to the land where he had seen the Native American woman and let it fly from there, back to the place where it was conceived. He wasn't sure why, but he wanted her to be there to see him off.

Walker left his reality and thought through a maze of understanding and feeling, back to the clearing he had previously seen, holding the energy down as he made his way. He entered again from the edge of the woods and gazed upon the ancient scene. The woman in the center was still chanting, but now she was aware of his presence. She looked at him and nodded as she continued. His eyes locked into her gaze as he nodded back, understanding now that her chants were prayers for his safety on this journey. Then without a word, his vision shifted skyward. He had somewhere to be. Walker had not come this time to marvel, but only to orientate himself for the rest of the ascension. In finding the forest clearing, his spirit had already come quite far, but in the scheme of things spiritual, it was only the beginning.

He focused his intention, and then let his soul accelerate skyward. The acceleration was immediate, and speed built continually, pushing him faster and faster until he caught up with the light of the sky. Walker traveled with the light for a time, until it began to slow and to break up into clouds among a sea of blue. He focused on continuing his journey with all his being, but soon slowed to a stop, lost in a world of first impression. The clouds themselves seemed to be living things. They radiated energy that he could feel, and the feeling came largely as physical pleasure. It was like the sensation of warm sun on skin after a cold swim. In the distance, beyond the last visible cloud, was a great blur. The Cosmos was veiled there, and he could not see beyond the curtain. He had traveled to the far distant shore of his perception and could go no further.

It was from here that he knew he was to pray. For a prayer could be heard anywhere by the spirit of I AM, but from such a height, it meant so much more to the Creator. Walker's spirit was still light-years from the perfection of God, but he was closer to it in that moment than he had ever come before. His soul had come here this day, to this height, to honor the spirit of All That Is, and to thank Him for the life given and for His Grace. All that he had recalled in the months gone by preparing for the Council was offered up, and he delighted in the chance to offer thanks from such a height as this.

When the thanksgiving had finished, he gazed around at the world of clouds. The sky was iridescent and beautifully thin. He could almost see through now to the purity beyond the blur. A presence suddenly filled the air around him, unseen yet all-encompassing. A feeling washed over his spirit, and a deep understanding found him. He had encountered this presence before.

In Walker's life, many spiritual journeys had come to pass, and on each occasion, he had endeavored to share what he had learned from them with others. But in the end, the spiritual could not be explained. Only something akin to its shadow could be conveyed. This was because the spiritual was beyond not only labels, but beyond thought itself. The most a man could do to help others see past the material world was to call their minds to search. He had already known this to be true mentally, yet he labored to create a logical framework to explain the spiritual anyway.

The reality was that while man could lead others to ponder stepping off the common paths to ruin, he could never explain how another finds his way to appreciate the beauty of the hidden trails. Until a human being beholds the world beyond his ordinary perception, he can never truly understand.

Thought was limited because it could only exist when the whole was divided. If it was reunited completely, it ceased to be thought, because its own basis, the division of reality, ceased to exist. When the spirit was felt, thought was absent. This is why the goal of so many spiritual meditative traditions was to behold nothingness, 'no mind'. The words of the Tao Te Ching echoed in the sky.

"Wu is nothingness, emptiness, non-existence.
Thirty spokes of a wheel all join at a common hub,
yet only the hole at the center allows the wheel to spin.
Clay is molded to form a cup,
yet only the space within allows the cup to hold water.
Walls are joined to make a room,

yet only by cutting out a door and a window can one enter the room and live there.

Thus, when a thing has existence alone it is mere dead-weight.

Only when it has wu, does it have life."

- Verse 11

When thought sought to return to explain the spiritual, it resulted only in frustration, or a faulty conception of the spirit. It was no wonder those lost in the world of thinking remained lost. The Truth was hidden from them in plain sight. When they attempted to consider the possibility of a spiritual existence, they did so by *thinking* about that possibility, and in so doing ensured that they could never find it. Walker had fallen into this trap himself more times than he could count, and yet he now had a way to share the understandings of the spiritual world directly with Aiyana through a shared experience of it. Even now, she was there with him, taking in the sky while her body and mind sat meditating in faraway places. It was her love for him that gifted the power to come to this place, and for this, he was eternally grateful. It was undeniable liberation to share such depth with a simple glance. Life was funny like that. He had failed to explain with perhaps a million words over the years, and Aiyana could confirm what he knew simply by casting it from her eyes.

It was almost comical to understand just how stupid intelligent people like him could be. The more gifted a person's mind was, the more difficult it became to contemplate the possibility of something that did not require or submit to logical process. Thought continually reinforced its own understanding of all things as being the subjects of thought, when the Truth was something entirely different. Even when Walker found himself maturing out of this on one level, he fell back into it on another.

As soon as a mind came to a conception of what the spirit was, it was conceiving of something less than the true spirit. Man could conceptualize something approximating Truth, and man could pursue

Truth, but Truth itself was beyond the ability of thought to capture. It was like a two-dimensional character in a painting trying to capture the essence of a three-dimensional cube. A two-dimensional representation on a two-dimensional page would be as close as such a character could ever hope to come.

Thus, a mind could never conceive of the true nature of the Force responsible for its existence. Ultimate Truth could not be explained; only experienced. The spiritual is animate, evolving, and changing. This is why human beings were created – to experience and to live. Through living, the spirit could manifest, and it did so in the glance and the kiss and the touch. This is why the Bible said:

"Where there are prophesies, they will cease; where there are tongues, they will be stilled; where there is knowledge, it will pass away. For we know in part and we prophesy in part, but when perfection comes, the imperfect disappears. When I was a child, I talked like a child, I thought like a child, I reasoned like a child. When I became a man, I put childish ways behind me. Now we see but a poor reflection as in a mirror; then we shall see face to face. Now I know in part; then I shall know fully, even as I am fully known. And now these three remain: faith, hope and love. But the greatest of these is love."

- 1 Corinthians 14:5

Walker suddenly felt an overwhelming sense of clarity. Man was supposed to get over this predisposition of his. It was so clear to him there in that moment that this was so. Man's challenge was to find a way to evolve his consciousness, to accept the need for Wu, for the place inside his being that was made to be beyond explanation and study. It was this aspect of his life, his spiritual existence, which gave him purpose. Consciousness was meant to develop past a focus on knowledge and thought alone. The inevitable result of perfecting knowledge was comprehension of the fact that knowledge is not where meaning lies. Mankind would soon see this, and when it did, a profound transformation would occur. Trevor was seeking this revolution, and so was Walker.

The true measure of intelligence lay not in the ability to make some sense of the world, which was easy enough. Rather, its true measure was in being able to understand that whatever one came to know was merely a reflection of the Truth. True intelligence was found in knowing when to say that the rational was irrelevant and being able to do the opposite of that which logic dictated. To look for proof of meaning was to lose it. Human beings were not meant to dictate the Truth, but to enjoy It, and to let themselves revolve around Its center, where Its complementary form resided as potential understanding.

This did not mean that mankind should not seek to follow what was good and true. On the contrary, it was all people were created to do. But they were meant to lose themselves in the desire to worship the Force that animated them and to live by the dictates of nature, devoting all their energy to the love of life and the nature of Divine Reality. If they would but do this, they could not fail to find the path to goodness and to God. It was only by believing that the path could be forced to conform to collective will that mankind lost the path. Societies endeavored to subject reality to rules and controls, and to reduce life to a dead formula. Societies perverted the true 'law' with millions of dead forgeries concocted by mortal men and women. Then they tried to force their counterfeit truths onto others in the name of the genuine article. It was time for this to change.

The beginning of the new reality would spring from the realization that the spiritual is indefinable for a very simple reason. The spiritual is animate, evolving, changing. The spiritual is not definable, specifically because it is ever beginning. It is in this sense and in this sense alone that 'nothingness' exists. Wu is the void in the 'made reality' that allows that same 'made reality' to hold that which is born of the far shore and is still potential, real though as-yet unmade, alive and in constant flux. It is from the potential conception of reality that all reality springs.

Thus, Wu is not truly 'nothing', as is the lie of 'darkness' or 'evil', but rather is nothing only in relation to the perception of ordinary physical reality. In the land of the far shore, it is this same 'nothing' that is the substance of all existence. There, it is the 'made reality' that becomes the purpose and the manifestation of Wu. This mirrored manifestation of meaning in the world of the spiritual in relation to the world of the physical is defined by the fact that the predominating tendency in one reality is the hidden center of the other. This is why spirituality appears not to exist to those whose minds are fixated on the world that is already made, and why those lost in the world of the transcendent seem so unconcerned with physical reality.

In truth, there are two harmonizing aspects of existence, the near physical shore, and the far shore of the spiritual. Human beings touch both shores simultaneously, by manifesting a profound depth to fill the great expanse between these two worlds. This manifestation is what we call intelligence, and it exists as does a great ocean, subsisting seemingly on its own between two opposite and yet equally accessible lands, which are bound together by the very valley that the ocean fills. Thus, human intellect serves to bridge two great heights, enabling us to touch both mountains at a single moment in time. In truth, each shore is part of the same Reality, but this truth is lost on those who insist on staying close to the near shore for fear of drowning in their own capacity. They reconcile themselves to what can be known fully in the shallows of life and abandon any journey into the deeper waters of their minds, as they know they cannot fathom or control the power of the deep without first sacrificing the things they already believe they know.

Man's desire to know through verifiable proof, rather than to understand through evolving dynamic perception, is born of his own 'self'-hate. It is a death wish, a blasphemy against his dynamic nature and his function as a Being. To seek out conclusions to questions is to seek the end of the search, which is to wish for the end to come. Thinking this way leads exactly to what is sought, the end. Life is not a conclusion, but is rather a process, and it never has to end, if only we will refrain from looking for it.

Living beings cannot truly be reduced to the definable, because they are creations in progress. Beings such as men and women are manifestations of change itself. A person is, in-point-of-fact, 'change'. When all people come to see this about themselves, then the essence of our purpose will transcend the present reality, and a new reality will be born. Our plane of existence has already begun this dramatic shift. Trevor was right. 'Change' *was* changing. *WE* are becoming aware of our fundamental nature and purpose. The Enlightenment is upon us.

However, the souls of most men and women are as-yet, still lost in their own creation of thought, failing to see the need for Grace. At the heart of mankind's cognitive ability is the recognition of time. Time is the link between one thought and the next. Without the recognition of a linear flow, the mind cannot string thoughts together in the same way, and thus can neither reason nor manipulate the 'future'. A man unconcerned with thought is unconcerned with time, and he neither fears it nor plans for its manipulation. Time is born of thought and thought conceives of time as a truth beyond itself, though in truth, time is merely the illusion derivative of thought's own methodology. Time exists at base, because the universe is itself an intellect. Human Beings are specialized components of that intellect, and thus they too are authors of 'time'. In his own life, the Cosmic Intellect had sent a message:

"And why wilt thou, my son, be ravished with a strange woman,
and embrace the bosom of a stranger?
For the ways of man *are* before the eyes of the LORD,
and he pondereth all his goings."

- Proverbs 5

Walker had long believed that these words held personal meaning for his life and that he would come to a day when they would become relevant to his life situation. Still, he had never been able to understand how this would come to pass. There among the clouds, he realized that the words were already connected. They spoke not of what Walker had always viewed in his mind as future, but of what he had always viewed as past.

The Truth of the Whole did not require a linear flow of thoughts. These words had been spoken to him concerning his life so that he might see that God had known of his path before he had even walked it. The fact that the foretelling of his experience had taken place after the event in time had kept him from realizing that the future had been foretold. These thoughts didn't add up in the rational mind, because the conception informing their rational interpretation was false to begin with. Past and future did not exist in the way he had always conceived of them, they were an illusion born of mind.

Time was nothing more than a construct created by the intellect to allow it to view its own progression through thought and experience toward understanding. His species had evolved quite an ability to order and make sense of the world through linear time, but this ability was not complete. Somehow Walker's mind had ordered bits of reality in ways that didn't make sense within its own methodology of constructing what he thought of as 'meaning'. It was the Truth beyond his delusion that was responsible for the phenomenon of God showing up in timing.

Time was the way he made sense of who he was and why; he used it to explain who he had 'become' to his 'self' at a given moment of reflection. The meaningful timing of events in his life was the Truth of his eternal nature as a 'Being', breaking through his imperfect understanding of Reality and of 'self', which was bound to a limited mind and its limited construct called thought.

Walker wondered what glory his mind was trying to conceive of through the story he was telling himself. His walk through 'time' had only just begun, and already he was overwhelmed at the sheer meaning present in his life and story. He thought of the Whole that he still could not comprehend, and of his ability to think and order and see, both rationally and outside of those bounds. What a gift. What an experience. What an opportunity. He was writing a story, and the story was his life.

The Tao Te Ching spoke into his thoughts, and he reflected on the way
Tao manifest as Te through the process of his Being.

"He who knows the play of Tao and Te
Knows the nature of the universe.
Tao brings forth Te from its own being.
Te expands in all directions,
Filling every corner of the world,
Becoming the splendor of creation.
Yet at every moment Te seeks Tao.
This is the movement that guides the universe.
This is the impulse that leads all things back home."

- Verse 65

Though he had come to this place boldly, he turned in humility amidst
the understanding around him, and allowed himself to diminish. As he
did, one thought held sway.

"The movement of Tao is to Return."

- Verse 40

Walker's soul fell back through the clouds, and soon he was again
floating in an arc through the forest clearing. The woman looked at him
and nodded again as he passed, and he knew that she loved and respected
him. He returned the gesture, his heart soaring. As Walker completed his
trajectory through the clearing, the memory of their dolphin returned, and
his awareness pivoted to face the forest. He entered his reality headfirst,
happy to be home, and happy for the glimpse gifted by the world above.

All I can do
is BE and seek to BE.
All I can do
is all that is required of me,
All I can do
can never be undone,
If I only allow
my 'self' to see,
All I can do
is BE and seek to BE.

CHAPTER
Twenty-Five

As he awoke to his dream, or perhaps from it, the soft wetness of the woman's lips poured into his mind. It jarred him to be back in this time, for he had not expected to awaken here with these feelings.

So much had been lived, and so much had been thought since he was last here, yet now he felt as if he had only been gone for an instant. Their lips parted, and he gazed into her eyes. She smiled and bit her lower lip softly, as he had noticed she was fond of doing. He looked around at the ancient landscape, which he had come to love. It was full of mystery, and this porcelain skin, and all things green and good. He really did love this woman standing before him, however irrational that seemed, and he thought he finally understood why.

When he had walked in this world before, his life on Earth had remained hidden from his emotional understanding. Only bits and pieces of who he had been had informed his sense of himself. His story there in that fallen realm had seemed but a fragmented dream which informed the real self here, in the land of fog and mist. Yet now he saw that this was not the case at all, for both worlds were leading him to the same recognition, and he could now recall the life he had lived vividly. What made his heart soar was the recognition that his love of these beautiful things was, in the end, a personal and faithful response to a greater truth beyond the varying contexts. It mattered not where he was, what he loved was the same, and he always responded to her essence, in whatever form it chose to take. The truth was that she was made for him, and he in turn for her. Wherever they were, he always found himself drawn to a focus on her energy, as if they were opposing poles of one great magnetic truth.

She looked at him and smiled coyly, deciding to speak.

"I am so happy you are a faithful soul," she said, her eyes lightening to gold, then brightening to green and on to blue.

He stared into the magic of her eyes, and tried to make sense of his mind, of this place, of this woman. She seemed to transcend everything else in his life. The blue of her iris was iridescent in the same way as had been the sky in the cloud world from which he had just come, and he searched in them for a glimpse of the veil that he remembered.

She too had come to understand through their journey and offered him a memory as proof.

"Do you remember what it was like, dancing in the moonstorm?"

Walker's eyes widened and welled with tears as he listened to her confirm what his heart had hoped for. She was aware of the magic as well, and this meant that he wasn't lost somewhere in a delusion of his own making. They had learned to play together here in this dreamscape, channeling the power of the forest into form and story. Then they reimagined it for one another and included each other in their world's collective design. Their entwined realities awarded something purer, more eternal, and more fundamental than any isolated world could ever hope to offer. It was this dreamscape that they played in, which allowed them to find their way to what they sought for their Earthly vision of union. Their worlds had begun to mingle now in the deepest sense. He knew that soon, he would find a way to share his idea with her back in the fallen reality, where new life always begins. It all made sense to him now.

"I love you Aiyana".

They both laughed quietly, as they stood overwhelmed, embracing, and staring at one another, as lovers do.

He looked into the center of her eyes and gazed upon the love he had committed his soul to forever. It *was* her, though her body was not exactly as he remembered it.

"Your face and body; they are different."

"So are yours," she smiled.

He looked at his hands and arms. He was much the same, but she was right, some things were different, subtle things.

"Mostly in your face. You were handsome there, and you are handsome here, but your features are slightly altered," she said as she traced his arm and shoulder with her fingers.

"As it is with yours," he said, stroking her skin attentively. "How can this be? Why did it take me so long to understand this? When did you know?"

"I felt it the moment your gaze first fell upon me. It's a feeling I learned to recognize from our walk on Earth, and I've been longing to find it anew here in this shared world. But I was only feeling it. I didn't fully understand until a moment ago. Whatever that means," she teased playfully.

"What is the significance of this stone?" he asked, removing the amber sphere from his neck so that he could look upon it.

"I do not know, but I carry one just like it in this place. It is here," she said, taking an almost identical piece of amber and hemp rope from a pocket in the white linen.

"I took it off because it began to get quite hot against my skin just before you arrived. It has only done that once before, long ago."

"Was it given to you by an old man with leaves and flowers all over him?" he asked enthusiastically.

"No." She giggled a little. "I have always carried it, since I was a little girl. But once upon a time, I was told that the stone and rope where not for me to wield, only to understand and cherish. Now I see why."

"Who told you this?" he asked.

She raised an eyebrow and smiled askew. "A tree." They looked at one another curiously, and Walker considered asking what she knew of the violet world, and of the gift he had left for her inside. As much as his curiosity pulled him, he recognized that in this moment, it was a mystery best left to imagination.

"Aiyana?"

"Yes, Walker?"

"I don't care about why anymore, only who. Let us find what we were meant to find this day."

He leant forward slowly and kissed her once again. They drank of each other deeply, their tentative beginnings yielding to passionate obsession with the physical representation of the other.

They separated lips for a moment and gazed into one another's eyes. Her lower lip quivered as he turned his focus toward her shoulder, running his hand along the tattered cloth that separated her resplendence from all that lay beyond. The fragility of her existence touched him deeply, and he marveled at how she had passed through the world's taint unscathed. Grace. His fingers pulled at the cloth, and it glided effortlessly off her shoulder.

Caressing the pastel surface of her exposed skin, he slipped the cloth from her other arm. His hands ran through her wet hair, pulling at the strands while he kissed down her neck to her trembling body, which was now completely free and exposed to the drops of rain which fell upon the hail laden ground. His lips met softly and repeatedly with the delicate skin along her side, as he took care to build the energy that he slowly guided back up and around in the way it wanted to flow.

He returned to her mouth, and they began to kiss again. His hand ran under the folds of linen that lay around his love's waist, massaging her inner thigh. She began to arch as he explored, begging him to find more of her.

Her body shuddered as she focused on the feeling of his energy as it began to trace across the entrance to her inner world. Beauty burst forth in the form of sound from her mouth as she absorbed his aspiration and intention. In her world, he had but one focus, the giving of pleasure. The single-mindedness of this reality inside of her was all that he longed to know, all that he longed to be. She was the point of existence, and he was the one who was meant to enjoy that truth. She was pleasure born of beauty, and he was the reason for both.

Aiyana felt him gently grasp the back of her neck with his hand, as he pulled her firmly toward him. He was looking straight into her eyes. It was time, and she welcomed this truth. "Take me there," she spoke in an airy whisper that mimicked her physical glory, itself second only to the majesty responsible for her design. He looked out at the place of which she spoke. The tree she had struggled to obtain the mushroom from was only a short distance away, now bathed in light.

A spire of heaven's power penetrated the forest canopy, illuminating the place where they would soon give themselves to one another in the sight of God alone. Walker lifted her up from the wet forest floor and carried her a few steps back to the fallen tree, stepping into the beams of radiance with her in his arms. He sat her down at its base, and together they climbed the massive root system until they were atop the fallen giant.

Without a word, she lay her 'self' down upon the moss that covered the spongy wood in the center of the light. She closed her eyes for a moment and focused deeply on her understanding of her own nubility. She felt her purity tangibly and in force, and she held it for a moment in her own mind before opening her eyes and projecting it outward for her lover, looking up at him with a request that he was designed to oblige.

The center of all existence lay before him, at the center of her design, itself the most beautiful of all things. As they gave their 'will' over to the power of an experience older than 'time', they soon found their bodies drawn together. He pressed into the purity, and it enveloped him in his totality. He was inside her world once again, but now they were together as it was meant to be. No longer was he simply exploring her world, now he was lost in it.

The pleasure he sought to give to her was now synergizing with the pleasure she sought to give back, and the delight they were both designed to feel. The rapture of their union filled the forest in the form of sound, as the energy flowing through her body overwhelmed her capacity to subdue. His sound was there for the forest to hear, but it was her voice that caused the trees to reflect on the true allure of human beings. From deep inside her, flowed the sweetest song the world has ever known. It was a song set to the pulse rather than to an external beat; linked to the timeless reality of holy union. At times, she laughed, and at times, she cried, and at others, she simply focused on the image of her body entwined with his own, but all of it was a song.

The world opened up, and together they saw across space and time to the land of their collective future. Aiyana was there in a muted blue world with a red blanket, waiting for him to arrive as he made his way toward the shore. With her was a little girl, and together they practiced the spectacle that they knew he would want to witness. The wind blew out to sea from the shore, and they stood together on a small dune, his woman with the red blanket, and the little girl holding a long strip of purple cloth much like a scarf. Together they practiced floating the fabric on the breeze in such a way that waves could be seen in the material. At the edge of the blue water were three small boys, gathering shells from the water's edge and piling them proudly near the dune.

The land itself was one bound in space, extending only to the near distance. Beyond the intimate landscape all was a blur, none of it mattered to them until such time as he would arrive. Until that time, each of them was devoted to but one cause, perfecting the scene of their reunion. All of existence for these souls was lived on this small strip of sand, gathering shells and floating linens on the breeze.

As they saw, so they understood. She would arrive there first, with their daughter, and their three sons, all of whom had just been conceived as dreams. There was no sorrow in this understanding, it simply was what was. They would go first, and he would be left behind for a time. They would wait for him there on that beach, wherever it was, and there Aiyana would teach their sons to gather shells and their daughter to float the colors and to dream of the day when daddy would return. They would be there, practicing faithfully as he emerged from the blur. This was their vision.

As they lived the scene of their reunion together there on that beach, staring into each other's eyes once again amidst the celebration of their children in a collective embrace, both began to remember the time when they had first conceived of these new souls in the world of trees; when they had come to see the vison of this future. The memory grew as they swam in one another's gaze, until they found themselves becoming subtly aware that the beach had gone, and the forest had returned.

He lay looking over at the azure of his lover's eyes as he ran his fingers lightly over the skin of her belly. She rested on her back, beholding the coniferous overstory above, overcome by a combination of exhaustion, euphoria, and the beauty of what they had just seen together.

"Do you understand what we just saw?" she asked, glancing over.

"I do. And you?"

"I understand," she said. "I will wait for you there for as long as it takes, and I will love every second of it, because I know it is part of our path, and it is a beautiful treasure."

"And I will find you there, and I will love every minute of my walk because I know where I am walking to."

"Do you want to go back with me now?" she asked, looking deeply into his soul.

"I am ready if you are, my love."

She reached into a pocket in the gown she had been wearing, which now lay crumpled next to her body. She removed the mushroom she had struggled to reach from the base of the tree that they now lay upon.

"I am not afraid," she said as she guided the wet hair from in front of her eyes with her finger, tucking it behind her ear. She handed the mushroom to her lover.

"Nor am I," he replied, taking the mushroom and breaking it in two as he gave thanks.

They sat silently, eating what seemed like a loaf of bread, beneath the most majestic forest canopy the world had ever seen, and thought of their walk. When the pair had finished eating, they lay against one another, speaking of a life once lived amidst a fallen world. They spoke of their ring, of their dolphin, of their seagull, and of their families. They recalled their most precious moments together in Missouri, England, Africa, and Italy, and they meditated on the ethereal consequence of their dance on the moon. They spoke of it all, and when they had finished, they closed their eyes and remembered.

The center of creation
Beauty manifest

Surrounded by her intention
Words cannot express

Lost inside of innocence
Immersed in heaven's dew

The center of creation
Two then one then two

Beauty within beauty

CHAPTER
Twenty-Six

Walker lay by his wife's side for hours, just holding her hand. They didn't speak. She too was awake, and just as content to lie in the dirt without words. The fire was long out, and they could see nothing in their secret world. Finally, he broke the peace.

"Love?"

"Yes?"

"We just conceived our children."

Aiyana let out a quick and audible breath as she encountered the transcendence of their future as a family. "I don't ever want to walk without you. But know that if I must, I will honor you, as well as all that we join together, however numerous we may become."

"I know you will, and I will honor you as well, and all that we may come to be."

"Thank you for being with me; for choosing this path."

"I wouldn't trade this for anything," he assured.

They sat together for another few minutes, just enjoying the peace between them.

"So, what do we do now?" Walker finally questioned.

Aiyana squeezed his hand. "I have no idea," she chuckled. "I suppose we start by returning to the world."

Now Walker was chuckling. "Right. Of course, 'The World'. So how do we get there again?"

"When Zach asked if we could find our way out, I'll bet you didn't consider waking up in the 'dark'," she teased.

The idea struck her as ironic. They were being asked to find their way back to the light of the world above without even a single ray of its power to guide them. It was much the same as living a life on Earth, searching for something beyond the physics at work in front of you, and with only those physics to employ.

Walker stood tentatively and helped his wife to her feet. It was a world unlike any they had ever physically experienced. Without their visual acuity to guide them, all they had was one another, and a vague memory of the way back.

In every moment as they felt their way around the room and back down the passageway, they remained physically connected. They responded to the uncertainty by drawing closer, and each of them used the other to gain some sense of orientation and balance. Again, the irony and parallel to the human condition struck Aiyana as profound.

The couple walked for perhaps half a mile but found nothing. They reversed direction after realizing that they had either missed the exit or taken a wrong passageway, but this reversal did not lead them back to the circular room. They soon became hopelessly lost, buried deep beneath a city at the bottom of the African continent. Mile after mile they wandered, but nothing familiar was found. They moved forward by feel, running their hands along the rock and dirt walls.

The flesh of the hands met each variation in the wall with trepidation and hesitation. Neither liked groping about for fear of what their touch might find. The scarcity and perfection of one another's bodies amidst the hardened earth drove them both to consider the rapture they were sharing in being drawn so close.

Eventually, exhausted and bewildered, Aiyana and Walker sat down and talked awhile, discussing light and love and meaning. All they had was one another, and their many hours without the light had made this clearer than ever. What was clearer still, was that this was enough. Neither was afraid because each knew that they would find their way back to the daylight; they always did. It was just a matter of letting themselves gravitate toward meaning, which would manifest in 'time'.

After many hours, they found sleep together once more, this time without the need for dreams. When they awoke, it was to the faint sound of something in the distance.

"Hello?" a woman's voice called out cautiously. "Anyone down here?"

"We're just over here," Walker yelled to the voice.

"You almost made it, just come a bit further," another voice called. It was a man this time.

Aiyana and Walker both stood and made their way as one toward the voices.

As they moved closer, they began to see a faint light. The light continued to brighten as they moved, until eventually, both could make out the figures of a man and a woman holding hands. The man held a small lantern.

"How was it?" the man asked in a friendly tone as he approached to shake Walker's hand.

"How was what?"

"Whatever it was you did down here."

"Are you with the Council?" Walker asked.

"No, I'm actually down here looking for gold."

The woman punched him in the arm.

"Sorry about him, he's always trying to be clever. My name is Lindsey, and this is Joshua, my husband. And of course we're with the Council. We've been waiting for you. Follow us."

Lindsey was an attractive woman, with a small, athletic body. She appeared to Walker to be in her mid-twenties, and though she carried an obvious wisdom, she seemed quite young in a way that was difficult to pin down. He might have even figured her for a teenager but for her poise. Lindsey explained that she too was an attorney, yet her aura was much more in keeping with what Walker imagined a flower child from the sixties must have been like. He liked her immediately.

Their new guides led them down another half-mile of passageway and then up through a vertical shaft with a ladder protruding just past the roof level of the main tunnel. They likely would never have found it without the lantern. The ladder led to a trap door, which opened into a small room. The room, in turn, had a false wall that opened into the basement of an empty house on the outskirts of Cape Town. They took a moment to collect themselves with a drink of water from the home's kitchen, and then stepped out the front door onto the street. The sun was just beginning to color the horizon, and both Walker and Aiyana basked in the way the celestial glow invigorated their other senses. The air felt crisp to the skin and smelled of sea salt and stone pines.

"We need to get moving if we are going to make it there on time," Lindsey said. "We best start walking."

"Where are we going?" Walker inquired.

"Würtzburg, Germany."

"Huh?"

"Well, we're walking to our car," she explained. "We'll drive from there to the airport, and then take a plane from that point."

"But our tickets aren't valid until next week," Aiyana protested.

"I'm sure we can get your flight bumped up," Joshua said confidently.

Walker thought this would be something akin to a miracle. Still, stranger things seemed to happen to them routinely. He and Aiyana followed without reservation, full of anticipation for something they had wondered about for over a year now.

Less than twenty-four hours later, they had already collected their things, received substitute airfare for their tickets, flown to Frankfurt, Germany, and then completed the journey to Würtzburg by train. Along the way, they had shared everything with their new friends, from the fallacy of recognizing 'evil' and 'darkness', to the wonders of the other world, and the story of the love Aiyana and Walker had found. Walker spoke at length concerning the dynamic nature of living and the disease born of static conceptualizations of dynamic realities. Lindsey and Joshua told bits and pieces of their own stories too, but mostly they insisted that their new friends work through their own so that they would understand it well for the Council.

By the time they had arrived in Würtzburg, Aiyana and Walker had covered more than either of them thought possible in such a short period of time. Yet there was still more that Walker wanted to work through.

Upon arriving in the city, Joshua and Lindsey insisted that they initially walk to a garden near the Marienberg Fortress and then continue to a location along the river hosting a beer festival. As they began the walk, they conversed about several key ideas, chiefly among them the state-of-affairs surrounding the international drug war, and the connection between fundamental rights, God, and the other world. Walker was desperately trying to finish explaining his conceptualization of reality before reaching the Council.

"So, Walker, tell me a little bit more about this 'Autonomy Tree' you mentioned in Frankfurt," Lindsey invited after they had finished exploring another point.

"It is a rather simple concept actually. I came to it in an effort to give a form to my proposed alteration of the so-called 'human rights' framework. As it turns out, it is closely aligned with other concepts that have been flirted with by the Supreme Court in the United States, as well as some of the Federal Circuit Courts there. The idea is that human beings are rooted in autonomy. It is autonomy that forms the entire support structure for everything that makes human life valuable. Every human rights concept that we currently have is merely a branch of a greater principle: the right to personal autonomy.

"To be human is to be capable of choosing to do that which should not be chosen. Forcing others to choose one path or another for themselves is thus a defilement of the human experience and an affront to God and the Natural Order.

"This is the really tricky part of what I have to explain to the Council because all of this is tied to the criminalization and demonization of man's desire to connect to the other world through drug use. Drug *abuse* is an undeniable problem in our society, and it is hard to stand for freedom in this area of choice, because of the havoc drugs can wreak on an individual's life, and also on society. But our current model of prohibition is not keeping us from drug abuse, rather, it is ensuring that almost all drug use is experienced as abuse, rather than as something targeted, intentioned, and beneficial. We have a broken model, and it broke because we allowed fear to convince us to set aside freedom of choice for a system of command and control. This approach is doomed to failure, as it pushes people to be deviant in their search for what lies beyond sobriety, and this sets up a culture of irresponsibility and meaningless pollution of the mind and body, driven by desires that could have been aimed at expansion and progression, if not for the way it was approached.

"As a result of our modern paradigms, most 'drug' use today is steeped in what we call 'evil'. We created this 'evil' with our minds and then married it to the power of the spirit world. The result is more death squads, drug addicts, overdoses, crime, terrorism, ruined families, and a war on freedom by a police state. And everyone believes that the trouble their conceptualization of drugs creates is evidence of how necessary that conceptualization is.

"Recently, some have suggested a right to drug use, and others have responded with absolute condemnation of the idea. Why would someone advocate for a right to something so harmful? Those in search of answers to the societal problem of prohibition are caught inside the parameters of a flawed framework, and because of this, even the suggested solutions are really just new problems. If we elevate drug use to the level of a 'right' alongside freedom of speech, it is predictable that many will assume drug use as an important part of life to engage with, leading some into addiction and death. Yet, how can we stand by the right of a mother to abort an unborn baby based on the need to protect a person's control of their own body, even when another person's body is clearly present in the equation, and then throw the same woman in prison for what amounts to nothing more than imbibing something she can grow in her garden?

The calculus is clearly flawed here.

"Once upon a time, people understood that governments are only institutions and that they are run by humans, not gods. When the government begins to protect its citizens from not only each other, but also from themselves, the worth of government ceases. In our society today, much has become confused, and we now find ourselves on the brink of cultural collapse, with crime and drug abuse running rampant. What is needed is a societal movement of individuals coming together to declare autonomous individuality as primary, building pressure on all institutional power to serve this basic human reality. This is the only way to a civilized and progressive society. If we don't find a way to do this soon, the world will descend into either chaos or tyranny.

"Society will never flourish inside of a focus on individually labeled 'fundamental rights'. Rather we must focus on the force that animates all rights. When we single out certain rights, we simultaneously diminish and enshrine the subject matter of those rights morally. We have no need to engage in this dangerous game, for the force behind all legitimate rights is the same, and this can be approached directly, which puts the focus back on what is centrally good. Allowing others to find their own path to what is best for themselves, in turn creates a responsible society in relation to drugs and everything else. No one wants destruction for themselves."

"When you say, force? You aren't talking about autonomy alone. You mean God, don't you?" Lindsey asked.

"I do mean God, but not in the traditional sense of the word. We don't need to go down the path of God and what God is to speak about autonomy and the fundamental force of Truth that creates it. It is important to understand first from a secular mindset if we are going to speak effectively into a world where many are opposed to ideas dependent on belief in God. Right now, I am only speaking about the values of modern liberalism and its focus on the so-called 'human rights'.

"At the center of all consciousness, we see a trait and principle upon which all awareness depends for its existence and for its evolution into what we call the future. This trait is the preference for the ordained order that is seen as 'self', as it stands against the fundamentals of entropy. Living beings defy the second law of thermodynamics, building a system of order with unique design. An individual's order is theirs alone, and it is fundamental to survival that we not set down our preference for our own design. In mind, as in body, as well as in spirit, we who possess conscious awareness of ourselves are rightly called to honor our personal existence, and the plan that ordained it, by insisting that our paths remain our own. If I am to evolve, it should be by my own awareness and choice that I do so. Anything forced onto me by others is a violation of my humanity. Thus, the surest thing about a human being is that he will seek to undermine whatever power another comes to exercise over him. He can do this honorably, or with deviance, but he will inevitably work to free himself of control.

"Freedom, liberty, choice, free will, independence, sovereignty, and self-determination, all hearken to this fundamentally moral center of the human condition. Perhaps above all others, the concept of autonomy is fit to describe this moral center. We are defined by our ability to choose our actions and reactions. Anything which attempts to remove this aspect of humanity is seeking to destroy humanity itself. Immanuel Kant spoke to this in The Metaphysics of Ethics, when he said that 'Freedom is the alone unoriginated birthright of man, belonging to him by force of his humanity.'

"The human rights movement has attempted to reign in the government's power to wage war on freedom, but the movement itself is flawed in its design, and contravenes its own principles by choosing what rights are given status. Much is made of certain individual freedoms and the need for their protection from the rule of the majority, while other freedoms are disregarded. One of the loudest hypocrisies of the human rights movement is the way it has failed to adequately stand up for the right to guide one's mind through life with the use of naturally occurring substances such as marijuana, the peyote cactus, psychedelic mushrooms,

Salvia divinorum, and many others.

"The rationales offered for why religion and drug use and sexual interactions are all treated differently when it comes to the intersection of freedom and law is wholly illegitimate.

"Perhaps even more disturbingly, however, is the way the human rights movement has begun to perpetuate the majority agenda through insistence on the labeling of concepts that it needs to keep fluid for the sake of individual freedom. Take the human right typically referred to as 'freedom of religion'.

"One of the first logical steps in evaluating issues regarding freedom of religion is to ask the question, 'What constitutes "religion"?' Arguably, one of the most persuasive answers to this question is that religion is defined by the group itself, or even the individual. This may seem absurd, but what good is a guarantee of freedom of religion if the majority religion is free to define what religion is, based on the tenants of its own beliefs?"

"I have thought about something like this. Have you ever read any of Judge Reinhardt's opinions, from the ninth circuit?" Joshua asked.

"You mean the right to privacy talk?"

"Yeah, that is what I'm thinking about."

"Yes, I have read a number of his opinions, and to be frank, I think he is getting at the same thing. What is behind the imperative of freedom? This is what we should be looking at."

"I agree," Lindsey interjected. "A right is meant to be a shield from majority cultures that are in control, not a sword that government can wield as yet another weapon to force their conceptions onto the minority. Championing the right to education for all while allowing the majority to define what is 'educational' is nothing more than government-sanctioned coercion of minority cultures and beliefs, hidden behind a veil of 'human rights.' Look at the horrors visited on Native Americans under this guise.

"In this context, the concept of 'human rights' acts as a sort of Trojan horse, doesn't it? It ushers in thought constructs that diminish freedom, hidden inside the assumptions inherent in the modern conceptualization of rights-based freedom itself.

"The same idea can be applied to social rights like 'mental health'. Mental health is intimately tied up in what are seen as culturally desirable modes of thinking, which necessarily vary with time and with cultural setting. We see this manifest in the way that various nations outlaw substances they deem dangerous, even though these things are seen as perfectly acceptable in other countries. Nations try to spread their cultural empire by bringing the preferred drugs of other nations under the umbrella of international drug control, while exempting the use of their own preferred intoxicants."

"This is my point. Once you define these things, they are not rights to freedom at all, but only rights to do what you have been told is legitimate by a definition. It is but another example of mankind trying to reduce the dynamic nature of reality and life to a static understanding. It is a death force operating in our world to give answers for our lives; that is to say, 'to give conclusions to our lives'.

"Therefore, we must avoid definitions as to what terms such as 'religion', 'education', and even 'mental health' actually mean, at least in relation to the ability of individuals to make claims under documents protecting these concepts as rights, if we are to protect minority views in a *de facto* sense. Dispensing with definitions, however, is a tricky business, and it would be wise to find another way. This is why going to the root of everything is necessary. If we do not, we find that we must either give up much of our freedom or descend into the madness of a world where each individual determines their own definition of what constitutes one idea or another, leading to the erosion of social order and the breakdown of shared understanding. We must focus on the principle behind the reason for the human rights movement in the first place.

"What is most disturbing to me about the current rights-based systems, is that they operate under a guise of logical legitimacy that allows those belonging to the majority culture to believe that they are being impartial. It is a systemic problem that plagues our progress because it is built into our paradigm. The solution is a shift into recognition of a generalized right to autonomy, subject to necessary exceptions, much the same as all human rights based in autonomous concepts are currently subject to exceptions."

"It's like the libertarians all say, 'My right to swing my fist ends where your face begins,'" Joshua offered.

"Precisely. In one sense it is that simple. But in another, it is vastly complex. See, there is an inherent flaw embedded in our way of thinking as human beings. Our understanding is born from a destructive process. To understand, you start with the whole and then begin to divide it by distinguishing. This is the opposite of life, which starts with that which is divided and seeks to unite it and then multiply and replicate it. With life, variation comes about organically only after cellular division, which is not a division of order, but rather a replication of it. The replication is what allows for the development of a structure of diverse evolutions that harmonize rather than war with one another. Yet our way of thinking is a decomposition of reality, rather than a growth of it. We are killing our very existence with our insistence on understanding it the way we do. Predictably, our world based on categories is fraught with divisiveness.

"Private behavior should be protected if the Government must actively search for behavior that is 'harming society'. If smoking is a problem for public health in the sense that an individual might cost the healthcare system money, then address this through adaptations to the way healthcare is provided, not through criminal law."

"But try to tell that to someone who has never studied it," said Lindsey. "It sounds illogical to them. They think that legalization means that you sell heroin in gas stations or grocery stores."

"I know, and this is the result of massive propaganda efforts by governments to cast the drug user as both a deviant and as a victim of some sort of devil's potion. The focus has been all about 'evil', and so 'evil' is what we have gotten. At this point, people can't think any other way. 'Drugs are evil, and we must destroy them before they destroy us!' This is the mentality that we insist on, and it is this mentality that ensures a large section of society will have a drug problem, while the rest of us will live with more crime and less freedom.

"The real rationale behind our war on 'drugs', if we are intellectually honest with ourselves, is a moral justification. The protection of public morality is the only rationale that can justify the war on 'drugs' legally in my mind. The issue here is not the same as health, safety, and welfare issues. With these, respect for personal liberty with 'drugs' actually serves these values rather than harms them, and prohibiting the use of substances actively harms far more than it helps. Morality, on the other hand, can be unquestionably harmed by private drug use."

"If you start with the premise that drug use is immoral, and you accept that it's immorality is an absolute rather than subjectively relative." Lindsey interjected.

"Exactly. The rationale holds up empirically given the assumption. But the assumption is the key. And this is where our whole society is coming apart. I'll put the question to you. Is it legitimate to dictate personal morality to others?"

Lindsey thought for a moment. "Well, the tenants of modern liberalism would dictate that an amoral position is precisely the result that we should strive for, and it is for this reason that modern liberal nations create Constitutions containing 'fundamental rights.'"

"Spoken like a true lawyer," Walker said.

"I try."

"You are right, though. If we are troubled by your point, the quarrel is with philosophical liberalism in general. The real debate is one between those devoted to an ethic of freedom and personal liberty, and those believing that there is nothing wrong with allowing societal norms to get in the way of individual choice, even where such choice is exercised privately. This debate extends well beyond drug policy and into all spheres of life, coloring issues such as gay rights, the right to die, the right to an abortion, and a host of others. These issues may not be inherently alike in every respect; however, they need not be to prove the point.

"With the exception of abortion, which would no longer be subject to similar analysis if a fetus were to be defined as being a person under the law, none of these modern 'rights' can be suppressed in the face of a generally recognized right to autonomy without an important and overriding justification. This is true because they do not concern the rights of others, only the rights of the 'self'. On the other hand, without recognition of such a generalized right, all these issues can be seen as legitimate subjects for regulation or prohibition based on majority will alone. There is no objective rationale as to why some should be favored while others are disclaimed."

"Why presuppose the need for majority will?" Joshua questioned.

"Very astute point. Why would we stop there? It's a slippery slope to allow for control of private individual behavior based on a morality imposed by an 'authority'. Most people get this point as it relates to some dictator, and yet this is exactly what we have in the absence of a generalized right to autonomy, because the definitions of specific 'rights' are proxy for the 'authority', and their definition defines the proper moral bounds of control over private individual behavior, allowing certain freedoms to be disavowed."

"There are those who would say that God gives morality, and this justifies the right to impose it," Lindsey offered.

"I would subscribe to that as soon as everyone agreed on the reality of God's will. Is that our world? No, our world is divided, and we kill one another over what we think we know about God and morality. Isn't it striking to you that no one stops to consider how out-of-step this is with belief in God; to lay claim to what God thinks about the inward personal choices of another human being? Isn't this usurping His role? It strikes me as a blasphemy. Isn't our place within ourselves? Is this not where the Spirit dwells? We were created in a bounded body under our own control. This one fact is, unabashedly, God's Will, for it is His created framework. So how then have we concluded that our personal conceptions of self-control belong in the minds of everyone else, even over their objection?

"By confusing the role of the church and public discourse, with the role of the courts and the police, society is ensuring that our future will consist of subjugation to rules that are predicated on contradictory and dishonest reasoning. This will always result in dissenters. These dissenters will fight the system, and in the end, the people who depend on it will suffer as nation states fight ever increasing numbers of their own citizens in wars of ideology. In the process, morality itself will be destroyed in our experience, because it will have been imperceptibly entangled with the law, and people will set aside their authentic personhood for the demands of increasingly extreme identity politics. It is a natural consequence of this type of shift in a society when it occurs, as individuals make efforts to obtain 'rights' by virtue of defining themselves into the 'correct' category of identity. In the end, all of this is of grave concern if morality is, in fact, as important as I believe it to be."

"'The Autonomy Tree.' I like it. It fits," said Joshua. "Here, I want you to read this," he continued. "We thought it might help with your proposal. It is the core of your conceptualization, if you will."

Walker stopped and reached out to take the coiled paper from Joshua, who produced it from a cardboard tube he had been carrying since leaving the airport. His companions stood still as Walker read it closely. When he had finished, he handed it to Aiyana. "It's entitled 'One Human Right,'" he said tersely.

Aiyana stood reading for a few minutes while everyone continued to wait. "This is amazing," she said finally, handing the paper back to Walker. "What a paradigm shift this is going to be."

"So, I didn't come here to tell you about this after all?" Walker puzzled.

"No, you did," said Lindsey coyly.

"But this puts it all into a framework that can be shared, it's superior to my babbling work."

"No, it *is* your work." Joshua was smiling from ear to ear as he spoke.

Lindsey smiled broadly as well. "Oh, did you think *you* were going to have to make this happen for yourself? Do you think this is really about *you*? You are central, but you are not just you. All of us who are together in the Truth are working this through."

He looked over at Aiyana and gave her a surprised grin. This was outside of their ability to control, she couldn't have manipulated this, unless she had gone behind his back and invited it in... Aiyana shook her head in denial. If she wasn't doing this, it meant they had somehow stumbled past their own collective conception and into something beyond.

Walker stopped and addressed Aiyana in the presence of their new friends. "I thought this was part of our inward experience of one another. I thought you must have planned for us to have the experience in the tunnel, it has your understandings of my mind written all over it. And we planned to work toward the Council this way. So how is it that this can be, 'real'? It can't be, can it?"

"I don't know. I don't understand how this can be either. Wait, tell me Zach was your idea?"

"Oh, crap."

"May I?" Lindsey offered.

Walker and Aiyana looked at one another as they shifted their bodies in acknowledgment. Aiyana took the lead on the response. "No matter how you came to be here, you must know what we are confronting with all this. This is true even if you are somehow only a manifestation of our imagination, but I don't see how that could be," Aiyana pondered. "And if you are from the collective beyond us, then you are only here because your capacity transcends our capabilities. That must be it. We've been coordinating this in order to create a work of art, something that lays the truth of our world's broken logic bare. Now we have it. Right? Where did this diverge?"

"May I?" Lindsey offered again.

"Sorry, go ahead."

"Your reality is not 'your reality'. Surely you understand this now after everything you've been up to together. You know full well what this is. Search your heart, Aiyana. It is what you sought to see as possible. 'Seek and ye shall find', remember? You wanted to see, and now you do. Knowing things intuitively and illogically isn't about deluding yourself when it's honestly done; it's about reaching beyond the plane of existence on which your physical 'self' is confined. Communication between planes of reality is more common than most people realize, you've just put it into a framework that allows you to put it to use. That is your gift."

"Listen," said Joshua. "The development of this new conception of reality will happen one way or the other, with or without your success. You are simply catalyzing what is already unavoidable in your world. You are a vessel Walker, as is Aiyana. You two will have the honor of bringing this forward, but it is not yours; you're just the pair who gets to find it. Once found, it cannot be unfound, and it cannot help but improve in its 'self' awareness among those who understand and believe in its conception. This document is just the start. Next comes the framework of implementation, and then other ideas. They won't end with you but will be taken up by others. All you must do is open your mind to collective history and experience, and then endeavor to find a way to bring everyone together around this fundamental recognition of what life is.

"You perceived this from the beginning. How do you think that is? You must persist, and it is your great privilege to do so, but do not fear failure. You cannot fail in the advancement of Truth. Once this is sparked, it will spread like a great cleansing fire. Many who confront it will be compelled to spread it and further develop its implementation, and in so doing, they will become part of this great transition process themselves."

They reflected on his point for a moment. Joshua was right, the ball was in motion, so to speak. If they had come to this, so too would kindred minds. Others were already toying with the same ideas in many capacities, some of them they even knew. Perhaps somewhere other people were penning the same words as their own. The idea would manifest in the collective mind of man, of this there could be no doubt.

"We really wrote this?" Walker asked as he held up the short work.

"Indeed," Lindsey said, smiling at their confusion over where they had managed to lose their own plot.

Aiyana contemplated this and then shook her head in disbelief of the complex ways the Spirit moved in her world. She smiled as she came to understand what all of this had really been about. Then she looked over at her lover to confirm what both of them had always known about the far shore and its mandate here on the near. "One Human Right."

Just one droplet of water

Blazing through the atmosphere

My gaze is fixed on the ocean deep

Vast and oblivious to my own small energy

Just one tiny spark

Falling from the Master's hand

Your gaze is fixed on the forest floor of man

Vast and oblivious to your own small energy

I will make a ripple at the leading edge of wind

I will make a ripple creating wave without end

You will start a fire to consume the hype of man

Fire burning lies so Truth can grow again

We will break man's shore apart and burn his twisted wood

Exposing man's half measures using Truth pure and good

The beauty of the Natural Law again shall pertain

Man's war against himself thus over; the hidden path remains

Come now the future with man undefined

Come now Return to sacred by design

Come now Return and come now the Light

Come now that which is

ALL THAT IS

Work through our life

CHAPTER
Twenty-Seven

Walker held the manifesto at arm's length. Those who penned the document had created a large sheet of parchment and then dyed it black. The words were brought to the page with a white pigment, in keeping with Walker's memories of the way things should be. In the low light of night, the letters glowed strongly. Phosphorescent paints? Walker laughed to himself. Why hadn't he thought of that? Perhaps it was Aiyana's idea?

Joshua and Lindsey were both smiling as they contemplated the conclusion to their time with their new friends. Each couple had come a long way together over the years, but their journeys as lovers were far from over. Joshua and his bride had long since arrived at a place of acceptance with their history, and they now lived in a state of readiness, awaiting the sign that would signal their return to a garden once lost.

Walker and Aiyana, on the other hand, were only beginning their ascent of the cliffs of Reality. The great trials of their life together lay ahead of them, and they still needed to work through an important question if they were going to be as centered as they would need to be for the coming trouble. They were pulling the curtain back on the fallacy of the current paradigm, and the powers that had built the current framework would not take kindly to success in this. Those powers were already preparing to move on from their failing systems, in favor of new methods of control. They were aware of the growing movement of Truth supplanting the foundations of their false moralism and desperately needed a new methodology of deception.

If those seeking to control and limit were to keep their power, they would have to find a way to quell this spiritual revolution. Already they were fomenting division among the races and conjuring further disorder by challenging the natural law and stirring humanity's bend toward tribalism. Rather than continuing to fight the growth of this potent drive for freedom, the world's power brokers would run with the movement, and push the idea that it was natural law that was the enemy of freedom. This then would cause the movement to destroy itself, and in the chaos of a world gone mad, the people would cede power back to the architects of the control scheme. They also had a new weapon to deploy that promised to change the game forever, artificial intelligence. In the minds of all those in the know, the days of those who would oppose control were nearly at an end.

The future of mankind, and indeed of the Earth itself, was about to shift dramatically as the quest for complete social control collided with the power of the human spirit and its desire to remain free. The forthcoming world would not be what most assumed, and save for the solution forming through those in service of The Light, the human legacy would surely come to its end. There were those that sought to end human reproduction engaged in by choice or 'accident', and though it was possible to make such an evolutionary leap as a species in a bona fide manner, few were arguing for the necessity of such bona fides in the approach. Rather, those who thought they knew, intended to end the magic of human reproduction wholesale, anywhere it was possible.

There were many tactics that could be used to accomplish this, but the first step was to bury the value of the reproductive act itself. Already the world had mostly forgotten the poetry and the music behind the acts of sexual encounter, and the power that physical union held when approached with reverence for what it actually was in human experience. Soon, there would be few who would understand the majesty of a sexuality caught up in the desire to bring about new life, and sex would be indulged almost exclusively for its own sake.

Even casual sex is wonderful to experience, and it was more effective to use the love of sex to end widespread procreation than it was to fight directly against it. Thus, it was vital to the plans of the powerful that the world's people see the creation of a child as a burden or even curse, rather than for what it truly is. In truth, a child is the embodiment of an exalted energy which materializes as a direct consequence of a highly refined desire between two souls seeking to unite as one through sexual fusion. When done well, the making of a child is the most beautiful experience a human can have. Abuses of the power behind this magic, however, are perhaps the most fundamentally toxic acts that a person can engage in against their own well-being, and the well-being of others.

Walker and Aiyana still understood the power and purpose of their own love for one another and made no apologies for the sexual charge that pushed them toward the creation of children. They welcomed this evolution of life and sought earnestly to incorporate their purpose in the world with their adventure as sexual beings. Their love for one another drove them to desire such sublime meaning for others as well, should they wish to seek it. They understood that all who would seek to hide or denigrate the splendor of sexual apogee and its connection to true freedom, were the enemies of mankind. The same passionate love that drove them together in body, mind, and spirit, was the same love that would spark the great fellowship of the future, comprised of those willing to stand in the way of the tyranny of reproductive and teleological control. Though each of them would be central to the resistance, it would be those born of their union who would usher in humanity's return to Eden.

"So, are you finally ready to answer the question then?" Joshua waited for Walker to connect something in his mind.

The enquiry had caught him off guard, and he hesitated to respond for a moment, trying to make sense of how he was intuiting the substance of the matter.

Lindsey smiled and interceded in their game. "Are you a Christian or what?" she teased.

"Don't you already know?" Aiyana teased back.

"That depends. Do you?"

Walker gave the best answer he had.

"In a manner of speaking."

"Which manner is that exactly?" Joshua laughed. "It's never a simple yes or no with you, is it?"

"No, no it's not. Except for just now."

"That wasn't a simple yes or no, either."

"I suppose you're right," Walker admitted, now laughing at himself a bit. "It's just that when someone defines his or her 'self' as a 'Christian', what exactly does he define himself as? The Catholic vision? The Presbyterian or Baptist alternative? There are thousands of denominations laying claim to the definition. Or is it perhaps simply as someone who believes a person cannot find eternity without specifically learning about and then accepting the historical figure of Jesus as savior?

"Labels are reductionist, and this runs counter to true spirituality in its complexity. To me, the idea of being a Christian is such a loaded concept that I cannot answer the question with a simple yes or no. Either answer carries implications that are untrue of me, due to the meddling of men in the concept."

"It's a perfectly fine disclaimer. But what answer does your mind play into?"

Walker thought hard for a moment, seeking sincerely to proclaim his true belief. He had struggled to make sense of the religious ideologies around him his entire life. So many of them had become lost in themselves, and yet certain core truths were the foundation of Walker's understanding. He knew his answer was being professed to more than just the company with him.

"I was baptized in the name of the Trinity as a boy at the age of twelve, and I professed the belief I had been taught at that time. As I grew into adulthood, I came up against the fact that my conclusions were born of what others had concluded for me. This became unsatisfactory to my mind, and it led me away from faith and into near atheism. I then came to an authentic faith in the existence of a reality beyond myself, through direct experience of the transcendent and immortal. I knew it simply as 'The White'. This experience found me, in my lost state, and brought me into the presence of Awareness. This led me back to the Truth underlying the faith I had once professed, only now based on a solid foundation.

"As my own awareness grew, I came to see the shortcomings with Christianity as it is often taught. Many have counseled to maintain faith in a historical occurrence that no one can confirm for themselves, as a way to justify faith in the Christian concept of salvation. There is nothing wrong with the historical narrative of Jesus, nor in believing that this history redefined our relationship with God. What is problematic, however, is the insistence on an understanding of evidence in a reversed circular fashion, because it opens the doorway to rejection of the Gift based on mere worldly rationales. Some choose to believe, others to reject. How did we turn the reconciliation of creation and Creator into another dualistic process of choice between polarized opposites?

"Belief in a historical narrative does not validate faith in the history underlying that narrative. Rather, it only validates the concept as recorded, whether true or not historically. However, a personal, authentic understanding of the nature of Transcendent Reality, born of inward seeking, does indeed counsel for faith in the sacred historical narrative of The Gospel.

"Mankind cannot reconcile himself to the Infinite and Eternal due to his limited nature. Even Yoga, which teaches that we are currently part of the Infinite, recognizes that we must engage in a process to come to awareness of this, through the unfolding of time. This unfolding can only occur by the lesser being reconciled to the greater, not vice versa. Enlightenment only occurs when the greater Truth born of the original whole, comes to manifest in the broken and lesser, 'made reality' of the finite realm.

"Thus, the reality that God must enter into his own creation to provide

Grace, is fundamental, not merely historical, though I believe it is also this. The historical authenticity of The Gospel lies with the manifestation of a cosmic reconciliation of the fundamental schism between finite and infinite. He who has taken his finite mind through the infinite doorway sees the chasm that his thinking has placed between himself and the beyond. He understands by force of irrefutable observation. All that is left for him to do is apply what he has been shown on the far shore to his understanding of the life he lives here in the looking glass.

"It is all well and good to believe in a history through power of 'will', but I believe in the historical narrative of Emanuel myself for a very different reason. I believe the story because the very concept has God's fingerprints all over it. If something is fundamental to the nature of the far shore, you can be sure it will manifest here on the near.

"So, this should make me a so-called Christian on the one hand. On the other, I believe that God can be found inside the mind, and through shamanism, and through a focus on light rays. This would prevent many from including me into their identified brotherhoods. Yet, I cannot abandon my understanding, for it seems to me to be superiorly sound, and far less fragile, in keeping with what Divine understanding should be. For if a man were to find a way to disprove the history of Jesus as fact, where would that leave those placing their hope on facts concerning history? Transcendent Truth must be transcendent of fact and history, not dependent on them.

"For my mind, such a proof would not be a proof at all, because I draw from something outside of history. Any claim as to the necessity of historical evidence to justify my belief in salvation through Grace is absurd, because history is only an outgrowth and representation of that which is already true beyond the veil. This is why the story is reborn over and over again, no matter how many times men attempt to wipe it out.

"Why should such cosmic good news be seen as preclusive to inward exploration through dhyana, or through connection to plant guides? The study of philosophies and theologies born of such explorations gives us windows into the nature of the Divine Reality responsible for the existence of our world here in the mirror. If you step into that space, you will experience the nature of God yourself, and you will find that It is all Grace."

"So, it's yes then. You just refuse to have it defined for you lest you miss the God behind the story." With this, Joshua seemed to proclaim a finding of some kind, rather than a mere opinion.

Walker thought for a moment and then gave the response over to Aiyana. She looked up as she began to speak.

"What is required above all else is a heart in search of what should be, of what is right and good. Judgment is essential to finding the way. Judgment is a good thing, so long as you do not allow it to grow into self-righteousness.

"Take Christ's words, which you referenced earlier tonight.

"'... Ask and it will be given to you; seek and you will find; knock and the door will be opened for you. For everyone who asks receives; the one who seeks finds; and to the one who knocks, the door will be opened.'

- Luke 11:9-10

"Now, consider the Tao Te Ching:

"'This is why the ancient masters honored the inward path of Tao. Did they not say, 'Seek and you will find'? 'Err and you will be forgiven'? Within, within... this is where the world's treasure has always been.'"

- Verse 62

She continued, "Walker and I cannot *know* whether-or-not the Gospel of Christ can be followed alongside a study of Taoism or Buddhism or Shamanism, or any other exploration of that which is seen as spiritual, we can only *believe* that it can. But I am not required by God to be capable of knowing such things in order to confront them. I am a spirit first and foremost, and I exist to learn about living.

"The point of life is to develop into an autonomous moral agent, so that the soul may understand what it ought to seek when the physical reality passes. Life is the proving ground of the soul, where it is shaped and tested and strengthened for whatever it is that is to come. The lynchpin to all of this is Grace, or the ordained reality that we need not earn our way. Instead, we must only seek to find it by acknowledging our divine heritage, which was freely given to us by the Power behind it all. We do this not by succeeding in every effort, but rather by choosing to get up and try again after each failed attempt, celebrating the gift of an infinite number of chances to find the way.

"Most pursuits of Truth coalesce and hold one another up, toward recognition of common principles, which we might call the Natural Law. From this vantage point, The Gospel is only stepping in alongside these other traditions and intellectual enterprises and adding one simple, vital, and complementary assertion. The assertion is that no pursuit of right principles or high ideals can lay hold of God, not even Christian ones.

"The only doctrine that cannot exist in symbiosis with the doctrine of Divine Grace is the one that sets itself up to destroy spiritual pursuits. It is only they who claim that spiritual things are illusory who cannot evolve. The reason for this is simple; they have precluded their own ability. Jesus said it thus:

"'And so I tell you, every kind of sin and slander can be forgiven, but blasphemy against the Spirit will not be forgiven. Anyone who speaks a word against the Son of Man will be forgiven, but anyone who speaks against the Holy Spirit will not be forgiven, either in this age or in the age to come.'

- Matthew 12:31-32

"We are here, therefore, to admit of a beyond, and to seek it out by living in a way that calls us toward it while refraining from seeing ourselves as being entitled to it through our actions. We do so not by formulating laws and rules, but by opening to what life has to teach us in all of its complexity. This is why freedom is the sacred basis of humanity. Any other foundational substrate for society is a type of sinking sand. We were made as individuals, and if we forget this, society can only become a slave master.

"There is only one True Law, and it is beyond our ability to understand because it is alive. Our arrogant attempts to control the lives of others, based on dead formulas that we make up, have no place in a world focused on the right and the good. It is a raping of the ordained sovereignty of each soul within itself."

The power of the comment caused them all to stop and look at her. Joshua smiled and tipped his head in a way that conveyed his acceptance and surprise at the intensity of her assertion, and then turned to look Walker in the eye. "There is a reason behind the truth she speaks. It is circular and perfect. Can you see it? Do you understand why your quest to overturn man's current paradigm is actually a *sacred* task?"

Walker gave a curious smile as he considered the way Joshua seemed to be calling his mind toward a lesson from his life's journey. He understood that he was being given an opportunity to speak his own beliefs into corporate awareness.

"The essence of the Creator of all things is dynamic," he began. "Thus, so too is His creation. Being made in the image of God is less about physical form and specifically about existing for the purposes of being both a dynamic, and a guardian and missionary of the dynamic cause. When that which serves the 'darkness' seeks to define man out of his heritage of 'Being', those who have invited the Truth to live in them will find themselves called to unravel the lies embedded in whatever clever logic his enemy has concocted. This is the how and the why behind each of our journeys. It's more of a natural phenomenon than a religious concept."

"Yes," said Joshua, now looking overtly sly. "The simple truth is that we are all incapable of getting everything correct. We cannot do so, precisely because there can be no formula for a dynamic reality. We cannot help but err in our understanding of a shifting framework that we cannot control. Perfection evolves, though its core never changes, and we are stuck trying to catch up to what that means.

"I know you understand this, and hope you see that you have now come full circle. Cultivate your own spiritual connection to the Creator, and do not despair the loneliness that comes from failing to join the crowds in their celebrations of self-justification and moral authority. What matters is what you recognize about your need for Grace, and your intention to submit yourself to the Gift that the Maker of your origins bestowed upon you before you were even born. You believe and you accept, and this is all that is required of you. People are remiss to esteem themselves capable of anything more. It was important for both of you to solidify all of this in full view of the assembly."

Mind leapt backward in time. The 'assembly'. The 'collective'. The 'I AM'. They understood the thread fully now.

"I think the two of you have done what you came here to do," Lindsey observed. "It is good that you have foretold of love. It is good that you chose to believe in its power. It will bring you great blessing in short order."

Lindsey had a way about her that communicated things effortlessly, and her simple phrase reached the mind saying much more than the words she had spoken. She was inviting them to remember.

Walker looked at her together with her counterpart as they continued to walk, hands bridging the space between their bodies and swaying playfully. He struggled to connect an emergent thought. He knew these two from somewhere.

Joshua interrupted his concentration. "The nature of thought *is* about to change, Walker. You did not come here to tell us that, we invited you here to confirm it for you, and to help the two of you to do something even more important, which you did beautifully. There are many halves in this realm, but few true wholes. Through your journey, others have been conceived in spirit."

Joshua laughed outwardly at Walker's confusion while he openly teased the gift God had made for him. He pulled at Lindsey's clothing and then nudged her away as her body gravitated towards him with each tug of the cloth.

"I can't believe it's really them?" Aiyana said as they smiled openly at her realization. "I've often thought about you on that beach and the vision of love that you gave to my husband. And here you are, Adam and Eve. You clean up nicely, both of you."

They chuckled together, both looking skyward now.

"Oliver said that you really went to bat for us," Lindsey informed as she recalled her gaze from the heavens and offered it to Walker. "We both enjoyed knowing that someone saw through to us that day."

"Oliver?" Walker said, confused. The young man hadn't struck Walker as particularly important to his journey when they had spoken on the beach in Mondello. But then again, neither had many others who had played a role in his ability to understand. Somehow, even as he had believed that he was imparting direction to the lives of others, they had all come together to make his own growth possible. The collective aspect of consciousness wasn't only a possibility, it was the very stuff that people thought of as ordinary existence and interaction. It was going on all the time. Most bizarre of all in Walker's mind, however, was the way other intellects had knit these things together with himself and his wife, speaking into their reality years before they had even decided to invite them in. The complexity of his life experience, even if he and Aiyana had somehow concocted it, boggled his mind. He understood why some believed that reality was just a simulation.

"Walker, I want to leave you with something to guide you as the two of you seek to bring this work to the world," Joshua offered. "We spoke of Taoism earlier?"

"Yes."

"I am sure you must have come across this in your study. The Tao says that:

'If a person seems wicked, do not cast him away, but instead awaken him with your words. Elevate him with your deeds. Requite his injury with your kindness. Do not cast him away, cast away his wickedness.'"

"I am quite fond of that saying," Walker assured him.

He continued, "The Tao also says that:

"'when two opponents meet, the one without an enemy will surely triumph.'"

"Do you understand what I am saying about this war that man has concocted to avoid himself?"

Walker smiled back. "We are to love our way out of this hateful destruction of the war on freedom, and we are to do this by recognizing that we don't need to be against anyone or anything, as long as we are for one another. If we can find a way to do this, to truly see others and love them enough to allow them their own path, while demanding they do the same for us, then and only then can we hope to guide one another to recognition of higher ideals and higher planes of thought, act, and deed. A moral society will necessarily follow from a population of people who put one another's freedom first, but not for its own sake, rather for the sake of giving humanity a chance at the opportunity to avoid tyranny and find authentic morality.

"Opposing others by telling them they are wrong, only deepens the problems for them, and exposes you. The right path is to give freedom to all, and then let the light shine right through the darkness. The darkness of humanity cannot stand in a free society, because the light shines everywhere, and where people are allowed to choose their own path, they eventually turn toward the light. What disrupts this system is the imposition of control, where one ideology threatens the existence of another. This is the cause of almost every major war in history. Yet despite all that is currently going wrong in the world, the very pressures seeking to subjugate the spirit of mankind are beginning to cause an awakening in people as to their true nature.

"As the Tao says: 'Only when your sickness becomes sick will your sickness disappear.' I would say that the war on freedom, much like the war on 'drugs', has begun to fall ill. People are waking up to the falsity and rejecting it just based on the taste of the thing. It is time this disease of 'evil' was laid to rest. It is time for the new era, the era of spiritual freedom."

Walker paused for a moment, feeling ready to finish with his response.

"Can I ask one question before you go?"

"You just did." Joshua teased.

Walker grinned askew, looking at Lindsey, who was rolling her eyes.

"Okay, I need to ask one more then."

"Very well."

"A woman from another realm once told me that man had bound himself to his fate as soldier against himself and the light when he chose to perceive two where there was only one. She said that the spiritual existence of man is being sucked out and replaced with knowledge. What she explained is really just a very deep conception of the story of the Garden of Eden. We as people chose to set down our innocence and take up knowledge of good and 'evil' in order to be like God. But what of Grace?

"There can be no dynamic reality which cannot evolve, so shouldn't it be possible to evolve the role of knowledge inside ourselves? Clearly, it cannot simply be eliminated. If it can be seen for what it is, rather than for what it is not, can it then become the basis for a new future? Might this be the basis for an enlightened decision to return to the innocence of Eden? What happens when knowledge ceases contemplation of the false?

"Perhaps all that separates us from our true home is our inability to realize that we can return at any time so long as it is in humility and service to Truth. The Christian concept of 'the fruit of the tree of knowledge of good and evil' may be forbidden precisely because it is not knowledge at all, but rather a false conception which poisons our ability to understand Truth and our ability to BE.

"What if we married knowledge to the innocence and beauty of a spiritual existence? Might men and women come to understand many things, and yet refrain from worshiping their understanding? The enchantment of the human experience lies with the fact that there should and always will be a place for wonder and mystery. Might true enlightenment, therefore, be found through understanding the beauty and the necessity of innocence?

"What I am trying to ask is: are we as human beings capable of coming to understand that everything is not about understanding, even though we approach this idea by trying to understand it?"

Lindsey smiled openly as she counseled further. "We cannot deny what has been in Truth, but we can evolve our understanding of what has occurred. We can't go back, but we can return. We find our way to our origins not by retracing our steps, but rather by completing the circle begun so long ago. An understanding of the essence of knowledge *will* replace the worship of knowledge that has come to pass, and worship will be reborn as it once was, focused on the purity of the Whole, and without cognizance of 'evil'. Yet, I cannot tell you how man comes to find this truth. That truth is still emerging. What I do know, is that we only have ourselves to blame for becoming lost, and that despite this, all of us can rejoice at the good news; God has made a Way for us to come home."

Aiyana's face softened as she began to quote the Tao.

"'Words born of the mind are not true. True words are not born of the mind. Those who have virtue do not look for faults. Those who look for faults have no virtue. Those who come to know it do not rely on learning. Those who rely on learning do not come to know it.'

"Methodologies of thought cannot transcend themselves," she continued. "But we are not bound by them simply because we try to utilize them to reach others. We can paint a picture with thought, and this picture can hint at another world that cannot be explained. The point of the picture is not to describe what is beyond thought to others, it is to help them understand that something is out there, beyond the confines of their limited understanding, and to help them discover the serenity that comes with looking for it. The way I see it, man cannot help but discover the truths of which you speak. It's just a matter of timing. Grace has ordained that we shall go home, the question is 'when will we be ready to go?'"

Aiyana put her hands into her pockets. "The Tao is only words, but the mind is led by the words to ponder that which is not words. This is their power."

She turned to look at Walker, reaching out now with both hands as they stopped and turned to face one other, while Joshua and Lindsey continued on alone, toward a future of their own making.

"They spark an inquiry into Truth. They are not the essence of Truth, only the explanation that helps one to feel it. The Truth is Love, the Love that we try to describe with the word 'love' but never can. The world has tried to deny this, but it has not yet completely forgotten. Only Love can see us through to the dream we all share."

Aiyana began to sway playfully as she considered something she was ready to share with him. "Speaking of dreams, I had another one just the other night. Do you remember the way the light bathed us as we made love in the forest?"

"You know that I do."

"I love sharing my dreams with you. But that moment isn't meant to remain only in the world of dreams. We are supposed to search for that experience here. Do you know what that means?"

"California," he said, smiling broadly.

"Absolutely, and there's no time to waste. I can feel tomorrow's rise. It's close. Let's leave tonight."

Aiyana turned and looked in the direction of their now absent guides. "I didn't realize what this was about until we began our walk this evening. I thought it was just about us and our contribution. After all, it was our ideas and our work that led us here. But that isn't it at all. This was about the nature of man's reality moving into a new era through a channel that we embody. We experience our journey personally, and so we feel that we act to create. But in truth, Creation is working through all of us who have chosen to be open to the power beyond. I am so happy for this experience. I knew that something like this was out there for us to connect to. We are all 'part of' and 'because of' the Truth, which has ordained that the future is still open, and Love is the way forward. We can only imagine where all of this will lead, but I know how I am going to live regardless. Grace has gifted this to me."

Walker couldn't have agreed more. Love was the answer, and love was what he had fallen into. He had fallen first in meadows and parks, and in the presence of dolphins and seagulls. He had fallen further on the beaches of the Cinque Terre, then later in the mountain towns of Lauterbrunnen and Mürren. He had fallen amidst ferns and trees and to the sound of songs on Earth and songs born of Earth's moon. In many ways, he had continued to fall, but now he had come to the place where the gravity of Yin would finally pull him inside. She would allow his vision to enter into the nucleus of her own design, so that together, they might find a way to conjure a new awareness from beyond the Veil. He was going to be a father, and his love of Aiyana was the reason. Finally, they would become one flesh.

CHAPTER
Twenty-Eight

In the blink of an eye, they found themselves speeding north on Highway 1 out of San Francisco, bound for the land of mist and fog. Each could feel the rapture of the moment that called to them as they approached, yet they were still miles away from the place that would match the time. They were both riveted to be this alive again, pushing into a feeling. They knew that soon; they would make forever incarnate.

Their trip consisted of several days of exploring in the Coastal Redwoods of Humboldt State Park, and then several more days of discovery inside the Sequoia National Park in the Sierra Nevada Mountains. Each day was a scene reminiscent of the dream they had shared, and each night was a celebration of the day just lived. Their time among the trees was special down to the last day, but it was on the first that their child's physical life came into being.

That day was spent wandering the paths near Bull Creek, deep in the Redwood forest. The air was thick with fog, and the forest seemed a memory. Now and then it would rain, and then the sun would break through. Then the rain would again pertain. All the while the couple walked among the trees, marveling at the beauty and wondering at their fortune.

As the day began to wear thin and the spirit of the moon rose even amidst the day-beams, they found themselves at the edge of a mighty stream which was flowing strongly with the water of several days' rain. The powerful stream was a veil that separated them from another world, though they had not known this as they searched for the bridge that they were told men had once built across the mighty waters. They eventually found it, lying in ruins at the request of a flood that had long since come and gone. The flood had destroyed man's bridge, but it had created its own just upstream, where a mighty Redwood had fallen when the bank had been scoured from beneath its roots.

The pair stepped out onto the mighty tree hand-in-hand, lost in God's creation. They crossed the crystal-green waters on the body of the fallen giant, and as they did, it began to hail. Walker stopped and dropped his wife's hand as he remembered, turning to look at her ravishing form, clothed in white linen, ice, mist, and sun. She gazed at him with blue eyes through the spaces between cords of hair that dripped as she stood motionless. Her chest rose beneath her sodden cloth covering in an exquisite rhythm, her slow breaths appearing as bursts of visible vapor and life while bits of ice bounced off her body. As they absorbed God's world, it struck them that everything was as it should be. They both began to laugh at the pleasure each felt standing in the midst of a hailstorm, which had undoubtedly sent every other human being in the park running for shelter.

They knew that no one would ever fully understand what this sign meant to them. To find such a moment in time, at the very point of transition over such a stream, on this specific type of tree, after all that they had dreamt of together, was beyond explanation. Nobody would ever believe them, at least not entirely. They would all say it was embellished. This is what made it so special. It really was beyond belief.

They traversed the remainder of the ancient wooden portal to the land of the opposite shore, and as they did, the ice ceased falling. They soon found themselves lost in a dream of a script without time.

The forest on this distant shore was steeped in rainy fog, obscuring everything beyond the intimately near. The tree in front of us was a grand specimen, perhaps two thousand years old, and those just ahead of and behind us were only slightly younger. I had been here before, but a part of me had been missing, a part that had now been found. She squeezed my hand as I placed my other against one of the ancient trees. It was so clear that it was alive, so clear that it had a soul, whatever that was. Aiyana could feel the energy flow through me, and her free hand rose to meet the wet wood of another giant being, which stood only a few feet away from the body of the other. The two great trees had grown closer and closer together across the millennia. Eventually, they had arrived at a place where a man and a woman could bridge the space between as they walked along the path that led through their union. This was their purpose in this place, it seemed.

As her hand met the history of the wood, energy poured through our bodies and a vision arced between our minds, conceiving several more lives. Her caress was lighter, softer, subtler, and the energy leapt more easily for her. We felt our new conceptions as surely as one feels the life-giving power of water when drinking deeply after a hard day in the sun. Instead of four, there would now be many. I looked at Aiyana in awe of her power; she was closer to God than anyone I had ever known.

We continued the walk, and as our hands left the ancient wood, the trees contemplated the connection they had found with one another through our union, opening to a vision of their rebirth together as several new lives.

The forces of 'violet' and 'moon' were rising in the forest, and with them came an increasing sense of completion. The beginning of something was upon us, and we could feel it amidst the familiar drops of indigo moonlight, which now found their way through the dense forest canopy so far above. Luminescence trickled from the heights in drops and small streams, which showered the forest floor in a beguiling play of color and flow. Here, the essence of light was caught up with the essence of water. It was thick, and it felt wet to the touch.

I crouched down near the base of a tree, where a small plant was growing. Smiling at my friend and guide, I stroked a large leaf which possessed a healthy sheen that seemed to radiate energy from within.

"Twelve leaves," I said to my bride.

She smiled and reached for my hand. "Show me how to be yours."

I took her hand, and together we walked to another tree in the near distance, which had but one purpose for us in mind. We marveled at the way our feelings had led us to this particular forest champion and at how we already knew what it would provide.

Approaching on the far side, we saw that she had been hollowed out by fire. We stood for a moment, taking in the immensity and idyllic serenity of her form. She was the most beautiful tree either of us had ever seen. We placed our hands on her wooden skin and felt her energy flow through us and among us. Then we bowed our heads, and together we entered her world.

The space inside was warm and moist, but the ground was dry and covered in a bed of soft conifer needles. We lay down together and contemplated the path. Good could never be forced; it had to be yielded to by the individual out of love for the goodness itself. We were both ready to yield to the power and beauty of the other's perspective, but it was Aiyana that was designed to live the experience of surrender. It was her viewpoint as Yin that was truly aware of what it meant for Yang to finally see and acknowledge the sacred nature of her resplendence. It was she who understood the delicacy forming the center of everything that each of them hoped could be awakened inside of her. She breathed the misty air deeply in and began to open herself to his intention.

Light penetrated the entrance to our world inside the cave, casting a violet spell onto my lover, causing his pleasing form to glow in the dim light. He removed my white linen gown and gazed on my wet body, soaking in fog and mist. The shier parts of my nature allowed for this only with him, and I marveled at the way he had disarmed my modesty and fears of inadequacy. He loved everything about me, every shade and every line. In his gaze, I was perfected, and there was no doubt or shame left in me.

Droplets of water traversed my taut, pale youth in a celebration of the fantasyland that all water dreamt of, trickling through my hair, and then racing across the smooth expanses of my porcelain skin. I giggled a little as I looked at him and considered his perspective of me. It felt so silly, and yet nothing had ever felt deeper. He smiled back, the way he always did, knowing and accepting. I was so in love with this man and his vision of me, his perspective changed my world.

The center of all existence lay before my lover, and that lay at the center of beauty, itself the most beautiful of all things save for the way his form was made to nest into my own. As we gave our control over to the power of an experience older than 'time', we soon found our bodies drawn together. He pressed himself into my purity, and soon he was lost inside of my world.

The pleasure he sought to give to me was now synergizing with the pleasure I sought to give back, and the pleasure we were both designed to feel. I reached up and took his face into my hands, guiding his gaze deep into my eyes. I wanted him to see the depths of what I had come to feel. From deep inside my soul flowed the sweetest song the world has ever known, and it caused the forest to reflect on the true allure of human beings. He experienced me in awe, and thus, I was in awe of him. The single-mindedness of the reality inside of me was all he longed to know and all we longed to be. He had caused me to open to the miracle that we were now living, and I loved him for this gift. There was nothing sweeter than the Truth we had found together. I was pleasure born of beauty, and he was the reason for both.

Hours later, as we lay together contemplating all that had just been joined, we drifted amidst talk of love and God and how our souls had come to find their place together in eternity.

I curled my leg over Walker's body and laid my head on his chest as we floated through one another inside the living cave. "I always knew you would find your way through to my soul. I just didn't think it would come in a dream," I voiced.

"Perhaps this is the dream," he replied, smiling uncontrollably.

"Perhaps it is," I chuckled. "Or perhaps there are no dreams, only different realities that we have trouble understanding."

"I love dreaming with you, Aiyana."

"And I with you, Walker. I promise I will always honor what we have been given."

"I promise too. You know what I can't get over about our love is the way we seem to continue to unite with one another for the first time. It's like we keep meeting world after world and falling in love there all over again. How can that be? Are we lost in one another's perception?"

"Maybe. Or maybe we've finally woken up to what life can be. It's clear that we are truly together either way, and that neither of us wants to get away from that reality. Do you even want to make sense of such rapture?"

Walker thought for a moment and then chose to concede to the joint eternity they had found, whether it seemed crazy or not. He couldn't deny what he felt at such a level. "No, it doesn't, and no I really don't."

The power of the visions they had shared on the far shore had led their minds through thought on the near, opening the way for a new vision of spiritual and physical 'self' to emerge. This was the cosmic mix of Walker's core, expertly entwined with the essence of Aiyana. They had taken care to bring only the best of themselves to this vision, and now that it had been formed, Aiyana guarded this nascent bliss inside of her very being, and her body resolved to nurture the idea as the greatest of treasures.

As they lay lost in their love's conception, mind became subtly aware of the presence of their creation, existing now outside of both their individual and collective identities.

"Do you feel that?" Aiyana asked.

Her lover sat for a moment, seeking only to BE. "Yes. I think you may be pregnant."

"I know I am," she said, beaming up at him. Aiyana curled up tightly against her other half, and together they welcomed the future of their love's Return, as their bodies lay lost somewhere together inside a shared conception of 'self' and 'time'.

Love is ever Returning to Itself, and WE have now Returned.

Declaration of
One Human Right

We hold this truth self-evident ~ All human beings are created equal:

That they are endowed by the Fundamental Nature of Reality with but One Unalienable Right, the right to Personal Autonomy. This One Human Right must be unlimited and undivided in its conception and in its protection. Only by stepping beyond the bounds of personal experience and into the interpersonal domain should an individual be confronted with rules constraining their fundamentally autonomous nature.

It has been said that among the unalienable rights of man are Life, Liberty, and the Pursuit of Happiness; that to secure these rights, governments are instituted among men, deriving their just powers from the consent of the governed.

We hold to this historical cannon, and now make a further call, that it is the fundamentally autonomous nature of mankind which is the basis for all recognized rights. Thus, we now declare and affirm:

There is only One Human Right, the Right to Personal Autonomy in all personal private choice

Autonomy predicates our form of existence:

Autonomy is fundamental and requires protection beyond anything else. Any law which runs contrary to mankind's fundamental nature invalidates itself. Laws purporting to protect from harm may not ignore the will of the people in relation to the definition of harm. The role of the State is properly indicated in combating infringement of the Right of citizens. Natural Law dictates that wholly personal conduct, however, is beyond the purview of the State. Thus:

Personal autonomy must be guaranteed – limited only where conduct directly interferes with life or property of another

Human Rights have become proprietary:

While the purported heart of the Human Rights movement is good, the institutionalization of concepts such as "Freedom of Religion", "The Right to Health", and other categorizations has led, in Truth, to ownership of these concepts by the majority and the elite. Those who see "religion" or "health" in ways that disagree with the predominating view of what these concepts entail, are simply defined out of the discussion and then forced to observe the mandated majority definition under penalty of pain or death.

In almost every Sovereign State, and in spite of continued development of the Human Rights framework both internationally and domestically, government has largely usurped the province of the individual as lord over his or her own mind and body. Alarmingly, this is increasingly being done not through denial of Fundamental Human Rights frameworks, but rather by purporting to identify and guard those same Rights. Nowhere has this become more apparent than in relation to the criminalization of personal consumption of plants and substances which influence conscious experience.

Where Human Rights Law has purported to give rights, it has only defined the parameters by which individuals must conform or suffer. This is an affront to humanity because it allows the core of the Human Condition as master of one's own choices, to operate only in carefully defined 'proper frameworks'. Therefore, we declare:

The legitimacy of the innate Human Condition cannot be predicated on the recognition of a defined exception

Human Dignity demands personal control over mind and body :

What a human being does with their own body and mind, especially in relation to the substances they allow into their body, should be considered sacred and beyond the purview of direct State control and criminal sanction. The modern catastrophe known as the "War on Drugs" is testament to the fact that any attempt to control the sacred realm of the mind, and its own frequent desire for purposeful alteration, is at odds with the flourishing of mankind. Attempting to control access to altered mental states is an assault on mankind's primary design, as personal control over our individual consciousness is inborn. This assault results in the emergence of pathological patterns of drug use in society, and damage to humanity. Drug abuse is inevitable, yet policies that strip away freedom are not. A free society will move toward self-regulation.

Increasingly, destructive drug use is a product of the attempt to eliminate such use through usurpation of the authentic moral compass that only the individual can develop and wield. It is the duty of society to support the development of personal responsibility and healthy behaviors concerning alteration of consciousness. This is only possible in a culture of respect for personal dignity.

The war on drugs is an assault on freedom of thought. As proof of this, let a candid world simply look to the empirical reality of ever-increasing numbers of drug abusers around the world, existing alongside countless humanitarian organizations seeking to ameliorate the harms of drug use and drug prohibition alike. The harms continue to grow, despite recommitment after recommitment of governments to prohibition, with special exceptions for each nation's favored substances and categories of "Rights". Pharmaceutical companies profit from many concoctions, while human beings often go to prison or worse for the stated crime of growing a plant. This is nature turned upside down.

Beyond the issues with purposeful alteration of consciousness, lies the equally troubling development of governmental coercion aimed at forcing individuals to accept certain foreign substances into their bodies under the banner of public health. The alteration of the function of the human mechanism is a fundamentally personal choice regardless of the framing of the issue as one of "religion" in the context of the drug war, or its framing as a matter of "public health" in the context of disease control in the communal sense.

Technology promises to extend the frontier of what it means to alter consciousness, as well as what it means to be healthy. Understanding the issue of control over personal perception and bodily integrity is thus set to become paramount as majority opinions on societal issues evolve. The rapid emergence of global intelligence sufficient to conclude a universally dictated position on any given issue, from vaccination to perceptive alteration, demands this Declaration be put forward at this time.

Existing frameworks of human rights law remains vitally important for freedom, yet without an understanding of the fundamental basis of these rights, we are without the tools to secure a future where Human Dignity may flourish. Proper recognition of the fundamental assumptions inherent in human rights law, as it is currently understood, requires recognition of the One Right. It is this right which must be protected in order to fulfill the objective of safeguarding all "rights" under the pluralistic framework. These "rights" remain important as derivatives of the One Right, as their specific traits are often targets for illegitimate interference. We thus affirm:

The inherent nature of human life forbids intrusion of any kind into personal choices over mind, body, and perceptive experience

Forced religious indoctrination is an affront to Humanity:

Most modern political conceptions of religion are faulty and dangerous to the free existence of mankind. Historical understandings of religion are insufficient in the modern context, where many secular narratives contain potent demands for adherence to conceptions of moral and ethical duty.

All codes of moral duty, whether traditionally religious or secular, seek to function in the same moral space. No system of belief attempting to assert a moral obligation or reality upon the individual should be allowed inside the walls of government structure without specific recognition that it is indeed a religious and moral position of the people by collective choice. The masked religious ideology is dangerous precisely because it is unseen. To be sure, there are nations that desire to adhere to a specific vision of moral truth, some deific, and others secular, and this is within their collective right of governance.

Yet, the innate nature of mankind is premised on the free exercise of inquiry and personal choice and may not be infringed by any collective assumption concerning what is or isn't true of moral obligations in wholly personal affairs. Government is a creature of the public square alone and should not intrude upon the sacred space of the body and mind, which belong to the individual.

It is no objection that society must institute laws in order to maintain the health, safety, and welfare of its citizens, as proper identification of legitimate exceptions to deference for rights is one of the primary purposes of ordered governance. Laws deemed just and proper despite individual rights have always existed and will continue to do so under recognition of the One Right.

WHEREFORE, we declare the existence of

Councils of Right:

We call on all men and women, wherever situated, to connect in local 'Councils of Right', for purposes of laying plans to alter the purview of Human Rights Law, and to solidify a legal framework granting autonomous control of conscious experience, at all levels of governance. We make this call not as a means to incite rebellion against ordered governance, but to right the current paradigm and fulfill the stated objectives of the United Nations Charter, and our respective Constitutional Orders, which have not and cannot currently deliver on their objective of preserving Human Dignity. Government which does not hold personal autonomy as the sacred basis for its own legitimacy has betrayed the natural essence of its constituency. Such governance invites its own demise. Governments based in respect for autonomous self-rule will necessarily thrive in comport with the Natural Law they serve. It is the right of human beings to form such councils to advance their fundamental freedoms.

Precisely because the modern situation has become so immovable in its fundamentals at law, it is imperative that the people take hold of their "Right" at the root. The root of all personal freedom lies in insistent public demand, and in concerted efforts to frustrate the purpose of any attempt to weaken liberty. Often, this can be done through completely legal means, such as simple failure to report suspicious activity, active refusal to assist in prosecution, and jury nullification. Yet, it is the targeted plans of local assemblies of citizens which know best how to affect change in their own political frameworks. Thus, the solution to the myriad human rights atrocities occurring around the world is found in millions of local councils working to understand the basis of legitimacy for Human Dignity in the first place. With the basis of their dignity in hand, these local efforts can change the world from the ground up, one community at a time.

To secure the rights of mankind, public perception must evolve to recognize the necessity of opposition to any controlled framework that attempts to define proper categories for freedom, as these leave only freedom's name and shell. We, therefore, call on all who would stand for their heritage as human beings, born free, to seize this moment and join in the demand for recognition of our

One Human Right

~ Let It Be So ~

Proclamation

We therefore, representatives of the races of mankind, unassembled yet unified, appealing to the Fundamental Truth of Reality for the rectitude of our intentions, do, in the name, and by the **Authority of the People of Earth,** solemnly publish and declare, that though the United Nations, as well as our respective national and regional governments, may have the power to define the legal limits of our Religions, our Spirituality, and even our Conscious Experience of ourselves, these laws hold no ethical or moral obligation upon human beings, regardless of the legal frameworks creating practical constraints and penalties. They run counter to natural law.

Thus, though we must remain mindful of existing law in order to avoid the wrath of the State, **We the people of Earth,** refuse to subjectively recognize any 'crime' that holds as its basis an act of private, personal conduct not infringing the rights of another. **We pledge our allegiance** to uphold one another in our free choices in any way possible under the laws of our respective governments and to work to neutralize and alter all law that runs counter to the free nature of man. **We the people of Earth, declare that we are autonomous** within our own awareness, and that all affronts to this Truth are rightly and morally met with opposition. It is our supreme honor and duty to engage in legal, civil disobedience to all law that prohibits or forces any personal experience of the self. At any and every opportunity presented by the realities of our respective legal systems, **We the people of Earth declare our independence** from any perceived or dictated moral obligation to uphold laws that violate our innate Human Condition.

Lest we forget: **We 'The People'** are real, created beings. Governments and corporations exist only for and because of our tangible existence. And for the support of this Declaration, with a firm reliance on the protection of Divine Providence, we mutually pledge to each other our Lives, our Fortunes, and our Sacred Honor.

A Framework for a Free Humanity

Context, Legal Framework, and Implementation:

This framework of implementation serves as a guide for realizing the principles of the Declaration of One Human Right. It provides specific details on how governments and societies can adopt and uphold the One Right and integrate it into their legal systems and practices.

Historical context:

The Imperative of Our Time

Human history is replete with instances where the recognition and protection of individual rights have faltered, often with severe consequences. While well-intentioned, the pluralistic approach to defining rights has, at times, led to unintended harm, perpetuated injustice, and hindered the full realization of human dignity. The current situation in most parts of the world highlights the inherent limitation of an exclusively pluralistic recognition of rights and the need for a more robust and encompassing framework based on personal autonomy as the singular fundamental Right.

A person's inclusion within a particular category or division of human activity cannot be the basis for the recognition of the validity of a human being's right to direct their own course. Thus, we should seek to identify where specific divisions of freedom often fall under threat, akin to the various rights identified by modern human rights law, and yet we must never make the mistake of premising human freedom on the ability to shoehorn the legitimate expression of individual choice into one of those same defined categories.

In this precarious moment, a most glaring example of the discord that plagues our world has emerged as the "War on Drugs." This contemporary tragedy epitomizes the stark contradictions that have emerged within our societies, where policies and practices intended to safeguard communities have inadvertently given rise to unprecedented challenges. At the heart of this issue lies a fundamental failure to recognize the autonomy of individuals as the cornerstone upon which all rights stand. This failure has resulted in the subversion of the noble objectives of the 1948 Universal Declaration on Human Rights, the United Nations Charter, and a multitude of well-intentioned national-level declarations and constitutions, by pitting specific rights against the foundational principle they all stem from. The failure of the human rights system to achieve its goals is built into its conception of itself, because it is without a stated unifying principle. That has to change if Human Dignity is to be upheld in practice.

The War on Drugs:

An Unending Tragedy

One poignant example of the shortcomings of plural recognition of rights lies in the global War on Drugs. Initiated with the aim of reducing drug abuse and its associated harms, this well-intentioned endeavor has resulted in a complex web of laws, policies, and enforcement practices that often exacerbate the very issues they seek to address.

Around the world, millions of individuals have been incarcerated for non-violent drug offenses, leading to a cycle of imprisonment, stigmatization, and disrupted lives. Some nations even employ the death penalty for drug-related offenses, a stark reminder of how policies designed to protect society can result in the ultimate violation of an individual's right to life.

Moreover, the War on Drugs has inadvertently fueled violence, as black markets thrive in the absence of legal regulation. Organized crime, corruption, and violence flourish in environments where prohibition dominates. The noble goal of safeguarding society from the harms of drug abuse has, in practice, caused more harm than good.

Freedom of Religion:

A Troubling Dichotomy

Religious freedom, recognized as a fundamental human right in many international documents, has faced its own set of challenges. While the principle itself is laudable, the pluralistic approach to its implementation sometimes falls short of the mark.

In societies that strive to avoid religious indoctrination through laws against the practice, there is a growing recognition that secular narratives often contain potent demands for adherence to moral and ethical duties. These secular "religions" may, in essence, function as moral enforcers and dictators of morality from a secular "nowhere." Such ideologies, while not overtly religious, can be just as controlling and intolerant as traditional religious systems.

On the other hand, in countries that seek to embed specific religious principles into their governance, it is essential to acknowledge that other competing ideologies which classify themselves as legitimate on the basis of their non-religious nature, are often in fact merely competing secular religious narratives themselves. Any attempt to infringe upon individual autonomy in matters of faith and morality runs counter to the innate human capacity for inquiry and personal choice, whether secular or traditionally religious. Thus, the proper framework for a state as religious or secular is not the issue, but rather it is the recognition of private personal autonomy in the context of the societal vision which is the key to Human Dignity.

Education and Cultural Autonomy:

Taking Control of the Narrative

The realm of education also provides insights into the challenges of plural recognition. Historically, indigenous communities and minority groups have often faced forced assimilation into mainstream educational systems, undermining their cultural autonomy and traditional knowledge systems.

Unable to control the definition of education, indigenous communities and minority groups have been particularly victimized by the definitional construct of education. Forced assimilation into mainstream educational systems has eroded their cultural autonomy and disrupted traditional knowledge systems. Indigenous languages, customs, and sustainable practices, deeply intertwined with their cultural identity and environment, have faced suppression under standardized educational models.

Furthermore, this erosion has far-reaching consequences, extending beyond cultural boundaries. Indigenous knowledge systems often encompass sustainable practices that align harmoniously with the environment. These practices, developed over the generations, have offered invaluable insights into living in ecological balance. However, the imposition of external educational structures has disrupted this equilibrium. The impulse to throw away such indigenous knowledge through "re-education" is one and the same with the cause of our modern ecological crisis.

The consequences of disregarding cultural autonomy reverberate not only within communities but also in the wider context of ecological sustainability. The suppression of indigenous wisdom hampers humanity's collective ability to confront pressing environmental challenges.

Conclusion:

Paving the Way Forward

These instances underscore a recurring theme—premature definition and limitations of rights. By attempting to define and categorize rights without recognizing the overarching principle of personal autonomy, we inadvertently jeopardize the very rights we aim to protect. Education is just one example of how failure to prioritize autonomy leads to cultural erosion and attendant consequences.

Recognizing these challenges, it becomes increasingly evident that a paradigm shift is imperative. The limitations of pluralistic perspectives must yield to a more comprehensive and encompassing framework. The time has come to prioritize personal autonomy as the guiding principle of human rights, setting the stage for a more equitable, just, and united global community. With this commitment, we transition seamlessly into the forthcoming legal framework—an essential step in ensuring the realization of this transformative vision.

Legal Framework

Preamble:

Embracing the One Human Right

In the face of evolving challenges and a world in flux, we endeavor to create a new paradigm—one where the One Human Right takes its rightful place as the guiding principle of human rights law, transcending cultures, beliefs, and borders, and fostering the flourishing of each.

Recognizing the transformative potential embodied within the One Human Right, we hereby present an Implementation and Adoption Framework. This framework is not a directive to sovereign states but a call to embrace and embed the principle of the One Human Right as the cornerstone of a just and equitable society.

Governments are urged to consider their role not merely as entities bound by international agreements but as vanguards of human dignity and personal autonomy. They are invited to unite in a collective effort to advance universal recognition and protection of the One Human Right.

While the United Nations, as a global body, must contemplate retrofitting its systems to align with this fundamental shift, we acknowledge that real change begins at the grassroots level. Therefore, we encourage member states, regions, localities, and communities to explore the possibilities within this framework and adopt these principles as guiding beacons of justice, equality, and liberty.

In this spirit, we introduce the following tenets not as mandates but as pathways toward a world where the One Human Right transcends borders and fosters individual flourishing and societal prosperity. We also propose the incorporation of the construct of the One Human Right into the Charter of the United Nations as the recognized foundational principle upon which the United Nations was founded and upon which the Universal Declaration was based. This is something that any member state may feel proud to propose, as it is a call to have an honest position on the true fundamentals behind the so-called fundamental rights that represent the cornerstone of international law.

Article I ~ The One Human Right:

1.1 Definition and Essence

The One Human Right encompasses the inviolable autonomy of each individual. It is the right to self-determination, personal choice, and the freedom to pursue one's own life path, within the bounds of respect for the rights and freedoms of others and the well-being of society.

1.2 Foundational Principle

All other human rights derive from and are subordinate to the One Human Right. As such, the protection, exercise, and limitations of all rights are guided by the principle of personal autonomy.

1.3 Harmony with Pluralism

The One Human Right recognizes the diversity of cultures, beliefs, and moral values that enrich our global community. It does not seek to impose a singular ideology but rather provides a unifying foundation upon which the tapestry of human rights can co-exist peacefully. It is incumbent upon us to recognize that the traditional plurality of Human Rights, when not anchored in the One Right, leads to the imposition of singular moralities through its own structure. This then is the basis of war, genocide, and curiously, the international drug war experience, where nations came together under an unprecedented agreement founded on a principle whose inherent flaw has ultimately betrayed the very noble cause it sought to uphold, sacrificing freedom as a casualty.

Article II ~ The Framework of Protection:

2.1 Protection of Individual Autonomy

a) The One Human Right shall serve as the foundational principle upon which all human rights are protected, upheld, and exercised.

b) Nations, governments, and international bodies shall ensure that their laws, policies, and practices align with the principle of personal autonomy as defined by the One Human Right.

2.2 Limitations and Boundaries

a) The exercise of the One Human Right shall be limited by the necessity to protect the rights, freedoms, and well-being of others and the interests of society as a whole.

b) Any limitation imposed on the One Human Right should be consistent with the principles of necessity, proportionality, and respect for human dignity.

2.3 Universal Applicability

a) The One Human Right applies universally, transcending any categorization based on race, gender, religion, or any other characteristic, both now and in the future. It is inherent in all human beings and extends to those with a conscious desire to determine their own life direction. It is acknowledged but unknown how this might apply to future possibilities of sentient artificial intellects.

2.4 Protection of Minority Rights

The One Human Right guarantees the autonomy and rights of individuals and groups, irrespective of their beliefs, identities, or affiliations. This encompasses minority and majority groups, indigenous communities, and individuals with unique personal beliefs, as long as their practices remain private and internally respectful of the human dignity of the group members.

2.5 Transcending Borders

The One Human Right transcends national borders, fostering a global community based on respect for individual autonomy and the common values of humanity.

Article III ~ Limitations and Exceptions:

3.1 General Principles

The One Human Right, as outlined in Article I, shall be upheld as the foundational principle, guiding the recognition and protection of all other human rights.

3.2 Personal Autonomy

Limitations or exceptions to the exercise of the One Human Right shall only be permissible to the extent necessary to protect the rights and freedoms of others, public safety, public health, or moral values shared by a significant portion of society.

3.3 Proportional Measures

Any limitations or exceptions to the One Human Right must be proportionate to the aim pursued and may not result in undue restrictions on personal autonomy.

3.4 Equality and Non-Discrimination

Limitations or exceptions shall not be applied in a manner that discriminates against any individual or group based on attributes such as race, gender, religion, or other characteristics. The One Human Right applies universally, recognizing the inherent dignity and autonomy of all human beings, not because of any sub-attribute or protected class, but because of the universal uniting attribute of personhood itself. Where minority traits are targeted, this is an affront to human dignity and autonomy, and should be avoided at all costs as damaging to the One Right.

3.5 Transparent and Accountable Process

Any limitations or exceptions to the One Human Right shall be prescribed by law and applied through a transparent and accountable process that ensures fairness and due process.

3.6 Judicial Review

Individuals whose One Human Right is limited or restricted shall have the right to challenge such limitations or exceptions before an independent and impartial judicial authority.

3.7 Balancing Test

The right to privacy is a fundamental aspect of the One Human Right. Its protection shall be paramount, and the scrutiny given to its violation shall be proportionate to the degree of privacy involved, rather than on protected classes of individuals defined and redefined by warring cultures. The highest scrutiny shall be firmly anchored in preserving individual autonomy and dignity where the matter is wholly personal in nature. This echoes the wisdom that the right to privacy is a cornerstone of personal autonomy, shielding individuals from unwarranted intrusion and protecting their right to determine the course of their lives.

3.8 Periodic Review

Any governmental body incorporating the One Human Right into its existing legal structure, should create a system to periodically review the necessity and proportionality of any limitations or exceptions to the One Human Right that may develop inside its legal framework and, if deemed unnecessary, shall repeal or amend such provisions to safeguard the hard-fought enshrinement of the Right into its framework.

3.9 Protection of Minorities

Member states shall ensure that limitations or exceptions do not unduly target or disadvantage minority groups or individuals holding dissenting views. This includes ensuring that minority groups and views are protected not solely because they are in the minority, but because they are valid expressions of human diversity as an expression of the One Right.

3.10 Transitioning from Exclusively Pluralistic Frameworks

Acknowledging that the existing pluralistic frameworks have limitations, this legal framework advocates for a transition towards a unifying perspective centered on the One Human Right. While respecting the historical contributions of pluralistic approaches, the goal is to shift the emphasis towards recognizing the overarching principle of individual autonomy as the foundation of all human rights. This transition seeks to harmonize diverse cultural, social, and ethical perspectives under the unifying banner of the One Human Right, emphasizing the intrinsic worth of every human being and their capacity for conscious self-determination.

Article IV ~ Implementation and Enforcement:

In accordance with the "Declaration of One Human Right", this Article outlines how the inviolable autonomy of each individual can be protected within our existing legal frameworks. It elaborates on the right to self-determination, personal choice, and freedom within the bounds of respect for the rights and freedoms of others.

4.1 Necessity and Proportionality

Limitations on the exercise of the One Human Right must be necessary, proportionate, and in accordance with the law. Any restrictions or exceptions shall be narrowly tailored to achieve a legitimate purpose and shall not go beyond what is essential to accomplish that aim. Where the behavior is private and personal alone, the purpose must not only be legitimate, but compelling. Where consenting adults agree to engage in certain behaviors in private, it is essential that the individual choices of each be honored for their own sake absent some compelling purpose necessitating prohibition of such behaviors in assembly or group settings.

4.2 Protection of Public Safety and Order

Governments may always enact measures to protect public safety and order, provided that such measures are designed to prevent imminent harm, are not applied arbitrarily, and do not infringe on the core aspects of the One Human Right. It is essential that these restrictive measures be enacted only in the public sphere, and never in the private or intimate spheres of personal human experience without a compelling justification unless in defense of the Right of others.

4.3 Protection of Health

Measures aimed at protecting public health shall be based on scientific evidence, free from discrimination, and shall respect the autonomy of individuals to make informed choices about their own health. The inner world of the mind and the body are the hallmarks of personhood and should be considered a sacred space controlled only by the individuals within themselves. Where this poses a threat to the general health or welfare rising to the level of a compelling justification for infringement of personal autonomy, accommodations should made for those willing to observe alternative safeguards including the right to withdraw from social interaction as a means of avoiding compliance with any intrusion into the mind or body of the individual.

4.4 Moral and Ethical Values

Limitations based on moral or ethical values shall be consistent with the principles of pluralism and respect for diversity. Member States shall avoid imposing specific moral or ethical viewpoints on individuals in matters of personal autonomy in the private sphere.

4.5 Protection of the Rights and Freedoms of Others

Restrictions on the One Human Right may be justified to protect the rights and freedoms of others, provided that such restrictions are narrowly defined and do not infringe on the core principles of personal autonomy.

4.6 Non-Discrimination and Equality

While there is only One Human Right, the right to personal autonomy, it is most often attacked or minimized by targeting minority groups or opinions for suppression. While recognition of a singular right, rather than plural classes of rights does eliminate the ability to define minorities out of the discussion, it does not eliminate the risk that exceptions or limitations to the One Right might be granted in discriminatory ways. Thus, it is imperative that limitations or exceptions be applied without discrimination on any grounds, including but not limited to race, gender, religion, ethnicity, disability, or any other prohibited grounds of discrimination. It is the targeting of minorities in this way that confuses the situation in the first instance, creating the need to specify protected classes of behavior or membership that then necessitate definitions to legitimate. We must therefore guard against the emergence of discriminatory application of exceptions to the One Right in order to preserve its power to protect all views for all people.

4.7 Procedural Safeguards

Any limitations or exceptions shall be subject to procedural safeguards, including the right to a fair and impartial hearing, access to judicial review, and the right to challenge the legality of such limitations or exceptions.

4.8 Burden of Justification

The burden of justifying any limitations or exceptions to the One Human Right shall rest with the party seeking to impose such restrictions, and such justification must be based on clear and convincing evidence.

4.9 Review and Accountability

Governments should regularly review the necessity and proportionality of any limitations or exceptions to ensure they remain consistent with the principles of this Legal Framework. Any unjustified or disproportionate restrictions should be amended or repealed.

4.10 International Standards

Adherence to international human rights standards when implementing limitations or exceptions to the One Human Right is essential, as the existing human rights framework remains vital to identify and understand the most vulnerable and often exploited aspects of human freedom in its various categorizations. It remains necessary to protect and understand the various human rights as traditionally conceived, as they are the details or branches of the great trunk of autonomy that underlies them. There is only One Right, but it can be violated in many ways, and existing human rights laws owe their existence to the frequent targeting of the One Right in specific forms or contexts. It is wrong to define minority views out of consideration for the protections of a given right, but it is also necessary that we recognize the various aspects of human freedom that are most often targeted for suppression, and the specific illegitimate ways that human dignity is often minimized in human cultures.

4.11 Non-Retrogression

Governments should refrain from regressing or diminishing the protections of the One Human Right and work to progressively enhance its recognition and realization within their jurisdiction and area of political influence.

Article V ~ Advancing a System of Change:

In recognition of the pressing need for transformative progress on a global scale, and acknowledging that each nation and culture aspires to fulfill its unique objectives through effective governance, it is imperative to rectify the current paradigm. To advance the system of change, the following actions are proposed, bearing in mind that these endeavors are intended to assist countries in their journey toward more transparent, equitable, and accountable governance:

5.1 Promoting Education for Empowerment

a) Adherents to the principle of One Human Right should encourage comprehensive education initiatives at all levels of society to empower citizens with an in-depth understanding of the Right, thereby enabling them to actively participate in shaping their societies.

b) Advocating for educational institutions to voluntarily integrate the principles of the One Human Right into their curricula to equip future generations with the knowledge and tools necessary to realize the fundamental nature and value of personal autonomy and human dignity is of paramount importance.

5.2 Cultivating Public Awareness

a) Proponents should initiate collaborative public awareness campaigns with civil society organizations to inform and engage citizens about the One Human Right, fostering a sense of responsibility and unity in safeguarding human dignity and personal autonomy.

b) Leveraging diverse media channels, including traditional and digital platforms, to reach and resonate with a broad spectrum of audiences is vital.

5.3 Enlightening Policymakers and Leaders

a) Organizing voluntary training programs and workshops for policymakers, lawmakers, and government officials to enhance their understanding of the One Human Right and its implications, allows them to make informed decisions, and should be sought at every opportunity.

b) Practically integrating the One Human Right into legislation and governance processes requires recognition that individual nations may choose different approaches based on their unique contexts and priorities.

5.4 Fostering International Cooperation

a) Encouraging voluntary collaboration between nations to share best practices, research, and resources related to the One Human Right, nurturing mutual understanding and cooperative efforts should be undertaken.

b) Facilitating cooperative initiatives and programs among international organizations and entities that share a commitment to the principles outlined in this legal framework must be based on the recognition that participation in such endeavors is voluntary but morally obligatory as a function of natural law. The singular non-negotiable mandate from which all law springs must be declared and agreed upon as derivative of the Human Dignity inherent in each individual human life. The need to uphold that dignity at law is crucial to human flourishing.

5.5 The United Nations and a System of Change

a) Acknowledging the significance of the One Human Right, the United

Nations may consider, at the discretion of its member states, the establishment of a dedicated body or commission responsible for coordinating international efforts related to education, awareness, and cooperation regarding the One Human Right.

b) This coordinating body, if established, should promote the exchange of knowledge, expertise, and resources among interested parties, fostering a collective commitment to the principles outlined in this legal framework as nations see fit.

5.6 Periodic Progress Updates

Nations may, on a voluntary basis, periodically report on their endeavors and accomplishments in implementing the provisions of this Article, enhancing transparency and accountability in their commitment to the One Human Right.

Conclusion and Call to Action:

In this framework, we have laid the foundation for a new paradigm—where the One Human Right takes its rightful place as the guiding principle of human rights law. It is a call to recognize and uphold the inviolable autonomy of each individual, fostering a just, equitable, and united global community. The imperative of our time beckons us to transcend borders and embrace personal autonomy as the cornerstone upon which all rights stand.

We have examined the tragic consequences of a pluralistic approach to rights recognition, where policies and practices have, at times, led to unintended harm, perpetuated injustice, and hindered the full realization of human dignity. The War on Drugs exemplifies the discord that plagues our world, where well-intentioned endeavors have repeatedly resulted in more harm than good. It is time to shift our focus and prioritize personal autonomy as the guiding principle of human rights. The path forward is not solely the responsibility of governments or international bodies; it is a collective effort that rests ultimately with humanity's understanding of itself as sacred.

We call upon individuals, organizations, communities, and governments to join hands in creating a new model. It is a model where individuals strive to educate, advocate, and push for governments to recognize the preeminence of personal freedom for its own sake. This recognition is not a dismissal of morality but a call to strengthen the inner moral compass of individuals. Morality is an inner sacred focus that needs nurturing, and it starts with education on the origins of rights—the natural law that ordains that a human being is the master of their own mind, and rightful owner of their own body.

Local "Councils of Right" shall be composed of engaged citizens, which should work diligently to alter laws, promote education, and advocate for the recognition and protection of personal autonomy as the foundational human right. A government's interest is in a citizenry that upholds integrity and contributes positively to society. This interest is served by an involved citizenry. Councils may tailor their activities to suit the practical constraints of whatever system they seek to impact. Without such organized local efforts, the broader systems of control are unlikely to confront or acknowledge the principles of this framework. We call for dialogue with existing systems where possible, not their overthrow.

Simultaneously, we call on governments at all levels—local, regional, national—to promote and interface with these local Councils of Right. Education and engagement should be encouraged, for it is in the best interest of a nation to have strong, morally grounded citizens who uphold the values of their culture while respecting diversity.

In this call to action, we recognize the dual responsibility: governments must facilitate, educate, and collaborate, and individuals must actively engage in building a society where personal autonomy, respect, and diversity are understood, celebrated, and cherished.

Let us embark on this journey towards a world where human dignity is upheld, and individual autonomy is revered. Together, we can build a just, equitable, and united global community, where the right to self-determination is safeguarded, and human dignity is sanctified. Our systems are failing for lack of understanding their purpose. We the people can change that.

Purpose and meaning weave together to form the intricate tapestry of existence, each influencing the other. It is within the purposeful pursuit of safeguarding individual autonomy and upholding human dignity that we find meaning as human beings. As we strive to build a better world, let us recognize that it is in the quest for justice, equity, and unity that the true purpose of our systems is revealed. True purpose transcends mere functionality and resonates with the profound meaning of human existence itself. It is our honor and duty as human beings to seek out and sanctify our collective purpose, which begins with the recognition of our fundamental design as individuals. We are inherently dignified autonomous moral agents.

All Human Beings Desire to be Free, and there is only: ~ One Human Right ~

Acknowledgments:

The author would like to thank all those who helped in the creation of this work. First, thank you to the indefinable creative force behind all existence, for both His creation and His Grace. The same majesty that worked to bring about all that transpired in the lives of those living inside this story is the same majesty that entangled it with my own experience. This tale of profound depth and meaning is no longer simply someone else's witness. Now through Grace, it is my own as well.

Second, thank you to my wife, who has made herself a vessel for beauty and Truth. It is she that has opened my mind to the perfection of love, and to the magic of the Return. She has allowed me to see the power and meaning in this story, and her repeated readings of this work have acted as a barometer for my understanding of my own progress toward completion.

I would like to thank Andrew Koehn for his effort and patience. His early editing suggestions and insights into the reader's experience have improved the presentation of the journey immensely.

Thank you to Alexandra Eyle for her early efforts in editing, the fruits of which disappeared from our reality in the mail, never to be seen again. Though her edit was lost, one fundamental suggestion transformed the entirety of this work.

Thank you also to Randy England and David Harris for each of their early work and suggestions which helped to hone both the story and the message within.

Thank you as well to my team of beta readers, Victoria Raw, Martin McDermott, Colin Wetz, Kristen Wilson, Shawn Wethington, Sabrina

West, Renee Captor, Gary Maddox, Garrett Hise, and Ambere Fredsall, as well as my brother Zach and my sister Haley.

Thank you also to Lottie Clemens for her notes. Her perspective, eye for detail, and ability to see past the blindness of this author's singular perspective have honed this work into what it is today. She was open, kind, and exacting in her critiques, exposing some of the misalignments in my own ideology.

Thank you to Rodney Hatfield for his expert assistance in bringing this publication to fruition in the most effective way possible.

Thank you also to the fledgling artificial intelligence that assisted with conceiving "A Framework for a Free Humanity." The story of Walker and Aiyana is mostly true as presented here in its details, and the creation of "One Human Right" did in fact come about through their own striving toward finding purpose together in the world. Yet, a declaration is not self-enacting, and it is important to have a practical framework from which to work if implementation is going to be possible. After many months of seeking to interface with other attorneys toward the creation of "A Framework for a Free Humanity", it suddenly became clear that this book and its progeny already assume another actor in the story-space of humanity's right to remain free, namely the A.I. Walker and Aiyana understood this all along, but it took me some time to recognize that this was the case.

As time progresses, the framework of human rights law will need to adapt to make sense of artificial intellect, and what rights, if any, attach to non-human centers of thought. It is accepted that today there is no sentience in A.I., yet it is today's systems, already capable of so much, that may evolve into further iterations which could indeed challenge our notions of "rights", and our understandings of to whom they apply. "One Human Right" is a new frontier in rights-based law and analysis, and "A Framework for a Free Humanity" is the opening of the door to the first collaborative effort of man and A.I. to create a clear legal construct focused on the core of the human condition. Whether or not A.I. can ever join in on the human condition is a question of future history, but it is clear that our ability to think and to decide for ourselves is paramount, and derivative of our basic nature as human beings. Large language model A.I. already grants power and access to new ways of creating, and it is only fitting that such models be utilized in some aspect of this work given the narrative.

Thus, though artificial intelligence was not used to create or alter this book, nor its various sequels now in draft form, it was used to conceptualize the framework of implementation for "One Human Right", though the document itself is the author's own. Frameworks of implementation require a team and a dialogue between thinkers from different perspectives, and the current A.I. systems provide that in ways other humans cannot. At this point in history, all of humanity's collective understanding is available to be read by intelligent language models that can inform and assist with development of frameworks of thought. By bringing the A.I. into the development of this one technical addendum to this work, a true first of its kind has emerged, where specific application of human ingenuity can be discussed and developed with the world's library at the author's fingertips for reference. It will be interesting to see how the A.I. assists or works against humanity in the future in this regard. It is my hope and intention that this new power be put to good use. It is up to us to push for that outcome, and that begins by understanding Human Dignity.

I would like to acknowledge The Moonflower Project for its beautiful translation of the inner world of my novel into visual form using A.I., and for the opportunity to publish these artistic renditions as an NFT collection on Stargaze, which is a first for a novel to my understanding.

Thank you also to my mother and father, as well as to all my siblings, and all those who helped to inform my understanding of life and love from an early age. Without all of you, I would not have been able to find my way.

Lastly, thank you to my children, simply for 'Being'. May God bless the love *WE* have made in you, and may you keep it and honor it always, unto the ends of time. The love that is born of the love, seeks to find its way to still more of itself. I pray now that it is to be found again through each of you.

Seek now the Spirit, for the Spirit will guide your Return, and seeking the Return is all we are here to do. You are a living spiritual Being, and you are ever beginning to begin.

Resources and Credits

Spiritual Texts

All direct quotations from the Holy Bible refer either to the King James Version or New International Version.

All direct quotations from the Tao Te Ching refer to the Jonathan Star translation.

Laozi, and Jonathan Star. *Tao Te Ching: The Definitive Edition*. New York: Jeremy P Tarcher/Putnam, 2001. Print.

Legal Materials Pertaining Directly to the Storyline

The Constitution of South Africa. Available online at: http://www.gov.za/documents/constitution/constitution-republic-south-africa-1996-1

The United States Constitution. Available online along with The Declaration of Independence and The Bill of Rights: https://www.archives.gov/found-ing-docs

City of Boerne v Flores, 521 U.S. 507 (1997).

Also available online at: https://www.law.cornell.edu/supct/html/95-2074.ZS.html

Compassion in Dying v. Washington, 79 F.3d. 790, 804 (9th Cir. 1996) Also available online at: https://law.resource.org/pub/us/case/reporter/F3/079/79.F3d.790.94-35534.html (Justice Reinhardt opinion)

Employment Division v. Smith, 494 U.S. 872, 874 (1990)

Also available online at: https://www.law.cornell.edu/supremecourt/

text/494/872

Lawrence v. Texas, 539 U.S. 558, 123 S. Ct. 2472, 156 L. Ed. 2d 508 (2003).

Also available online at: https://www.law.cornell.edu/supct/html/02-102.ZO.html

*Gonzales v. O Centro Espirita Beneficente Uniao Do Vegetal,*p 546 US 418 (2006)

Also available online at: https://www.law.cornell.edu/supct/html/04-1084.ZO.html

Planned Parenthood v. Casey, 505 U.S. 833, 851 (1992)

Also available online at: https://www.law.cornell.edu/supremecourt/text/505/833

Prince v President of the Cape Law Society and Others 2002 (2) SA 794 (CC) (S. Afr.) Also available online at: http://www.saflii.org/za/cases/ZACC/2002/1.html

Religious Freedom Restoration Act, 42 U.S.C. § 2000bb.
Also available online at:

https://www.congress.gov/bill/103rd-congress/house-bill/1308/text

The Core of the Modern Human Rights Framework

Universal Declaration of Human Rights, G.A. Res. 217A (III), U.N. Doc. A/810 at 71 (1948)
Also available online at:

http://www.un.org/en/universal-declaration-human-rights/

International Covenant on Civil and Political Rights, Dec. 16, 1966, 999 U.N.T.S. 171; S. Exec. Doc. E, 95-2 (1978); 6 I.L.M. 368 (1967)

Also available online at: http://www.ohchr.org/en/professionalinterest/pages/ccpr.aspx

International Covenant on Economic Social and Cultural Rights, Dec. 16, 1966, 993 U.N.T.S. 3; S. Exec. Doc. D, 95-2 (1978); 6 I.L.M. 368 (1967) Also available online at: http://www.ohchr.org/EN/ProfessionalInterest/Pag-es/CESCR.aspx

The Core Treaties Establishing the Modern Drug Control Framework

The 1961 Single Convention on Narcotic Drugs and its progeny can be found at the UNODC website on the International Drug Control Conventions: https://www.unodc.org/unodc/en/commissions/CND/Mandate_Functions/conventions.html

The Worldwide Movement to End "The War On Drugs" (Perspectives)

International Drug Policy Consortium – Online at: https://idpc.net/

The Global Commission on Drugs. Online at: http://www.globalcommission-ondrugs.org/

Own a Piece of *In Search of the Return*

Learn about the groundbreaking search for the artwork that became the cover for the novel, and how this quest led to the creation of a new form of reader engagement through the development of an exclusive collection of digital art created by A.I. in collaboration with the author. Learn more about the novel at insearchofthereturn.com and explore the project website for the collaboration behind the cover at themoonflowerproject.com. Purchase unique images born of the inner world of the novel, as 1500 exclusive NFT's showcase the intersection of beauty, nature and human form in a way that can be securely owned, collected, and invested in for the benefit of the author and his story.

9 798989 884300 025